THE DEATH OF DISTANT STARS

A Legal Thriller

Deborah Hawkins

The Death of Distant Stars © 2016 by Deborah Hawkins

Formatting by Polgarus Studio

Published by Deborah Hawkins
ISBN 978-0-9889347-7-1 (ebook)
ISBN 978-0-9889347-8-8 (print)

"A star's light shines the brightest,
When it's starting to collapse."

Supernova, Erin Hanson

* * *

"Revenge is an act of passion; vengeance of justice."

Samuel Johnson

NOVELS BY DEBORAH HAWKINS

THE WARRICK-THOMPSON FILES
(Legal Thrillers)

DARK MOON
MIRROR, MIRROR
KEEPING SECRETS
THE DEATH OF DISTANT STARS

AWARD-WINNING WOMEN'S FICTION

DANCE FOR A DEAD PRINCESS

Foreword Reviews, Book of the Year, Finalist, 2013
Beverly Hills Book Award Finalist, 2014
Paris Book Festival, Honorable mention, 2014

RIDE YOUR HEART 'TIL IT BREAKS

Winner, Women's Fiction, Beverly Hills Book Award, 2015
Honorable Mention, Paris Book Festival, 2015

Contents

PROLOGUE

Wednesday, August 1, 2012, Black's Beach, San Diego, 7:30 a.m.

He looked like any other blonde California surfer in his black wetsuit as he made his way down the Glider point trail with his board. His suit was unzipped and hung around his waist, revealing his broad shoulders and perfect six-pack abs. He was healthy and fit and only forty years old that day as he descended to the hard-packed sand at the edge of the water where he had surfed since childhood. He could have been the model for the covers of women's romance novels instead of a Stanford-educated lawyer with a job he loved.

At seven-thirty, there were only a handful of fellow surfers in the water. They looked like seals in their wetsuits as they floated far from shore where the waves began to form. They were focused on catching a ride on the perfect wave.

He stood for a few moments, breathing in the cool ocean breeze and feeling it fan his cheeks, hot from the exertion of climbing down the trail. He listened to the throbbing cry of the seagulls overhead and watched the sleek, gray dolphins arcing joyfully into the air above the sun-streaked ocean before disappearing into its depths.

He loved this place, and all the creatures who lived here. He'd never been far from this ocean. For that reason, he had refused to accompany Paul and Tom to Harvard in bone-chilling Boston. He slithered into the top of his wet suit and zipped it up. He waded into the water and launched his board into the waves. As he paddled farther and farther from shore, closer and closer to the joyful dolphins, he felt his soul join with the ocean as it always did. He belonged here, and here he always found peace.

Then he saw it, the first wave of the day. He paddled into it, positioning himself over the swell just as it was about to break. He popped up on the board as he had done thousands of times and began his ride.

* * *

Wednesday, August 1, 2012, San Diego Breaking News, 6:30 p.m.

Lifeguards found the body of forty-year-old Stephen Cooper washed up on Black's Beach at 4:30 this afternoon. Stephen, a graduate of Stanford Law School, was a staff attorney for the National Resources Defense Council. He was part of a famous trifecta of champion surfers who grew up together in Pacific Beach. Stephen, along with his childhood friends, Paul Curtis and Tom Andrews, had won multiple national and international surfing competitions since the age of twelve. He is survived by his sister, Amanda Cooper.

THE FILING OF A LAWSUIT

CHAPTER ONE

Friday, January 10, 2014, P & J's Brewery, The Gaslamp District, San Diego

Paul was always late. Kathryn Andrews wished she had remembered that before she walked into P & J's Brewery and Tasting Room in the Gaslamp alone at the appointed hour of six p.m. But what did it matter, she asked herself, as she allowed the indifferent waitress with a host of Goth piercings to show her to a table and hand her a list of designer beers. She did everything alone now, and waiting for Paul in a brewery on a Friday night packed with singles looking for dates did not faze her. She could feel the male eyes at the bar checking her out, but she refused to look their way. They weren't Tom; and so, by definition, she was not interested.

Forty is too young to give up on love, the grief counselor had intoned over and over again in those black days after Tom's death not quite two years ago. Dr. Nina Ferguson, sixty, if a day, a tiny bird of a woman who perched on the edge of her chair and peered at Kathryn with beady, black bird-eyes, insisted she had many years of life left. And maybe she did. But they would all be spent alone, holding back the tears the way a dam holds back a river.

The heavy wooden doors with the frosted glass panels swung open, and Paul appeared. He smiled and waved and began to make his way through the half-sitting, half-standing throng in the tasting room. He and Tom had not been blood brothers, but they had grown up together in Pacific Beach as inseparable as siblings, with the same chiseled, blonde surfer good looks that made heads turn. And the female heads were turning as Paul crossed the room to her. A young litigation partner at Warrick, Thompson, everything about him said money.

"Sorry, I'm late. A phone call I had to take."

"I knew you would be." She stood up to accept his kiss on each cheek.

The no-longer indifferent waitress' eyes never left Paul's face as he folded his six feet into the chair opposite Kathryn's and accepted the beer list from her with his usual casual grace. He gave the hovering Goth his charming smile. "And would you bring us the food menu, too?" She scampered off, happy do his bidding.

Paul took off his obviously expensive navy suit coat and loosened his maroon power tie and studied the beer list. "Have you ordered?"

"No, I was waiting for you to make sense of it. I'm a wine girl."

"Two pale ales," he told the waitress when she reappeared. "Some fried calamari to start and two burgers, medium. Does that work for you, Kath?"

"Perfect." Tom was the only other person who had known

her well enough to order for her. But then the three of them had been inseparable since their first month of law school at Harvard, twenty years ago.

"So you knew I'd be late." He settled back in his chair and smiled at her.

"You always are. A Warrick, Thompson partner never sleeps." She smiled and sipped the ale, finding it surprisingly smooth and mellow.

"It feels like that." He suddenly looked sad.

"What's wrong? You wanted Warrick out of law school. You got the offer. You've made partner and more money than you'll ever spend. You knew the life you'd have to live to do that."

"Guilty on all counts. But I guess I didn't think my marriage and losing Jodie were the price I'd have to pay."

The waitress returned with their appetizer.

Kathryn looked around at the hopeful throng, sipping beer and taking flirting to a new level. "There are plenty of women in here who'd be interested."

But Paul shook his head as he finished a calamari and wiped his fingers on a napkin. "I can't say I'm in a hurry to get married again. As much as I hate to admit it, Carolyn had a point: I wasn't around enough to be good husband material."

"Wasn't she a bit of a hypocrite, though? She very obviously married you for the money and the lifestyle."

Paul frowned. "Is that what you thought?"

"It's what Tom and I both thought from the beginning. To put it bluntly, she didn't love you."

He sighed. "Couldn't you have tried to tell me?"

"Would you have listened?"

He gave her a little grimace. "Ouch. No. Okay. How many ways do you want to say I-told-you-so?"

"None. You had to do what you had to do to learn what you had to learn."

"She's getting married again, by the way."

"Barely a year. She hasn't wasted any time."

"I think this one was waiting in the wings."

"Another lawyer?"

"No. Real estate investor. Net worth thirty million. He'll be around a lot more."

Kathryn smiled. "He'll probably get under her feet, and she'll wish for the old days when she could spend your money behind your back."

Their burgers arrived, and Paul ordered more beer for them both. "I don't really care what she thinks or feels. It's Jodie I miss."

"But you get to see her, don't you?"

"In theory. But every other weekend with a five-year-old is a pipe dream for someone with my caseload and work hours. For the past six months I've been mostly living out of a suitcase in Chicago, taking depositions in a case that may go to trial next month. When I do get to come back, Jodie has some vague idea that I'm her 'real' daddy, but she calls Carolyn's new guy 'daddy,' too. It hurts."

Kathryn reached across the table and squeezed his hand. His deep blue eyes, so like Tom's, looked up at her full of anguish. "I know it must. Have you thought about leaving the firm?"

"Thought about it, yes. Would I leave, no. There's no point. Carolyn has set in motion what she wants for Jodie's life. My leaving the firm and hanging out a solo shingle wouldn't change that."

He put his burger down and waved his hand toward the tasting room where the frantic flirting seemed to be reaching a fever pitch. "I've come in here a few times, and tried that." He nodded toward the bar. "Waste of time. What about you? Getting out at all since—"

"Since Tom died. You can say it."

"It's been a year and a half, so I thought maybe—"

"Maybe I'd decided it's time to move on? You don't move on from someone like Tom. You know that, Paul."

He emptied his beer and called for another.

"Be careful if you're driving home."

"Oh, I'm not driving for a long, long time. I'm going back to the office to read deposition transcripts until midnight. I've never told you this, but I've always wished you'd picked me instead of Tom."

"What?"

"Oh, come on. Don't tell me you didn't know I was waiting for the two of you to break up throughout law school. But once you met Tom, I never had a chance. I should never have introduced the two of you. Should have kept you for myself."

"Paul," Kathryn put her hand over his again, "this is just the alcohol talking. We've never been anything but very close friends. And I think now we're closer because we're both missing Tom so much."

"Is it getting any easier for you?" His blue eyes, full of sympathy, held hers.

"I tell myself it is, but it isn't. I keep expecting to turn the corner at work and see him in his office. There's someone else in there now, and it breaks my heart every time I look in and Tom's not there. I keep trying to remember the sound of his voice. I'm so afraid a week from now or a month from now or a year from now, I won't be able to remember."

"Maybe you should sell the house. Start fresh in a new place."

"Maybe, but I can't afford to. You know what public defenders earn. It's hard without Tom's income."

"Didn't he have some life insurance?"

"A little. I put that bit away toward retirement. If I ever get to retire."

"You need a new job. Why not talk to Alan Warrick? You've got the same background I do. And you graduated higher in our class than I did."

Kathryn smiled. "And what would I do at Warrick, Thompson? Defend drug companies who murder people like Tom?"

"Ouch. You make me ashamed of myself."

"But don't you ever think about him when you're defending those corporate monsters in depositions where plaintiffs' attorneys are asking those fat-cat executives why they released a drug they knew would kill people?"

"All the time. It's been a lot harder to do this job since Tom died."

"Well, I certainly couldn't do it."

"But you could be a star in white-collar crime. Look, there's not much difference between negotiating plea bargains for people who can't afford a lawyer and for those who can. You'd be able to put a lot of money away for retirement or anything else you wanted to do."

She sighed. "You've got a point."

"And the surroundings wouldn't remind you of Tom."

"True."

"Want me to talk to Alan about setting up an interview for you?"

Kathryn sighed and studied the tasting room where couples were beginning to form at the bar. "Not yet. There's something else I have to do first."

"What?"

"Sue Wycliffe Pharmaceutical."

"You mean a wrongful death claim for Tom?"

She nodded.

"But that's crazy. You're a fantastic criminal defense attorney, but you don't know the first thing about a wrongful death suit."

"Actually, I do know the first thing. I know how to draft a complaint, and I know where the courthouse is. But, you're right, I couldn't take it to trial. Guys like you would chew me up and spit me out in under ten seconds. But the truth is, I've been trying to find someone to sue them for me. No luck so far. The attorneys I've talked to who want the case are incompetent ambulance-chasers who think they'd get some attorneys' fees by filing suit and then settling without going to trial. The attorneys who have the expertise to try the case won't talk to me."

The check had arrived, and Paul studied it for several seconds as if reading tea leaves. Then he pulled out his American Express card and plunked it down on top of the bill. He studied

Kathryn's face for a few seconds. "I hesitate to say what I am about to say."

"Why?"

"Because if you don't already know, wrongful death litigation can get very nasty. The drug companies always try to put the dead person on trial for every possible sin he or she ever could have committed. I know. I'm ashamed to say I've done it."

"Are you saying don't do it?"

"I'm saying it won't bring Tom back, and you'll relive his death countless times if you do. Not to mention every quarrel, every spat the two of you ever had."

Kathryn stared at her empty glass. "Tom suffered horribly before he died. I want to throw that in Wycliffe's face in front of a jury."

"So you're determined to bring a wrongful death suit?"

"Yes."

"Well, then, the attorney you need to talk to is Hugh Mahoney. Biggest plaintiff's attorney on the West Coast. Probably in the whole U.S. He does big drug and securities cases. And he is superb at both. To be honest, when we in the defense bar see his name on the pleadings, we immediately advise our clients to settle for the best deal Mahoney is willing to offer."

"I've tried to make an appointment with him, but his secretary always says his calendar is full."

"That's because you told her you want to bring a wrongful death suit based only on Tom's death. Hugh prefers to take class action plaintiffs because the actual plaintiffs receive virtually nothing in damages, but the attorneys make countless millions in attorneys' fees. Hugh has built his law firm and his personal fortune on class action litigation."

"So since Hugh won't see me, who else should I go to?"

Paul shook his head. "Hugh and Hugh and Hugh. He's the only attorney I know who has the guts and resources to take on a giant like Wycliffe Pharmaceutical. If you can get in to see him, Hugh will realize that if Wycliffe's drug ate up Tom's liver–and we know it did–then there are likely thousands of other victims out there. He'll be happy to represent you."

"But I have no way of finding out how many deaths Myrabin caused besides Tom's."

"You need to go see Dr. Richard Peyton. He is Hugh's medical expert whenever Hugh tries a drug case. He mostly works for Hugh, but to keep himself looking unbiased he sometimes crosses over to the defense side. I've actually used him in a couple of my cases. Smart guy. I'll call him and introduce you. Then make an appointment to go see him. Tell him about Tom. I'm pretty sure Rick will get you in to see Hugh. But fair warning, Kathryn. You won't like Hugh Mahoney. He's the nastiest, meanest plaintiff's attorney on earth with an ego that defies description. But if he takes your case, he'll fight for Tom and for you like a rabid pit bull."

CHAPTER TWO

Friday, January 17, 2014, Scripps Clinic, Rancho Bernardo

A week later, a nurse in purple scrubs printed with kittens holding balloons ushered Kathryn into Dr. Richard Peyton's plush office in the ultra modern Scripps Clinic Building in Rancho Bernardo at two p.m. Kathryn took one of the leather chairs in front of Peyton's long, marble-slab desk and stared out at the pine trees level with the windows. Irrationally, she resented a medical professional dressed to suggest that the business of treating disease was playful. If a nurse in kitten scrubs had come into Tom's room during those last, long, agonizing days, she would have strangled her.

The door stirred, and the great man himself appeared in a business-like white lab coat. He was six feet tall, but stooped a bit as if to hide his height. He had a long narrow face and very dark eyes that took in everything around him. A shock of black hair streaked with gray flopped messily over his left eye. He wore large, dark-rimmed glasses that seemed to suggest he really was an expert on any subject he cared to claim. She guessed he was in his early fifties.

"Richard Peyton, so nice to meet you." He smiled and extended his hand.

She returned the gesture. "Kathryn Andrews. We spoke on the phone about Myrabin."

"Of course. I remember. Have a seat. Sorry to make you wait. I still see patients as an internist, and sometimes they need immediate attention. Would you like my assistant to fetch you a drink? Tea? Water? Coffee?"

"No, thank you. I've come to talk about my husband's death." Those words were almost impossible to utter because hearing them destroyed her precious fiction that somehow Tom would return to her.

"So sorry for your loss. Paul told me you think his hypertension medication caused his liver to fail. Why do you think Myrabin played a role in his death?"

"Because Tom's cardiologist thought so."

"And who was treating him?"

"Bruce Myers here at Scripps."

"Good man, Bruce. But were there any other possible factors? Genetic disease, alcohol, hepatitis?"

"No." Kathryn used her courtroom voice designed to put a stop to any and all time-wasting tactics.

"But how can you be so sure?"

"Obviously Tom and I shared the same house and the same bed. And we even shared the same job. We were public defenders. I passed his office twenty times a day until the day he was too sick to show up for work."

"And when was that?"

"The end of May 2012."

"How long before he died?"

"Four weeks."

"No transplant?"

She shook her head. "He was too sick for the surgery."

"But what led Dr. Myers to point the finger at Myrabin? I suppose he told you it is one of the most widely prescribed drugs in this country for hypertension."

"Yes."

"When did your husband develop high blood pressure?"

"In February 2012. He was only forty. It didn't make sense because he was athletic and in great shape."

"Hypertension is still not well understood," Dr. Peyton observed. "So how did Bruce Myers decide on Myrabin as the cause of his liver failure?"

"Tom started on Myrabin in February. It was the only medication he was taking. He got sick about ninety days after he started taking it. Dr. Myers said the timing of Tom's illness led him to suspect Myrabin. He researched the drug and found it was originally developed in 1991 by Laboratories Suchet, a French company headquartered in Paris. Suchet abandoned work on it in 1993, but Wycliffe Pharmaceutical bought the rights in 1994 and got approval from the FDA to market it in 2007."

"It was hailed as the wonder drug for hypertension," Dr. Peyton observed.

"But Dr. Myers found a reference in the literature to a researcher at Suchet who had concluded it attacked the liver in rats. He thought that was why Suchet stopped working on it. He tried to run down the name of the scientist to get a copy of his research, but no luck."

"So you think a lawsuit will uncover this lost research?"

"It must be at Suchet somewhere."

Rick Peyton nodded. "But what if Wycliffe bought the rights to the drug without knowing about the problem?"

"I highly doubt that."

"I think Hugh Mahoney will be interested in this."

* * *

Kathryn didn't feel like going back to work after her meeting with Rick Peyton. Instead she drove home to Pacific Beach, pulling into her driveway at three-thirty. She sat in her white, five-year-old Mini Cooper and studied the tiny blue cottage with white shutters surrounded by the white picket fence at 1845 Ocean Place that she had shared with Tom. The iceberg climbing roses over the front door that they had planted together a month after the house became theirs, swayed softly in the light, briny breeze. Although their little house had barely twelve hundred square feet, all property in proximity to a beach was pricey. With an under-the-table loan from Tom's parents that the mortgage company could not detect, they had scraped together the down payment; and it had become theirs a year after they joined the public defender's office. Tom had wanted to live in the neighborhood where he grew up, close to the ocean, so he could get in some early morning surfing before going to work. Most days he went with Steve, who also lived close by, because Paul's Big-Firm Lawyer Schedule left him little time for anything but work. She studied the little house in the late afternoon sun with its cheerful window boxes full of red geraniums and purple statice and the white roses surrounding the red front door, and remembered all the days she had watched Steve and Tom ride away on their bicycles, their boards somehow balanced under their arms. Tears stung her eyes.

She didn't want any more tears. To hold her emotions in check, she resolutely gathered up her briefcase and went inside. She hurried down the narrow hall to the kitchen at the back of the house, her heels clattering on the tile floor, and dropped her purse and briefcase onto a chair. She took a wine glass out of the cabinet and poured herself a glass of chilled white Two-Buck Chuck. Granted it was close to four o'clock and she had a rule about drinking alone before five-thirty, but the meeting with Dr. Peyton had unnerved her. Talking about Tom's death was never easy.

She considered sitting at the tiny white shabby chic table in the little breakfast nook, but the memory of Tom, Paul, and Steve sitting in the green, red, and black chairs that she had painted, drinking beer and laughing together, was too strong. Instead she wandered back down the hall to their small living room and threw herself on the dark blue, slip-covered Ikea sofa. But there were memories here, too. Cuddling with Tom on crisp fall nights, a fire in their small white-washed brick fire place. Super Bowl parties with Paul and Carolyn and Steve and one of his string of girlfriends. Kathryn could hear the laughter, see the chips and beer bottles on the scuffed pine coffee table, and smell the garlic in Tom's special chili at their last Super Bowl party, a few weeks before the shadow of Myrabin crossed their lives.

Kathryn looked over at the antique glass-front cabinet under one of the windows that faced the street. It had come to them from Tom's parents' house after his mother passed away. It held all of the trophies and medals Tom had earned in surf competitions in high school and college. By law school, Tom had given up competing, so she had never shared that part of his life. But she knew how much those gleaming symbols of athletic prowess had meant to him, and now to her, because they were something tangible she could hold on to, not like the sound of his voice which she struggled to remember.

Her eyes went from the trophies to their wedding picture on the mantel. According to Dr. Nina, it should be out of sight by now, an admission that her life with Tom was irretrievably lost. But she couldn't yet bring herself to hide it away. She smiled at the image of Tom. His hair was blonder than hers because of all his time on the waves in the sun. The fresh smell of sea and wind always clung to him. He was most alive when he was gliding across the water. "I'm a simple man," he told Kathryn not long after they met. "I love the ocean, and surfing, and the law. And now you."

She swallowed the last of the cheap wine, put her head down on one of the sofa pillows, and sobbed.

CHAPTER THREE

Friday, January 31, 2014, The Penthouse, Emerald Shapery Center, San Diego

Goldstein, Miller, Mahoney & Fitzgerald occupied the penthouse of the 30-story Emerald Shapery office tower, well above Warrick, Thompson's offices on the twenty-sixth, twenty-fifth, and twenty-fourth floors. It took Kathryn two weeks after winning Rick Peyton's approval to gain access to Hugh Mahoney. Finally, at four o'clock on Friday, January 31, she stepped into the pale gray and blue marble lobby, ready to announce herself to the receptionist, only to find the receptionist's chair empty.

She heard the sound of champagne corks and ragged laughter and looked across the deserted reception area to find a party underway in the conference room that opened off the lobby. People were milling around the long table, loaded with food, in the center of the room. A bar with an attendant in a white jacket was off to the right. A loud cheer went up as additional corks popped, followed by drunken mirth. Apparently this party had been underway for some time.

Her heart sank. She'd had a feeling all along that Hugh Mahoney wouldn't help her. She'd endured the wait to see him and had cancelled all her late afternoon court appointments and jailhouse visits for nothing. She sighed and turned back toward the elevators.

"Wait! Where are you going? Come join the party!" Kathryn was looking into mild gray eyes, a wide smile, and an expressive face with a lock of light brown hair flopping toward his right eye. He looked to be about her age. His expensive gray pants said there had once been a gray suit coat over his starched white shirt. But the coat was long gone and his conservative maroon tie was loosened.

"I'm Mark Kelly." He stepped toward her with an outstretched hand. Professional courtesy kicked in automatically, and she gave him her firm, no-nonsense handshake.

"Kathryn Andrews." She realized she should have worn her one and only Calvin Klein suit that she'd paid fifty dollars for at Ross Dress For Less. She had forgotten she'd be moving in expensive circles at Goldstein, Miller.

"And you're one of my plaintiffs, and you got the email to come celebrate with us! Come on in and have a drink!"

"One of your plaintiffs?"

"I just won a forty-three million dollar jury verdict this morning in *Besser versus Capital Energy Development*. The firm sent out an email inviting any plaintiffs in town to come down and celebrate this afternoon." He kept smiling as if he were the most affable human on earth rather than a tiger of an attorney who had just brought a major corporation to its financial knees.

21

"I gather that was a class action lawsuit?"

He nodded. "The firm's specialty. Come on in and celebrate."

Kathryn tried to imagine what forty-three million dollars looked like. Her convicted murder clients freaked out when the judge ordered them to pay a one-hundred-dollar restitution fine, a sum which didn't even begin to cover the burial costs of their victims.

"No, thanks. I can't. I had an appointment to see Hugh Mahoney at four, but this doesn't seem to be a good time."

Mark Kelly's eyes remained affable, but he now seemed to be appraising her. "Are you a client of Hugh's?"

"Maybe. I don't know. Potential client."

"Ah, I see. Well, he's inside. Come with me, and I'll introduce you. I'm sure he wants to talk to you. There's nothing Hugh loves more than a new client and a new lawsuit. Want something to drink first?"

"No, thank you." She was suddenly miserably nervous as she followed Mark into the crowded room. Judging from the looks of the partiers, none were clients. They were all expensive lawyers in various stages of coats on and off, ties tied and not, and hair slicked back in buns and lose, flowing like the champagne. Why should she be intimidated, she asked herself. She'd gone to school with people just like this. Paul, her best friend, was one of them. Why was she suddenly miserably conscious of her cheap suit jacket from Forever 21 and her unpolished black flats, a DSW bargain at fifteen bucks?

Mark threaded his way through the high-priced legal talent toward an ungainly man, six feet-four, if an inch, in the corner of the room, with a glass of champagne in one hand and an arm draped over the shoulders of a twenty-something blonde in a breathtakingly expensive red suit.

"Hugh, you've got an appointment with this lady at four!" Kathryn was embarrassed when eyes turned to appraise her, but the most penetrating of all belonged to Hugh Sean Mahoney.

His dark eyes, walled-up behind small coke-bottle glasses, studied every detail of her face and clothes. Kathryn couldn't help staring back at this mountain of a man in a rumpled white shirt that had once been crisp with starch and expensive suit pants that, like Mark's attire, were missing the polish their jacket had offered. She guessed his loafers, as bright as mirrors, were the kind of Gucci's that high powered criminal defense attorneys wore. He had short, wiry gray hair that defied taming.

"Hugh Mahoney." He undraped his arm from the blonde, who looked disappointed, and offered her his hand.

"Kathryn Andrews."

"Oh, that's right. Rick sent you."

"If it's a bad time—" But she knew she wouldn't be back. This whole episode had been a mistake. Tom wouldn't have wanted her here among the sharks who fed on the injuries of little people to line their expensive pockets.

"No, of course not. We have an appointment. Come this way to my office where we can talk. Want some champagne?"

"No, thanks." Kathryn followed him down the winding halls where she could glimpse expensive, empty offices through open doors. *I'm not here to celebrate* she wanted to say. *I'm here because Big Drug killed my husband, and I want you to do something about it.*

Predictably, Hugh had an office as big as a small apartment that overlooked the city on one side and San Diego Bay on the other. A glass door gave him access to the roof of the thirty-story building.

He folded his large body into the chair behind his pristine cherry-red mahogany desk that glowed like a jewel in the late afternoon light and got out a yellow legal pad. Kathryn thought of her chipped oak counterpart, loaded with thirty-five case files, at the Office of the Public Defender just six blocks away.

"Rick said you are thinking about a wrongful death suit."

"Yes, my husband Tom died a year and a half ago. Liver failure. He was only forty."

"Okay, so why wrongful death?"

"Tom's hypertension was diagnosed in February 2012, and he was given Myrabin to lower his blood pressure. By Memorial Day, his liver had failed. He died on June 18. His cardiologist believes Myrabin destroyed his liver."

The big man's ears, which protruded from his head like an elephant's, seemed to perk up. "Who makes Myrabin?"

"Wycliffe Pharmaceutical. They are based in Seattle."

"Right." Hugh nodded as he made notes on his legal pad. "Rick told me about Myrabin. Tell me more about your husband. Excessive alcohol consumption? Risky sex?"

Kathryn tried to control her irritation. "Of course not. We met at Harvard when we were One L's. We got married a month after we graduated. We were married for fifteen years."

"You went to Harvard?" His dark brown eyes studied her carefully. She could see he was trying to reconcile her cheap clothes with her expensive legal pedigree.

"I did."

"Who do you work for?"

"I'm a Senior Deputy Public Defender. Tom was, too."

Hugh sat back in his chair and frowned. "What were the two of you doing over there? Your classmates are all over here working for me or downstairs at Alan Warrick's."

"It was Tom's idea. We clerked for big Wall Street firms when we were in school, but a lifetime of pushing paper for corporate giants seemed so empty. We wanted to do something to make a difference."

"And the public defender's office allows you to do that?" His voice dripped with skepticism.

"You already know the answer to that. My clients don't care if I went to Harvard or the YMCA Night Law School. They all think I'm trying to sell them down the river because the best I can do is negotiate a plea deal for them. I can't do magic and get guilty people off. I can't make what they've done go away. My clients resent me because I can't pull out a wand and send them home as if nothing ever happened. They all think I can 'beat the case' for them. The word 'grateful' is not in their vocabulary."

"So why stay in the public defender's office with a background like yours and your husband's?"

"I stayed because Tom stayed. He still thought we were doing some good with our high-powered degrees."

"And now?"

"And now my entire life is up for grabs. The only thing I know for sure is I want Wycliffe to squirm in front of a jury for what they did to Tom!"

He was silent in the face of her fury, as if observing and

calculating the depths of her emotion. Finally he observed, "You didn't grow up here."

"No, Tom did. He wanted to come home after law school. I'm from Atlanta."

Hugh nodded. "You've got a little bit of an accent left. I think mine's all gone. My Boston Catholic father was unmerciful in schooling it out of us. I grew up two hours north of you in Chattanooga. Are Tom's parents alive? Did he have brothers and sisters? Did you and Tom have any children?"

"We didn't have any children." But not for lack of trying, she thought bitterly. "He was an only child, and his parents passed a few years before he died. I'm glad they weren't here to see Tom die."

"How do you know Rick Peyton?" Hugh asked.

"Through Paul Curtis."

A flicker of recognition danced through the otherwise inscrutable eyes behind the small, thick lens. "I know Paul. Fine attorney. Yet to beat me, though. Like everyone else." He grinned.

"Do you always win?"

"No, and you don't always lose."

"But most of the time."

"And most of the time our firm gets a favorable result for our clients. No one can outspend us, and no one can out litigate us. And we are careful about the cases we take. Obviously thorough screening increases our chances of winning. What did Paul say about me?"

Most successful trial attorneys had huge egos, but Hugh Mahoney's was the biggest she had encountered, and he wanted it stroked. "I'm going to give you an honest answer."

"Those are the only kind I like."

"Paul said, 'You won't like Hugh Mahoney. He's the nastiest, meanest plaintiff's attorney on earth. But if he takes your case, he'll fight for Tom and for you like a rabid pitbull.'"

The minute the words were out of her mouth, she regretted being that frank. But Hugh threw back his head and laughed until his whole body shook. Finally he looked at her again. "I'm delighted by that description. And do you dislike me?"

Kathryn thought of the ostentatious champagne party probably still going strong in the conference room. Above all, she thought of Hugh's wedding-ringed hand draped over the blonde as Mark Kelly had introduced her.

Hugh spoke before she could. "Never mind. I see the answer on your face. You'll be happy to know you're in the majority. When I tried cases, I lost a few because jurors don't like me. I think I'm just a teddy-bear of a guy, but jurors find me abrasive. I take depositions and plan case strategy, but I put the appealing guys like Mark Kelly out front in the courtroom to wow the jurors. Juries really like your friend Paul, too. He wins when he isn't up against me and my partners."

Although he was being affable about her opinion, she knew she'd blown it. She felt as if a job interview was over, and she was about to be shown the door.

And she was exactly right. Hugh unfolded his six imposing feet from his leather chair and stood up, extending his hand across his desk. She rose, too, and returned the handshake automatically.

"Thanks for coming by. I'll give your case some thought. I need to talk to Rick some more about Myrabin. It's not a drug that's on my current hit list. But maybe it should be. As I said, we do a lot of research before we agree to take on a case. I forgot to ask when your husband died. Is there a statute of limitations problem?"

"Possibly. He died on June 18, 2012. Dr. Myers told me about Myrabin in mid-July, so I have to file by July 15 of this year."

Hugh nodded. "There are a lot of good plaintiff's attorneys in Southern California. I've worked with most of them. Best of luck to you, Mrs. Andrews."

She felt like an intruder being escorted off the premises as he walked her back to the lobby, shook hands once more, and pressed the down call button to summon the elevator. He turned back to the party as she entered the lift; and, just as she'd guessed, the festivities had ramped up into an even higher gear. The sound of champagne corks had been replaced with the intoxicating smell of filet mignon, making her empty stomach rumble. She knew that if Hugh had planned to take her on as a client, he would have invited her back to the party to chat and get to know her. Being shunted into the elevator depressed her. Although everything about Hugh and his grandiose firm turned her stomach, her lawyer's instincts said that he was the one who could make Wycliffe swing slowly in the wind. Well, she'd call Paul later tonight and tell him she was back to square one on finding an attorney to tell Tom's agonizing story. She saw Mark Kelly come forward to welcome Hugh back to the festivities with a glass of something that looked like scotch. As the elevator doors began to slide together, she saw Mark cast a curious eye in her direction while Hugh shook his head "no."

CHAPTER FOUR

Friday, January 31, 2014, Coronado Island, San Diego, California

At midnight, Hugh Mahoney stood in his bedroom, sipping scotch and staring out at the night-dark Pacific. He had bought the oceanfront Crown Manor more than ten years ago in the fire sale that had been Larry Lawrence's estate. Lawrence, a Chicago real estate developer with a taste for pretty women and a warmer climate, had bought the Manor, just down the street from his other Coronado investment, the Hotel Del, so he could keep his eyes on his prize. But his third wife, who managed the hotel, loathed the Manor; so it stood empty until said third marriage went belly up because he was having an affair with his soon-to-be-fourth wife. He was forced to renovate the Manor for his new bride because his Rancho Sante Fe mansion had become the property of Wife Number Three.

Hugh had pulled down the brick wall that Larry had built around the sprawling house to ensure the privacy of visiting presidents. Like Larry, Hugh had vast sums to contribute to presidential campaign war chests; but unlike Larry, Hugh rarely entertained the victors themselves. No, Hugh would much rather take depositions where he could watch corporate executives squirm, hour after hour, under the onslaught of his surgically precise questions, designed to reveal where the bastards had hidden their shareholders' money. Then he preferred to come home to his scotch and this breath-taking view of the infinite Pacific. Hugh Sean Mahoney was no longer the boy who had grown up poor and land-locked in Tennessee. He was an attorney as powerful as the vast black ocean stretching into the dark night. He was the majority owner of an eight-hundred-attorney firm with offices in San Diego, New York, Los Angeles, Chicago, Atlanta, Miami, Washington, D.C., and London. And in the past six months, his attorneys had won verdicts in excess of three hundred million dollars in securities and pharmaceutical class actions. Mark's verdict today had been the cherry on top. Hugh smiled as he sipped his scotch. Under his leadership, Goldstein, Miller, Mahoney & Fitzgerald had become unbeatable. He had only to pick his next target, and it would fall at his feet.

But Wycliffe Pharmaceutical was not going to be his next target. Although very little penetrated the armor of his invincibility these days, meeting Kathryn Andrews had unsettled him unlike any meeting he had ever experienced. But his unease didn't come from her beauty, although Hugh was a connoisseur of beautiful women; and Kathryn's shoulder-length, honey-blonde hair and almond-shaped, hazel-green eyes and perfect oval face ranked her at the top of the beautiful scale. He was equally intrigued by the way she carried her lean, lithe five-eight frame. Her grace and poise said she must have been a dancer at some point in her life. She was the only woman he had ever met who could look elegant in a cheap gray suit.

No, Hugh was uneasy because meeting Kathryn Andrews had brought him face-to-face with an uncomfortable truth: becoming the most powerful lawyer of his generation had stripped his heart of the ability to feel anything. He could remember the days at Vanderbilt when his relationship with Elizabeth "Buffy" Chapin, a banking heiress from Atlanta, had been brand new and when he had still believed himself to be the luckiest man in the world because she was in love with him. And he could remember their wedding day and the days his children, Elise and Erin, had been born. He could remember how full of love he'd been on those days as he'd vowed to be the best husband and father on earth. But his desire to hunt Big Corporate Game and to bring home million-dollar verdicts had defeated all of those vows. Little by little, the words "I love you" became empty, their meaning wiped out by his insatiable lust for power and money.

He had spent his marriage on the road, deposing witnesses. When he had been at home, he hadn't slept with his wife often because he had been up at all hours planning trial strategy. Without complaint, Buffy had raised Elise and Erin alone and filled the rest of her days with volunteer work for charity in return for the privilege of spending as much of Hugh's money and her own as she pleased. Her mother had lived that life, and Buffy had felt entitled to the same. Now asleep down the hall in her own room, she never raised an objection to Hugh's absences, or to his many affairs, including the current one with second-year associate, Logan Avery. After so many years, Buffy was as devoid of feeling as he was.

Elise, who was now twenty-nine, had always been closer to her mother. Even if Buffy was comfortable with their arrangement, Hugh knew Elise judged him for being unfaithful. On the other hand, Erin, who was twenty-seven, idolized him even if he had missed most of her birthdays and her high school graduation because he had been nailing major corporations to the wall ostensibly on behalf of their shareholders, large and small, although in truth his purpose had been to fill his firm's coffers even higher with the spoils of attorneys' fees from class-action victories.

He watched the vast Pacific, reduced to nothing but curling shadows at low tide, lap the wide ribbon of gray sand at land's end and willed himself not to let meeting Kathryn disturb his comfortable, numb peace. *Sometimes people come into your life who remind you of what you have lost, or have never had, or have never been.* He sipped his scotch and smelled the soft briny air drifting through the open windows and remembered how her fierce anger over her husband's unjust death had made him realize that his own heart was nothing more than a dark, empty hole. His empty heart twisted as he remembered the way her hazel eyes had flashed fire as she'd vented her rage at Wycliffe Pharmaceutical. Her husband had been more than lucky to have been loved like that. He wished someone could yet love him that much. But that was impossible. Women like Kathryn Andrews had much more depth than the wet-behind-the-ears associates like Logan, who were Hugh's willing prey.

Hugh didn't respect the women who gave in to his advances. Their real aphrodisiac was money. He had grown up lanky, plain, and spectacled, driving a Dodge clunker of a car. It was not until his bank account swelled, and he owned a Porsche and a Mercedes that women like Logan flocked to him in droves. It was an important lesson: a man with a paunch, coke-bottle glasses, and a wedding ring could have all the sex he wanted if he had the bucks. Women with perfect bodies and vacant hearts didn't take to "poor." And Hugh knew way too much about "poor."

Although it was midnight, his phone began to ring. He looked to make sure it wasn't Logan. She'd been upset because he hadn't wanted to continue the victory party in a suite at the Westgate. Thankfully, she'd taken "no" for an answer. It was his older brother Patrick calling from San Francisco.

"You're up late, little brother." Hugh could still hear the faint purr of southern vowels in Patrick's speech. He smiled at being called "little brother" by his sixty-four-year-old sibling.

"As are you. Up late worrying about some slimy plaintiff's attorney alleging you all have infringed their software patent?"

"There probably aren't going to be any software patents after the Supreme Court hears *Alice v. CLS Bank* at the end of March." Patrick was the general counsel of Fisher Technology Group, the multimillion dollar software-development child of twenty-nine-year-old, San Fran boy-wonder, Marty Fisher.

"Never heard of it."

"No reason you should. It doesn't involve a drug that has killed people or manipulating corporate assets to screw the shareholders. I keep Marty and the accountants on the straight and narrow. Believe me, little brother, they know you are out there lurking."

Hugh smiled. He loved to hear that Corporate America was terrified of him. "So why the call? Are you going to be in town?" He hoped so. Patrick was the one person with whom he could be his genuine self.

"No, unfortunately. I'm heading over to London with Marty in the morning for a week-long summit with ten or twelve international software development firms. I just called to congratulate you on the *Besser* case. Stunning victory."

"Thanks. We had a big party at the firm tonight. Wish you'd been there."

"I'll take a rain check until the next time Marty sends me south. I actually thought you'd be holed up at the hotel with that 'friend' of yours."

"You don't have to beat around the bush. You know the arrangement Buffy and I have."

"Yeah, sorry. I just feel awkward about it. All that Catholic upbringing and Saturday afternoon confessions are still hiding inside me somewhere. Doesn't it ever feel odd to be sleeping with someone your daughter's age?"

Patrick's words stopped Hugh in his tracks. He thought for a moment. "No and yes."

"How no and yes?"

"No, because I don't think about the age gap when I'm with someone I'm attracted to. It's there, but I don't think about it. Yes, because when it's over and I try to give them something to make up for ending it, I thank God Elise and Erin would never sleep with an old guy like me who ought to know better."

"That's honest, at least."

"It is. But I have to confess I met a woman today, late

thirties, early forties, taffy-blonde, with melting hazel eyes, who makes all the rest pale in comparison."

"I believe you," Patrick said. "Your voice changes when you talk about her. Who is she?"

"A Harvard graduate working at the public defenders' office, of all unlikely places. She and her late husband wanted to 'make a difference' by being PD's."

"And are they 'making any difference'?" His soft sarcastic vowels said it all.

"Of course not. She's thoroughly disillusioned with that notion."

"What about the husband? Does he still see himself as the Ivy League Knight in Shining Armor?"

"He's dead. Died in June 2012. She came to see me about a wrongful death suit against the drug company that she believes killed him. Wycliffe Pharmaceutical."

"That should be right down your alley. Wycliffe is one of the biggest. They are even a client of ours. We make an inventory tracking product for them."

"Know anything else about them?"

"Not a lot. I've met some of their execs. Typical MBA suits. The R & D Ph.D.'s are all in the trenches, developing drugs. Wycliffe is tough to sue because their litigation war chest is bottomless."

"Hmm. You're right. Sounds like my kind of lawsuit."

"If you pick them off, it will be your biggest coup yet."

"I'm not going after them."

"*What*?"

"I said I'm not going to take this one. Rick's mixed up in it.

He's the one who sent her to me."

"Oh, and you're still backing off of those arrangements with him? But you want to take her case?"

Hugh stared out at the neutral ocean and asked himself what he wanted: to feel something other than blood lust for taking down Corporate America. He wanted to feel the kind of passion for someone that Kathryn Andrews had felt for her husband. He wanted a relationship about real love, and not about the size of his bank account and the cars he drove. And then he came to his senses and silently laughed at his middle-aged self with the gray hair and the noticeable paunch and the coke-bottle glasses. How ridiculous could he be?

"No, I don't want it," he lied. "It's just that she reminded me of how much Dad cared about Mom. I always thought they were lucky to fall in love with another Catholic. You didn't marry outside the church back then."

"Yeah," Patrick agreed. "And there was no birth control. Mom lost three babies between you and me."

"She never told me that."

"No reason to. But I was nine when you were born. I was old enough to be shocked when they came home with you. I didn't think you'd live either."

"Not only did I live, but now I tower over your puny six feet."

"True. Remember those soggy fish sticks we had to eat every Friday?"

"All the charm and taste of shredded paper." Hugh's voice changed to the angry, bitter tone he used when he talked about William Mahoney's death. "What I remember best is the day

Dad lost the dealership."

"You were only ten."

"Yeah, but it's as clear as if it happened yesterday."

"I was away at college."

"At least you had a scholarship and got to stay. It was losing the dealership that killed him." Hugh's bitter tone was back. "Ford screwed him royally on his contract."

"So you grew up to build a mega law firm based upon pure hatred for Big Business. And that's the reason you're going to take Kathryn Andrews' case. But be careful, little brother, your eye for women is going to be your downfall one of these days."

CHAPTER FIVE

Friday, February 7, 2014, Hugh Mahoney's Office, Emerald Shapery Center, San Diego

"You have to take Kathryn Andrews' case," Rick Peyton said as soon as he sat down in one of the chairs in front of Hugh's massive desk. The wan winter sunlight cast long shadows over its polished red mahogany surface.

"No, I don't have to," Hugh said. "Would you like some coffee?" The door swung open at that moment, and his secretary appeared with a silver carafe and two sturdy black mugs.

"It's going to be an important case," Rick insisted. "There's been talk in the medical community about Myrabin ever since it was approved."

"What kind of talk?"

"That Suchet was right to stop working on it. That Wycliffe has hidden the truth about the number of deaths it has caused."

Hugh sipped his coffee and frowned. He opened the top drawer of his desk, pulled out a flask, and poured a healthy helping of scotch into his cup. He held the flask toward Rick, who shook his head.

"You need to lay off of that stuff."

"So my cardiologist says." Hugh recapped the flask and put it back in the drawer. "Look, I'm not saying Wycliffe's hands aren't dirty. I just don't think this case is for us. For one thing, this is just one plaintiff."

"But I'm sure it will turn out to be a lot more. There are probably hundreds, if not thousands, of people out there who've been injured by this drug. Lots of liver transplants."

"And how do you prove that?"

"The usual way. Discovery. Talking to other experts."

"And I gather you want to be the expert who testifies at trial?" Hugh frowned slightly.

"According to our usual arrangement, yes. I sent this one to you, after all."

Hugh sipped his drink and stared out at the magnificence of San Diego at his feet in the soft, late afternoon sun. A lawyer reaches the pinnacle of his career when he can walk away from litigation worth millions. "We are taking a risk if we follow the usual procedure. You know that. The U.S. Attorney has been sniffing around us for two years. The statute of limitations has run on all of our past arrangements. As of now, we are in the clear."

Rick squirmed in his chair and crossed and uncrossed his legs. "I know, and I wouldn't ask for one more if things weren't—well—desperate."

"I told you the last time not to get into financial trouble again."

"All I need is five million."

"All? You're kidding."

"Look, Hugh, for you five million is nothing. You're worth five hundred million at least. We've been friends a long time. We've never turned our backs on each other."

"But this kind of thing is getting too risky."

"Last time. I promise. Besides, Kathryn is a perfectly legitimate plaintiff, and you know you want to take down Wycliffe. I'll lose everything if you don't."

* * *

After Hugh walked Rick to the elevator, he wandered back down the halls of his empire to Mark Kelly's junior-partner, glass-box corner office. It was spacious, but not as spacious as Hugh's; and the view of San Diego through its glass walls was slightly less spectacular. Mark was on the phone when Hugh entered, but he gave him the sign to wait, so Hugh sat down in one of the chairs in front of the desk.

"I'm glad you came by," Mark said as soon as he hung up. "I was going to come see you this afternoon about splitting the attorneys' fees for the *Besser* case."

Hugh leaned back and studied his protégé. "What were you thinking about the split?"

"Five million for Hays, Price. Two for Lane, Turner. We keep the rest."

Hugh frowned. "No way I'm approving five for Hays."

"But they took three years worth of depositions for us. They actually asked for eight million."

"I don't care how much work they did or what they asked for. Bill Hays tried to settle behind my back, if you recall."

Mark pressed his lips together, considering what to say next.

"I don't agree with that assessment of Bill's thinking. He only talked to *Besser*'s general counsel about what it would take to settle the whole thing without a trial. He didn't actually make an offer to settle."

"Don't care. I didn't authorize him to do that, and we were the lead firm and I was the lead attorney."

"He was trying to do a good thing, Hugh."

"Give Hays, Price the same as Lane, Turner."

Mark opened his mouth to protest but closed it again. "I don't think you came to talk about the *Besser* fee split."

"No, I didn't. I came to talk to you about the Tom Andrews' wrongful death case."

"I thought you'd already decided not to take that one."

"Rick asked me to. He's in financial trouble–again. He needs this one last case."

"It sounds like a good one based on what we know so far."

"Which isn't much."

"True. But if Rick wants it so badly, he must have a good reason."

"He says there's been talk about Myrabin for years. He insists we can convert all that hearsay into solid expert opinion."

"Well, an expert can rely on hearsay in giving an opinion."

"Sure. But right now, we don't know if the hearsay Rick thinks is out there actually exists."

Mark smiled. "I'm betting Rick is right. Let's take it."

Hugh grinned back. "Can't resist a good fight, can you, just like me? Okay, I'll have Patty call Kathryn Andrews and set up a meeting with all of us to sign a retainer agreement. Something in the late afternoon, so you can take her to dinner afterward.

Only make it seem spontaneous."

"Why, may I ask?"

"Obviously we're going to have to know the state of her marriage. She's not going to be willing to talk about something that personal in a cold conference room in front of me, you, Patty, and Logan."

"So that's the team for this case?"

"As of now, yes."

"Okay, I'll take her to dinner and see what I can find out."

CHAPTER SIX

Thursday, February 27, 2014, Conference Room, Emerald Shapery Center, San Diego

The main conference room at Goldstein, Miller, Mahoney & Fitzgerald looked very different from the last time Kathryn had seen it. There was no party this afternoon at four o'clock. Flanked by his minions, Hugh Mahoney sat at the head of the table, serious in his navy suit and gold-striped navy tie. Mark Kelly, junior partner, was on his right; Patricia E. Fox, slightly more junior partner, was on his left; Logan Avery, second-year associate, occupied the chair next to Patricia. All eight-hundred-dollar suit coats were on; all hair was wound and pinned into chignons; all Rolex watches were visible above starched pima cotton or silk cuffs; fabulously expensive pearls were in ears; wedding rings were displayed only on Hugh and Patricia's fourth finger. The tailoring, alone, probably cost around sixteen thousand dollars, Kathryn thought. Tom must be hovering above them in his Men's Wearhouse two-hundred-dollar suit, wondering if she had lost her mind.

Kathryn sat a few chairs down from Logan as if space were

needed to delineate the status of being a client from being a member of the Goldstein, Miller litigation team. Although she wasn't even close to the sartorial splendor around her, at least she had remembered to wear her black, off-price Calvin Klein today, with her on-sale Anne Taylor silk blouse and Halston pumps, culled from Nordstrom's semi-annual sale last August. She tried not to think about every other female foot in the room, shod in Manolo Blahniks.

Since her January meeting with Hugh, Kathryn had become resigned to finding someone else to go after Wycliffe. Paul had agreed that the thunderous silence from the Plaintiff's God-On-High meant Tom's case had been turned down. He'd given her a list of five alternate plaintiff's attorneys who ate raw meat and corporate giants for breakfast, acknowledging none of them could gut Corporate America with Hugh's style and grace. Or success rate.

And then on Monday, when Kathryn had come back to her office at four-thirty, too exhausted to think because she had spent the day splitting legal hairs for a client on trial for murder, she'd found the message in a half-inch stack of pink phone tickets the receptionist had left on her overflowing desk. Please call Patricia E. Fox at Goldstein, Miller. And ten minutes later, in the crisp vowels of Brahmin Boston that Kathryn recognized from her own time at Harvard, and which explained why she was not plain Patricia Fox, Mrs. E. Fox had informed her that Hugh Mahoney would, indeed, accept her as a client in the wrongful death of her husband. She was to appear in the firm's main conference room at four o'clock on Thursday afternoon to sign the retainer agreement.

And now it was signed. Hugh stood up, indicating the meeting was over, and told her Mrs. E. Fox would set up another meeting early next week to go over the details of her husband's death so that Logan could begin to draft the complaint and interrogatories to send to Wycliffe. Kathryn shook Hugh's hand, smiled at everyone in the room, and allowed Mrs. E. Fox to escort her to the elevators, thanking the Universe all the while that she had allowed Tom to drag her into the public defender's office so that she hadn't spent the first three years of her career drafting dry and boring documents for men like Hugh.

She stepped into the lobby a few minutes later only to find Mark Kelly waiting for her. Gone was the serious face he had worn for the last forty-five minutes in the conference room. He was grinning mischievously.

"Beat you."

Kathryn considered whether to respond in lawyer-mode or person-mode. Lawyer- mode would have sent the signal to bug off. But his shining gray eyes and round boyish face, full of himself because of the prank he'd pulled, melted her professionally very hard heart. Tom liked to surprise her, and no one had done that since he had died.

So she chose person-mode. "You ran down twenty-nine flights of stairs?"

"Not exactly. I cheated and took the freight elevator. Goes much faster."

"I'll have to remember that next time. Thanks for the tip."

"I wanted to offer you a lift. My car's downstairs. And it's pouring outside."

She saw he was holding his Burberry. She had shrugged into

her own bargain London Fog in the elevator on the way down. The sky, indeed, was falling.

"No thanks. It's only a few blocks to my office where I left my car."

"A few wet blocks. Let me drive you. Better yet, let's go for a drink."

"Not P & J's."

Mark laughed. "Of course not. You can't be heard in there during Happy Hour. There's a much quieter place in the Gaslamp, Bice Ristorante. I like Italian food on a rainy night. Come on, let's start the tab rolling for Wycliffe. We want to make sure this suit is as expensive as possible for them. And you look like you could use a glass of good Chianti."

So Kathryn followed him to his black BMW with the heated leather seats, which they quickly abandoned to valet parking a few blocks later at Bice. As if she had melted into some sort of fairy tale, she let him lead her to one of the more out-of-the-way white-linen topped tables in the simple, but elegant, dining room.

He ordered a bottle of Chianti which probably cost as much as a month of her salary and waved his hand over the appetizer menu and ordered all of them.

"We'll share," he smiled.

"I probably won't be hungry for anything else after all that."

"Then Wycliffe will have gotten off much too lightly. But the night is young. When you see the minuscule portions they bring, you'll understand why you won't be able to leave without having one of the entrees."

The waiter appeared with the wine and conducted the de

rigeur tasting ritual. Mark raised his glass as soon as both were filled, "To victory!"

Kathryn joined his toast but frowned slightly.

"You seem hesitant," Mark said.

"I just don't think it's going to be as easy to vindicate Tom as snapping our fingers."

"No, it isn't. It's going to be months and months of depositions and slogging through the records Wycliffe has to turn over in discovery, but we will win this case."

"Because Wycliffe killed Tom or because Hugh is unbeatable?"

Mark's eyes never stopped laughing, she noticed, once he was out of professional mode. "Actually, I'm unbeatable."

Kathryn sipped her wine and thought about the implications of that statement.

"You?"

"You're surprised."

"Paul sent me to Goldstein, Miller because of Hugh. He didn't mention you."

"Paul who?"

"Paul Curtis."

"Say no more. The defendant's wonder-attorney at Warrick, Thompson. I've been up against Paul. Talented guy. So far I've beaten him, though."

"How many times?"

"Once."

"Then he'll get you next time."

"It could happen. So you went to Harvard with Paul?"

"And Tom. Paul introduced me to Tom."

"And lived to regret it, I bet."

Kathryn wondered if her cheeks turned pink. Could a woman of forty-two blush? She would simply say it was the wine if he noticed.

But he didn't. The appetizers had arrived, and Mark began to portion aged prosciutto, thin slices of ahi tuna, and fennel and pear salad onto her plate.

"The prosciutto is the best," he said as he handed her the cocktail plate.

And he was right. For a few minutes she was absorbed in the smoky flavor of the ham, the lightness of the tuna, and the contrast of the sweet pear in the salad.

"Good?"

"Fantastic."

"Then Wycliffe is off to a good start making amends, whether it knows it or not. Tell me more about Tom."

"I will, but before I do, tell me about you. I don't like to talk about something this personal with a stranger."

Mark's gray eyes became serious for a moment. "Good point. I apologize. We'll be together for months and months in this litigation. We should introduce ourselves properly. Mark Hayden Kelly. Hayden was my mother's maiden name, and being the good daughter of the South that she was, she made sure it attached to her oldest son.

"Grew up in Charleston, South Carolina. Father was a small-time corporate lawyer. One sibling, a sister, MaryBeth, now a mom of three, married to a doctor, living in Savannah. Graduated from the University of South Carolina and finagled my way into the University of Virginia for law school. Clerked for Hugh one summer, fell in love with the idea of plaintiff's litigation against major corporations, and have never looked back. What did you do before Harvard?"

Kathryn smiled. "I grew up in Atlanta, no siblings, a father who vanished when I was two. A fantastic mother who taught the third grade for thirty years until she retired, now happily living in Miami with the love of her life, whom she met three years ago. I loved gymnastics until I blew out my left knee in competition in high school. Graduated from William and Mary as an English major without any idea of what I wanted to do. So I tried law school, got into Harvard, and met Paul on my first day in Contracts. One week later, I met Tom, who was with Paul at O'Leary's Pub and Wine Bar. What happened to your accent?"

"Same thing that happened to yours. Too much time out here without enough practice."

Kathryn smiled. "Hugh says he can hear mine."

"Hugh is full of it sometimes." Mark signaled to the waiter who appeared with menus as if he had read his mind.

"For an entree I would recommend the halibut."

Kathryn looked down at the menu and read the description of the most expensive item Bice offered: Pan Seared Halibut with Clam, Mussel, Wild Salmon, Shrimp and Jumbo Lump Crab in a Lobster and Saffron Broth. Oh, well, why not. She could step out of the gray metal, stale sandwich world of the public defender's office for one night.

"Sounds good."

Their order for their second course now dispatched to the kitchen, Mark got back to the serious business of getting acquainted. "So Tom stole you from Paul right away?"

Kathryn smiled. "It wasn't quite that sinister. Tom and I just knew from the beginning we belonged together. And Paul did, too. He and Tom and Steve seemed to know how to read each other's minds."

"Who is Steve?"

She closed her eyes to summon her courage to answer his question. When she opened them, she met his kind gray ones in the low light.

"Don't talk about it if you don't want to," he said.

"No, it's hard, but I want all of you to know everything about Tom. He was the most wonderful person you could ever imagine. There was no one like him."

His eyes radiated warmth and sympathy which she tried not to let her tired, empty heart respond to. She went on. "Tom and Paul and Steve Cooper grew up together in Pacific Beach. From the time they were in middle school, they were winning surfing championships all over California. By high school and college, they were international champions. I have a case at home full of Tom's medals."

"Impressive."

"Very. The three of them went to Stanford as undergraduates, and then decided to go to law school. Paul and Tom went east to Boston, but Steve didn't want to be away from surfing, so he went back to Stanford."

The entrees had arrived, and for a few minutes Kathryn was absorbed in the exquisite seafood. But Mark wanted to hear more.

"Does Steve work for Alan Warrick, too?"

Kathryn sighed. "No, Steve was passionate about environmental issues. He went to work out of law school for the National Resources Defense Council here in San Diego. He loved that job."

"So I gather you don't see him anymore?"

"No, I do. In my imagination, when I walk down to the beach where he and Tom used to surf. I look out at the dots in their black wetsuits against the horizon just where the waves start to form, and I pretend that two of them are Tom and Steve. And I convince myself that before long, they'll come riding their bikes back to the house, sandy and laughing, and ready to sit at the kitchen table and drink beer. Only in reality, none of the spots on the horizon are Tom or Steve because Tom died in June 2012, before Steve died in August."

Mark looked at her in shock and without thinking reached out and took her hand. It was only a friendly gesture, but for a full ten seconds Kathryn wanted it to be more until he realized touching a client was inappropriate and let go. "I'm sorry. What happened?"

Kathryn took a sip of wine and then said, "He drowned, and no one knows how or why it happened. The waves were not even very big that day. And of course, like Tom and Paul, Steve was an expert swimmer."

"So no one saw it happen?"

"No. The guys in the water with their boards were some ways off. They saw Steve catch a wave, but they just assumed he rode it in. No one saw him go under."

"How hard for you. Your husband and one of his best friends within months of each other."

"Yes." She ignored the tears in her eyes. She didn't want him to see her cry, but it couldn't be helped. Mark squeezed her hand again, and she gave him the tight little survivor's smile that she had perfected since her husband's death.

"Do you surf?"

"No. Tom and Steve tried to teach me not long after Tom and I were married, but my knee wouldn't cooperate. Tom went out with Steve more than with Paul because of Paul's hours at Warrick."

Mark nodded. "Makes sense." He turned to the hovering waiter. "No, we don't need to see the desert menu. We'll have the Molten Pistachio and Chocolate Lava Cake with two forks. And coffee. Decaf or caf?"

"Caffeine, please."

Mark smiled. "It will keep you up all night."

"That's okay. I'm in trial tomorrow on a murder case, and I have to go over the witness's police statement tonight so I can impeach him on the stand tomorrow."

He looked at her with renewed respect. "Murder one?"

"Murder one with gang special circumstances. Life without parole if convicted."

"Wow. Heavy lifting."

"I'm used to it. I've been a public defender for seventeen years."

"Who are you defending?"

"A real jerk. Javier Andre Lopez, twenty-eight years old. A Crip since age thirteen. He has a rap sheet as long as both of your arms."

"Who did he kill?"

"A rival Blood who was in the wrong place at the wrong time in Barrio Logan. The DA offered him a 25-year-to-life deal which meant he might be able to live outside of prison in his lifetime, but he turned it down."

"And so he's going to get convicted?"

"Without any doubt. The prosecutor has already tainted the jury with how bad gangs are. And there is surveillance video of my client's car at the murder scene with the shooter's hand out of the front passenger seat window and a tattoo on his forearm that matches Javier's."

"Wow, you've got nothing to work with."

"I know. But the client doesn't. He keeps bringing motions to get me relieved as defense counsel because I'm not trying to 'beat the case' for him. The trial judge tells him I'm doing all I can every time we go into chambers to listen to him complain."

"You've tried a lot of cases, I take it."

She smiled. "More than you, for sure."

He laughed. "True. Ours settle. Especially when defendants see Hugh's name on the complaint."

"Paul told me that."

"Then maybe Wycliffe will fold, too," Mark smiled.

"Somehow I doubt that. Rick Peyton said Myrabin is one of Wycliffe's biggest moneymakers."

"Then they'll fight hard to keep anyone from saying it's not safe."

Dessert, a puddle of melted chocolate sprinkled with pistachio ice cream, arrived with two forks. They were silent as they ate.

Finally Kathryn sighed, "You finish it. I've never been so full."

Mark laughed. "Okay." And he scooped the last bite into his mouth.

"I had better go," she said. "Trial preparation for tomorrow. And I bet your wife is wondering where you are."

He signaled for the check and laughed. "My ex-wife could care less where I am. I would bet my life on that. Jan and I were college sweethearts. Married, made it through law school, and then came out here so I could work for Hugh. She got sick of my hours and of living in California and went back to Charleston."

"Children?"

"No."

"Then you're lucky. Paul's ex uses his hours to keep him from seeing his five-year-old daughter, Jodie."

"Jan would have done that if we'd had children. Glad I dodged that bullet. Maybe he'll be lucky enough to meet someone like Rachel."

"Rachel?"

"My fiancée. She was a paralegal in the corporate section when we met, so she understands everything about my career: my hours, my travel, and client dinners like this one."

"Everything?" She suppressed a tiny hiccup of disappointment that this had turned out to be a strictly professional dinner after all. She had had the impression that he had used the get-acquainted-with-the-new client excuse for personal reasons. Wrong.

"Yes, everything."

* * *

They went out into the damp dark. The rain had stopped, but the air was heavy with moisture. Mark swung his BMW into the light traffic, but didn't head for Kathryn's office.

He turned and smiled at her. "Just a short detour."

Within minutes, he pulled over and parked in a no-parking zone in front of Petco Park. He gave her the mischievous grin he'd greeted her with when she'd gotten off the elevator as he opened the driver's door. "Come on."

"But won't you get a ticket, parked here?"

"We'll only be a minute. I'll take the risk. Come on."

She wondered about Rachel waiting at home as she followed him to a door that said "Employees Only." He produced a key and motioned for her to follow him inside.

They went up flights and flights of stairs until they came out on the top deck, overlooking the dark stadium. A full moon had broken through the clouds, and the silver light made the rows and rows of seats into magical ghosts in the dark.

Mark smiled and motioned for her to join him at the rail. "I love to come here. I have a key because I've done some work for the Padres."

Kathryn said nothing as she stared over the park.

"I wanted to play baseball when I was a kid. Made it to the team in college. Never got beyond that."

She nodded, still staring down at the thousands of empty seats. She felt the tear form in her left eye and did nothing to stop it when it trickled down her cheek.

His face went from beaming to contrite. "I'm sorry. I wasn't thinking. Bad memories?"

She shook her head. "No, good ones. Tom and I came to

games a lot. And Steve often went with us. Paul and Carolyn not as much."

"Carolyn the ex-wife?"

"Yes."

"What was Tom like?"

She smiled. "Special. Really special. He had the biggest heart in the world, and he would listen for hours if someone needed comfort. He was six feet tall, and he stayed in great shape so he could surf. He tried to go every day, but sometimes work got in the way. He loved everything about the ocean, the waves, the sea creatures, and what he called the broken-hearted cries of the gulls. He had big hands and long graceful fingers, and his smile lit up a room. He was fair and decent and a good lawyer, and everyone loved Tom."

"You said he influenced you to become a public defender. Why did he choose that job?"

Kathryn looked out over the empty seats and focused on the moon shining through the rain clouds. "I always give the official explanation: he wanted to 'make a difference.'"

"What is the unofficial explanation?"

"Steve got into some trouble when he was fourteen. His father left when he was a baby, and his mother struggled to work and take care of Steve and his sister, Amanda. Steve needed money, and he started selling drugs. At first, it was just marijuana, but he and Paul and Tom went to school with kids from rich families. Steve figured out cocaine would bring him a bigger profit."

"Did he use drugs?"

Kathryn gave him an ironic smile. "No, of course not. He

wanted to compete in surfing competitions. Selling drugs was pure financial gain for Steve and nothing else."

"So I gather he got caught?"

"He did. He sold to an undercover female cop who looked like a high school student and got arrested. The court sustained a juvenile wardship petition, and he should have had some sort of custody time, but his public defender managed to get him on probation instead. But it wasn't just what his lawyer did for him in court. Gary Johnson became a sort of father-figure to Steve. He inspired him to improve his grades and eventually to get that scholarship to Stanford. Gary's kindness to Steve was Tom's inspiration to join the public defender's office."

Mark was silent for a few minutes. The moon slipped behind the ragged remnant of rain-cloud. Finally he said, "When I went to work for Hugh, I was hoping I'd be able to do something to make a difference in people's lives."

"And have you made a difference?"

"I'm not sure. Have you?"

"Not as much as I thought I would when Tom talked me into becoming a public defender. I'm tired of the ingratitude of guilty people."

"So do you regret your decision?"

"Not when Tom was alive. Now the job seems meaningless. What about you? Do you regret your decision to work for Hugh?"

"No. I admire Hugh, and he's one of the best plaintiff's attorneys around. I've learned a lot from him. But he's vindictive. If you cross him, you are going to pay a big price."

"Paul said I wouldn't like him."

Mark shook his head. "It's not that simple. Hugh is complicated. He keeps Corporate America honest even if sometimes he goes too far with his personal grudges."

"I just want him to make sure Wycliffe doesn't get away with what they did to Tom. And to me."

"He will."

* * *

Thursday, February 27, 2014, Crown Manor, Coronado, California

When Hugh's phone rang at midnight, he assumed it was Patrick. His brother had been on a trip to China with Marty Fischer for the past two weeks, and Hugh had missed talking to him. He was due back today.

But it wasn't Patrick. It was Mark Kelly.

"You're calling late."

"Sorry. I had to pay my dues when I got home. Rachel didn't like the idea of me taking our new, very attractive client to dinner alone."

"You told her I made you?"

"Yes, but that excuse isn't very persuasive since Rachel works at the firm and knows all about you and Logan. She figures you wouldn't hesitate to encourage me to follow in your footsteps."

"Kathryn's a client. That's different. We don't date our clients."

"I explained that to her. Look, it doesn't matter. She's returned to planning our blowout wedding in November. I called to tell you I couldn't shake Kathryn's story. Tom was exemplary in every way, and they were very happily married."

"H-m-m. I don't buy that."

"Well, I can only report what I saw and heard. She didn't look as if she was lying."

"My gut says otherwise."

"I think you're too skeptical, Hugh. Maybe marriage didn't work out to be happily ever after for you or me, but who's to say Kathryn and Tom Andrews didn't have what we all wish for?"

"So you think I'm just being a big cynic?"

"Based on what I saw and heard tonight."

"Well, keep your eyes and ears open. I still think there's a lot more to this story than she's telling."

"I will. Look, I have to go. I'm getting the evil eye from Rachel. See you at the office, tomorrow. Good night, Hugh."

MOTION FOR SUMMARY JUDGMENT

CHAPTER SEVEN

Monday, April 7, 2014, Edward J. Schwartz Federal Courthouse, U.S. District Court, Southern District of California, San Diego, 9:00 a.m.

It was odd to sit on the plaintiff's side of the courtroom, Kathryn thought. She had spent her career at the defendant's table where Robert McLaren now sat with Annette Fry, a senior associate at King and White, and Emma Talbert, an in-house attorney for Wycliffe. Hugh, who now occupied the lead counsel's chair at her table, and Mark Kelly, in the chair between her and Hugh's, had introduced her to opposing counsel while they waited for the judge to take the bench. As the introductions progressed, she had had to remind herself this was civil law. While she might nod to the deputy district attorney as they took their places each morning for trial, introducing her shackled client was unthinkable.

Patty E. Fox had called her last Monday to say Wycliffe had wasted no time in filing a motion for summary judgment.

"They're trying to knock this out of the water without providing any documents in discovery. That means there's something in their files they don't want us to see. Hugh and Mark are going to argue the motion. Hugh wants you there, if you want to be."

Of course I do, Kathryn thought. *I want to hear their sleazy excuse for murdering my husband.*

She'd decided on her off-price Calvin Klein suit that morning, realizing she'd have to haunt the outlet stores more often in the coming months to have a wardrobe that would show herself worthy of being a Goldstein, Miller client.

The clerk announced the entrance of the judge, and Elizabeth Weiner, an attractive brunette in her late forties, took the bench in her impressive black robes and looked down at the parties.

"We are here this morning on a motion for summary judgment," she observed. "Mr. McLaren, you're the moving party. I'll hear from you first."

As Kathryn watched five-foot-five, supremely cocky, gray-eminence Robert McLaren assume the podium, she wondered how wise it was to appear before a federal civil servant in several thousand dollars worth of navy sartorial splendor. On the other hand, Hugh and Mark had pulled from the back of their closets the kind of low-budget gray suit that Tom would have worn, had he been there that day.

"I don't have much to add, Your Honor, beyond what we've laid out in our moving papers. We are sorry for Mrs. Andrews' loss, but Myrabin had nothing to do with her husband's death. I have attached the FDA data on Myrabin. There have been no reported deaths."

Judge Weiner turned over a few pages of Wycliffe's motion

thoughtfully. Then she looked at Hugh. "I expect you've got something to say about this, Mr. Mahoney."

"I do, Your Honor."

Bob McLaren went back to his seat, allowing Hugh to take the podium.

"Your Honor, this motion is untimely. Wycliffe has failed to answer even one interrogatory or turn over even one document in discovery. And as you can see in our opposition, we have affidavits from Dr. Bruce Meyers, who prescribed Myrabin for Tom Andrews, and from Dr. Richard Peyton, an internationally recognized medical expert, stating the known risks of Myrabin. Facts are in dispute here, Your Honor; and with the full discovery that we're entitled to, I have no doubt that a jury will find in favor of Mrs. Andrews."

Judge Weiner gave Hugh an ironic smile. "You're a bit far down the road, Mr. Mahoney, but I agree you've shown facts in dispute, and Wycliffe must turn over discovery to the plaintiff. Motion for summary judgment denied."

* * *

Wednesday, April 9, 2014, 1845 Ocean Place, Pacific Beach

At eight p.m. Kathryn and Paul settled comfortably on the sofa in her living room after supper. He had been out of town almost constantly since they'd met at P & J's in January. He'd called on Monday, anxious for news about the case and anxious to see her.

The cozy aroma of chicken roasted in olive oil and oregano blended with the cool night breeze blowing through the open window. Paul poured two glasses of the Napa merlot he had brought and handed one to Kathryn.

He lifted his glass. "Congratulations on your first victory in Tom's case."

She returned the gesture, but her smile quickly melted. "I think it's going to be a long, hard slog."

He nodded. "Yeah, probably. They brought that motion way too early, before they'd even produced any documents in discovery. There's something in their files they don't want you to see. They'll fight even harder next time to avoid turning it over."

"That's what Hugh said. And Mark."

"Mark Kelly? Is he on your case?"

"He's going to try it because juries don't like Hugh. Or so Hugh says."

"At least he's honest. Mark's a good trial attorney. And an attractive guy." He didn't look happy about the latter.

Kathryn frowned. She'd avoided Mark since their dinner at Bice because the next morning she'd felt used in a way she couldn't explain. To her relief, he seemed to be avoiding her, too. Patty E. Fox always called with news about the case. Despite her Brahmin pretensions, Patty was struggling to keep up with the responsibilities of being a young Goldstein, Miller partner and the mother of two children under four. Kathryn had grown to like her for it. Patty was far more human than her clothes, her pretentious middle initial, and her Brahmin accent advertised.

"Mark's very engaged to a firm paralegal. No interest in him here."

Paul smiled. "I'm relieved to hear that."

THE DEATH OF DISTANT STARS

Kathryn drank her wine and stared at Tom's trophy case.

Paul followed her eyes to the display of his friend's medals. He reached out and took Kathryn's free hand gently. "Do you think there'll ever be a chance for us, or will he always be in the way?"

Her eyes remained fixed on the case. "I don't know. I wish I knew, but I don't. I still wake up and find his side of the bed empty and think he's out surfing with you and Steve. I can't tell you how it hurts when I'm fully awake, and I know he's not coming back."

Paul kept her hand in his. "I know what you mean. I keep thinking I'll call Tom and Steve to catch a few waves. And then I remember they're both gone."

"It's coming up on two years. When do you think we'll get used to being without them?"

"I don't know," Paul said.

The silence stretched on between them until Kathryn removed her hand from his and asked, "Do you ever see Shannon?"

He frowned, and she could tell the question surprised him and made him uncomfortable. "Not often. She's moved to Coronado and opened a surf school for kids. She calls from time to time and begs me to put Jodie in it. And she wants to surf with me."

"And do you surf with her?"

"Only twice. Both times I ran into her on the beach. It wasn't planned."

Her cell phone began to ring.

"Don't answer it."

But she shook her head. "I have to. It might be the office with an emergency."

"Can't they get another Senior PD to tell whatever idiot has been arrested tonight not to talk to the cops?"

But she had already picked up her phone and said, "Kathryn Andrews."

"Kathryn, Hugh Mahoney here. Is this a bad time?"

"Well, I have company. Paul Curtis came over for dinner."

"I apologize, then, for the interruption. I just wanted you to know that Wycliffe called today and is demanding I make you available for deposition right away."

"I–I see."

"I won't pull any punches. Being deposed is not going to be fun or easy."

Kathryn felt her stomach churn. "I understand."

"Not really. You couldn't possibly understand what it's going to be like at this point. We need to get together to begin preparing. I was hoping you'd be free to come to dinner at my house on Friday night. I'd love for you to meet my wife. She grew up in Atlanta, too. You'll find it easier to talk over a good dinner than in a cold conference room at the firm."

"Of course I will be there, Mr. Mahoney. What time?"

"Seven. And please call me Hugh."

Kathryn punched the end-call button and looked over at Paul.

"I gather that was Hugh Mahoney."

"Wycliffe wants to take my deposition right away."

Paul nodded. "That would be their next step."

"Why?"

"They'll be looking for even the faintest crack in your marriage to use against you. Being deposed won't be an enjoyable experience."

"That's what Hugh said."

"Hey, you look worried. Don't be. You'll be in the best possible hands. They'll give you all the do's and don'ts."

She gave him a wry smile. "Funny, I went to one of the best law schools in the country, and I don't know how to have my deposition taken."

"You'll do fine. Come on, let's stop being sad and serious. Let's walk over to Cass Street, find a bar with a loud band, and dance. You know that's what Tom and Steve would want us to do."

She smiled. "You're right."

"And give some thought to 'us.' Tom and Steve would want that, too."

CHAPTER EIGHT

Thursday night, April 10, 2014, 1845 Ocean Place, Pacific Beach

Her house was deadly quiet when Kathryn got home from work at seven. She'd deliberately lingered at the office because she had dreaded this moment of walking into the too-quiet house suffused with the last orange-pink rays of sunset.

She hurried to the kitchen and poured herself a glass of her usual cheap white wine from Trader Joe's. She'd nearly finished it by the time she'd shrugged out of her suit and pulled on black yoga pants and a green hoodie. She stared down at the empty glass and considered whether to pour herself another. She was drinking too much, but fortunately she was the only one who noticed. At first she'd told herself she'd stop when the pain stopped. But when the pain didn't stop, she told herself drinking was pain management.

She went back to the kitchen and poured another glass. The wine was all she wanted, but to make herself feel less guilty, she threw a frozen lasagna into the toaster oven. White wine and lasagna. Tom would laugh at her.

She looked around the silent kitchen, wondering if his spirit ever came back to hover here. In the early days, she had talked to him, hoping by some miracle there would be a response. But the silence night after night drove the stake of grief deeper and deeper into her heart. Tom was dead. Tom wasn't coming back.

The oven dinged, and she fished out the sagging paper tray of tomato sauce and noodles. She balanced it on a plate and went into the living room and curled up on the sofa.

The first bite had all the charm of cardboard. She looked over at Tom's medals and trophies and said, "We'd have gone out before we'd have eaten this."

Tom had been an excellent cook, and he had prided himself on fast, healthy meals even after a day on his feet in trial. "If the law thing doesn't work out, I'll make a fortune as a short-order cook," he'd always teased her.

She went on chewing the tasteless pasta, thinking about Paul's warning of the night before. "And they'll be looking for even the faintest crack in your marriage."

Had she given enough thought to that risk before she'd decided to sue Wycliffe? Of course she'd had a vague idea that the drug company would try to show she was unhappily married to reduce the amount of her loss if the jury held the company responsible for Tom's death. But unhappily married was so far from the truth that she'd discounted the possibility all together. Until last night when Paul had said, "faintest crack."

She and Tom had not set out to be childless. The day they had planted the white roses around the front door, they had also planned their family: three children–boys or girls–it didn't matter. But they had wanted a few years alone as a couple. Time to get their feet on the ground in their new jobs. Time to spend the weekends pulling up the dingy wall-to-wall carpets and putting down wood-laminate floors. Time to take out the molding 1960's tile in the bath and a half and put in shiny ceramic tile in patterns they designed themselves. Time to put in new kitchen cabinets with glass-front doors and new appliances.

But thirty came, and Kathryn began to hear the clock ticking. They agreed she should stop the pill. And three months later, to her great joy, she was pregnant. Tom came home one night with a tiny little surf board, and they put it in the spare bedroom that was going to be the nursery. She joked the baby had a surf board before he or she had a bed.

Two weeks later, the cramping and bleeding began in the middle of the night. Tom rushed her to the emergency room. By morning, she had miscarried. When he brought her home that afternoon, he'd hidden the little board in a corner of the garage. Except it wasn't really hidden. Kathryn saw it every time she did the laundry or took out a bag of trash. Her heart ached.

Still, they'd been confident it wouldn't take long to become pregnant again. But thirty edged upward, year-by-year, until Kathryn was thirty-five. Now they made love in time to her ovulation schedule. Tired or not, romantic or not, they labored to make a baby where they had once spontaneously and joyfully expressed their passion for each other.

The grim discipline wore them down. Tom escaped to the ocean more and more often after work or first thing in the morning instead of obeying the demands of her ovulation clock. Thirty-five edged upward to thirty-six. Kathryn realized their life as a childless couple had solidified. They went to Rosarito

Beach for Memorial Day and the Fourth of July. They spent Labor Day in Carmel. They went to Cancun for Thanksgiving and sometimes for Christmas. They gave parties on New Year's Eve, Super Bowl Sunday, and each other's birthdays. And at Christmas. On the day in August when Kathryn celebrated her thirty-seventh birthday, she found the tiny little surf board gone. And her heart broke all over again.

"Oh, I gave it to Shannon," Tom said a few days later when she summoned the courage to ask.

"Who is Shannon?"

"She's Steve's new girlfriend. Or soon-to-be new girlfriend. They just met, but they seem perfect for each other."

"Does she have children?" Kathryn demanded, making no effort to hide the bitterness in her voice.

Tom laughed. "No, of course not. She's only twenty-six. She teaches kids to surf."

Kathryn tossed and turned all night, thinking about the little board and Tom's signal that he'd given up on having a family. The next morning after he'd left to surf with Steve, ignoring her few fertile hours for August, she lay miserably alone, haunted by the little surfboard, until she got up, put on a hat and sunglasses, and followed him to the beach where she caught her first glimpse of Shannon Freeman.

Shannon's slim form rose up out of the ocean and onto a surfboard like a goddess in command of her kingdom. She was six feet of wiry, lean muscle. Her wet suit hugged her taught body like a second skin. Her long blonde hair was pulled up into a ponytail that sat high on her head.

She rode her wave into shore, confidently navigating every

dip and curl without falling off. At the end of her ride, she squatted gracefully over the board and leaped into the shallow water. She looked back at Tom, who was just behind her, and laughed, shaking her ponytail so that her blonde hair gleamed like gold in the sun.

Kathryn watched Tom come up beside her and give her a hug that seemed to last a moment too long to be just friends. But Steve rolled in just behind them and didn't react as if anything were amiss. The three of them lay down on their boards and paddled back into the waves. Kathryn didn't wait to see any more, and she didn't want Tom to know what she had seen. Overwhelmed with guilt for spying on him, she turned and hurried away, feeling with gut-wrenching certainty that this woman's presence in their lives meant there would never be a baby.

* * *

Friday, April 11, 2014, Crown Manor, Coronado

Next evening, at seven p.m., Kathryn parked her Mini on the sweeping drive in front of Crown Manor, a red-brick copy of a Tudor palace, surrounded by tall palm trees with a breathtaking view of the Pacific. Although the sun had not set and the long June twilight lingered lovingly like a pink shadow over the house, its battery of lights around the entrance were already on, giving it even more the air of a royal residence. Like one of the high kings of ancient Ireland, King Hugh had summoned her.

He met her at the door and gave her the theatrical California air kiss aimed first at one cheek and then the other, a gesture that reminded her she was in the land of civil law where attorneys could trust their clients not to pull weapons on them. Although his tan casual pants and open collar knit shirt must have been expensive, like the suits she had seen him wearing in the office, his big frame still looked sloppy and unkempt. His mane of gray hair was too stiff to stay down; his collar flopped to the left as if one shoulder were higher than the other.

Behind him in the black and white marble hall stood a sleek middle-aged woman in an obviously expensive yellow knit pants suit. The woman's light brown hair was swept up in an elegant fifties chignon. Her makeup was perfect. Her smooth jaw line and forehead screamed expensive plastic surgery.

"Come in, come in. This is my wife, Elizabeth."

The vision in yellow extended her hand like an empress. "Buffy," she insisted in the vowels of Kathryn's native state. "Please, everyone calls me Buffy."

Kathryn followed Hugh and his wife down the long chessboard hall to a glass-walled room at the rear of the mansion with a battery of French doors opening onto a large stone patio where red bougainvillea and a riot of cerulean morning glory blossoms tangled themselves over gigantic trellises.

"Please sit down," Buffy gestured toward one of the large sofas facing the patio, covered in a flowered print that mimicked the bougainvilleas and morning glories outside.

"Red or white?" Hugh asked. "We're having grilled salmon for dinner, if it matters."

Kathryn accepted a glass of French Bordeaux that even Paul would have had trouble affording and answered Buffy's questions about Kathryn's life in Atlanta and her mother's happy retirement to Florida.

Buffy shared photographs of her elder daughter Elise, a comparative literature professor at Duke, married to an English professor; and of Erin, a second-year associate at Craig, Lewis, and Weller in New York. They were both beautiful because they resembled Buffy, with heart-shaped faces, high cheek bones and caramel hair. The only trace of Hugh was in Erin, who had her father's imposing height.

"My old firm," Hugh said with pride, now well into his second scotch.

A shadow crossed Buffy's perfectly tailored face. "Yes, following in her father's footsteps." *Law had not been kind to this marriage,* Kathryn reflected.

The patio was warmed by tall propane heaters that kept the chill of a San Diego June night at bay. Hugh was solicitous of her comfort, but she insisted her light sweater over her simple green dress was adequate. Buffy narrated the history of the organic vegetables from the large garden their gardener maintained at the rear of the estate and the origin of the organic salmon the chef served on cedar planks.

Thankfully dessert was omitted, and Buffy grew tired of gardening trivia and headed upstairs to rest.

"Shall we talk out here?" Hugh asked after requesting coffee from the housekeeper who cleared away the dinner dishes. "I like to listen to the ocean."

"Yes, of course."

"But you looked troubled somehow."

She reminded herself she was in the presence of one of the top attorneys ever to practice law, so of course he noticed the nuances in people's faces.

"I was thinking that the sea is a jealous mistress."

"Was she a rival, then, for your husband's affections?"

Kathryn looked down at the coffee that had just been poured into the thinnest of china cups. She took a sip of its rich perfection. "Now that you put it that way, I'd say yes, she was."

Hugh sipped his own coffee and studied her face. "Were your husband's activities as a surfer a source of conflict between the two of you?"

"No, of course not."

He raised one eyebrow above his thick glasses, and she wondered if that meant he knew she was lying. "Wycliffe's attorneys will probe for all the sore spots in your relationship. Better to tell me now, so I can help you be prepared to answer those questions."

"We didn't have any," she went on lying.

"Every marriage has them. What about money?"

"We agreed on money."

"Careers? Any conflict over working for the public defender?"

"We agreed while we were still in law school to work for the indigent. We were both Senior Deputy Public Defenders. No one's career took off at the other's expense. Besides, Tom was a fantastic trial attorney. I'm sure he was as good as anyone in your office. I had nothing but respect for his work."

Hugh nodded as if absorbing the magnitude of what she was telling him. "What caused his high blood pressure? Did he do recreational drugs? Drink too much?"

"No, to both. He ran, he surfed, he ate well. Dr. Myers couldn't explain it."

"Bruce Myers, at Scripps? I think Rick mentioned him."

"He was Tom's cardiologist."

"And he was the one who suspected Myrabin?"

"Yes."

"Who treated him for liver failure?"

She sighed and scanned the stars for a moment. "It was a whole team because they thought he was going to have a transplant. I'm trying to remember all their names. Dr. Karl Martin was the one who saw Tom the most often."

"And does the firm have all of your husband's medical records?"

"I signed a release during that first interview with Mrs. Fox."

"Then I'm sure we have them. Patty never misses anything. Wycliffe is going to want those before your deposition. I'll make a note to Patty to take out anything we don't want Wycliffe to get its hands on."

She was surprised. "It's been a long time since first-year civil procedure, but aren't you supposed to turn over all of those records?"

"Supposed to, maybe. Will I, no. How are they going to prove I've got something they've never seen?"

"I doubt there is anything damaging to Tom in them."

"You never know. Everyone has secrets."

"Tom didn't. At least, not from me."

He refilled his cup from the silver pot the housekeeper had left on a warming stand. Kathryn saw his mind working as he sipped. She sensed he could tell she was lying. Finally he said, "My parents are the only the couple I've ever known who didn't have secrets from each other. Buffy and I have too many to count."

She thought of Logan Avery, but said nothing.

"You're thinking about Logan."

"Are you a mind reader?"

"Sometimes. Buffy and I have had an arrangement for years. I don't hide what I'm doing."

She thought about his arm around Logan at the party. "I see."

"No, you don't. And sometimes I don't either. My parents loved each other the way you and Tom did until the day my father died. Buffy and I lost whatever we had for each other a long time ago."

"So that's your excuse for Logan Avery?"

"And Patty Fox before her, and too many others to name. After things are over, I make sure they are looked after."

"As in making partner?"

"When appropriate. Patty is everything the firm could want in an attorney. And I think Logan is on the way to proving she is, too."

"But isn't that awkward for you? Being surrounded by so many ex-mistresses?"

He sipped his scotch and shrugged. "We have offices in San Diego, New York, Los Angeles, Chicago, Atlanta, Miami, and London. Transfers are easy to arrange."

Kathryn shivered even though she wasn't cold, and he noticed. "My indiscretions upset you?"

"No."

"And you don't like me?"

"No."

"We are going to have to work on your ability to lie before

you get in front of Wycliffe's deposition cameras."

"It's not what you've done. You and Logan Avery were obvious the first night I came to the firm. I'm uncomfortable because you're so frank with me about you private life."

"But why shouldn't I be? I'm trying to get you to tell me everything about yours. It's much easier to open up to a friend than to a stranger."

So he wanted her to like him. But she didn't.

"I don't have anything more to tell you about Tom and me."

"Yes, you do. You loved him. You loved him so much that you're willing to go through the hell of this lawsuit for him. Ugh! This coffee is cold. Let's go back inside. I need another scotch."

She followed him past the glass-walled room that led onto the patio, deeper into the house, to his study. The walls were covered with awards and pictures of Hugh with politicians and other famous lawyers. He motioned for her to take a seat on the small sofa in the corner of the big room, away from his monstrous desk. He poured himself a scotch from the open drinks tray.

"One for you?"

"No, I'm driving."

He sat down again on the soft leather chair facing her. Despite the coffee, he'd had a lot to drink, and Kathryn knew the alcohol was talking. "So here's the story of Hugh Mahoney– in his own words. William Mahoney, my father, who was always called 'Bill,' grew up Irish and poor in Boston. He met my mother at a USO dance in Fort Ogelthorpe, Georgia, during World War II. He was a private in the army on his way to the

European theatre. She was a kindergarten teacher from Chattanooga. He fell head-over-heels in love with Sharon Murphy.

"He managed to stay alive, even during the Battle of the Bulge; and he kept his sanity after the horror of liberating Dachau, in order to make his way back to her after the war. Later he would say that knowing my mother was waiting for him was the only reason he had to stay alive.

"Because they both were Catholic, their families gave them their blessings, but Mom didn't want to live in Boston although Dad desperately wanted to go back home. To make her happy, he scraped together enough cash to buy a twelve-hundred-square-foot tract house and to open a Ford dealership on Ringgold Road in East Ridge, a suburb of Chattanooga. My brother Patrick was born in 1950. I was born in 1959. My father did his best to make a living selling cars, but we only scraped by. In a word, we were poor; and poor people are powerless, I quickly discovered."

* * *

Mid-October, 1969, Chattanooga, Tennessee

Hugh perched on the arm of the saggy living room chair that sat in front of the picture window, a position which allowed him a panoramic view of the street in front of 4507 Maple Court Drive. He was waiting for his father to come home. Decimals, the obsession of his fifth-grade teacher, had all the charm and comprehensibility of ancient Greek for him; so he looked to his father night after night to get him through his homework.

Although Hugh hated math, he spent the day anticipating those hours alone with his father, who was otherwise too busy to spend time with him.

Nevertheless, Hugh had no doubt his father's lack of time had nothing to do with how much Bill loved him. Or Patrick or his mother. At ten, Hugh was too young to fully comprehend his father's extraordinary capacity to love. But even then, he sensed that Bill's enormous heart set him apart.

Hugh squirmed on his uncomfortable perch and wondered when his father would be home. The house smelled of boiling cabbage and potatoes, a meal his parents loved, but he hated. The ugly, round, plastic black clock on the cheap veneer oak end table by the sofa said six-fifteen. His father was late. He was always home by six. Every night he drove up in one of the brand new dealership cars and hurried straight to the kitchen to kiss Hugh's mother and to get a Pabst Blue Ribbon out of the fridge. By six-thirty, Bill would be seated on the saggy brown sofa watching Walter Cronkite on the CBS evening news with Hugh perched adoringly at his feet. By seven, his mother would have supper on the red linoleum table in the kitchen. By seven-thirty, Hugh would be deep in the throes of his math homework with his father.

But that night, six-thirty came and went without Bill. Hugh's mother wandered in from the kitchen and stood next to Hugh, peering into the chilly autumn dark where maple leaves detached themselves and drifted into piles on the lawn.

"He's late," Hugh said.

"Probably traffic," Sharon observed.

She turned to go back to the kitchen but paused for a moment. "Hugh?"

"What?"

"Tell him I'm in the kitchen when he comes in."

He nodded, and then once again was alone with his thoughts in the living room.

A gray car pulled into the drive with a dent in the back bumper that made it look as if it had been kicked in. Bill Mahoney, looking tired and haggard, got out with a six-pack of beer.

"Mom!"

Sharon hurried in from the kitchen.

"He's home, and something terrible has happened."

At that moment, Bill's key turned in the front door; and he stepped inside, his face worn and deeply lined.

Sharon ran to him and put her arms around him. He hugged her while still clutching the six-pack.

"What's happened?" she asked.

Bill looked down at her. "Ford's taken over the dealership. Their people arrived from Detroit today and told me to leave."

Hugh's mother sucked in her breath. "Twenty-three years," she whispered. "Why come and take it over after twenty-three years?"

Bill Mahoney shook his head. "They didn't say. They just told me to empty my desk and go home in the used car they said I could keep."

"But you have a contract for another seven years!" Sharon frowned.

"I told them that, but they didn't care. They claimed I was underperforming, but I know my sales numbers are as good as Perkins Ford in Fort Ogelthorpe."

Bill looked over at Hugh's frightened face. "Don't worry, son. Everything will be okay. Your mother has her job, and it won't take me long to find something else."

But, in truth, Hugh could see his father was very worried. He barely touched his favorite supper of corned beef brisket with the boiled potatoes and cabbage. He told Hugh that Sharon would have to be his homework tutor for the night. He sat on the sofa, blankly staring at the television and drinking himself into a stupor.

* * *

Friday, April 11, 2014, Crown Manor, Coronado

It was midnight when Hugh paused the story of his father and got up to pour himself yet another scotch. He was an absorbing storyteller, Kathryn reflected. She felt as if she'd actually been in the little house the night Bill came home defeated. She could smell the boiling cabbage and potatoes.

"What happened after that night?" she asked.

Hugh settled back into the soft leather chair. He took a sip of his drink and propped it on his knee. "For a while he stayed in bed all day, too depressed to get up. The profits from the dealership had always been an up and down sort of thing, so we were used to getting by on my mother's teaching salary. It wasn't easy, but we made it.

"Finally, my older brother Patrick came home from college for Thanksgiving. He was a sophomore at UT in Knoxville. Full scholarship, so his education went on as planned. Somehow he managed to cheer Dad up enough to get him out of the house.

In December, my father started selling door-to-door for Fuller Brush. I bet you don't even know who they are."

"I do. One of their salesmen used to come to our apartment when I was pretty small. I can barely remember my mother buying some hair brushes."

Hugh smiled. "My dad was a gentle giant of a man with kind brown eyes and a great smile. He actually did pretty well selling for Fuller Brush. But he was fifty-one, and it was hard on him physically to drive everywhere, hefting those big cases door-to-door."

"Didn't he ever think of suing Ford?"

"No, of course not. The only lawyers my parents knew anything about were the ones who wrote wills. In their world, you only saw a lawyer to write your will or when someone died and left one to probate. There were no firms like Goldstein, Miller to take on giants like Ford for a man with nothing like my father."

"Is that why you do it?"

"You mean why I'm a plaintiff's attorney?"

She nodded.

"I didn't start that way. I worked for Craig, Lewis, and Weller in New York when I got out of law school. I defended big business."

"So how did you cross over to plaintiff's work?"

"It took me a long time. Craig, Lewis sent me to San Diego to defend a pharmaceutical company that had made a defective surgical implant. I liked the weather so much, I took a job at Warrick, Thompson and made partner in their litigation section. But I was still doing defense work, like your friend Paul.

"Then I met Rick Peyton. His wife committed suicide after taking an antidepressant that Rick was sure had caused her death. I left Warrick and opened my own shop, so I could take Rick's wrongful death case."

"Wasn't that a big gamble?"

"The biggest. But I'd been waiting for a chance like that since my father died."

"Why?"

Hugh settled back in his chair, took a sip of scotch and said, "My dad lugged those big black cases around for two years. Then one morning, in May of 1971, he got up with the worst stomach ache of his life. The doctors found a tumor, but they couldn't know how bad it was without surgery. A week later he died on the operating table because they had given him the wrong anesthesia. He had told them the ones he couldn't tolerate, but the anesthesiologist was an arrogant SOB who refused to read the nurse's notes."

"So your mother sued the hospital?"

Hugh shook his head. "Like I said, lawsuits didn't exist in my parents' world. The hospital handed her a check for $2,000 and made her sign a release. The hospital's lawyer said that was all my father was worth because he had cancer and would have been dead within three months anyway. I was twelve when I saw her take that check, and I vowed I'd find a way to get revenge. When I won Rick's case, I realized I'd found my calling."

"Is that why you took Tom's case?"

"It was one of the reasons."

CHAPTER NINE

Early Hours of Saturday morning, April 12, 2014, Coronado, California

It was one-thirty a.m. when Hugh walked Kathryn to her, car parked in the magnificent drive. He repeated the air kisses of his original greeting and patted her on the shoulder.

"Don't worry about the deposition. But make an appointment to come in next week and do some preparation with Mark or Patty. I will try to come by to help out."

"I will. Thanks." She slid into her little car and moved forward toward the turn onto Ocean Boulevard. In her rear-view mirror she saw Hugh standing in the drive, watching her leave.

She was tired, but emotionally unsettled. She was having trouble pigeonholing Hugh back into the arrogant, aggressive, money-making machine she'd seen that first night with his arm around Logan Avery. He'd just shown her a human and very down-to-earth side she had never dreamed existed.

She felt as if she needed protection from the racing thoughts threatening to transform Hugh Mahoney from a cold-hearted, big-firm lawyer into a flesh and blood man with a heart. She drove down Orange Avenue, past the dark and shuttered businesses of the little town, and turned left onto First Street, where the homes on the right side of the street had sweeping views of the bay and the lights of downtown.

She counted the houses to her right until she reached 817 where Paul lived. The house sat on a small private street that ran parallel to First. Kathryn swung her little car onto the private road and looked for a parking spot. She needed Paul at that moment. She needed his arms and his warmth and his steady reassurance that everything was going to be all right. He was the one person in the world she could turn to at this hour of the morning.

But just as she switched her engine off, she saw it parked in Paul's drive behind the low gates that allowed the house to be visible from the street but kept tourists from occupying his driveway. Her heart sped up, and her stomach churned. Shannon Freeman's sleek red Corvette was nestled in for the night. The old hot waves of jealousy overwhelmed her.

* * *

December 2009, 1845 Ocean Place, Pacific Beach

By December, Kathryn knew Shannon well. She knew the way she wrinkled her nose when she laughed, the way she tossed her waist-length blonde mane, and the way she brushed up against Tom in doorways or at restaurants when the four of them went out for brunch. She knew the way Shannon smiled at Tom with her heart in her eyes, and she wondered if Steve ever noticed.

He didn't seem to. The two of them gave the appearance of a happy couple. Not long after that August morning when Kathryn first saw Shannon with Tom, he told her Steve had asked Shannon to move into his cottage, not far from 1845 Ocean Place.

It had been a Saturday in early September, and they'd walked up to The Yellow Café on Garnet for brunch.

"I never thought it would happen," Tom said over scrambled eggs. "I never thought Steve would actually ask someone to move in with him."

Kathryn scanned his face for signs of jealousy, but there were none. His lovely eyes were clear and blue, his smile genuine and happy. "What made him do it?"

"All I can say is he really, really likes her. She can surf with him."

"But he's had other surfing girlfriends."

"Shannon is world class. She can keep up with us."

Kathryn hoped she didn't flinch when he said "us." "She's a good bit younger, isn't she?"

"Eleven years. I don't think Steve even thinks about it."

What about you, she wanted to ask. *Do you think about a woman who can do all the things with a surfboard that you can and who has a lot more time to have children than I do? And who looks at you as if you hung the moon?*

As the days stretched into California's version of autumn, Tom began to surf with Shannon and Steve six days a week. Sunday was the only day she woke to find his side of the bed still occupied. She knew Paul was rarely with them because Tom had mentioned he was living out of a suitcase in Dallas doing discovery in a case that might go to trial in a few months. And his marriage was starting to crumble.

As the days went by, she tried not to think about the child she so desperately wanted. But one Saturday morning in late October when the few precious fertile hours came round again, she reached out and pulled Tom back into bed.

"Don't go." She smiled at him, hoping he would understand what she wanted.

The trouble was, he understood all too well. "Not this morning."

"But this morning is important."

He sighed. "I'm sorry. I know what this means to you, but I just can't. Not anymore. We took temperatures, we lived our lives around the calendar, we made love when it wasn't love at all. I can't get back on that merry-go-around again."

"But it's not a merry-go-around. It's now. Once. This morning."

But he shook his head and got up. "I would if I could, Kathryn. But I can't."

* * *

Early Hours of Saturday Morning, April 12, 2014, Crown Manor, Coronado, California

Hugh watched Kathryn's tail lights disappear through his impressive entry gates, then turned back to the house. He poured himself a Glenlivet nightcap with a twinge of guilt because he had an appointment with the cardiologist on Monday, and his blood pressure was working its way to new heights. Dr. Tilson would give him another lecture about how much the heart hates alcohol. Although Hugh doubted the truth of that. Without scotch, the pressures in his life would drive his blood pressure even higher.

He walked upstairs to his room where the light by the bed burned softly. In the dimness, he put on pajamas and brushed his teeth. He stared at his reflection in the bathroom mirror. He looked so old. The old-man pj's didn't help. He shouldn't be sleeping with Logan. She couldn't possibly have any interest in him other than to advance her career. He should stop pretending she found him attractive.

He sighed and got into bed with the remainder of his Glenlivet and a Tom Clancy novel. But Jack Ryan did not hold his interest. He kept thinking about Kathryn. She was lying about her marriage. Something had been wrong. Hugh guessed it was something badly wrong since she was working so hard to cover it up, and she obviously didn't trust him enough to share her secret. They desperately needed to teach her damage control. She was a transparent liar. They had their work cut out for them.

CHAPTER TEN

Monday, May 5, 2014, Office of Hugh Mahoney, Emerald Shapery Center, San Diego

Mark Kelly was annoyed by Hugh's summons at eight on Monday morning. He'd spent the weekend fighting with Rachel over the nuptial extravaganza she was planning. Two hundred guests and a sit-down dinner at the Hotel Del made him queasy, although not because of the cost. He could handle that. But more and more, he wasn't sure that he was in love with Rachel. If he went through with the wedding and it turned out to be a colossal mistake, fewer witnesses to his folly were far preferable. Two days of turmoil had made him long for the moment when he'd hit the peace and quiet of his own office at eight that morning. He needed some solitude before putting on his lawyer-face for the week.

But no luck. He was summoned like a first-year associate to the great man's office the minute he arrived. Patty was already seated in one of the chairs in front of Hugh's desk. She looked impeccable as always, hair slicked into a tight bun, perfectly tailored black suit. She was cradling a Starbuck's cup in her heavily diamonded left hand and listening to Hugh, who looked up when she entered. Was it ever weird, Mark wondered, to work with the man she'd slept with for her first two years at the firm?

"Ah, there you are. Logan will be along in a few minutes. She's found something in Wycliffe's documents that she wants to tell us about." Hugh sipped from his own paper-lidded Starbuck's Café Americano.

Mark pulled up a chair from the conference table in the corner of Hugh's office to leave the remaining chair for Logan. He wondered if he had time to retreat downstairs for his own cup of coffee.

But the answer was no. The door burst open, and Logan appeared, looking like Patty's opposite number. Instead of a suit, she wore a bright red dress that hugged her curves. She shook her shoulder-length hair out of her eyes and looked at Hugh seductively.

Mark felt uncomfortable when Logan was coming on to their boss. And Monday morning was way too early for seduction.

Hugh refused to make eye contact with her, and Mark noticed her big brown eyes became stormy. He had been through enough of these affairs to tell when Hugh was ready to wind it down. Patty had had the good sense to accept the message, but Logan was making the mistake of fighting it. She should have realized Hugh held all the cards.

Logan flounced down on the empty chair and looked over at Patty, whose dark eyes remained expressionless. She'd get no sympathy in that quarter, Mark thought.

"So tell us what you've discovered in Wycliffe's documents," Hugh said, still without meeting her angry eyes.

Logan made a great show of powering up her laptop and opening a file. She studied her notes with a perfect pout that was too obviously for Hugh's consumption. *Logan is overplaying her hand,* Mark thought.

"The paralegals and I have been through the ediscovery and the paper copies that Wycliffe handed over. There are huge chronological gaps in the clinical trial information. Wycliffe pulled out almost all their documentation about the trials they conducted while they were trying to get FDA approval. Rick thinks they were getting adverse results that would have prevented approval of the drug."

"Those bastards at King and White!" Hugh thundered, this time, banging his fist on his desk. "Who do they think we are that they can behave this way? Get busy drafting a Motion to Compel Discovery, Logan. And call the judge's clerk and get us on the calendar as quickly as possible! Patty, be sure to tell Kathryn as soon as you've confirmed a court date."

"Will I be arguing this one?" Mark asked.

"No, I want the pleasure of burying Bob McLaren, myself."

* * *

Friday, May 9, 2014, Office of the Public Defender, 450 B Street, San Diego

Kathryn's cell phone began to ring at exactly five o'clock as she was heading for her car, looking forward to the weekend. Caller ID identified Paul, and she considered not answering. It had been exactly four weeks since she'd seen Shannon's car in his drive. He had called and texted her numerous times, but she'd either ignored him or sent excuses.

But now the weekend loomed ahead, lonely and empty with no one to talk to about the bad news from Patty: Wycliffe was refusing to play fair in discovery. Civil litigation was Paul's world. He could tell her how much she should worry about this new development. So, in a moment of weakness, she pressed the answer button.

"Thank God! I was beginning to worry about you. Why haven't you answered my calls?"

Because on a night when I really needed you, I saw Shannon's Corvette in your driveway, she wanted to say. But didn't. "I've been busy. I've been in trial for the past two weeks."

"Is it over?"

"Yep. Today. Verdict for the prosecution. My client is going away for life."

"Sorry."

"I'm not. He killed two people. I'm just glad it's over."

"Then come for dinner tonight. I've missed you."

* * *

Against her better judgment, she decided to go. Paul met her at the door with a hug and what would have been a kiss had she not turned her head and pulled away.

He looked hurt but said nothing as he led the way to the kitchen. "I've cheated and gotten carry-out lasagna from Il Fornaio. You know the awful truth: I'm a rotten cook. I'm hoping this very expensive Chianti makes up for it."

She sipped wine while Paul served the food and carried the plates out to the deck.

At seven-thirty, the sun was just setting, leaving delicate trails of gold and orange streaming across the sapphire waters of the bay. Kathryn sat down in one of the two chairs and studied the San Diego skyline in the twilight. Her eye went almost at once to the Emerald Shapery Center, ablaze with the last fire of the sun, and she wondered if Mark Kelly or Patty or Logan or even Hugh himself were there, trying to find out the truth of what Wycliffe had done to Tom.

"You seem worried."

"Patty Fox called me earlier this week. They are going to have to go back to court to make Wycliffe turn over things they apparently are hiding."

"What kinds of things?"

"The data from the clinical trials, pre-FDA approval."

"Wow! So Bob McLaren thought he could get away with that! He's not always on the side of the angels. He can be sleazy."

"Will he get away with this?"

"No way. Judge Weiner is no-nonsense about discovery. She'll go through the roof. Maybe even impose sanctions. When is the hearing?"

"Monday the nineteenth, in the morning."

"I'd go, if I were you. There'll be fireworks for sure. In fact, I'd go if I were going to be in town."

Kathryn was comforted by his open optimism, but the Corvette in the drive still haunted her.

Paul ate thoughtfully for a while and then said, "The discovery problem isn't the only thing on your mind. Are you upset because I told you I had run into Shannon a few times? Look, Kathryn, Shannon is harmless–”

“No, she isn't!” She slammed her hand down hard on the glass table making all the dishes rattle.

Paul sat back in his chair and studied her face in the deepening twilight. Finally he said, “Tell me why she isn't harmless.”

“Because after dinner at Hugh's, I was upset.”

“What upset you?”

“Talking about Tom. Talking about having my deposition taken. Talking about having to say out loud that Tom is dead.”

Paul reached for her hand, but she pulled it away. He looked surprised. “Wow. I must have done something unforgivable.”

“You have.”

“What?”

“I don't want to talk about it.”

“Then I can't apologize. And I want to apologize. I wouldn't do anything in the world to hurt you.”

“That isn't true.”

He looked at her as if she were speaking a foreign language. “It would help if I had some idea of what you are talking about.”

“After dinner that night at Hugh's, I was upset. He dismissed his wife on cue after the meal and took me to his study to tell me private details about his life.”

“Such as?”

“His father was screwed over by The Ford Motor Company and finished off by Our Sisters' of Charity Hospitals; but his family was too poor to hire a lawyer, so Hugh vowed one day to get his revenge on Big Business.”

"So that's why he became such a fierce plaintiff's attorney. Why did that story upset you?"

"Because he wanted me to feel close to him, so I would talk about me and Tom. He wanted me to like him."

"And did you like him?"

"Mixed feelings. But the whole evening, after his wife went to bed, had a distinctly personal overtone that made me feel uncomfortable."

"I don't think you have anything to worry about. Hugh is a womanizer, but he limits himself to the young associates at his firm. He's never been known to hit on a client."

"I'm not saying he wanted to hit on me. It did feel like a little bit like that, but I think it was more about changing my opinion of him. He said he wanted to tell me his personal history because he was asking me to tell him about mine with Tom. He was trying to level the playing field to make me comfortable telling him the details of my marriage. He talked for a long time. When I left, I was upset, and I wanted to talk to you."

A funny look came over his face as he finished the last of his lasagna. "Did you call?"

"No. I just drove straight here."

Now he looked uncomfortable. "What time did you come by?"

"Between one and one-thirty. I saw her car in the drive."

He got up and came over to her and tried to pull her to her feet and take her in his arms, but she resisted and remained seated. "Don't touch me."

Defeated, he went back and sat down. "I don't suppose you'll let me explain?"

"I'll listen. I won't promise to believe you."

"I got home from work around ten that night and found Shannon waiting in the drive. She was upset and lonely and had come looking for someone to talk to. I asked her in because I didn't want to be alone. I was upset because I was supposed to have Jodie that weekend, and Carolyn had refused to bring her. I hadn't had anything to eat, and Shannon was hungry, too; so I made a couple of omelettes. We wound up talking and drinking too much wine, and all I can say is I wish it hadn't happened."

"But it did."

* * *

December 2009, 1845 Ocean Place, Pacific Beach

Kathryn didn't feel like a Christmas party that year. The tradition had started in their second year of marriage, when they'd been proud of the work they'd done on their house and wanted to show it off. Now all their friends expected an invitation for the second Saturday evening in December. They had colleagues from the public defender's office, and Paul and his wife and a few Big-Firm types who had been law school classmates, and a handful of Tom's surfer friends, most of whom Kathryn barely knew.

It was a lot of work to get the house cleaned, the Christmas tree up, and food either purchased or made. At least after more than ten years in the public defender's office, they could afford something better than trays of Costco frozen quiches.

The house was always stuffed to the gills with guests. They

spilled onto the front and back lawns, drinking and laughing so loudly that the neighbors would have complained in any neighborhood other than Pacific Beach. But here parties were a daily occurrence. So the Andrews party fit right in. And, besides, Kathryn made sure to invite her neighbors, just in case any of them had thought of going to bed.

She had steeled herself for Shannon's entrance. She came an hour after Steve arrived because her bartending shift at the PB Saloon did not end until eight. Kathryn watched her circulate through the guests, eventually taking up residence in the dining room where Tom and Steve were picking off hors d'oeuvres and drinking beer.

Kathryn nursed a glass of red wine slowly in the living room, standing in the circle that Paul's Warrick, Thompson friends had formed around him and Carolyn. She tried to concentrate on Big Firm gossip about lawyers she didn't know and cases she didn't know, but her eyes kept straying to Shannon, beer in hand, one arm draped loosely over Steve's shoulder, but her eyes fixed solidly on Tom. She was the picture of confidence.

"Gorgeous, isn't she?" Carolyn said.

Kathryn tried to hide her embarrassment at being caught watching the three of them. "Yes."

"I'm glad Steve has finally found someone. Paul never thought he would."

How could she not see that Shannon's attention was fixed on Tom, not Steve, Kathryn wondered. But she would sound paranoid if she said anything. "They've only been together a few months."

"That's true." Carolyn cocked her head to one side as if to

get a better view of the dining room. "Paul said this one feels different to him. And I agree. The two of them just have that air of belonging together. I'm going to predict this is going to work out."

* * *

Cancun was cheap in December, so they went for Christmas and stayed until New Year's. Kathryn knew that Tom had asked Steve and Shannon to come, too; and it would not have been the first time Steve and a girlfriend traveled with them. But to her great relief, Shannon begged off, saying she wanted to spend her first Christmas with Steve alone. Ever since the Christmas party, Kathryn had been sternly reminding herself that Carolyn had seen nothing out of place between Tom and Shannon. She decided her own eagerness to have a baby was making her imagine things.

But when they came back, Tom's morning surfing trips began to grate on her again. The glow of love-making during their week-long holiday had vanished. On the morning in January when the window of fertility was open for those few precious hours, Tom left her to surf. She wondered obsessively if he was out alone with Shannon. That night at bedtime she went into the room that was to have been their nursery but had become an office that they shared. Tom had been working at his desk. He was preparing for a trial scheduled to begin in the morning.

"What's up?" He smiled and rubbed his tired eyes.

"I was hoping you're ready for bed."

"Not quite yet. I haven't finished my opening statement."

"Couldn't you do that in the morning?"

"I'm going surfing in the morning."

"Before trial?" He normally went straight to the office when he was in trial.

"I think it will clear my head."

Her gut told her he wanted to see Shannon, but she had nothing to gain by calling him on it. She sat down on the chair next to the desk and tried to find the words she wanted.

But he broke the silence first. "You're going to bring up the fertility stuff, aren't you?"

"We've stopped trying. And you gave away the baby's surfboard."

He sighed and took her hand. "It made me too sad whenever I looked at it. I've gotten used to things the way they are. Just you and me. We've tried so long to have a child that I'm worn out with trying. Sex isn't fun anymore. It's just mechanics when hormones and the calendar demand it."

"Is that why you've stopped making love to me?"

"But I haven't. When we were in Cancun–"

"But that was the first time in months."

"It was different there. No pressure. No deadlines."

Kathryn took a deep breath. "I want to try in vitro."

He frowned. "But that's horribly expensive. And the hormones will make you miserable. You know what it did to Leslie Hopkins. She took so many sick days she lost out on promotion to Senior Deputy PD.

"But she and Bill now have twin boys. If you ask her, she'll tell you it was all worth it."

"I gather you have asked her?"

"Yes. And I have the names of her doctors."

Tom sighed. "If we'd gotten pregnant three years ago, I'd have been happy about it. But now, to be honest, I don't want children any more. We're happy together. I don't want to rock the boat."

She wanted to ask him if Shannon was the reason he no longer wanted a child. But she had nothing to go on except the unconfirmed suspicions that tormented her daily.

She felt Tom studying her face. He reached out and pulled her onto his lap and held her close. "I can't stand to make you unhappy. We'll try in vitro if that's what you want."

CHAPTER ELEVEN

Friday, May 9, 2014, 817 First Street, Coronado, California

The rest of the evening had been awkward with the two of them trying desperately to avoid the subject of Shannon. At ten o'clock, Kathryn made her excuses and headed home.

As she drove onto the graceful arc of the Bay Bridge, she felt the first tears behind her eyes and struggled to hold them back. She didn't want to cry. But at that moment the uncertainty of everything overwhelmed her. What if the unthinkable happened, and Hugh lost the motion to make them hand over all the clinical trial data?

And what if Shannon was now coming between her and Paul the way she'd– But Kathryn stopped herself in mid-thought. Shannon had not come between her and Tom. Or had she? Paul had said "faintest crack in your marriage." Was Shannon more than a "faint crack"? Had she been a split so wide and so deep that even if Myrabin had not taken Tom from her, Shannon would have? Would Kathryn inevitably have been overwhelmed with grief and trapped in the nightmare of Tom's loss? Was Shannon, and not Myrabin, the real reason her life was now nothing more than an empty shell?

Wycliffe would want to know about Shannon. She racked her brain to figure out who could give that secret away. Carolyn knew Shannon had flirted with Tom, but nothing more. Paul, likewise, knew only that there had been a flirtation. And, besides, Paul had dubbed Shannon harmless. Wycliffe would never get Shannon's name from either of them.

No, she decided, there was no one to tip off Wycliffe about Shannon. And besides, she was probably overreacting. Tom's warmth and charm had drawn everyone to him, especially lost, lonely women. He was kind, so he listened. He was the shoulder to cry on. But his compassion was one of the qualities that she had loved most, and so she had accepted his desire to help others, whether women or men, without complaint. Except for his friendship with Shannon. During all the years of their marriage, that relationship had been the only one that had left her questioning his motives. But Tom had told her repeatedly that she'd been wrong about his relationship with Shannon, she reminded herself.

She had known why Hugh had taken her aside at Crown Manor and told her personal stories. He'd been trying to inspire her to tell her most closely guarded secret: her fears about Tom and Shannon. But she wasn't going to tell Hugh because now she realized her fears had been baseless. She'd transformed her disappointment over failing to conceive into an imagined affair between Shannon and her husband. But no affair had ever existed.

She had reached the graceful center arch of the bridge when she glanced in her rear- view mirror and realized a black

Suburban was closing in fast. She was in the outside lane, the one closest to the edge of the bridge. If forced too far to the right, she would plunge over the side and into the bay.

She sped up but the Suburban continued to close the distance between them, bearing down on the rear of her little car. Her heart beat faster, and she shifted to the middle lane to give the big black car a clear field to speed past her. Obviously, the driver was drunk. The answer was to get out of his way.

But instead of passing her in the open space she had created, the Suburban moved to the left, going behind her car and weaving into the third lane, menacing her bumper on the driver's side. Her heart raced faster. The car's swerving back and forth between lanes began to seem intentional.

And then she felt a jolt. She looked into her rear view mirror and saw the Suburban swerve back into its lane, speed up, and start toward her again just as it drew next to her door on the driver's side. It was coming right at her. This was intentional.

She turned the wheel and moved her little car as far to the right as she could, knowing that if the Suburban hit her at its current speed, it would send her into the water. She pushed the accelerator as hard as she could, and the Mini, ever ready to race, took off.

It hummed along contentedly at a hundred miles an hour as it tore along the bridge's curved mid-section. Kathryn gave thanks for the Cooper's stability as she rounded the last turn and headed onto the mainland.

Suddenly she heard a crash behind her and looked in her rear-view mirror. The top-heavy Suburban had flipped over as it sped into the bridge's last curve, apparently trying to catch up with her. It rolled uncontrollably across the empty lanes, no longer a threat.

Her heart began to slow as she merged onto the 5-North and headed for home. Had she been the victim of a drunk driver's road rage? Or had the Suburban been sent to kill her?

* * *

Friday May 9, 2014, Crown Manor, Coronado, California

Jose swung the big black Mercedes into the circular drive at midnight, got out, and opened Hugh's door. Jose, who had lost his job as a cab driver when Uber's entry into the market forced his employer to downsize, had been hired by Mark Kelly a month ago to make sure Hugh and his scotch no longer got behind the wheel of Hugh's Mercedes at the end of the day. Hugh had bowed to Mark's judgment to avoid the DUI bullet he had been dodging for years.

"Thanks," Hugh smiled as he swayed up the front walk. Too much good scotch at Fred Akers' informal fund raising reception for Hal Edwards had done its damage. Of course, Hal, as the sitting President of the United States, was being coy in public about his plans to run for a second term. But through the junior Senator from California, Hal had privately let all his big donors know that he wanted to be in the White House for four more years. He had made a video appearance to tell them how much he needed and appreciated their support. Remaining in Washington had prevented press speculation about his plans for a re-election bid.

Unsteadily, Hugh wound his way up to his bedroom on the

second floor, threw off his clothes, and donned his old-man pajamas. Was it his imagination, or was his paunch starting to decrease? He'd told his personal trainer to push him harder in hopes his Alfred-Hitchcock silhouette might melt away.

As he brushed his teeth, he considered his faux pas of the evening: he'd taken Logan to the reception instead of Buffy. Fred had raised his eyebrows slightly when Hugh introduced her as an associate attorney at the firm. And Hugh could see why. Although she'd managed to wear a black dress, as Hugh had requested, the plunging neckline and figure-hugging curves still shouted "Mistress" instead of "Professional Colleague" to everyone in the room.

He'd made a mistake. Nowadays, he rarely made a mistake. But today he undoubtedly had. He'd looked like the foolish old man he was in a room full of people whom he wanted to respect him.

Besides, he wanted the affair with Logan to end. He'd been sending her all the hints that usually worked, but she seemed oblivious. He knew the time was coming when he'd have to be direct. Or at least as direct as his position would allow him to be.

Kathryn. His mind went to her constantly even in the midst of deposing CEO's with millions of attorneys' fees at stake. Gymnastics had given her that graceful dancer's body that he could not forget. He'd been jealous when Mark had recounted the details of their dinner at Bice. And he could tell Mark was developing feelings for her, too, despite the diamond on Rachael Roberts' left hand. But Kathryn was a client, and therefore as remote as the stars for them both. The firm's reputation had taken a hit tonight because of his bad judgment. But dating young associates was forgivable; having an affair with a client was not.

"Hugh? Are you awake?" Buffy rapped softly on his door.

"Yes, come on in." His guilt over his evening and his thoughts about Kathryn tightened his gut. He felt the way he had in the early days of his marriage, when he'd been dependant upon Buffy's money, when pleasing her at all costs had been his objective.

She slipped into the room, thin and regal in a red embroidered Chinese robe. Her light brown hair was loose around her shoulders, instead of up the way she wore it in the daytime. It gave her an air of youth and innocence, and Hugh hated himself as he thought of Logan in her tight, black, fuck-me dress.

"You're back late. Did you go to Fred's reception for Hal?"

"Yes. I thought you might be bored."

"So you took Logan."

Hugh sighed and moved toward the simple white couch and chairs in the sitting area of his bedroom. "It sounds as if you want to talk. Let's sit down. Scotch?"

"No, thanks." Buffy folded herself gracefully onto one end of the couch. Hugh poured himself another drink and took the chair opposite.

She frowned at the glass in his hand. "Do you think that's a good idea?"

"You mean 'haven't I had enough?'"

"To put it bluntly, you're drinking too much, Hugh."

"Agreed. But that's not something I want to talk about

tonight. Is that why you came?"

"No. It's your affairs. I haven't said anything. We've always had our own lives, and it's suited us. But we've made appearances together when it mattered. Until tonight."

"I know. And I regret what I did. It was a mistake."

"I think you should stop stringing these girls along," Buffy said. "Even though they are well-educated, they are still young and vulnerable. They're Erin and Elise's age."

He winced when she mentioned their daughters. "You're right. I've been thinking for some time that I need to end things with Logan."

Buffy shrugged. "And not start anything with someone else."

His well-practiced poker face slipped, and he could tell she was pleased that she'd surprised him. He struggled to banish all emotion. "There isn't anyone else."

"You don't really expect me to believe that. Don't forget I saw you with the new client at dinner. I almost didn't go upstairs when I was supposed to because I didn't want to leave you alone with her."

Hugh caught his breath, suddenly terrified that someone at the office might have seen the same thing. "I–"

"Don't make excuses. We've known each other too long. Besides, when you tire of one mistress, there's always another waiting in the wings."

"Okay, look. I admit I'm attracted to her. I have a weakness for beautiful women. She's a beautiful woman. But she's a client, Buffy. You know what that means."

"*I* know what it means. I'm reminding you in case you've forgotten."

He sighed and took a long pull of scotch. "Look, I admit I was indiscreet tonight. I'm going to put an end to Logan. And there won't be any more."

She smiled. "I wish I could believe you."

I wish you could, too, he told himself.

They were silent for a few minutes, Hugh drinking scotch he didn't need, and Buffy gazing at the priceless Persian rug. Finally she said, "What if we did something together?"

"Sure. How about a cruise in August?"

"No, I don't mean a vacation. You're well-connected politically. How about running for Fred's seat? Hal's going to give him a cabinet appointment next term."

Buffy had never been this full of surprises. "How do you know that?"

"You forget that Edith and I go back a long way."

Hal's wife. Of course. He'd been an idiot to forget all the charity balls and silent auctions those two had planned.

Before he could say anything, she went on, "She was actually the one who suggested it."

"So you were complaining to her about me and Logan." He felt chastised.

"I'm not going to tell you what I discuss with my friends. But running for Fred's seat was Edith's idea, and I like it. Hal would endorse you."

He studied her in the low light in her magnificent red robes. She looked like an empress. She was still a stunning woman at fifty-five. He had the consummate political wife sitting across from him.

"I'll give it some thought, Buffy. I'm not sure I'm ready to leave law. But I'll give it some thought."

After she left, he rolled into bed and thought about Kathryn until he fell into an uneasy, drunken sleep.

Buffy went to her own room and reminded herself to call Edith tomorrow and thank her for the suggestion to hire the firm of private investigators she used to keep tabs on her own husband, the President of the United States. According to Edith, they were better than the Secret Service. Over the years of her marriage, Hugh's wandering ways had tempted Buffy to track him, but she'd always decided against it. But then she'd seen him with Kathryn Andrews. This was different. This was truly dangerous. Edith had been exactly right: the time had come to keep herself fully informed.

CHAPTER TWELVE

Saturday, May 10, 2014, 1845 Ocean Place

Kathryn woke late. Her head ached, and she remembered she'd drunk some more wine after she'd gotten home to calm her nerves. When she closed her eyes, she could see the black Suburban positioning itself to ram her off the bridge. Thank God her quick reflexes and the Cooper's ability to outrun the top-heavy truck had prevented that.

She pulled on her robe and went to the kitchen to make coffee. She started the kettle boiling while she ground the beans. Tom had preferred coffee from an automatic drip pot. And truth to tell, it had been fine for her, too. But she'd taken to making it with a French press, so she wouldn't think about Tom standing at the pot waiting to catch the first drips in his mug. No one had loved good coffee more than Tom.

For a few minutes, the concentration of grinding and boiling and brewing kept her mind off of last night. But when her mug was full of equal parts half-and-half and chocolaty, medium roast coffee, her thoughts defaulted once more to the terror on the bridge.

She carried her cup into their study and sat down at her own smaller desk across from Tom's. She sipped her coffee as she studied his big oak desk. She still hadn't had the courage to go through all the drawers. She realized she was kidding herself if she thought she was anywhere close to accepting Tom's loss. But wasn't that why she had sued Wycliffe? To give herself the opportunity to wallow in her grief and rage, so she had no chance to move on and start a new life with someone else.

She flipped open her laptop on her own desk and entered her office's private database which could access new police reports before they were available to the public. She found the one for the accident: a 2013 Suburban rolled over on the Coronado Bay Bridge at approximately twenty-two hundred hours. She shivered as she realized the whole episode had not been a figment of her imagination. Someone had come close to killing her. But the report offered no clue as to who that someone was. When the police found the vehicle, it had been empty. How had anyone managed to climb out of that wreck and escape on foot from the middle of the bay bridge? It didn't make any sense.

She closed her computer and realized her coffee had gotten cold. She felt frightened and small and very alone. She wanted to tell someone what had happened. But who?

She looked over at Tom's empty desk and said out loud, "Someone who disappeared tried to kill me last night. Who should I tell?"

Paul.

"Why Paul?" she asked the empty air. "Paul slept with Shannon. Did you? Did you sleep with Shannon?"

But her only answers were silence and brilliant, early-morning May sunshine streaming in through the blinds.

Kathryn got up, went into her bedroom, and slipped on a pair of shorts and a baggy t-shirt. She slid into her beach sandals and walked the few blocks to the ocean, thinking all the while about Tom and Steve and Paul. And Shannon. She made her way across the soft sand until she came to the hard-packed surface at the water's edge. She slipped off her sandals and waded in. Even on a May morning, it was like ice around her ankles.

She looked out at the horizon, shielding her eyes from the bright sun with her hand. She watched the black wet-suited surfers as they floated on the waves, waiting to catch the next big curl. Her heart seemed to swell and burst as she stared out at them. And slowly it dawned on her: she couldn't put Tom and their marriage behind her as long as she was living in their house and doing their job and sleeping in their bed. Changing a coffee pot was just a useless gesture. Paul was the only person she could call. But with Paul, came Shannon. Just as it once had been with Tom. Tom was dead, but she was still trapped in the nightmare triangle Shannon had so expertly created in her life. A child. If she and Tom had had a child, Shannon would have had to stay away. Tom would have made her. He would never have turned his back on his child.

* * *

December 31, 2010, 1845 Ocean Place, Pacific Beach

Another year of trying, and nothing but disappointment to show for it. Kathryn had not felt like going out on New Year's

Eve. She and Tom had met at the fertility clinic that afternoon to learn that their third in vitro attempt had failed. The year 2010 had been devoted to shots, out-of-control hormones, and surgical procedures, yet Kathryn was not pregnant. And now, on the very last day of the year, they discovered they were out of options.

"After three tries, we suggest adoption," Dr. Lee, a small bespeckled Filipino, told them.

They drove home in silence until Tom said, "Do you still want to have dinner at George's At the Cove tonight?"

If they didn't give a party themselves, they had a tradition of splurging on New Year's Eve. It was part of the routine of being a childless couple.

"No, not tonight."

"Can I do anything to make you feel better?"

"Help me find another fertility clinic where we can try again."

"But you heard Dr. Lee. Three times is the maximum. Those shots and hormones are powerful. They take a toll on your body, Kathryn."

"I don't care."

"*I* care." He said it so quietly she almost didn't hear him.

"What did you say?"

"I said *I* care. I don't want them to put any more of those injections into you. And I don't want you sedated again for those egg harvesting procedures. Your body wasn't built for that kind of punishment. And besides, sweetheart, we've used up every penny of our savings. We can't afford another in vitro even if someone out there is willing to do it for us."

Kathryn sighed. "Promise me to keep trying!"

"But I hate all that counting and temperature-taking stuff."

"It's all we have left."

DISCOVERY,
THE FIRST MOTION

CHAPTER THIRTEEN

Monday, May 19, 2014, Edward J. Schwartz Federal Courthouse, U.S. District Court, Southern District of California, San Diego, 9:00 a.m.

Judge Weiner listened attentively as Hugh explained how Wycliffe had handed over thousands of documents about Myrabin with most of the critical clinical test data missing. As Her Honor listened, her gentle brown eyes strayed from Hugh's face to Kathryn's. Was she trying to size up the genuineness of her grief, Kathryn wondered; or was she just curious about a woman who had the courage to take on a company as big as Wycliffe? In the end, she'd convinced herself the incident on the bridge had been a random act of road rage, and she'd told no one.

When Hugh finished, Robert McLaren took the podium, once again dressed in thousands of dollars worth of sartorial splendor. Kathryn wondered if he was relying on his full head of gray hair to establish his credibility as a gray eminence who had earned enough victories in the courtroom to command respect for his pricey clothes.

"Your Honor—"

And that was as far as he got. "Tell me, Mr. McLaren, does Wycliffe believe that its data on the clinical trials of Myrabin are irrelevant to Mrs. Andrews' claims?" Judge Weiner's eyes had gone from gentle to hard.

"Well, no, Your Honor." Whatever smooth presentation he had planned evaporated.

"Then why are we here this morning, Mr. McLaren? Why haven't you provided these documents in discovery?"

"I was about to explain that, Your Honor. They're proprietary. They are full of Wycliffe's trade secrets. And since the FDA's data shows there have been no deaths from Myrabin, there is no compelling reason to jeopardize those trade secrets by turning them over to the plaintiff."

Kathryn enjoyed watching the judge flame into anger. "That's ridiculous, Mr. McLaren. Mrs. Andrews alleges that Myrabin killed her husband. She has a right to see the clinical trial data from Wycliffe. Are you telling me that you never thought of turning over that data with an agreement that the plaintiff would not disclose the material?"

"I—we—" Paul had told her McLaren charged clients eight hundred dollars an hour. Kathryn wondered how anyone could pay that rate for stammering in court.

But Emma Talbert, Wycliffe's in-house attorney, was quick to protect her client and her investment in pricey outside counsel. "Your Honor, if I might add something?"

"Please, Ms. Talbert. I'm at a loss to understand Wycliffe's decision to block discovery. I'm considering sanctions. Very expensive sanctions."

Standing at counsel table to bail out her hired gun, Emma looked very credible in her regulation Ann Taylor navy suit and tightly wound bun. "Your Honor, the documents not only contain trade secrets, they are protected by attorney-client privilege."

Judge Weiner frowned. "Really, Ms. Talbot? What sort of legal advice was your client seeking when it submitted scientific documents to its in-house attorneys? Are you a research scientist as well as an attorney?"

"Uh, no, Your Honor. But the documents were sent to us for review."

"Review is not legal advice, Ms. Talbot. It sounds to me as if your client is trying to misuse attorney-client privilege to avoid providing discovery to the plaintiff. I am ordering the documents turned over immediately. If Wycliffe thinks any portions are actually trade secrets, I will entertain a further motion. But for now, as far as I can see on this record, nothing here is privileged and all of it must be turned over to the plaintiff's attorneys. Today."

* * *

Monday, May 19, 2014, Hugh Mahoney's Office, Goldstein, Miller, Emerald Shapery Center, San Diego

"She's hiding something!" Hugh insisted, throwing a pen onto his polished expanse of desk in frustration. Kathryn had refused an invitation to lunch with him and Mark after the hearing.

"I did my best to get it out of her," Mark countered.

"I know, I know. I'll find an excuse to talk to her again, one-on-one."

Mark realized he was being dismissed, but he wasn't ready to go. "There's something else we need to talk about."

Hugh raised his eyebrows in that irritating way that said *you're an idiot for bothering me.* "What's on your mind?"

"Bill Hays called me on Friday about the fee split in *Besser.*"

"I don't want to talk about Bill Hays. The money's already been divided up."

"Hugh, Bill's a good lawyer. And Hays, Price is a good firm. Surely you remember we researched firms in Raleigh-Durham before we offered them a piece of the *Besser* case."

"So what?"

"So we may need them again some day. Stiffing Bill Hays three million dollars after all the work they did for us on that case is not a good idea."

"Bill went behind my back."

"No, he didn't, Hugh."

"Don't argue with me. The split's been made, and that's that. Bill needed to learn a lesson."

"But it's a lesson his firm can't afford."

"What do you mean?"

"Bill called me on Friday to say they'd committed so many resources to *Besser,* as we asked them to do, that they're struggling now financially because their client-base has dropped off. In other words, they put all their eggs in our *Besser* basket."

"It's Bill's tough luck if he made a bad business decision."

"Not if it's a decision you asked him to make. You asked him to devote his entire firm's manpower to our case."

"Yes, but I asked for loyalty, too."

"Bill is loyal to you, Hugh. That's my point. Come on,

another three million to Hays, Price will let them survive as a firm. And that sum is nothing to Goldstein, Miller. We'll never miss it."

Hugh shrugged. "Bill betrayed me. The answer is no."

Mark stalked to his office and closed the door a little too hard, a show of temper he could indulge because Hugh was too far away to hear the angry bang. He sat down behind his desk and took deep breaths to control his rage.

He and Hugh had hit it off almost immediately the summer Mark had clerked for the firm as a third-year law student. And as Mark had developed as a trial lawyer, Hugh had realized that Mark's reasoned, gentlemanly courtroom presentations were far more appealing to jurors than his own. Hugh had no sons, and at times Mark felt a bond with Hugh similar to the one he had with his own father. But Mark was never blind to his mentor's faults; and Hugh's unbridled arrogance, along with his womanizing, sometimes irritated Mark so much that he had to do what he was doing now: go into his own office, close the door, and remind himself that Bill Hays wasn't his responsibility even if he truly believed Hugh owed Bill and his firm every penny of that three million.

* * *

Monday, May 19, 2014, 1845 Ocean Place, Pacific Beach

Kathryn came home at six that night to find a mixed bouquet of pink orchids and white roses on her doorstep. Intrigued, she carried it inside, placed it on the coffee table and opened the card.

"Please forgive. Paul."

She threw the card down on the table without putting it back in the envelope and went to the kitchen to microwave a bowl of last night's mac and cheese. She poured herself a glass of red wine and carried her food back to the living room where she curled up on the sofa and studied the flowers. He had called constantly since the night they'd had dinner, but she had refused to answer. She'd focused only on her anger as she pictured over and over again the red Corvette in his driveway. But as she ate, she thought about the consequences of not answering his calls. He was the only other person who knew Tom as well as she did. He was her only living link to the years of her marriage. Was she willing to give up that link because of Shannon? Why did it always come down to Shannon, she thought angrily. When, if ever, would she be out of Kathryn's life?

* * *

Monday, January 17, 2011, 1845 Ocean Place, Pacific Beach

Although Martin Luther King Day was a court holiday, Kathryn had to go to the office anyway because she had a trial beginning the next day. But Tom had the day off, and he'd promised to fix the leaky faucet in the half-bath and pick up some groceries after a morning run. The waves weren't good enough for surfing, and Kathryn had sat in the deserted Public Defenders' office preparing for trial, relieved that he had no reason to be with Shannon that day.

She came home at five, hungry and tired, and hoping Tom would be in the mood for an early dinner at The Yellow Café.

As soon as she walked in the front door, she heard male and female voices in the living room.

She took off her coat and dropped her briefcase in the hall and went to see who was with Tom. He and Shannon looked up in surprise when she walked in. They were seated on the sofa. Two half-full glasses and a bottle of wine were on the coffee table between them.

Tom stood up and crossed the room to give her a kiss on both cheeks. "Hey, sweetheart. Shannon dropped by to talk to me about a problem she's having at work, and I opened some wine. I'll get you a glass."

Kathryn sat down on the chair opposite the sofa and worked to keep her jealousy in check. How long had this conversation about Shannon's supposed problem been going on?

Tom was back from the kitchen with a fresh glass within seconds. He poured some wine for Kathryn and handed it to her.

"How did trial prep go?"

She shrugged. "Fine. Nothing out of the ordinary." She looked over at Shannon.

"What happened at work?"

"Oh, nothing, really." Shannon fidgeted with her wine glass, slowly turning it as she held it. Her wide blue eyes were fixed on some paper lying on the coffee table.

Tom picked it up and handed it to Kathryn. "Take a look at this."

"What is it?"

"It's a contract," Shannon asserted defensively. "A guy came into the bar last night, claiming he was a hotshot L.A.

photographer and talent agent. He wants to sign me for some headshots. He says he can get me work as a model in L.A. I was skeptical, so I asked Tom to take a look at it."

"What did Steve think?" Kathryn tried to keep the barb out of her voice.

"Oh, I haven't talked to him about it, yet. I wanted to make sure the offer was legitimate before saying anything. He won't like the idea of me in L.A."

Kathryn looked over at her husband. "So was the guy a con artist?"

"Apparently not. We researched his company together this afternoon, and he checks out. Robert Harris, Photography and Talent Management."

She tried not to focus on the words "we" and "together." "So are you going to do it?"

"Tom suggested letting him take the headshots before I sign a contract to see if they are any good."

"The contract terminates if her photos aren't any good," Tom explained. "There's no point in signing anything if he ultimately decides he's not going to represent her."

Kathryn could not imagine Shannon taking a bad photograph. She was the archetypal model: thin, tall, beautiful eyes, perfect mouth, perfect nose, long blonde hair.

"I should go." Shannon put her wine glass on the table and stood up. "I have to be at work at six. Thanks, Tom."

"Glad to help. I'll walk you out."

Kathryn had to fight down a particularly strong surge of jealousy when Tom put his arm around Shannon as they walked toward the front hall. It was no more than a friendly gesture, but even that display of easy intimacy made her uncomfortable.

But that night, Tom insisted on taking her to dinner at the expensive and romantic Marine Room in La Jolla. And afterward, they came home and made love as if Shannon Freeman did not exist. Kathryn dearly hoped they'd make a baby that night, and the headshots would take Shannon to Los Angeles and out of their lives for good.

CHAPTER FOURTEEN

Tuesday, June 3, 2014, Conference Room, Emerald Shapery Center, San Diego

"The video camera makes me very uncomfortable," Kathryn said. She was sitting at the mahogany conference table in the Goldstein, Miller conference room with Mark Kelly and Patty Fox facing her. She was learning how to be deposed.

"Sorry," Patty said. "It makes everyone uncomfortable, but we have to use it. There'll be a camera running during your actual deposition, so it's a good idea to practice in front of one. And Mark and I need to go over these tapes of the practice runs so we can tell you how to improve."

Kathryn realized she had just squirmed in her chair like a kindergartener. No one said anything, but she was pretty sure that behavior was out at a deposition.

"There are just a few basic rules," Patty went on, "and I expect most of them are the same things you say to your clients before you put them on the stand at trial."

"So we apologize for telling you things you probably already know." Mark gave her his reassuring smile, but Kathryn still felt nervous. The pair had all the ambience of good cop/bad cop, even though they had shed their high-priced suit jackets and were appearing in less intimidating monogrammed custom shirts and thousand-dollar silk blouses. She laughed inwardly at the fiction that all lawyers make seven-figure incomes. She didn't.

"Listen carefully to the question," Patty began. "If you don't understand it, ask for it to be repeated."

"And don't be afraid to say you don't know. Above all, don't guess or speculate," Mark added.

"Right," Patty jumped back in. "And pause for five seconds before you begin your answer to give us time to put an objection on the record if we need to."

"And there will be lots of objections," Mark said. "Bob McLaren does not play fair. He is going to try to push your emotional buttons whenever he can, and he will ask a lot of questions that we will have to instruct you not to answer."

"And you will need breaks," Patty said. "I'm not going to try to sugarcoat it. This will be an hours, and probably days, long ordeal. So whenever you need a time out, let me or Mark know. Don't go on when you are upset or too tired to think before you speak."

"That latter point is crucial," Mark agreed. "Think before you open your mouth. Don't just blurt out answers."

"Now," Patty said, "and this is the hardest part, so I apologize in advance. We have to find out what the weak points in your story are going to be because obviously these are the things Bob McLaren will be probing for."

"Weak points?" Kathryn frowned. "I don't understand."

"Bob wants you to make his case for him," Mark said. "He'll be looking for facts that will prove Myrabin had nothing to do with Tom's death. He's sure to ask you a lot of questions about how much Tom drank."

"Tom had a beer or two, now and then. But nothing more."

Mark nodded and typed a note into his laptop. "McLaren will also be pressing you to admit you or Tom or both of you were involved with other people. He's really going to press you hard on that one because even if we can show Myrabin caused Tom's death, you won't recover much in damages if your marriage was on the rocks when Tom died."

"I realize he'll be after that kind of information. But there isn't any!" Kathryn tossed her head contemptuously.

"Okay," Patty agreed. "That's good. That's fine. But don't let that kind of emotion into your voice and body language. That would let McLaren know he's touched a nerve. And if he finds a spot like that, he won't back off. He'll push you to tell him more."

"Well, there isn't any more." Kathryn worked to keep her voice even and her head still. She was angry with herself for making such a classic mistake. She was a lawyer. She should know better. "Tom and I were happily married. That's all there is to it."

"Did Tom take Myrabin as prescribed?" Patty asked. "He didn't double up on the dosage on his own, did he?"

"No, he took it exactly the way Dr. Myers told him to. The insurance paid for 30 pills at a time, one each day for a month. I picked up his refills once a month."

"How old was Tom when he was diagnosed?" Patty asked.

"Forty."

"Did he have a family history of hypertension?"

"No."

"What about stress?" Patty continued to ask the questions, but Kathryn felt Mark's eyes on her, studying her face for cracks in her story.

"Tom was a Senior Public Defender. His clients were all facing sentences of life without parole or the death penalty. And like everyone in the office, he was overworked. We all have more cases on our dockets than we can really handle."

"Any other major stresses in his life?"

"No." She kept her eyes steadily on Mark's so he could not tell she was lying.

* * *

Late February 2011, 1845 Ocean Place, Pacific Beach

The headshots were far from being the ticket to removing Shannon from her world. Steve was incensed when he discovered Shannon had gone to Tom for advice and even more incensed when he learned Tom had encouraged her to give modeling a try. Kathryn heard the two of them arguing one morning as they got off their bikes after surfing.

Steve was so angry he could barely speak. "She's just a kid with two years of junior college who knows how to do two things: surf and tend bar! L.A. is not the place for her! The sharks up there will chew her up and spit her out in a heartbeat! What were you thinking, telling her to go for headshots?"

"She asked me to look at the contract to see if it was a real offer. It was. The decision to pursue it was hers alone."

* * *

June 2011 - 1845 Ocean Place, Pacific Beach

Kathryn came to bitterly resent Tom's support for Shannon's modeling foray. Because her head shots were successful, Shannon had to travel to Los Angeles for modeling jobs, sometimes several times a week. She and Steve began to fight regularly, and Shannon turned to Tom for advice and support. She spent more time with him than ever before, and Kathryn felt more and more uneasy about what that meant for their marriage. Finally, one Saturday morning in late June after she had been awakened by Shannon and Steve squabbling as they returned from the beach, she decided to confront her husband.

It was nine-thirty. He was alone in the kitchen in board shorts and a t-shirt, making coffee. He turned when she appeared in the doorway, hair tousled, robe cinched loosely around her waist. He looked guilty the minute he saw her.

"Sorry. I think Shannon and Steve woke you up. Sit down, and I'll make some breakfast. The coffee will be ready in just a second."

Kathryn watched him bustle around the kitchen. When he put the coffee mug in her hands, she drank several long sips before she said, "Now that Shannon and Steve aren't getting along, I don't think you should spend so much time with Shannon."

"What?" Tom was so surprised he dropped the spatula he was using to turn the bacon.

"I said, I don't think you should spend so much time with Shannon. You need to let her work things out with Steve on her own."

He stared at her. "But she's my friend, too. She needs my help."

"No, she doesn't. She's using her problems to get close to you, and that's coming between you Steve."

"That's ridiculous!" He turned back to the stove and began to scramble the eggs. A few minutes later, still silent, he refreshed her coffee and put two plates on the table. He sat down and took a thoughtful bite of egg. "She hasn't come between me and Steve!"

"That's not true. I've heard the pair of you arguing over Shannon and her modeling career. And you've been meeting Shannon for lunch or drinks at a moment's notice whenever she's upset about something Steve has said to her."

His beautiful blue eyes studied her for a moment. "Are you jealous?"

"Yes. And I expect Steve is, too."

He took a long drink of coffee as he considered what she had said. "Thanks for being honest."

She said nothing while he drank more coffee and ate a few more bites of egg. Finally he said, "So you think I've been wrong to let Shannon cry on my shoulder?"

"Absolutely."

"Why didn't you say something before?"

"Would you have listened?"

"No."

"Why are you listening now?"

"I've got a gut feeling you're right. And Steve might be right as well."

"What is Steve right about?"

"He thinks the modeling stuff is a waste of her time. Harris paid her a big signing bonus, and she bought the Corvette instead of paying off the loans she took out for junior college. She thought the money was going to start rolling in, but it hasn't."

"Isn't she getting modeling jobs?"

"Yes, but by the time she travels to L.A., does the job and pays the agent his cut, she could have stayed here and given surf lessons or tended bar for a night and made more money."

"And she hasn't figured that out, yet?"

"She gets mad at Steve when he tells her."

"And haven't you told her?"

"I told her to go back to school and get a four-year degree so she won't have to be a bartender for the rest of her life. She's twenty-eight. We'd been Public Defenders for three years by the time we were twenty-eight."

"Since she likes modeling, why doesn't she move to L.A. where she can do it full time?"

Tom finished his bite of toast, put his plate in the sink, and poured them both more coffee. He seemed oddly quiet, and that made Kathryn uneasy. "I don't think she wants to leave Steve."

Steve or you, Kathryn thought.

CHAPTER FIFTEEN

Tuesday, June 3, 2014, Hugh Mahoney's Office, Emerald Shapery Center, San Diego

Hugh was keenly aware all afternoon that Mark and Patty were prepping Kathryn Andrews for her deposition in the small conference room. If he was honest, he'd admit he'd flown back from D.C. a day early to try for a chance to see her. But junior partners like Patty and Mark prepped clients for deposition. If he went into the conference room where the most senior partner in the firm was *not* needed, he might give away the deadly secret he hadn't been able to hide from Buffy. But he longed to see Kathryn even at a distance. He felt the way he had in junior high when he'd held his breath during every passing period hoping to catch the merest glimpse of Lisa Jenkins, the prettiest girl in the seventh grade, as he and three hundred other students jammed themselves through the narrow halls.

He imagined her now, sitting under the relentless lens of the video camera at the end of the glossy mahogany conference table, facing Patty's cold efficiency and Mark's southern charisma. Mark Kelly was a fool if he did not pursue Kathryn's honey-blonde, hazel-eyed charm. If Hugh had been twenty-years younger and free of Buffy–but he made himself stop before he could complete the thought. He was who he was. Powerful, rich, but fifty-five and the owner of a paunch, unruly gray hair, and coke-bottle glasses. He was an object of desire only for predatory women like Logan. And nothing more.

His phone rang, and he picked it up. His secretary said, "Senator Akers on the line."

And what did the junior senator from California want with him at four-thirty on a Tuesday afternoon?

"Hi, Fred." Hugh went on the offensive before his caller could speak. "Are you in D.C. or San Francisco?"

"Just arrived in San Fran," Fred Akers said. "There's a fund raiser tonight for Governor Bishop. I'm surprised you're not here. With Buffy."

Hugh winced at the emphasis he placed on the last two words but did not rise to the bait about his appearance with Logan at Hal Edwards' private fund raiser. "Sent my contribution and my regrets. Is that why you called? To make sure I'd put my money in the reelection fund?"

"No, but I'm glad to hear you're supporting Les. He's done a good job for the state and deserves another term. I called because I want you to run for my seat when Hal appoints me Attorney General. I was hoping you'd be here tonight so I could introduce you to some people who could help you with fund raising and putting together a campaign team."

"So that's the cabinet post Hal has in mind."

"How did you know the president had promised me a cabinet appointment?"

"Buffy. She's pressuring me to leave the firm. She and Edith cooked up the idea that I should run for your seat."

"Well, it's a great idea. I'll endorse you, and so will Hall."

"Why are you so anxious for me to run?"

"Because I want to leave this seat in the hands of someone loyal to me and the president."

"I'll think about it."

"It would help you mend fences with Buffy."

"Why do you say that?" Hugh knew he'd spoken more sharply than he'd intended.

"She talks to Olivia as well as to Edith."

"So the wives' club is massing against me."

"To be blunt, that little tart you brought to Hal's private fund raiser didn't do anything to enhance your image."

"I know. Logan is a junior associate at the firm, but she likes to dress like a hooker."

"Olivia said Buffy and Edith have concocted a plan to embarrass you if you don't run."

"I know. Edith's going to book my wife on all the talk shows to give all the lurid details about my affairs. Some innocent people I love will be smeared on national television if I don't run for your seat."

"Look, don't worry. You'll like the Senate."

"I like law practice more."

"You can't say that until you've been a senator. Besides, there are plenty of babes on the Hill who find senators nothing but sexy. If Buffy forces you to become Senator Mahoney, you can have plenty of fun on the side."

"I'd like to give up that pastime."

"Suit yourself. But I can give you some introductions to women who'll make your little Logan tart look homely. Give it some thought, Hugh. And come to the next fund raiser, so I can get you started with the right campaign people."

* * *

Hugh sat watching his silent phone for a few minutes, waiting for his blood pressure to go down. His doctor had been all over him about stress at his last visit. I'm a trial lawyer, he had shot back. I eat stress for breakfast, lunch, and dinner. But now, as he felt the blood rushing through his temples, he wondered if he was as immortal as he believed. And he hated knowing Buffy had outsmarted him again.

Suddenly his desire to see Kathryn overrode all his common sense. He got up and wandered down the hall to the small conference room, trying to think of an acceptable excuse for why he had come.

But he didn't need an excuse. He slipped in unnoticed. Kathryn was sitting at the end of the small conference table in tears. Patty was standing by the video camera, which she had just turned off; and Mark was sitting beside Kathryn, offering her the box of tissue. Even in tears, she looked elegant in a simple beige dress and navy jacket. The part of him that couldn't stop thinking about her wanted to tell Mark to move over, so he could hand her the tissue. But his ever-vigilant lawyer side was glad they'd made her cry. Now she'd be much harder to shake in the actual deposition.

Suddenly everyone noticed he was there.

"We're taking a break," Patty said.

Hugh nodded. "Of course. This is bound to be emotional stuff."

Kathryn looked up at him with her lovely, hazel, teary eyes and gave him a faint smile. "I'm sorry. I didn't think I'd become emotional."

"No need to apologize. Better to be emotional here than on the day of the real thing. That's why we do these preparations."

He wondered if Patty and Mark had gotten the secret of her marriage out of her. He looked over at Mark, who seemed to guess his thoughts. Mark shook his head "no" ever so slightly.

Hugh looked back at Kathryn, overjoyed that he had the perfect excuse to say what he was about to say. "Hey, I've got an idea. I'll take you to dinner tonight, and we can finish talking about your deposition over some good food and better wine."

* * *

Logan had been furious when he'd cancelled their plans that evening. He'd made a reservation at the Marine Room, so he could tell her she was being transferred to the Washington, D.C. office. He had made sure not to see her often since Buffy's ultimatum. He liked the Marine Room for breakups. The romantic surroundings gave the dumpee hope that the split was only temporary and discouraged scenes. Hugh hated scenes. But now his heart was soaring at the thought of an evening with Kathryn under low lights with the ocean just steps away.

"You promised!" Logan pouted when he called to tell her of the change in plans.

"Kathryn Andrews had a rough day in depo prep. And I've got some things I need to talk to her about. She's upset and nervous. It will go better if the firm buys her a nice dinner, and we talk over a bottle of wine."

"You like her," Logan accused.

"She's one of the nicer clients," Hugh agreed.

"No, you *like* her," Logan insisted.

"Don't be insulting. She's a client, Logan. You know very well we don't get personally involved with our clients. Tell you what, I'll be done with dinner by ten. I'll stop by your place on the way home." He hung up and wondered why the richest, toughest plaintiff's attorney in America was afraid of a junior associate in his firm. Probably because he had dirt on Logan, but she had far more on him.

* * *

Now as he sat across from Kathryn in the soft light of the Marine Room with the ocean rolling onshore just beyond the glass, he no longer had any desire to go by Logan's afterward. And he fervently wished he looked like Mark Kelly and wasn't Kathryn's lawyer.

"Sorry for today. I know it was difficult." He'd ordered a French Bordeaux to impress her. He hoped she was impressed.

"It was." She took a long drink of the wine, but did not reward him with a compliment. He could tell her mind was elsewhere. "I've had cases where clients confessed to crimes they didn't commit, and I've wondered how anyone could be pushed to say things that aren't true. And today I experienced what they must have in the interrogation room."

"Then Mark and Patty did a good job."

She nodded. "They did. But Tom and I were happily

married. It angers me beyond words to have anyone insinuate otherwise."

"Then be prepared for Bob McLaren because he will give you no quarter in that department."

"I know. I understand what he wants to do. And I hate myself for thinking lawyers must show some respect for the truth on the civil side. Truth is nothing but fiction in criminal law."

"You've been an attorney long enough to see that we aren't engaged in a search for the truth. It's all about who has the most money, civil or criminal. You know that."

"I wish I didn't."

The waitress appeared.

"You'll want the lobster," Hugh said to Kathryn. "The firm is picking up the tab. And I'll have the same." He smiled at the waitress, who scurried off.

Years of experience had taught him the direct approach was often the best. "What made you cry today?"

She shrugged. "Nothing in particular. I was tired. They asked a lot of questions."

"What was the last one they asked before you started crying?"

"They asked me what the stresses were in Tom's life."

"And you said?"

"Our jobs. I mean, you just said it yourself. Money is the key to acquittal. How do you think it feels to represent someone facing the death penalty with nothing but a part-time investigator and an overworked paralegal and lying cops on the other side?"

"So your husband took his job seriously?"

"Very."

"But aren't most of your clients guilty?"

"Most. But a few aren't. And guilty or not, the Sixth Amendment requires us to do everything we can to raise a reasonable doubt about our client's guilt. That's hard to do when you have too many cases assigned to you. And Tom and I both had too many."

"So you think that kind of stress raised your husband's blood pressure?"

"It certainly contributed to it."

"Was there a specific incident in late 2011 that led to his diagnosis in 2012? Anything at work or at home?"

"No." She wouldn't meet his eyes as she spoke, and Hugh knew she was lying.

The entree arrived, and Hugh allowed himself to be absorbed by the exquisite blend of lobster and truffle sauce accompanied by roasted potatoes and broccoli puree. When the plates were cleared, he ordered decaf for them both.

He stirred his coffee thoughtfully and then said, "Wycliffe's fight to keep their clinical trials out of our hands means we are going to find a lot of helpful information in them. But I have to warn you, I think we are wading into deeper waters than I first thought when you came to me about your husband."

"Are you suggesting we give up on Tom's case?"

"Of course not. But I want to be sure you understand there may be risks beyond the ordinary ones."

She pictured the Suburban behind her on the bridge. But that had been only an act of road rage. It was over. It would not happen again. "My husband is dead. I have no children. I'm a public defender with a list of former clients as long as your arm who'd like to kill me. I'm already living with 'risks beyond the ordinary ones.'"

* * *

Tuesday, June 3, 2014, Midnight, Logan Avery's Downtown Condo

Wearing nothing but his boxers, Hugh stood in front of Logan's spellbinding view of San Diego's night skyline, sipping a scotch he'd poured for himself and thinking about Kathryn. He hadn't meant to come to Logan's tonight, and now he was sorry he wasn't home in his own bed.

After watching Kathryn drive away from the Marine Room in her little car, he had suddenly felt lonely. He'd gone through the mechanics of sex with Logan and then waited for her to fall asleep. But he'd chickened out of telling her about the transfer. He sighed as he drank and watched the cold lights of the city. Was he the only lonely, rich old man who'd lost his soul? Were there any others awake as the last seconds of Tuesday night slid into the first minutes of Wednesday morning? Did they, too, have voluptuous mistresses asleep in another room, whom they had tired of?

What was Kathryn hiding? What if her marriage had been all but over when her husband died? At best, the damages award would be nominal even if Mark could convince a jury Myrabin was responsible for Tom's death. The firm would take a financial bath.

The businessman in him screamed *don't risk it*, but the old warrior who loved to gamble and win said *go for it*. Besides, if he pulled out of the Wycliffe litigation, he'd lose contact with Kathryn. And although she would never consider him as anything but a loud, brash, smart-ass, he wanted to look into those big hazel eyes and hear her soft voice talk about the man she loved, even if it could never be him.

Suddenly Logan was behind him, her arms around him, her hands in places he wished they weren't. He could feel she hadn't bothered to throw a robe over her nakedness.

"Come back to bed and play some more."

He turned and pulled away. "Not now, Logan. I've got something on my mind."

"Something or someone as in Kathryn Andrews?" She wrinkled her nose at the name.

"Kathryn's got a secret she's not telling us. That matters to me."

* * *

Buffy checked her email one last time before turning out the lights and saw the pictures her investigator had taken of Hugh and Logan from a balcony across the street from Logan's condo. Hugh didn't look good naked. But then, he hadn't realized he was being photographed.

The more disturbing pictures were of him walking Kathryn Andrews to her car after dinner, somewhere. She couldn't tell where. He was standing a little too close as he leaned on the driver's side door, apparently after he closed it for her. And the look on his face as he stood in the parking lot watching her drive away said way too much about how he felt.

Logan Avery wasn't a threat to Buffy's status as the wife of a rich and powerful man, but Kathryn Andrews was.

CHAPTER SIXTEEN

Early Morning Hours of Wednesday, June 4, 2014, 1845 Ocean Place, Pacific Beach

After she got home, Kathryn could not sleep. She put on her pajamas and wandered the house in the dark. The clock on the stove said one a.m. when she pushed open the back door and went outside to sit in the cool mysterious dark under the stars.

She wasn't hungry or thirsty. She'd had more than enough expensive wine. She was exhausted and drained from the ordeal of deposition preparation and Hugh's probing at dinner. But Shannon's relationship with Tom, whatever it had been, was her closely guarded secret. Besides, she owed it to Tom's memory to accept his reassurances that he had only been Shannon's friend and nothing more.

* * *

October, 2011, Halloween Night, The Yellow Café Pacific Beach

By September, Shannon had given up the modeling gigs. She took on more surfing students and worked more hours at the PB Saloon, so she could make the payments on the Corvette.

She and Steve seemed to be in a state of perpetual conflict that required her to seek constant advice and attention from Tom.

There were many mornings when, as Kathryn got dressed for work, she could hear the rise and fall of Shannon's voice in the kitchen as she drank coffee with Tom after surfing and explained her side of her latest row with Steve. And on those mornings Kathryn's stomach would tighten when she walked by Tom's office and saw it was still empty at ten o'clock.

To make matters worse, on the weekends, Tom began to bring Shannon back for breakfast. Kathryn did her best to sit through the meal with the two of them locked in a discussion about Steve and Shannon's latest conflict, but she was up and out long before Tom walked Shannon out to her bicycle, one arm around her shoulders.

Halloween had become an increasingly difficult holiday for Kathryn. Children coming to the door in their costumes were yet another reminder of the baby she wanted and could not have. By this point in her marriage, Kathryn had thought she would have at least two, and maybe three, children. Instead, the man she loved was at the beck and call of another woman.

Kathryn summoned her courage to confront him on Halloween night. They left treats in a big bowl on their porch and walked up to The Yellow Café for dinner.

They were halfway through the meal when Kathryn said, "I thought I'd better let you know Millie came looking for you at ten o'clock this morning. When she didn't find you in your office, she asked me where you were. She said it's the third time this week she's been looking for you, and your office has been empty."

Tom flinched at the news that Mildred Fletcher, head of the

San Diego County Public Defender's Office and his boss, had noticed his absence. "What did you tell her?"

"Well, I didn't tell the truth: I didn't tell her you were sitting in the kitchen playing therapist for Shannon. I told her you were interviewing a witness in the Pepe Jackson murder case."

"Thanks." He looked genuinely relieved.

"But I'm not going to lie for you again," she added.

Tom put his fork down on his plate of half-eaten meatloaf. He seemed to be thinking about what to say next. Finally he said, "You warned me about letting Shannon cry on my shoulder too much."

"And you didn't listen."

"It's hard, sweetheart. She doesn't have anyone else to turn to."

"You mean you're her only friend."

Tom's blue eyes studied her face. Finally he said, "I guess if you put it that way, yes. When she and Steve aren't getting along, she only has me."

"And do you always take her side against Steve?"

"I–I don't think so."

"But Steve has stopped coming over. I warned you that Shannon was coming between you and Steve, and now she has."

Tom took another bite of meatloaf and thought about what she'd said. "I don't think she's come between us. Steve knows I want them to get along. I know he's busy with work right now. He has a case that may go to trial in a couple of months."

Kathryn studied her husband across the red-checked table cloth. "Making you late for work isn't the only problem Shannon is creating. It looks like you've given up completely on trying to have a baby."

In the light of the single candle in the Mason jar, Kathryn saw his eyes darken and become guarded. He sighed and put down his fork again. "I don't think I made a conscious decision to stop trying. But I told you before, I can't get back on the merry-go-round of tests and fertility windows. I feel more like if it happens, it happens. And if it doesn't, I'm happy being just the two of us."

"But what if I'm not? What if I want a baby?"

Tom reached out and took both of her hands. "Kathryn, we've tried everything including being wait-listed at adoption agencies. According to all the doctors we've seen, there is no biological reason why we shouldn't be able to conceive. But after years of trying, we've had no success. It's time to go on with our lives and just be happy we have each other. All this emphasis on getting pregnant has become way too stressful."

"But you don't mind listening to the stress of Shannon's problems instead of staying home with me and trying to have a baby!" She pulled her hands away.

Tom sighed. "It's not Shannon. It's the sea. It's surfing. That's where I find peace from all the stress of how little I can do to help people in my job and from the stress of not being able to make a baby with you and from the pain of your disappointment."

They finished the meal in silence, skipped coffee, and walked home in the dark, still without saying anything. A block from their house, Tom reached over and took Kathryn's hand and gave it a reassuring squeeze. But his gesture didn't relieve the knot in her stomach because she realized that to keep Tom she would have to accept the fact they would always be childless.

CHAPTER SEVENTEEN

Monday June 16, 2014, Conference Room, Emerald Shapery Center, San Diego

Mondays were beginning to be a relief from the weekends for Mark Kelly. Rachel's wedding planning continued unabated, and he increasingly felt he had become merely the excuse to fulfill her lifelong dream of an extravagant social event designed to make her the envy of all her friends. He wondered what she would devote herself to for the rest of their marriage after the honeymoon.

At Hugh's command, the Andrews litigation team had assembled in the small conference room at ten a.m., and Kathryn had been invited. Wearing an attractive but conservative black suit and white blouse, she was sitting on the opposite side of the table, two chairs away from Stewart Lipscomb, a tall, skinny third-year associate who had replaced Logan. Stewart had been pre-med as an undergrad, and Mark knew Hugh had shamelessly used his superior medical expertise as an excuse to bundle Logan off to the D.C. office. Patty in a light gray dress, had Mark on her left and Hugh's empty chair on her right. She was tapping her pencil impatiently on her legal pad. They were waiting for Hugh. Everyone had a mug of coffee served from the pot in the center of the table.

Mark studied Kathryn, who was checking messages on her phone. He had not seen her since the day they'd rehearsed her deposition. She was thinner than the first time he'd met her, and her eyes looked tired. Stress was taking its toll on her beautiful face. She stared at the phone, reluctant to make eye contact with any of them.

One of the big mahogany doors stirred slightly and then swung wide as Hugh strode into the room. His commanding height immediately established a dominant presence, but the way he surveyed his assembled troops with satisfaction also left no doubt about who was the commander-in-chief. He motioned for everyone who had slightly risen to sit as he took his place at the head of the table. Mark watched his boss's eyes go immediately to Kathryn's face. He could tell Patty had noticed, too. But Patty, who never lost her appearance of cool impartiality, gave him the slightest of shrugs as if to say, *there's nothing we can do*, and quickly looked away.

Hugh smiled jovially at everyone. "Good morning. I hope you had a good weekend. Thank you for joining us, Kathryn. I'm happy to tell you we've put off your deposition until mid-September. Patty will work out the details with you. Do you know how your trial calendar looks for the second week?"

She smiled and looked genuinely relieved. "I don't recall anything right now, but I'll have to check to be sure."

Hugh nodded. "Well, try to protect that week if you can. Wycliffe wasn't happy about moving things from August to

September, but we need time to get through the documents that they've been so reluctant to give us."

Hugh looked over at Stewart, who had opened his laptop and powered it up. "I know you haven't been on this case very long," Hugh began, "but you told Mark you had some information to share."

"I do." Stewart gave them all his geeky, but ultra-confident, smile. "Wycliffe has turned over very little of the work that Suchet did initially on the drug. When I contacted Emma Talbert to find out where the rest of it is, she claimed Wycliffe did not receive complete documentation from Suchet. According to her, they've given us everything they have."

"Ha!" Hugh snorted. "Like we really believe that! We need to talk to the head of the Myrabin development team at Suchet."

"True," Stewart agreed, "but there's a problem with that. Wycliffe is trying to hide his identity. On the few documents they've given us, the name of the head of Suchet's research team has been blacked out."

"Those bastards!" Hugh banged his hand on the table. "This is going to take another motion to compel. Damn! They're making us pull the information out of them bit by bit. Judge Weiner is not going to be happy with Bob McLaren. I bet she even imposes sanctions! Patty, call the judge's clerk and get us on her motions calendar as soon as possible.

* * *

On a ridiculous whim, Mark took the freight elevator to the lobby after the meeting broke up, hoping to run into Kathryn. But there was no sign of her. *It was just as well* he told himself.

* * *

Wednesday, June 18, 2014, 1845 Ocean Place, Pacific Beach

At eight p.m., at the moment the sun was setting, Kathryn tossed the white rose petals into the waves. She had walked down to the beach from her cottage alone. Paul had called frantically for the past week, leaving messages about how much he wanted to share this day with her. But despite the orchids a month ago, she wasn't prepared to forgive him for Shannon. Yet. Maybe never.

She watched the water swallow the last bits of the flowers that were as fragile as Tom's life had been while the sun sank into the gray-blue water in a blazing ball of crimson fire. She gazed at the water and tried to feel Tom's presence. Surely if his spirit had returned today, it was out there, hovering above the ocean he loved. She had never given much thought to spirits until Tom was gone, and she so desperately wanted to see or hear or feel him near her again.

"Tom." She called his name aloud to see if it would bring any sign of him.

But nothing. As of today, he'd been gone two years. Was that too long for him to come back to her? Couldn't the spirit world cut her a break on the anniversary of his death?

She didn't feel Tom's presence, but her intuition said something was not right. Out of the corner of her eye, she noticed a middle-aged man standing at the edge of the soft sand, wearing the ridiculous floppy hat tourists over fifty favored. He had a serious-looking Nikon with a long lens that he seemed to be pointing toward the sunset. He was snapping pictures in rapid succession. But she felt uneasy because the lens was pointed in her direction, too. He might be the eccentric tourist he appeared to be. But, then, again, he might not.

She turned and walked home without looking back. As she reached the cottage and put her key in the lock, she glanced across the street. He was there in his floppy hat with his long-lensed camera. It was pointed at her. Her stomach flipped-flopped as she hurried inside and closed and locked her door. She thought of calling the police, but her house had been marked as a public defender's residence. The cops might show up if she were actually dying. But then again, they might not.

DISCOVERY,
THE SECOND MOTION

CHAPTER EIGHTEEN

Monday, June 30, 2014, Edward J. Schwartz Federal Courthouse, U.S. District Court, Southern District of California, San Diego, 9:00 a.m.

"Back so soon, Mr. McLaren?" Judge Weiner looked down at Bob McLaren, Annette Fry, and Emma Talbert at the defendant's table just after she took the bench and the lawyers were seated. Kathryn, who had the chair between Mark and Hugh at the plaintiff's table, looked over at Bob McLaren, who actually seemed to squirm slightly under Her Honor's steely gaze.

But the judge was not ready to hear from Wycliffe. It was the plaintiff's motion, and Hugh had designated Mark, seated on Kathryn's left, as the point man.

"Mr. Kelly, why don't you explain what Wycliffe hasn't turned over in discovery that you think you're entitled to. It's been barely a month since you were here on a motion to compel. I thought I made it clear I wasn't going to tolerate anyone playing games by withholding documents. Explain to me what's still missing."

"Thank you, Your Honor." Mark stepped up to the podium which Kathryn could see he occupied comfortably in his navy suit. "As Your Honor may recall, when we were here before, Wycliffe was refusing to turn over the reports of their clinical trials for Myrabin, the drug we allege caused the death of Mrs. Andrews' husband. Since then, we've received some, but not all the reports."

"Which ones are missing?" the judge demanded in a tone that did not bode well for Wycliffe, Kathryn thought.

"Our expert has compiled a list of the Wycliffe work that's missing. But in addition to that, there are reports missing from the company that originally developed Myrabin in the early 90's, Laboratories Suchet. Wycliffe bought the rights to it in 1994, a year after Suchet stopped working on it. Wycliffe has turned over some, but not all, of Suchet's reports. And, most importantly, the name of the head of the team that developed Myrabin at Suchet has been blacked out on the few documents that have been turned over."

"Anything further, Mr. Kelly?"

"No, Your Honor."

Mark smiled at Kathryn and Hugh as he sat down beside them. Bob McLaren made his oily way to the podium.

Judge Weiner looked down at her notes and then at McLaren. "Looks like you have some explaining to do, Mr. McLaren."

"I know, Your Honor. And I can explain."

"Get busy, then."

"As Mr. Kelly said, Suchet developed Myrabin before my client purchased the rights. Suchet did not turn over all of its reports to Wycliffe."

"But Suchet did turn over the name of the head of its research team, did it not?"

"That's a delicate matter, Your Honor."

"How so?" Judge Weiner frowned skeptically.

"The scientist who led the work on Myrabin was let go from Suchet in 1993. He made inappropriate sexual advances to a female colleague who was the number two team leader on the project. She complained, and Suchet terminated him."

"And you've turned over the name of this woman whom you say complained?"

"Well, no, Your Honor. Both scientists are highly regarded in their fields, and the incident is long over. They would be embarrassed if the plaintiff were allowed to rake it all up again."

"But the plaintiff's suit is wrongful death, Mr. McLaren, not sexual harassment. The plaintiff is entitled to know who worked on development of the drug that she has alleged killed her husband."

"But, Your Honor—"

"No 'buts,' Mr. McLaren. If you make Goldstein, Miller bring a third motion to compel discovery, I'm going to impose heavy sanctions on Wycliffe and on King and White. You are an experienced litigator, Mr. McLaren. You know the rules. Your client has ten days to turn over any reports that have been withheld and the names that have been blacked out."

"But, Your Honor—"

"Court is adjourned, Mr. McLaren. Another word from you, and I'll hold you in contempt."

* * *

Monday, June 30, 2014, Hugh Mahoney's Office, Emerald Shapery Center, San Diego

At four p.m., his secretary told him Logan was on the line. He considered not answering it, but knew she would persist until he talked to her.

"Miss me?" she cooed into the receiver as soon as he picked it up.

"I hope you're settling in," Hugh replied.

"Okay, I get it. You don't."

"Logan, I explained how I felt when I told you about the transfer."

"I thought you didn't mean it."

"Well, you were wrong. I did. Buffy knows about us, and she objects. I can't make her unhappy."

"But you can do that to me?"

"You're not unhappy, Logan. I'm buying you a townhouse in Georgetown. I've arranged for you to work with Bill Snyder, our top litigation partner in D.C. And he's single, by the way. And I'm planning to put in a word for you when partnership comes around in a few years. I'll shorten up the time for you the way I did for Patty. Just do a good job, so I can. You're a good lawyer, Logan."

"I sure am," she agreed. "And you're going to find out just how good."

He was relieved when she slammed down the receiver. Most of the women in his past had taken the breakup better than this. She'd been so angry about the transfer that he'd agreed to buy her San Diego condo immediately to get her out of town. He really hoped Bill Snyder would take a shine to her and get her off his hands.

He got up and went over to the drinks tray and poured himself a double scotch. It had been a long day. He was tired, and he had promised Buffy he'd take her to dinner that evening. He had to show her he was trying now that Logan was safely on the other side of the country. He was powerful, but men like Fred Akers and Hal Edwards were also powerful. They stuck by their wives, and they expected the same from anyone they endorsed. He didn't want them against him. He had to keep Buffy as happy as she'd been when he'd been dependent upon her money.

His phone rang again, and his secretary announced Bob McLaren. Hugh sighed. He wasn't in the mood to deal with McLaren. He thought of transferring the call to Mark, but then he remembered Mark had left early to deal with some sort of wedding-planning emergency Rachel had created. If Mark had any sense, he'd get himself out of that fiasco as quickly as possible.

He sighed and picked up the receiver. "Hugh Mahoney."

"The judge was kind of rough on us this morning," Bob McLaren began without ceremony.

Hugh sat down at his massive desk, took a long drink of scotch, and watched the tiny people and cars far below him. He said nothing in response to McLaren's complaint, knowing that his silence would make his opponent more uncomfortable than any words he could utter.

"Anyway," McLaren plunged on, "I've got Emma Talbert here with me in my office."

Hugh heard the speaker phone button being pushed, and then Emma said, "Good afternoon, Mr. Mahoney."

"Ms. Talbert," Hugh greeted her in return. "I assume the two of you have called to discuss turning over the reports and the names you've been ordered to give us. How soon do you plan to provide that information?"

"We have ten days," Emma Talbert said defensively.

"There's a lot of material missing," Hugh warned her. "And the judge made it clear she isn't going to give you more time."

"Look, Hugh, Wycliffe doesn't want to hand over those documents and the names of the researchers. It would drag up a lot of bad memories for the people involved. They've gone on with their lives. They don't want to relive an old mistake."

"Are you saying you won't give them to us?" *Surely even McLaren was not that ballsy,* Hugh thought. The judge had threatened sanctions. White and King would be very upset if McLaren brought those down on the firm. McLaren would be wise to play by the rules from now on.

"No, I'm not saying that. But I'm calling to see if we could settle this."

"Wycliffe is prepared to offer half a million," Emma Talbert spoke up.

Hugh laughed his deep belly laugh. "No way."

"Okay, a million," McLaren offered.

"Nope, not enough."

"Oh, come on, Hugh," Bob cajoled. "Your guy went to Harvard, but he tanked his lifetime earnings by working as a PD. Face it, he just wasn't worth that much."

Hugh pictured the $2,000 check the lawyer had handed his

mother with the words, *he wasn't worth that much.* "You are forgetting Mrs. Andrews' damages for the loss of her husband."

"We'll offer two," Emma Talbert interjected. "But that's as high as I'm authorized to go."

"Not enough," Hugh said. "They were very happily married. I'm expecting to see documents and the name of the head of the Suchet team at eight in the morning."

CHAPTER NINETEEN

Tuesday, July 15, 2014, Conference Room, Emerald Shapery Center, San Diego

"Dr. Maurice Giles Vannier. He's a world-famous biochemist," Stewart Lipscomb announced to the Andrews litigation team, assembled once more in the large conference room. Hugh had his customary place at the head of the table. Rick Peyton was seated to his right. Mark and Patty were on his left. Stewart was next to Dr. Peyton so they could share the stack of documents in front of them. Kathryn had the chair next to Stewart.

Dr. Peyton spoke up, "Dr. Vannier was head of the team at Suchet that did the initial work on Myrabin. He left Suchet in 1993, just as Wycliffe claims. I've gone over all of his work that has been turned over and there's still a lot of missing information. We need to talk to him right away."

"Do you know how to find him?" Hugh asked.

"Of course," Stewart spoke up. "He's the chairman of the Department of Biology at the École Normale Supérieure in Paris."

"Patty, see how quickly you can get an appointment with

THE DEATH OF DISTANT STARS

him for Mark, Rick, and me. And book flights and a hotel."

Kathryn saw Patty grimace slightly, and their eyes met across the conference table. Hugh apparently had forgotten Patty was a full equity partner, and no longer his mistress at his beck and call.

Kathryn felt another pair of eyes on hers and looked up to see Mark Kelly giving her a slight smile. He'd seen her spot Hugh's faux pas. He glanced over at Patty and then at Hugh and said, "I'll have my secretary take care of the flight and hotel arrangements since I'm the one going. I'll telephone Dr. Vannier's office to make an appointment to see him. Patty has enough to do right now. She's defending the depositions of the staff who treated Tom Andrews at the hospital."

"Okay, fine." Hugh shrugged as if to minimize his social ineptness. Patty gave Mark a grateful look.

"I want to go, too," Kathryn said quietly. She knew taking a client on an investigative trip was unheard of, but she didn't care. She desperately wanted to know if Dr. Vannier could explain how Myrabin had killed Tom.

* * *

Wednesday, July 23, 2014, Mark Kelly's Office, Emerald Shapery Center, San Diego

At six p.m., Hugh wandered into Mark's office just as he was about to leave.

"I need to talk to you."

"Can't it wait? Rachel is sitting in the bar this minute at WhisknLadle in La Jolla, waiting for me. We have a dinner reservation in a half hour."

"Tell her you'll be thirty minutes late. Let's go downstairs for a quick drink."

As expected, Rachel was livid. If he didn't show by seven, she was leaving. Mark wondered if "leaving" meant the bar at WhisknLadle or him. He hurried downstairs to meet Hugh in the Westin Hotel's Lobby Bar. As he'd expected, Hugh was already seated at an out-of-the-way, marble-topped table, in one of the neutral, stone-gray chairs, a scotch in front of him.

"You caught hell from her," Hugh observed as he summoned the waiter. "Bring my friend a double scotch."

The waiter turned to go, but Mark held up his hand. "Wait, wait. A beer for me. I've got to drive to La Jolla to meet Rachel." He turned to Hugh, hoping to get the conversation over quickly. "What did you want to tell me?"

"A couple of things. One, I know Hays, Price went under today. They sent us an official notice of dissolution."

"I saw their announcement." Mark worked to keep his face impassive although he was seething. Hundreds of people were out of work because of Hugh's baseless paranoia.

"I thought you might come to me about it."

"It's too late. They've closed their doors and sent their employees home. If you sent them every penny Goldstein, Miller owes them tonight, they'd still be out on the street. Besides, you made it clear I couldn't change your mind."

"And you didn't. I just wanted to be sure we understood each other on this."

"If that's all, I don't want to make Rachel wait any longer."

"That's not all." Hugh waived at the waiter, who quickly brought him another drink.

"Hey, go slow on those, even if Jose is driving," Mark counseled.

But Hugh shook his head. "No, I need this. You don't know how I need this. I've got to take Buffy to dinner after we're through here. And she's on the warpath."

"Warpath? Why? Logan is a continent away."

"It relates to the second thing I wanted to bring up with you. Buffy wants—no, insists—that I run for Fred Akers' seat as the junior senator from California."

"Where's Fred going?"

"To a cabinet post after the election, assuming of course, Hal is re-elected."

Mark sipped his beer and tried not to appear as stunned as he felt. "Whose idea was it for you to run?"

"Edith put the bug in Buffy's ear."

"Edith as in First Lady Edith?"

Hugh nodded grimly. "Right."

"Do you want to run?"

He shook his head. "I'd rather be drawn and quartered."

"Then why even ask me for my opinion?"

"Because Buffy is turning all the years of my affairs around on me. If I don't run, she's going to broadcast my indiscretions around the world."

"How?"

"By leaving me. And giving lots of TV interviews. Edith's press people are poised to line them up."

"What will she say?"

"You don't have to ask. You already know. She will say I'm a randy old lech who slept with Patty and Logan and a lot of other females who are now our partners."

"Patty will sue her for libel and slander."

"Truth, unfortunately, is a complete defense. And you know my story with Patty."

"So you have to run for office to avoid ruining yourself and Patty and the others?"

"Something like that. Buffy wants to be a senator's wife."

"Why are you telling me this?"

"Because I'll want you to take over my role at Goldstein, Miller."

"*What?*"

"You heard me. I want you to be the firm's guiding force."

"You mean, I'll be your puppet. You'll tell me who to ruin, and I'll do your bidding." He couldn't help letting that much bitterness through.

"No, I don't mean that at all. I know you'll always follow your conscience, Mark, even when it creates friction between us. If you'd been in charge, Hays, Price would not have gone under."

"Then why did you let them?"

"Because Bill deserved it."

Mark bit his lip and decided not to comment further on Hugh's paranoia. He felt his phone buzz, and saw a text from Rachel: "Not here in ten minutes. I'm done."

He texted back, "Still with Hugh. Be there as fast as I can."

Hugh frowned. "What's going on? What are you doing?"

"Rachel has given me ten minutes to make it to WhisknLadle in La Jolla. I've got to go."

"No, no, there's one more thing."

Mark sighed. "Could you make it quick, then? I don't want a big row with the fiancée tonight."

"I want you to try again to find out what Kathryn isn't telling us about her marriage."

"Look, Hugh. The Paris trip isn't on until September 16. Dr. Vannier and his wife are in Greece on their summer holiday. He said he'd be happy to meet us, but not until the university term starts. Are you thinking I can somehow take Kathryn aside in Paris and get her to tell me a secret that you don't even know for certain exists?"

"She's hiding something," Hugh insisted.

Mark's phone buzzed and he saw a warning from Rachel, "I'm leaving!" He stood up. "I've got to go. Rachel has lost patience. Tell you what I'll do. I have a passing acquaintance with Paul Curtis. If she's hiding something, he'll know. I'll get him to meet me for a beer and see what he says. But I want you to promise me something."

"What?" Hugh signaled for a third scotch with a frown on his face.

"That you'll accept whatever Paul tells me. If he says there's no secret, you'll stop bugging me."

"Okay, okay!"

* * *

Twenty-five minutes later, Mark pulled up at the valet stand at WhisknLadle and ran into the restaurant. He pushed past everyone waiting for a table and rushed to the mahogany reception desk, startling the tall blonde goddess in black who ordained who should be seated and who should not.

"I'm sorry, sir. You'll have to wait your turn."

"I know. I apologize. It's an emergency."

The goddess raised one eyebrow but otherwise remained impassive. "What kind of emergency?"

"My fiancée has been waiting here for me for over an hour. I need to find her."

The goddess pulled her full, red lips into a pout and picked up a small coin-sized envelope lying on top of the reception desk. She handed it to Mark and said, "I'm very sorry, sir. She left a message."

He opened the envelope and stared down at the thirty-thousand-dollar diamond solitaire that he'd traveled all the way to Los Angeles to purchase from Harry Winston. He felt the blonde goddess's eyes on him as he studied the ring. He looked up into her sympathetic, dark brown eyes.

"I'm off at nine," she said. "I could set you up with free drinks in the bar until then, if you'd like to wait."

"No thanks."

CHAPTER TWENTY

Friday, July 25, 2014, 1845 Ocean Place, Pacific Beach

Kathryn got home from work at five-thirty. She was angry and frustrated. She didn't want to wait until September to go to Paris to interview Dr. Vannier. She wanted to know now, right this minute, just exactly how Myrabin had killed Tom.

She threw her briefcase onto the hall bench and stormed into her bedroom to change into yoga pants and a sloppy, gray sweatshirt with the hem out. She pinned her hair into a messy bun on top of her head and poured herself a very large glass of merlot. She took her cell phone and her wine into the backyard and settled into one of the two Adirondack chairs that she and Tom had painted bright yellow, one late September afternoon in 2011. It had turned out to be their last autumn together.

She made herself sip the wine slowly as she contemplated Paul's text.

"Are you ever going to forgive me? Shannon was a mistake. I'm sorry. I only want you in my life. You know Tom would want us together."

She closed her eyes and sipped her wine in the softening

summer dusk. And she remembered what she did not want to remember.

* * *

Saturday, December 10, 2011, 1845 Ocean Place, Pacific Beach

The Christmas tree was up. Platters of hors d'oeuvres covered the dining room table. Scallops wrapped in prosciutto, mini quiches, seared steak lettuce cups, bacon deviled eggs, crab beignets, potato croquettes, zucchini and goat cheese tarts, and chipotle chicken on soft tacos. And they had hired one of Shannon's colleagues to tend bar. It was, Kathryn thought, the most ambitious party of their marriage, and she tried to feel festive as she circulated among their guests. Since October she had struggled to accept Tom's decision that they would never have a child. But instead of growing closer to her after she'd come to terms with his bleak decree, Tom had continued to answer Shannon's midnight calls and texts in the name of giving her advice about her relationship with Steve. At least he hadn't made himself late to work again on Shannon's account.

Kathryn tried to put all of that out of her mind and focus on enjoying the party. The surf crowd was hanging out with Steve and his environmental friends in the dining room. Shannon held sway by the food in a skintight red sheath she had probably ordered from the Victoria's Secret catalogue. For a while, Tom stood with Kathryn by the Christmas tree as they listened to their colleagues from the public defender's office talk about their hopeless cases. But after she went to replenish the food, he joined the surfers. When Kathryn came back with fresh trays of hors d'oeuvres, she found him standing between Shannon and Steve. Shannon had draped an arm around each of them.

Kathryn arranged the food quickly and headed for the opposite side of the room where Paul and Carolyn were talking to some friends from Warrick, Thompson. The group was huddled in a circle in front of the fireplace. With her back to the dining room, she tried to lose herself in Big Firm gossip about people she had never met, until Carolyn nudged her.

"You might want to watch what's going on by the food. Shannon is making a play for your husband." As she spoke, Carolyn slid her arm through Paul's.

He looked over at her, startled. "What's going on?"

"I'm making sure Shannon doesn't put any moves on you." Carolyn tossed her auburn mane in the direction of the dining room and took a sip of wine.

Kathryn saw Paul's eyes shift to the group around the table. He studied the situation and then shrugged, "It's just Christmas, and they've had too much to drink."

Tom looked up at that moment as if he had felt their eyes on him. He disengaged himself from Steve and Shannon and the surfer crowd and came to join Kathryn, who breathed a sigh of relief.

The party spun on until the wee hours as it always did. Shannon and Steve were the last to leave at one-thirty. Kathryn and Tom put the leftovers in the fridge and fell into bed, leaving the rest of the cleanup for morning.

At three, Tom's phone began to ring. Kathryn pushed away the cobwebs of heavy sleep to find him sitting up in bed answering it. "Okay. I'll be there in a second."

"Where are you going? It's three in the morning."

"It's Shannon." He was already getting out of bed and picking up the pants he'd laid over a chair earlier. "She's had a blazing fight with Steve. She's out front, and she needs me."

* * *

Friday, August 8, 2014 P & J's Brewery and Tasting Room, San Diego

At six p.m., Mark walked the few blocks from his office at the Emerald Shapery Center to P & J's on Columbia Street. He thought it would have made more sense to meet Paul Curtis at the Westin Lobby Bar in the Emerald Shapery Center itself since Warwick, Thompson was also at Emerald Shapery, but Paul had proposed P & J's.

As Mark sipped his first IPA, a light citrusy brew, and listened to the escalating hum of happy hour, he smiled as he recalled Kathryn's aversion to P & J's. He sipped some more and crossed over into relaxed euphoria as he remembered that no angry Rachel would be waiting when he got home that night. She'd come with a truck and her aggrieved extended family the Saturday after she had decided to give the ring back, and they had spent the afternoon eliminating all signs of her from his house. Moreover, Harry Winston had agreed to accept the ring for sale-on-consignment with a sizable cut for the store if the staff found a buyer. Having Rachel and her ring out of his house and out of his life was a great relief.

Paul Curtis pushed open the heavy P&J's door. Mark noticed that most of the female heads at the bar turned to watch him stride confidently through the milling Happy Hour throng in his perfectly cut gray suit that reeked of expensive hand sewing. Mark made a mental note to get the name of Paul's tailor.

"Hey, buddy, glad you could make it. Let me buy you a beer." Mark rose to greet Paul's striking, blonde good looks, happily aware that the single female population was studying them both.

Paul shook his hand and loosened his maroon tie. "Sounds good, and thanks." He settled into the seat opposite Mark in the booth and asked, "I hope this isn't bad news about Kathryn's case."

"Oh, no. In fact, there's good news. We managed to wrangle the name of the French scientist who worked on the development of Myrabin out of Wycliffe. He's agreed to meet with us."

"So you think you'll get something helpful out of him?"

"Suchet accepted his recommendation to stop development of the drug. So, yes, we're pretty optimistic that we're going to get news that will help our case."

The waitress appeared with Paul's beer and lingered for a moment longer than necessary. Mark was happy that she found him and Paul attractive. There was hope for meeting someone new. And then he wished he wasn't Kathryn's lawyer.

"Who's going to Paris?" Paul asked as he sipped his beer.

"Me, Hugh, and Rick Peyton. And Kathryn."

Paul frowned. "Why is she going?"

"She asked, and Hugh said yes." So Paul was interested in Kathryn, too. Mark was not surprised. In fact, he was jealous.

They had a history that he could never have with her.

Paul frowned again. "There's a rumor down our way that Hugh sent Logan Avery to Outer Mongolia in your D.C. office because he's warming up for someone new."

"Logan's gone, that's true. Hugh found a better associate for Kathryn's case. Stewart Lipscomb was pre-med undergrad, and he sees a lot more in the Wycliffe documents than Logan did. But Kathryn's a client. You know what that means."

"I know, but does Hugh Mahoney know? He doesn't live by the rules. As you are aware."

Mark winced, thinking of Bill Hays and the demise of Hays, Price all because Hugh's paranoia had made him go back on his word. He wondered how much of the truth he should share with someone in another firm. But he was about to ask Paul some very personal questions about Kathryn and Tom, so he opted for sweetening the pot by being the first to share gossip.

"The truth is Hugh's wife has given him an ultimatum. He has to clean up his act and run for Fred Akers' Senate seat, or Buffy is going to leave him and air his dirty laundry on all the talk shows. Hal Edward's wife is Buffy's close friend, and she thought up the perfect revenge."

Paul sipped his beer thoughtfully for a moment, while Mark signaled the waitress for another. He tried to decide how to launch into the personal questions he was supposed to ask, but Paul created the opening he needed.

"I assume you wanted to talk to me about something in particular."

Mark took his second beer, sipped, and said, "Yes. As I understand it, you knew Tom Andrews very well."

"We grew up together. Neither of us had any siblings. We were the brothers each of us never had. Along with Steve Cooper. He had a sister, but he was like our third brother."

"Steve passed away not long after Tom?"

Paul's face clouded. "In August, after Tom died in June. A surfing accident."

"And you also know Kathryn well?"

Paul gave him a wry smile. "She is the girl I lost to Tom. I met her when we were One L's. But I had the bad judgment to ask her to meet me at O'Leary's Pub and Wine Bar a week later where I was hanging out with Tom. The moment they saw each other, they fell in love. I was there. I saw it happen."

Mark's stomach tightened. He was about to ask a question purely for his own personal information although he knew he shouldn't. "What about you and Kathryn now that Tom's not in the picture?"

Paul shook his head. "She keeps Tom between us. And I made the stupid mistake not long ago of having a one-night hook up with Steve's old girlfriend. I was lonely, I'd had too much to drink, and so I did something stupid. Kathryn doesn't trust me now because of that. I'm trying to win back her trust, but it's an uphill battle."

Mark told himself he didn't feel relieved at the news. "Hugh thinks Kathryn is hiding some deep, dark secret about her marriage."

Paul raised his eyebrows. "Such as?"

"Was either of them having an affair?"

"That's ridiculous!"

"Are you sure?"

"I couldn't be more sure. I told you, those two had eyes only for each other from the day they met in September 1994."

"Kathryn told Hugh the sea was a jealous mistress. Was Tom's interest in surfing a source of conflict between them?"

"Not at all. Kathryn supported Tom in everything he did, one hundred per cent. I'm afraid Hugh's wrong on this one. There were no deep, dark secrets in the Andrews' marriage. They were the most in-love couple I have ever met."

* * *

Friday, August 8, 2014, 610 First Street, Coronado

At seven thirty, Mark opened yet a third beer and went out to sit on his deck, so he could watch the afterglow of the sunset reflected in the glass towers across the bay. He hadn't been surprised to learn that he and Paul were neighbors on First Street and had been for several years. Lawyers who made their kind of money liked the pricey, exclusivity of Coronado Island. And those with the money to buy the San Diego skyline view, anted up for the prestige of the address. And no one in California knew their neighbors. So he was not surprised that neither he nor Paul had been aware of the other's presence.

He contemplated whether he should have gotten the waitress's phone number. She made it clear she was willing to give it to him and to Paul. But Paul hadn't shown the slightest interest. Paul, of course, still had a shot at having Kathryn in his life, whereas he remained only her lawyer. At least he'd have the Paris trip with her. Hugh liked to throw money around when he traveled, so Mark had taken advantage of his mentor's weakness to make sure Kathryn would have one of the premier suites in the small, family-owned, luxurious Hotel de Bertrand in the Fifth Arrondissement. He wanted to lift her out of her drab public defender world at least for a few days. And maybe if she saw what Goldstein, Miller had to offer, she'd consider a job with the firm. He could at least have contact with her as a colleague, even if nothing more.

As he regretted his decision not to ask for a phone number that might have led at least to a date with a woman who found him attractive, he remembered he needed to tell Hugh the outcome of his meeting with Paul. He was still angry with him over Hays, Price, so he was happy to think of Hugh at dinner, at this very moment, working hard to dance to Buffy's tune.

Mark looked down at his phone and smiled. Hugh was old school and hated text messaging. So a text was absolutely the best way to torment him with the news. He wrote, "Per Paul Curtis, they were the most in-love couple he has ever met. Investigation closed." And then he hit 'send.'

* * *

Friday, August 8, 2014, 1845 Ocean Place, Pacific Beach

At midnight, Kathryn walked home from the PB Saloon feeling tired and defeated. She had dared herself to sit at the bar that Shannon had once ruled to prove she had let go of the past. She'd spent three hours there, toying with her wine glass, fending off pickup lines, and dancing a couple of times with an unattractive fortyish man who did not understand the word no. But her antics had done no good because she'd pictured

Shannon behind the bar all night even though Shannon had stopped working at the PB after Steve died.

Now as she plodded along toward home, she heard the inevitable footsteps behind her. She'd grown used to them, so she didn't turn around.

* * *

Saturday Morning, December 10, 2011, 1845 Ocean Place, Pacific Beach

Kathryn did not even attempt to go back to sleep after Tom left. She got up and resumed the after-party cleanup. By eight, the work was done, but Tom had still not returned. She decided to call Steve, who did not answer.

At nine, Tom finally came straggling in, looking tired and worn, his face covered in stubble. Kathryn heard the front door close as she was making coffee in the kitchen. A few seconds later, he appeared in the doorway. She remained facing the coffee pot and didn't turn to greet him.

"I see you're angry with me."

She poured herself a cup of coffee, taking a long time to choose a cup from the cupboard above her head. She could feel him watching her.

"Would you pour some for me?"

She stepped away from the pot and went to the refrigerator to get milk. As she measured it into her cup, she said, "Help yourself."

He crossed the room and poured a mug for himself. He took a long sip as if he needed to be revived. Then he said, "You didn't have to do all the cleanup by yourself."

"I couldn't sleep." She bit off every word.

He leaned against the counter and frowned into his cup as if the answer lay in the dark liquid. "You're angry because I tried to help Shannon."

"I thought we had decided in October that you would stay out of her conflicts with Steve."

"No, that's not what we decided. We did not decide I would stop being her friend or stop being there for her when she needs someone to help her sort things out."

"I see. And what did she need your help sorting out at three in the morning?"

He sighed and sat down at the kitchen table as if the weight of the whole problem was too much to bear. "Steve asked her to marry him last night after the party."

"Why did she need your help, then? The answer to a proposal is a simple yes or no."

"She told him she wasn't sure, and he stormed out. She came over here to find me because she needed someone to talk to. I took her back to Steve's and tried to help her figure out why she wasn't sure about marrying him."

"And did the two of you decide what made her hesitant?"

"No. She was still confused when I left. But I couldn't stay any longer. I guessed you were already upset with me for being gone so long."

"Did Steve come back by the time you left?"

"No."

"I told you before, she's come between you and Steve. You hardly ever surf with him or spend time with him anymore.

You're always with Shannon instead."

He ran his fingers through his disheveled hair. She wondered if sorting out Shannon's feelings for Steve had included sex.

"I told you before, Shannon is only a friend."

"She's the only 'friend' who can take you out of the house at three in the morning. Paul and Carolyn are having their problems, but Carolyn doesn't call you in the wee hours to hold her hand while she cries over her litany of all the things she hates about her husband."

Tom was silent, staring into his cup. His jaw worked in tense circles. He seemed to be considering something else he wanted to tell her; but instead he said, "I'm sorry I've upset you." He got up and walked out of the kitchen. A few minutes later, Kathryn heard the water running in the shower.

THE INVESTIGATION, PART ONE

CHAPTER TWENTY-ONE

Wednesday, September 17, 2014, École Normale Supérieure, Paris

At ten a.m. on a crisp, mid-September morning, when Paris smelled of autumn tinged by the edge of coming winter, Kathryn, Hugh, Mark, and Rick Peyton crossed the beautifully landscaped green quadrangle at the heart of the École Normale Supérieure at 45 Rue d'Ulm, France's oldest institute of higher learning, on their way to see Maurice Vannier. As she walked just behind Mark and Hugh, Kathryn glanced at the tranquil Court aux Ernests, the fountain at the center, where the goldfish, known as the "Ernests," swam peacefully in their famous circle.

In less than a minute, their group had left behind the École's magnificent 1841 stone-facade and had crossed the narrow street to the modern beige and glass box at 46 Rue d'Ulm which housed the Department of Biology. They made their way to the second floor and down the hall to the reception area outside the office of the head of the department. An attractive blonde in a black dress tight enough to rival any of Logan's offered them coffee and explained Dr. Vannier would be a few minutes late.

Fifteen minutes later, he appeared, apologizing for the faculty meeting that had run long. He invited them into his office, sent the receptionist for a fresh pot of coffee, and settled everyone companionably on the two sofas in the corner of his very large office. He was only about five-foot-five, Kathryn noted, balding on top with otherwise closely cropped gray hair around the sides. He had the wiry build of a runner, almost no body fat, and small, round wire-rimmed glasses that made him look scholarly. He was wearing soft tan corduroy pants, a blue plaid shirt, and a light gray sweater. The Goldstein, Miller contingent had adopted the business casual uniform of dark pants, variously colored shirts without ties, and navy blazers.

Hugh began by explaining the litigation. Whenever he mentioned Tom, Dr. Vannier's light blue eyes studied Kathryn's face kindly. When Hugh finished, Dr. Vannier said in his delightfully accented English, "I extend my condolences, Madame Andrews."

"Thank you."

"And you have come because you want to know if Myrabin killed your husband," he went on.

"Yes. Dr. Myers, his cardiologist, believed it did based upon a reference he found to some of Suchet's original work on Myrabin."

"Your husband had an exceptional physician, Madame. I am surprised he was able to find that link to my work. Wycliffe worked very hard to bury any references to it after they bought the rights to the drug."

"According to the little we know," Mark said, "you were the head of the research team."

"I was," Dr. Vannier agreed. "Suchet saw a market for drugs to control hypertension in the late eighties and early nineties, and they paid me a small fortune to take a sabbatical and work on one for them."

"We know they stopped developing the drug that became Myrabin in 1993," Rick Peyton said. "Do you know why?"

Dr. Vannier smiled. "Because of my work and the work of my team. The prototype for Myrabin caused liver failure in our animal studies."

"Is there any doubt about that?" Hugh asked.

"None whatsoever. I'm guessing Wycliffe didn't turn over my work to you, Dr. Peyton?" Dr. Vannier turned to Rick.

"Only very insignificant parts of it. Nothing that told even a tenth of the story."

Dr. Vannier nodded wisely. "I suspected that. I have had everything copied for you." He motioned to a large box sitting on the table between the two sofas. "You must take that with you. It is the story of Myrabin, short and sweet. It looked quite promising in the beginning. But we quickly determined that the rate of liver failure in the test animals was extraordinarily high. We modified and modified, but we could not reach an acceptable level of tolerance. I and my team recommended abandoning it, and Suchet agreed. I returned to my teaching and research."

"Wycliffe told us you were fired for sexually harassing a woman on the development team," Hugh said.

Dr. Vannier looked blank for a moment before he burst into laughter. "No, absolutely not. Suchet lured me away from my own research here with the promise of a lot of money. But when the drug didn't work out, I grew disillusioned by the idea of making a quick fortune with the big pharmaceutical companies. I much prefer the combination of teaching and research I have here. And, by the way, if you doubt my reason for leaving Suchet, the name of my female co-chair on the project was Aimée Girard. She's at Stanford now. And both of us were and are very happily married. That is why I can only imagine the pain you've been through, Madame Andrews. And I want very much to help you."

"But not everyone who takes Myrabin experiences catastrophic liver failure," Rick Peyton said. "Can you explain why it is safe for some people?"

Dr. Vannier shook his head. "It is not a safe drug. Some people have a gene that affects the way the liver metabolizes toxins in their bodies. For those people, the liver processes Myrabin so that it becomes toxic to them. They are the ones who experience catastrophic liver failure and who will die if they do not receive a transplant. I am certain your husband was carrying that gene, Madame Andrews. It is quite common. But even if a patient doesn't have that specific gene, the drug itself has an adverse effect on the liver and always produces a certain degree of damage. It is not a safe drug," he repeated.

"Why did Wycliffe buy the rights to Myrabin if Suchet thought it was lethal?" Hugh asked.

Dr. Vannier frowned. "I contacted Phillip Teague, a colleague at Wycliffe, when I heard his company was interested in Myrabin. I told him about my research and the decision to abandon work on it. He said Wycliffe thought their team could improve it and make it safe."

"Was Teague part of the Myrabin group at Wycliffe?"

"No, he was just a personal friend. But I warned him we at Suchet had concluded it could not be manufactured in a way that made it safe. It was just toxic, no matter how you combined the various ingredients."

"Did you ever write an official letter to anyone in charge at Wycliffe?" Mark asked.

"Aimeé and I did. It's included in the material that I copied for you. And their response essentially said we French scientists didn't know what we were doing." Dr. Vannier chuckled.

"Was that all you did to warn them?" Hugh was glancing through the top folder as he spoke.

"That was the extent of my contact with Wycliffe. But when I learned they were submitting Myrabin for approval, I sent my research to the FDA."

Hugh stopped looking at the folder and focused sharply on Dr. Vannier. "You mean the FDA knew about your conclusions?"

"Absolutely. The letter Aimée and I wrote to them is also in the material I gave you."

"Did they ever respond?" Mark asked.

"No."

"Do you think Wycliffe was able to modify Myrabin to make it safe?" Hugh asked.

"Absolutely not. Phillip Teague sent me their formulation of the drug and insisted they had made it safe to take, but nothing substantive had changed."

"Wycliffe claims there has never been a death from Myrabin," Hugh said.

"Based on my research, that's not possible."

* * *

Wednesday Night, September 17, 2014, Hotel de Bertrand, Fifth Arrondissement, Paris

The black Mercedes limo that Hugh had booked for their stay deposited them at their hotel at nine-thirty. Still dazzled by dinner in the elegant white and silver dining room at the Hotel Le Meurice, featuring sautéed blue lobster with champagne and gold-leaf risotto, Kathryn grew restless in her suite with the blue brocade Louis Quinze love seats in the living room and the marble claw-footed tub in the bath. She snuggled into a furry black sweater and slipped out to walk the narrow streets of the Fifth Arrondissement in the crisp autumn air under Paris' golden streetlights. As she walked along, hands in her pockets, she thought of her trip here with Tom for their fifth wedding anniversary. No Shannon, then. No decision to remain forever childless.

She passed only a few people as she walked, mindful of the concierge's warning of how far it was safe to go. She replayed the meeting with Dr. Vannier and smiled to herself, knowing he was the key to vindicating Tom. And, equally importantly, he was willing to do it. She knew only too well that key witnesses often refused to come forward when they were needed. She'd lost cases she should have won because a witness she desperately needed had refused to testify.

At first it was a low hum that seemed to be coming toward her. She moved to the left, as close to the curb as she could get, sensing that whatever was approaching was fast-moving and would overtake her quickly. And she was right. Within seconds, an enormous BMW motorbike came roaring out of the darkness, straight toward her.

She stopped and made herself as small as possible at the curb while she waited for the behemoth emerging from the darkness ahead to pass by.

But then, in one horrible moment, she saw the bike's headlamp blazing toward her like a light saber. She didn't have time to think other than to realize she was its target. The heavy machine was closing the distance between them in tenths of a second.

She looked around for an escape. As counterintuitive as it seemed to move toward the monster speeding in her direction, she hurried forward until she reached the doorway of L'Artisan Parfumeur. If the bike were determined to hit her, it would have to go through the two glass windows loaded with perfume bottles that jutted out to form a little alcove that sheltered the shop's entrance door.

Her mouth dry with terror, her heart hammering, she flattened herself against the door and waited. The bike continued to scream toward her, but at the last second, the rider swerved when he saw the glass windows he was about to hit. He roared off into the night.

She huddled in the safety of the perfume shop's alcove for what seemed an eternity. Finally, praying the bike would not return, she ventured into the street cautiously. And there he was, across the street, snapping photos, the man in the floppy hat from the beach. So whoever had sent the motorbike would know the mission had failed. Without looking back, she hurried to the hotel. She went to the rooftop bar and ordered a Bordeaux. She sat down at one of the little tables with the view of the Eiffel Tower and the rooftops of Paris and tried to convince herself that the bike's rider had just been drunk. *Sure, just like the Suburban driver on the bridge,* her inner voice mocked her.

* * *

Wednesday Night, September 17, 2014, Hotel de Bertrand, Fifth Arrondissement, Paris

A little after ten, Mark made his way to the rooftop bar for a drink and a last look at Paris. Their plane would take off at six the next morning.

To his surprise, he found Kathryn alone at one of the small tables, wrapped in a fluffy black sweater to ward off the chilly autumn night, and nursing a red wine. She was staring out at the yellow streetlights as they warmed the creamy off-white Lutetian limestone buildings into glowing, golden jewels. She was lost in thought, but Mark noticed her hands were shaking.

"May I join you?"

He had startled her, but she recovered quickly. "Please do."

He sat down in the other chair at the small table with his own glass of wine and studied her tired, drawn face. Her hands were still shaking. "Are you cold?"

"No." She frowned as if she didn't like being asked.

"Then why are your hands shaking?"

"They're–" She looked down and realized denial would be useless. "I was feeling restless after dinner, so I took a walk. A motorbike went by too fast and too close, and it frightened me."

He looked concerned. "Are you all right?"

"Fine. Just a little shaken up." This was the moment to tell him about being followed on the bridge and about the man in the floppy hat. But she didn't want to admit there was any connection. After all, she did not know for sure that the incident on the bridge had not been road rage, unconnected to tonight.

"Is this your first time in Paris?"

"No. Tom and I spent our fifth wedding anniversary here. We stayed in a cheap little hotel in the Seventh Arrondissement and took the metro everywhere. No limos. No five-star restaurants. We loved it."

Mark smiled. "Hugh likes to do everything first class. He grew up poor and wants to enjoy his money."

Her lips quivered with the tiniest of return smiles. "Makes sense. And I must say, thank you for the lovely suite you booked for me. I've never slept in a Louis Quinze bed under a brocade canopy."

"I'm glad you liked it." He wanted to say more. He wanted to say, *I was hoping you'd see what life is like on this side of the fence and join us. I was hoping I'd get to see you every day and talk to you at work. I know it can't be more, but that would make me happy.* But he thought of Paul Curtis and remembered that he was her lawyer and so said nothing.

She sipped her wine slowly and stared down at the miniature world of tiny cars and tiny people awash in the yellow glow of the street lights. He noticed her hands were steadier now. She said, "I'm glad you and Hugh let me come. Somehow it helped to hear Dr. Vannier explain it all today."

Mark nodded. "I understand. He'll make a terrific witness for us."

"Hugh is taking him on as an expert to testify, isn't he?"

"Absolutely. It would be malpractice not to. Why do you ask?"

"I overheard Hugh and Rick having a few words before we went in to dinner at Le Meurice. It sounded as if Rick didn't want Dr. Vannier because his fee would reduce Rick's."

"I don't know what you overheard, but I promise you Hugh is going to rely on Dr. Vannier's testimony. Dr. Vannier is the heart of our case. We have nothing without him. That was obvious from the interview today."

"If Hugh hasn't mentioned it, he and Rick go way back. Sometimes they disagree, but it means nothing. Hugh is always very generous with Rick because they are old friends." *Being Hugh's friend is essential to getting paid,* Mark thought, remembering the fate of Bill Hays and his firm.

They were quiet again, like the city below them. Mark thought about how comfortable it was to sit with her in the stillness. Finally he observed, "I think we are going to be looking at more than compensatory damages for the loss of your husband."

"You mean punitive damages?"

"We're certainly going to ask the jury for them. Dr. Vannier was very clear. He warned them Myrabin wasn't safe, and they ignored his warning."

She looked sad and tired. After a bit she said, "I wonder where the FDA fits into all this. Why did they ignore Dr. Vannier's warning?"

"We're going to Washington in a week or two to talk to them."

"I want to come."

He smiled. "You realize that's unorthodox."

"I don't care. I want to hear everything. I want to understand how this happened." There were tears in her eyes. She looked away toward the city as soon as she realized he had seen them.

"Wrongful death suits are hard on the survivors." He wanted to put his hand on her arm to comfort her but knew he shouldn't.

"Paul warned me." She gave him a little smile as she wiped her eyes. "I just didn't think it would be this hard."

"It keeps you stuck in the past."

"I'm beginning to realize that. But even without the wrongful death case for Tom, I am stuck in the past. I'm living in the house where he and I lived together. I am doing the job he and I did together. My friends are the friends we had together. If I'm ever going to move on, I'm going to have to make changes. But I'm afraid to make them."

"Why?"

"Because if I change my life, I'll also have to admit Tom is really gone. If I keep everything the way it was when he was alive, I can keep change from coming. And if I keep change from coming, I don't have to admit that my life as I knew it with Tom is gone forever."

"Except it is."

"Yes." Her eyes, now wet with tears once more, met his. "Except it is."

"What about coming to work for us when all of this is over?"

"Hugh mentioned it. Paul did, too. I have to admit I'm tired of the low-paying slog Tom and I opted for. The job made more sense when he was here. He thought what we were doing as public defenders was important. But I don't any more. No one listens to us because the clients are guilty. Period. I'm just not sure what I'd do at Goldstein, Miller."

"White collar crime. Or civil litigation. You've tried more cases than I have. You should think about us. Or Warwick, Thompson. Alan would probably love to have you as much as Hugh would." *And Alan wouldn't try to start an affair with you,* Mark thought. He doubted Hugh's new-found commitment to Buffy would last long, especially if Kathryn was no longer a client.

"I'll think about it. I don't know what I want to do if I leave the public defender's office. But for right now I have to stay focused on suing Wycliffe. I have to make them face up to what they did to Tom. And to us."

"Of course." Mark nodded, and then took a personal risk he hadn't intended to take. "Even if you lost your husband, at least you had something with him most of us never find."

"But you and your fiancée–"

"All over." He smiled ruefully. "She lost patience with my lack of interest in a large, expensive wedding, and followed my ex-wife's footsteps out of my life."

"You sound relieved."

"I am. It wasn't right. And she did me the favor of leaving and making a clean break."

"So you miss her?"

"Not at all. I sometimes wish I did. I wish I'd loved her the way you loved Tom. Then I could miss her. But I didn't, and I don't. I have my work and more money than I'll ever spend. But it's not enough. I wish I had a woman in my life who I could love the way you loved Tom." The wine was talking. He was taking fearful risks. He made himself stop.

"Love Tom," she corrected him. "The way I still love Tom."

Paul Curtis was right. Tom stood between her and anyone new.

* * *

Thursday, September 18, 2014, Crown Manor, Coronado, California

The limo deposited Hugh at Crown Manor at ten p.m. He had insisted on seeing Kathryn home after the flight from Paris. She haunted him. Even just two days of traveling with her had left him feeling desperate to see her again.

But Hugh abided by the rules. He wasn't some cheap divorce hack who rolled every attractive would-be ex-wife who came his way. Still, even if he couldn't see her socially, he could dream. He'd had that one precious day of being with her for breakfast, of watching her sleep on the long transatlantic flights, of seeing her delight and relief when Maurice Vannier had said her hunch about the cause of her husband's death was correct. He'd walked through charming, crooked Paris streets with her the afternoon after their interview with Dr. Vannier, and he'd bought her a glass of wine in a small French bistro. Her laugh, her smile were forever etched on his old man's heart, which still longed for young love.

CHAPTER TWENTY-TWO

Friday night, September 19, 2014, Il Fornaio, Coronado, California

Paul Curtis had had first-date nerves all afternoon. He'd downed a scotch to take the edge off before Kathryn arrived in her Mini at seven-thirty. He'd been relieved that she had finally agreed to see him. It had been months since she'd run out of his house after he'd been forced to confess to that night with Shannon, and he'd missed her terribly. He'd been haunted by the fear he would not see her again.

They'd decided to walk from his house to Il Fornaio at the Ferry Landing. Now, at eight o'clock, they had a corner table overlooking the lights of the city and the winding arc of the bridge. She was breathtaking in the soft light. Her black dress highlighted her hazel eyes. Her light golden brown hair fell in luxurious waves around her shoulders. But she was thinner than she'd been in May.

They had ordered a bottle of Chianti and were enjoying the first glass as they waited for their salads.

"You look very beautiful tonight."

"Thank you."

"How was Paris?" He felt a twinge of jealousy knowing she'd been traveling with Mark Kelly.

"Beautiful. Exciting. Sad."

"Sad?"

"It made me miss being there with Tom. This trip was so different. Flying first class, limos, five-star hotels, only the best restaurants."

Their salads arrived, and Paul took a bite before he observed, "Hugh spares no expense."

"As Mark said, Hugh grew up poor and wants to enjoy what he's earned."

"Can't blame him for that. I feel the same way. I've always been grateful for the salary Alan Warrick pays me—and very willing to enjoy it. Have you given any more thought to leaving the public defender's office?"

"Some. I'm pretty burned out at this point."

"Do you want me to talk to Alan?"

"Not yet. I'm not sure what I want to do when I leave."

"If what you suspect about Wycliffe is true, you'll probably wind up with so much money you won't have to practice law any more."

"But it's about Tom, not the money."

"I know. I didn't mean it that way. But you deserve some financial breathing room, Kathryn. You said it's hard without Tom's income."

"That's true."

The empty salad plates made way for the main course, pasta filled with free-range chicken, sun-dried tomatoes, ricotta, pecorino, smoked mozzarella and organic spinach, finished with béchamel, marinara and mushrooms. For a few minutes, Paul watched her enjoy the food.

"How is it?"

"Fantastic."

"But not as good as Paris."

"I wouldn't say that." He decided to interpret her statement as a metaphor that meant being with him was at least equal to traveling with Mark. The thought made him happy.

"Did you find out anything that helps your case? Anything that you can tell me, I mean."

"I don't think it's meant to be a secret. The names of our experts will have to be turned over in discovery." She told him about meeting Dr. Vannier and his willingness to be an expert witness.

"Wow. That's huge. You've found the smoking gun."

She smiled at him in the candlelight. "We did. No wonder Wycliffe tried to keep Dr. Vannier's name a secret."

The waiter whisked away their empty dinner plates and waved dessert menus at them.

But Paul put up his hands. "We don't need them. Coffee and tiramisu and two forks." He didn't ask her if she wanted dessert because she might say no, and he wasn't ready for the evening to end.

But she seemed happy with his decision to prolong their meal. They shared the tiramisu in comfortable silence until she put down her fork and smiled. "You have to finish. That was delicious."

The waiter had just poured the last of the bottle of wine into their glasses. Paul noticed she chose the wine over her coffee, her eyes fixed on the twinkling lights of the city beyond. She had that dreamy expression that he'd seen so often when she'd looked at Tom, and he wished she was wearing it now because she was with him. He had decided not to tell her about Hugh's suspicion she was hiding something. After all, she wasn't. He felt that familiar wave of jealousy that swept over him whenever he thought of how happy Tom had been with her. Paul had loved Tom and could never have wished for his marriage to fail, yet he'd wanted Kathryn so desperately for himself.

"I've missed you."

She sipped her wine and kept looking at the bay and said nothing.

Her silence made him uneasy. Things weren't yet right between them. He decided to face whatever it was head on. "You're still angry about the night you saw Shannon's car in the drive?"

"I don't want to talk about Shannon." Her eyes came back to his, no longer dreamy but hard and determined.

"But I told you. I didn't mean to have Shannon stay over. There's nothing between the two of us except friendship." He reached out and took her hand, but she pulled it away. He was hurt.

"Did you know Steve asked Shannon to marry him the night of our last Christmas party?"

"No. She told me Steve didn't want to get married."

"She lied. She told him she wasn't sure, and when Steve left the house, she came running to Tom at three in the morning. The last year of Tom's life, she fought with Steve almost constantly, and she was always crying on Tom's shoulder."

"I admit she's not the most grown up person in the world. And Tom had a soft heart. But Tom never had eyes for anyone but you from that first day. Believe me, I know."

Her eyes met his, and he could tell she was startled by the depths of his emotion. He took her hand again, and this time she didn't pull it away.

"So you don't think Tom and Shannon—?"

"Oh, God, have you been tormenting yourself with that? No and no and no. Don't ever think about it again. Ever. You were Tom's only love." And mine, he added to himself.

CHAPTER TWENTY-THREE

Saturday, September 20, 2014, 1845 Ocean Place, Pacific Beach

It felt strange to be coming home at noon unshowered, in last night's clothes and makeup. Kathryn parked in her drive and contemplated her little house. Everything was there just as Tom had left it on that desperate day she'd driven him to the hospital. If he came down the walk this minute, he'd see nothing had changed.

But, of course, it had. She'd spent the night at Paul's, and now she was dragging herself home in the middle of the day like some college kid after a hookup. At least Paul wasn't a stranger.

She went inside, peeled off her clothes, and stepped into a steamy shower. She felt the hot water wash away the layer of sweat that still clung to her. She tipped her head back and washed her hair, too. She'd let Paul persuade her to walk back to his house for a nightcap. But she'd already had too much to drink with supper, and she was nearly asleep minutes after she finished her first glass as they sat side by side on Paul's deck, watching the lights of the city in the cool dark.

He'd tucked her into bed in his guest room, and she'd awakened to the smell of bacon and eggs. They had lingered over breakfast, and Paul had asked her to come back tonight for dinner, and she had agreed.

She felt lighter and happier than she had felt for a long time because Paul had cleared away her doubts about Shannon and Tom. She spent some time thinking about what to wear to Paul's. Suddenly it seemed important. Suddenly it seemed possible that her future lay in his direction.

Still full of anticipation for the evening ahead, she went into the bedroom and contemplated Tom's big desk. She had resisted going through it and discarding his things. But the news that Tom hadn't been in love with Shannon and that Paul cared for her made her feel as if her life was moving forward again. She summoned the courage to sit down and open the drawers. It was mostly full of odds and ends. But in the bottom drawer she found a small blue box decorated with sea shells. When she opened it, she found an inscription on the lid, "To my darling Tom. I made this for you with shells we found together. With all my love. Shannon."

Her hands began to shake as she picked up the cards and letters inside. A quick glance through them revealed they were mostly birthday and Christmas cards Shannon had sent Tom. But some were letters. The first one was dated January 1, 2012.

My darling Tom,

It's a new year, and I can no longer go on pretending I do not love you. I've realized that's the reason I can't say yes to Steve. I'm writing instead of emailing to make sure no one in your office reads this.

All my love,
Shannon

Two weeks later Shannon wrote again.

My darling Tom,

When you said we should stop seeing each other, I told you it wouldn't work. I know you don't want to hurt Kathryn and Steve, but we are hurting them more by not telling them the truth. We belong together. You know that.

All my love,
Shannon

Kathryn thought back to January 2012. Tom had been very stressed, and he'd kept himself locked away in his office at work or in his office at home. He hadn't had much to say, and there had been no sex, but there had been no sign of Shannon, either. When she had brought up the subject of Shannon and Steve, he'd told her angrily he didn't want to discuss it. He'd seemed like a kettle about to boil over all month long, but she'd attributed that to his feverish preparations for the Pepe Jackson capital murder trial that had been starting on February 6. Pepe was on trial for his life for killing a police officer, but Tom had believed Pepe when he said he had acted in self-defense. The officer who pulled him over for a burned-out tail light had ordered Pepe out of the car, put his gun to Pepe's head, and threatened to kill him for being poor and black. Certain he was about to die, Pepe went for the gun and fired at the officer. The police community would be furious if Pepe wasn't convicted, but forensic evidence told Tom his client was innocent. Then, just before the trial began, he'd been diagnosed with hypertension. Kathryn had thought it was the stress of defending an innocent client in a high-profile murder trial where the client likely would be convicted regardless of the evidence because he was poor and black.

The next letter had been written on February 23.

My darling Tom,

I can't tell you what it meant to spend last Monday with you. A whole day together! I wish you had court holidays more often. But more than that, I wish you would just decide we should tell Kathryn and Steve the truth.

All my love,
Shannon

That Monday would have been President's Day since it was the third Monday in February. So Tom had lied to her. He'd told her he was going to the office to work on his cross-examinations in the Jackson case. But in truth, he'd spent the day with Shannon.

On March 30, 2012, Shannon wrote again.

My darling Tom,

I know Paul told you to wait six months and think things over before telling Kathryn and Steve. But Paul was wrong. We shouldn't have to wait. We belong together now.

All my love,
Shannon

A slow tide of anger seeped in through her fingers as they held the letter. It traveled up her arms and spread through her entire body. Paul had lied to her last night. The most important piece of comfort she'd received since Tom's death had turned out to be a monstrous falsehood.

The last letter was written on April 30, exactly three weeks before Tom had gotten sick.

My darling Tom,

Please don't listen to Paul anymore. He wants you to think fifteen years of marriage can make up for growing apart. But you know it can't. Kathryn wants children. You don't. And I don't. Kathryn has never been able to share the peace of the ocean and surfing with you. But I can. And I do. Don't listen to Paul. He's unhappy with Carolyn and afraid to leave her because of Jodie. He wants you to be unhappy, too. We can't wait any longer to tell Steve and Kathryn.

All my love,
Shannon

Kathryn gathered up the letters and put them in her purse. It was five-thirty, and she wasn't supposed to be at Paul's until seven, but she didn't want to wait. Or take time to change clothes. It no longer mattered that she was wearing jeans and a sweater and didn't have on any makeup. The only thing that mattered was confronting Paul.

* * *

Saturday, September 20, 2014, 817 First Street, Coronado, California

"Oh, my God, he kept those!" Paul said when she threw the letters at him.

She had come raging through his front door like a spitfire bent on vengeance.

"You lied to me!"

He looked up from re-reading the letters. "Not entirely. You were Tom's only love."

"Not according to those letters."

"Look, Shannon wrote these. She was putting her spin on the situation, trying to get what she wanted."

"And what she wanted was my husband! Why did you lie to me?"

"Let's go into the kitchen and make dinner like we planned, and I'll try to explain."

"I don't want to eat! I can't eat! I'm too upset. I trusted you, Paul. Why did you lie to me?"

"Well, at least let me pour you a glass of wine, and we'll sit on the deck and talk."

"Okay."

She swept ahead of him through the house and planted herself in one of the chairs overlooking the bay. For a moment she forgot about being angry when he came through the door with two glasses of wine. The jeans and gray hoodie made her remember the day they'd met in contracts class. She had definitely been interested, until she'd met Tom.

"Here." He handed her the glass and sat down in the chair beside hers. "I'll start by explaining why I lied."

"Okay."

"Tom came to me after he got that March letter. He told me about Steve's marriage proposal, about the way Shannon had reacted, and about all the time he'd spent with her since. Steve had stopped surfing with them.

"He said he'd started out trying to help Shannon see that Steve was the best choice for her. He knew how much Steve loved her, and he wanted them to get together. He thought if Shannon cried on his shoulder, he'd have a chance to put in a good word for Steve."

"But he didn't do that, did he?"

"Oh, he did. Quite a lot of words, in fact. But the more good things he said about Steve, the more Shannon's attitude against him hardened. Tom realized if Steve had any chance at all with Shannon, Tom was going to have to keep his mouth shut about him."

"Then what happened?"

"Shannon went after Tom as hard as she could, pressing him to leave you."

"Was he going to leave me?"

"No."

"How do I know you're telling the truth?"

"Because he didn't leave you."

"But he thought about it, didn't he?"

Paul's silence fueled her rage.

"Tell me the truth. He thought about it, didn't he?"

"He felt guilty because he knew you were disappointed that he no longer wanted children. He wondered if you would be happier starting over with someone who wanted a family."

"So he did think of leaving me for Shannon!"

"He thought about a lot of things that winter, Kathryn. He was under enormous pressure from the Pepe Jackson case. You know that. He wasn't thinking clearly. His blood pressure was high, and he didn't feel well. That's why, when he came to me, I told him not to do anything rash. I figured when the trial was over, he'd feel better and be able to see things clearly again."

"The Pepe Jackson trial ended in early March. And Shannon was still writing letters in late March and April."

"Look, I can't tell you everything that was in Tom's head that winter and spring. He was stressed and tired and hurt and confused. Deep down, I knew he didn't love Shannon. Not the way he loved you."

"Did Steve know?"

"Not that Shannon had her sights set on Tom. He knew she was hesitant about marriage. Shannon's a bartender and a flirt, and some man somewhere is always after her."

"Why did she keep on living with Steve if she wanted Tom?"

"She moved out of Steve's place in late January. Didn't you know?"

Kathryn felt as if she'd been hit by a rock. "No. I knew Steve had stopped surfing with them in the mornings, but I didn't know Shannon had gotten a place of her own. That gave her more chances to see Tom alone, didn't it?"

"Look, Kathryn, don't torment yourself. It's in the past. Tom didn't leave you even if he spent some time with Shannon that winter."

"He used to go over there at night during the Jackson trial, didn't he? He'd tell me he was preparing for trial, but he was with Shannon, wasn't he?"

"I don't know all the details. Tom has always known how much I care about you, and he was ashamed of what he was doing. He wouldn't have ended it with you, Kathryn. I know that. Read Shannon's last letter. She was desperate at that point because she had begun to realize he wasn't in love with her."

"Who else knew about Shannon and Tom?"

"Just me."

Kathryn put down her empty wine glass on the small table between them and stood up. All her good feelings from the night before had vanished. "I'm not staying for dinner."

He put his glass down and stood, too, as he tried to put his arms around her.

"Don't!"

"Please stay."

"I can't." She had tears in her eyes. "Everything I believed in has been blown to bits. And the worst part is, I trusted you; but you knew the truth and never told me."

"But what good would it have done?" He demanded, his voice beginning to rise to match hers. "What if I had broken

Tom's confidence and come to you with these letters? Would it have changed anything?"

She wiped her eyes and shook her head. "No, I guess not. I always suspected the two of them, but it was better when I couldn't prove anything."

"And there was nothing to prove, Kathryn! He didn't leave you. I keep telling you, he didn't love Shannon. He wasn't going to leave you."

She shook her head again. "I'll never know the truth."

"Don't make yourself unhappy. The truth is he stayed with you."

"But what if he hadn't gotten sick? What if he was planning to leave when he got sick?"

"He wasn't planning to leave."

"You don't know that for sure. I've got to go. I need to be alone. I need to think."

"I understand. But think about forgiving me because I love you. And I want your future and my future to be together."

"I don't see how I could ever trust you, Paul. Maybe you had a reason to keep Shannon and Tom from me when he was alive. You were his friend. He confided in you. But after he died? Why didn't you tell me then?"

"You mean tell my best friend's grieving widow that her husband had a few months out of their fifteen-year marriage when he wasn't sure what he wanted? What good would that have done? Losing Tom was enough of a blow. Why make it worse with something that never happened?"

She shivered in the deepening dusk. She remained stubborn. "I think you should have told me."

"Look, Kathryn, all this is in the past. As much as it hurts, you need to let go and move on. Tom isn't here any more. You are. And I am."

"I'm going."

"Wait!" He reached out and touched her arm. "There's one more thing. It's just practical lawyer advice."

"I'm listening."

"Hugh Mahoney has radar for emotional conflict. He told Mark Kelly he thought you were hiding something from them about your marriage when they prepped you for your deposition. Mark took me out for a beer to pump me for information."

A look of horror came over Kathryn's face. "So they know, too?"

"No, of course not. There was no reason to tell them. I told Mark that Hugh was imagining things. Wycliffe has no way of finding out that there was anything between Tom and Shannon. You can say under oath your marriage was fine. And it was."

"Wycliffe could find out if they could find Shannon."

"But they don't even know who she is. And if they did turn up her name, it would be as Steve's girlfriend. Trust me, Kathryn, it was never what you imagined it to be between Tom and Shannon. Never."

CHAPTER TWENTY-FOUR

Sunday, September 21, 2014, 1845 Ocean Place, Pacific Beach

Kathryn drifted in and out of sleep although the sun was streaming in through her bedroom window. Her mouth was dry, and her head was pounding. She didn't want to admit even to herself she had a hangover. She reached over and patted Tom's side of the bed and smiled when it was empty. He was already up and had gone out with his board.

And then the sickening memories flooded in. Tom was dead. And if he hadn't been, he'd have been in the waves with Shannon, who could no longer pretend she did not love him.

And the man she'd brought home last night to punish Tom for Shannon and who should have been on Tom's side of the bed was already gone.

* * *

Saturday, September 20, 2014, Half Moon Bar in Pacific Beach, 11 p.m.

She had slammed Paul's front door behind her and blazed back across the bridge, nearing ninety miles an hour. She hurried into the house and poured herself a glass of her usual cheap wine. The clock in the kitchen said seven-thirty. Her mind was whirling. Thoughts tumbled together so rapidly she had no time to focus on one before another took its place. She paced the living room, absorbed by grief and fury, for more than an hour. The two men she loved most in the world had betrayed her. She longed for the days when she hadn't known the truth about Shannon and Tom, when she'd been able to allow herself to accept Tom's explanations. As much as she didn't want to admit Paul might have been right about his decision to lie to her, she could see how comfortable life had been before the tsunami of truth had washed her into the depths of grief once more.

The walls of the cottage began to close in on her despair as she paced and thought of all the lonely nights she'd spent waiting up for Tom in February, March, and April of that last year. He'd insisted he had to work, and she'd watched the hands of the clock pass midnight and then one a.m. and then one-thirty, night after night, before she'd heard his key in the front door. He'd slept in the guest room on a lot of those nights, using as an excuse his reluctance to risk waking her.

Finally, when she couldn't stand the thought of Shannon and Tom anymore, she showered, changed, put on her makeup, and walked up to the Half Moon Bar on Garnet Avenue. She plunked herself on a stool, and ordered an extra large glass of red wine. Then she turned to observe the partiers thronging the main floor.

A wave of disappointment washed over her. The men were all too young for what she had in mind. Somewhere in her grief-wracked brain she had formed the intention of finding a hookup. She'd been faithful to Tom for seventeen years, but now all she wanted was to pay him back for his infidelity. Unfortunately, the dance floor was full of college kids.

And then her luck changed. She felt a pair of eyes on her and turned to see a handsome, dark-haired man lounging on a stool farther down the bar. He looked to be close to her own age; and, unlike the board-shorted males throughout the bar, he was wearing a professional, casual navy sport coat and tan slacks. He gave her a mischievous grin and pointed to the empty stool next to her with a questioning look. She smiled and nodded, and a few seconds later he came to sit beside her with a drink that she assumed was scotch.

"Dan Ayers. Sorry if I was staring, but you look so lovely in that dress."

"Kathryn Andrews," she smiled. Even if the pick-up line was cheesy, she wanted herself and her deep green wool dress to be admired.

"Are you from San Diego?" he asked.

She nodded, throwing all caution to the wind even though she realized the alcohol was starting to overtake her judgment. "I live a few blocks away. What about you?"

"I'm from Seattle. I'm a computer software engineer and an attorney. My firm represents a software development company here in town. I came down to do some work for them and wound up staying over tonight because my flight got cancelled."

"Bet the wife or the girlfriend was disappointed."

He grinned broadly. "I have neither. What about you? A teacher, I bet. No, a college professor. You have that beautiful, but intellectual, air. And where's your significant other?"

"I'm a lawyer, too. A public defender for the last seventeen years. And my husband passed away two years ago last month."

His face softened. "Sorry. Hey, I have an idea. You look as if you could use some fun. Let's dance and eat and hang out, and never once mention the law."

"Deal!" She was overjoyed.

The music had softened and lost its frantic beat. Dan led her onto the dance floor where colored lights raked softly over the dancers. Kathryn let him pull her close and laid her head on his shoulder as they moved around and around under the shifting rainbows.

When they stopped the music at midnight, Dan insisted on buying one last round of drinks and appetizers. Under the spell of the wine she had already drunk and the romantic music, Kathryn agreed. They chose a small table in the back of the bar where they laughed and drank red wine and ate greasy cheese quesadillas with red salsa.

When they finished, it was one a.m.

"I'm not letting you walk home alone," Dan said. "My rental car is parked a block away. I'll drive you."

Kathryn smiled and nodded, happy to be with him a little longer; and when he stopped in front of the cottage, she invited him in.

"Are you sure?"

"Absolutely. This is my first even kind-of date since—well, you know. Come celebrate with me." She heard the alcohol talking, and she didn't care.

He followed her inside but put his arms around her in the hall before she could turn on the light. He pulled her close and gave her a long, long kiss. Every part of her wanted only one thing.

She led him down the hall to her bedroom, all without turning on the lights. She started to unzip her dress, but he reached out and stopped her.

"Wait. One thing before we do this."

She looked up at him in the dark, expectantly.

"I really like you. I come to town pretty regularly for this client. They are important to the firm. I don't want to do this unless I can see you again."

"I'd love to see you again."

* * *

Odd how you can sleep with only one man for fifteen years and then one night find yourself with a stranger, Kathryn thought when it was all over. Dan was a thoughtful, gentle lover. Much better than she had expected from a random meeting in a bar, but she burst into tears the minute they finished.

"Hey, hey, what's wrong?" He pulled her close as he turned on the light by the bed. "Did I hurt you?"

"No, oh, no. I am so sorry, I never expected this."

"It's okay. It's your first time after—"

"Yes, but don't say it. It's not your fault. I'm just a little upset and confused right now. But it has nothing to do with you."

"Why don't you tell me about it?"

She settled back into his arms and narrated the whole story of Tom, Paul, and Steve and Shannon. He listened thoughtfully, tightening his arms around her gently when she gulped back tears.

"Do you want to know what I think?"

She looked up into his kind, dark eyes through her tears. "Yes."

"I think your friend Paul is right. Your husband may have been temporarily confused, but he never intended to leave you. You are an amazing woman. He would never have wanted to give you up."

His words were balm poured into her wounds of grief, loss, and betrayal.

"Thank you."

"I mean it. And I'm going to count the days until I'm back in San Diego. Now, let's get some sleep."

* * *

But he was gone when she woke without any sign he'd been there except for the crease in the pillowcase on the other side of her bed. And he left nothing, not even a business card, to tell her how to contact him. At first she thought he had been only a figment of her alcohol-fueled imagination. But then she found the note he'd left stuck in the frame of the mirror on the coat rack in the hall. "Can't wait to see you again. Dan."

THE INVESTIGATION, PART TWO

CHAPTER TWENTY-FIVE

Tuesday, October 21, 2014, First Class Cabin, San Diego to Dulles International Airport

Hugh had chivalrously offered Kathryn the aisle seat in their row in the first class cabin. Mark and Rick Peyton were in the row behind them. They were on their way to interview the Food and Drug Administration team that had approved Myrabin. The big United jet sped eastward as they settled themselves for the flight. Hugh was drinking scotch and checking messages on his iPad. Kathryn was sipping red wine and trying not to think that a month had gone by, and she'd heard nothing from Dan Ayers. She knew she'd only intended a hookup, but it had seemed like so much more.

"Tomorrow should be very interesting," Hugh said as he closed his iPad. "I can't wait to hear what they have to say about Dr. Vannier's research."

"Do you think they will actually address his conclusions?"

"They'll have to. When Wycliffe sought approval for Myrabin, the company had to first submit what's called an 'IND' or 'Investigational New Drug' application to the FDA's

Center for Drug Evaluation and Research. The IND had to be based on laboratory work from Wycliffe that demonstrated the proposed drug showed promise and was safe to put into clinical trials. No matter what Wycliffe sent as its own laboratory data, Vannier's work should have caused the FDA to prevent Wycliffe from initiating clinical trials."

"But it didn't."

"Right, and I can't wait to hear them explain why they didn't stop the clinical trials as soon as they saw Dr. Vannier's research."

Kathryn listened to the jet engines hum and tried not to think about Dan Ayers' silence.

"I'm glad you wanted to come on this trip," Hugh said. "I thought you might say no because it would stir up too many painful memories."

"It's deposition preparation that stirs up the memories."

"I know, and I'm sorry. I was able to postpone it, so we could meet with the FDA, but the December first date is now set in stone because we've postponed twice already. Mark and Patty will take good care of you."

* * *

Wednesday, October 22, 2014, The FDA's Center For Drug Evaluation, Silver Spring, Maryland

Next morning, Kathryn followed Hugh, Mark, and Rick Peyton into the modern, angular glass and brick tower of Building 51 in Silver Spring, Maryland, the headquarters of the FDA's Center for Drug Evaluation and Research. Even on an October rainy day, the glass walls made the lobby light and bright. While Mark and Hugh dealt with the security arrangements for entry, Kathryn looked up at the offices visible through the large windows above her that faced the lobby. In addition to offices, she could see conference rooms on every floor with long, polished shiny wooden tables that looked sterile enough for surgery. People in this ultramodern glass and brick box had set in motion the chain of events that had cost her Tom. Unexpectedly, she felt tears in her eyes and reached up to wipe them away, hoping no one saw.

The members of the team who had approved Myrabin's New Drug Application in 2006 were already waiting for them in the conference room on the third floor that overlooked the lobby below. Through discovery, Kathryn already knew who they were. Dr. Fred Butler, round and bald, an M.D. in his early fifties, wearing a light blue shirt and gray cardigan sweater, sat at the head of the table. Mary Lancaster, an elegant brunette in her forties with a Ph.D. in pharmacology, wearing a simple wool skirt and black sweater, sat in the chair to his left. Frank Reynolds and Harrison O'Connor, both Ph.D. organic chemists in their late forties wearing plaid shirts and v-neck pullovers, sat to Dr. Butler's right. Their casual dress and the way they all leaned back comfortably in their chairs told Kathryn they were confident there were no holes in their story. Myabin was safe, and the FDA had been right to approve it.

In contrast to government-confident-casual, Hugh and Mark had adopted an aggressive-conservative look. They had dressed one notch down from power suits in well-tailored navy blazers and gray or black pants. Rick Peyton's lanky frame, on the other hand, in his ill-fitting gray suit did not convey the same air of power and assurance.

Ever concerned about looking the part of lawyer and client, Kathryn had splurged on a new dark gray dress and black blazer from Anne Taylor. She thought it gave her the Patty E. Fox Harvard Brahmin look.

"Thank you for meeting with us this morning," Hugh began after the initial round of handshakes and introductions.

"We're glad to answer any questions you have," Dr. Butler smiled. "As a preliminary matter, I should make sure that you received everything you requested from us."

Hugh glanced over at Rick, who had told Logan how to write the Freedom of Information Act Request. "Yes, thank you."

"Good." Dr. Butler glanced around the table at his staff, who smiled back. Their demeanor said this meeting is going to be easy.

"Why don't you start by walking us through the chronology of the approval process for Myrabin," Hugh began.

Dr. Butler's eyes went to Dr. Lancaster, who opened a folder in front of her. "Let's see. Wycliffe Pharmaceutical filed their IND in November 1997. We gave them approval for clinical trials a month later. Phase I trials began in January 1998 with fifty volunteers. The trials lasted one year. Phase II trials with two hundred and fifty patients began in January 2000. Phase II lasted two years. Phase III trials with two thousand patients began in January 2002 and went on for three years. Following Phase III, Wycliffe filed its New Drug Application on January 15, 2006. We reviewed it, and based on the strength of the data, we gave it expedited status. We approved the NDA for Myrabin six months later. The drug officially went on sale in January 2007."

"And what were the adverse effects reported during the trials?" Hugh asked.

Dr. Lancaster looked down at her notes. "Not much. Skin rashes, primarily. Some patients developed a cough."

"Were there any deaths?" Rick Peyton spoke up.

"Of course not. You know that we would have halted clinical trials if there had been."

"Dr. Vannier told us that Myrabin would necessarily have caused deaths," Hugh insisted.

"Well, I'm sure he said that, but he's wrong. His conclusion that the drug was not safe cost Suchet billions of dollars. Myrabin is one of the top-performing hypertension drugs in the world." Dr. Butler looked directly at Kathryn as he continued, "We're sorry for the loss of your husband, Mrs. Andrews, but we feel confident that Myrabin wasn't the cause of his death. Did his doctors consider outside factors like alcohol or hepatitis or recreational drug abuse?"

Kathryn wanted to slug his smug oiliness. She clenched the arms of her chair to avoid the temptation. In her best courtroom defense-lawyer disparaging tone she put him in his place. "Those were all ruled out. Tom's treating cardiologist felt strongly that Myrabin caused his liver to fail."

"How did you factor Suchet's laboratory work on the drug into your approval process?" Hugh asked.

Dr. Lancaster was quick to respond. "We didn't. The application was from Wycliffe. We relied on their lab work to initiate clinical trials."

"But back at the Investigational New Drug or IND stage, you were obligated to look at all the laboratory data surrounding the development of the drug. Suchet originally formulated and tested Myrabin."

"True," Dr. Butler agreed. "But Wycliffe bought the rights from Suchet in 1994 and worked on it in their laboratories for three years before they submitted an IND. We only looked at Wycliffe's research."

Hugh and Mark exchanged looks, and Kathryn realized Hugh was cuing Mark to ask the next question.

"We interviewed Dr. Maurice Vannier who was head of the development team for Myrabin at Suchet from 1991-1993."

"Of course, we know Dr. Vannier," Dr. Butler conceded.

"He gave us copies of his team's work on Myrabin."

"That's fine, but they are irrelevant to Wycliffe's application," Dr. Butler insisted.

"No, they are relevant. Very, very relevant." Hugh insisted. "Dr. Vannier's lab work showed that Myrabin was toxic."

Dr. Lancaster chimed in, "Wycliffe's scientists reformulated Myrabin to make it effective and safe. There have been no deaths from Myrabin."

Hugh had his head down, writing furiously on his legal tablet. Kathryn had the sense he was again cuing Mark, who spoke up.

"Did the FDA ever compare the Suchet version of Myrabin to the Wycliffe version to determine how Wycliffe modified the drug?"

Dr. Lancaster shook her head. "We never saw Dr. Vannier's work. Our focus was on our applicant, Wycliffe. Their clinical trials showed the drug was safe. There were no deaths linked to the drug. That was all we needed for approval."

Hugh looked up from his legal pad. "So you are certain no one at the FDA ever saw Dr. Vannier's work? He never sent it to you himself?"

"Never," Dr. Butler smiled benignly at everyone at the table.

* * *

Wednesday night, October 22, 2014, The Lounge at Bourbon Steak, The Four Seasons, Washington, D.C.

Around nine-thirty, Kathryn grew restless in her impressively expensive Georgetown Four Seasons room and wandered down to the bar, hoping she might run into Mark Kelly as she had on their last night in Paris. Instead, she found The Lounge empty except for Hugh on one of the stools at the most distant end of the bar, nursing his perpetual scotch. His back was toward her, so she could not see his face. But his big lanky frame folded awkwardly over the stool projected an aura of profound sadness and loneliness into the dimly lit, empty week-night bar.

He turned and smiled and gestured for her to join him, and she realized he had seen her reflection in the mirror behind the bar when she walked in.

As she slid onto the stool next to his, he summoned the bartender, who hurried over.

"Scotch?" Hugh invited, shaking the ice cubes in his own drink.

"No, thanks. Red wine; a merlot is fine." Kathryn told the hovering attendant.

"Don't worry about today," Hugh began.

"It wasn't what we were expecting, though."

He heaved his massive shoulders in a shrug. "They're lying. I'm never surprised when the other side lies."

"So you see the FDA as aligned with Wycliffe? They aren't neutral?"

"Ha!" Hugh shook his big head. She could tell he had moved from lonely to enjoying himself as he interpreted the facts for her. "They can't be neutral. They approved Myrabin. They have almost the same stake Wycliffe has in proving Myrabin didn't kill your husband. Even if the FDA is not on the hook for wrongful death damages, it still doesn't want the public to know that unsafe drugs make it through their review process."

Out of the corner of her eye, Kathryn saw a man enter the bar. At almost the same second, she realized Hugh had seen him, too. They couldn't discuss the case with a stranger present unless he settled himself at the far end, away from them.

But the man walked toward them; and as he did, Kathryn had a momentary shock of recognition. This man looked exactly like Harrison O'Connor, the organic chemist they'd met at the FDA that morning.

The man continued over to Hugh and sat down on the empty stool beside him. He handed Hugh a business card. Kathryn could see the name: Harrison O'Connor, Ph.D.

"Let me buy you a drink," Hugh said.

"No. I need to talk to you, but not in public."

"Let's go up to my suite." Hugh picked up his scotch and headed for the elevator with Harrison. Kathryn followed closely behind. Although Hugh seemed completely unfazed by the sudden appearance of the FDA's organic chemist, Kathryn's heart was pounding.

Once the elevator doors had closed behind them, Hugh dialed Mark's cell.

"Someone has come to talk to us, and you're going to want to hear what he has to say. Get Rick and meet us in my suite in five minutes."

Mark and Rick were standing at the door of Hugh's West Wing Presidential suite when they arrived. They all went inside and settled on the soft yellow brocade couches in the living room. Harrison declined Hugh's offer to order something from room service.

"I can't stay long. I'm worried I was seen coming here."

"How did you know where to find us?"

"I called your office here in D.C. after you left."

"Why are you worried about being followed?"

"Because I've been pretty sure someone has been watching me since you set up the meeting on Myrabin. And someone is also following Mary Lancaster and Frank Reynolds."

"Did Mary and Frank tell you they thought they were being followed?"

Harrison nodded.

"Why would someone surveil three FDA research scientists?" Hugh asked.

"Because we worked on Myrabin. And because you guys are now coming around asking about the approval process."

"So I take it the approval process was not strictly by the book as we were led to believe today?" Hugh polished off his drink and set it on the table, waiting expectantly for the answer to his question.

"That's right. It wasn't by the book at all. We did receive a packet from Maurice Vannier. I opened it and studied it. And, as you said, Dr. Vannier and his team found the drug caused liver failure in rats. Sometimes rapidly, sometimes more slowly. But it was not a safe drug."

"Then why did Dr. Butler lie to us today?" Mark Kelly spoke for the first time.

"Because he was instructed to ignore Dr. Vannier's materials."

"Who told Dr. Butler to do that?"

"Charles Lawson, who was head of the FDA at the time. Lawson also instructed him not to shut down Wycliffe's clinical trials after two people died from liver failure, one in Phase One and the other in Phase Three."

"So there were deaths!" Rick said.

"Absolutely," Harrison O'Connor said. "But we were not allowed to investigate them. Mary, Frank, and I resisted. By law we can't ignore deaths in clinical trials. But Dr. Butler said that if we wanted to keep our jobs, we'd accept those deaths as alcohol-related and not recommend suspending the trials."

"Why did you come to us?" Mark asked.

"Because I'm worried about the people who are taking the drug. When I met Mrs. Andrews today, it was the first time I'd met a person who'd lost a loved one because of what Mary, Frank, and I did to keep our jobs. I felt so guilty that I decided to come and tell you the truth."

"How many deaths have been reported since Myrabin's approval?" Hugh asked.

"I have no idea. Mary, Frank, and I receive reports, and we input them into our database, but they never show up after that."

"Do you know why that happens?"

"No idea. I just know it allows the FDA to go on saying there have been no reported deaths. Listen, I've told you all I know. I need to get going."

Hugh nodded. "Mark will walk you out. Thanks for coming. Would you be willing to testify at trial?"

"No, I'm sorry. I don't want to lose my job, and I would if I told the truth about Myrabin. And, since people are following me, there's a good chance I wouldn't survive if I testified."

CHAPTER TWENTY-SIX

October 23, 2014, The Amtrak Morning Train to New York From Washington, D.C.

Next morning, Hugh chose Amtrak's 2154 Acela Express for their three-hour trip to New York. He had used his Craig, Lewis, and Weller connections to get them an appointment with Charles Lawson. Hugh sat with Rick Peyton in the larger business class seats, using the time to decide how they would pose questions to Lawson. Mark and Kathryn sat behind them.

Yesterday's rain was still with them. Kathryn sipped coffee and watched the drops hit the windows as the early morning world sped past. The drops smashed themselves against the glass, spreading into long tears that slipped down the window. She thought about Tom and those last awful, agonizing days, and a tear of her own betrayed her.

She felt a gentle hand on her arm and looked over at Mark. She gave him a little smile. "You weren't supposed to see that."

"But I did." He smiled back. "Don't worry. We'll get to the bottom of this. I know what we heard last night was upsetting, but it did prove what we've suspected all along: irregularities in the approval of Myrabin. And there were deaths in the clinical trials."

"But Harrison won't testify, so how do we prove it?"

"We don't know yet." He was looking at her with his kind, gentle grey eyes that made her feel something she didn't want to feel.

She changed the subject. "When I found Hugh in the bar last night, he was alone. He looked sad."

"I think he is," Mark agreed. "But I don't know exactly why. I know his wife is pushing him to run for the Senate, and he doesn't want to. Maybe seeing Erin today will cheer him up."

The train rolled on through the rain to its own comforting rhythm. The big car swayed gently in time to the clacking wheels. Kathryn watched the rain drops dissolve into their own sad little puddles and decided any more personal discussions were dangerous.

So she said, "Tell me about Charles Lawson. Why was a lawyer appointed to be head of the Food and Drug Administration?"

"Lawson is a Harvard M.D. and J.D. He's well connected in political circles. He was a natural choice to head the agency."

* * *

Afternoon of October 23, 2014, Manhattan Offices of Craig, Lewis, and Weller

At three o'clock, Kathryn followed Hugh and Rick and Mark into an elevator that deposited them on the thirtieth floor of the Manhattan offices of Craig, Lewis, and Weller, deep in the glass towers of Wall Street. The receptionist, who was presiding over the lobby on a throne behind a marble desk, instructed them to be seated on the soft leather couches directly under her watchful gaze. Kathryn studied the fresh flowers on the table and wondered how much it cost the firm to keep orchids in the lobby year round. Outside, the incessant rain hammered against the glass walls in the deepening early afternoon twilight.

Fifteen minutes later, the double glass doors to the inner sanctum opened and Charles Lawson himself came striding toward him in all of his expensive Brooks Brothers splendor. He was around five eight and heavyset with salt and pepper hair and scholarly wire-rimmed glasses.

Hugh stood to shake his hand and introduce everyone. Dr. Lawson greeted them as cordially as if he actually wanted them there. He had them all follow him down the winding Craig, Lewis halls to his enormous office at the end of the corridor.

The five of them settled around a small conference table in one of the corners of Dr. Lawson's office. A secretary appeared with a pot of coffee and poured some for everyone without asking if anyone actually wanted any. But the brew was deep and rich, and warming on the cold rainy afternoon.

Hugh leaned back in his chair, legs crossed, coffee mug balanced on his knee. He looked relaxed and comfortable as if he owned the space he occupied. "Thanks for making time to see us, Charles."

"Not at all, Hugh. I'm afraid I'm not going to have good news for you, though. My secretary indicated you're pursuing Wycliffe over a wrongful death claim based on Myrabin."

"Yes. Mrs. Andrews' husband died as a result of taking

Myrabin. Liver failure within ninety days of starting the drug."

Dr. Lawson looked over at Kathryn. "My deepest sympathy, Mrs. Andrews. Ninety days after commencing treatment is an indication a new drug may be to blame, but this one is very, very safe. There are no deaths associated with Myrabin since its approval by the FDA."

"Dr. Maurice Vannier, head of the biology department at the École Normale Supérieure, does not agree with you," Hugh said. "He believes there are many deaths caused by the drug."

Dr. Lawton smiled and shrugged. "The American scientific community does not find Dr. Vannier's work all that remarkable."

"In other words, American science is better?" Hugh raised his eyebrows.

"If you want to put it that way, yes. Dr. Vannier was out of his element when he worked for Suchet. They fired him, you know."

Hugh looked over at Mark, a gesture Kathryn had come to understand cued him to speak. "That's not our understanding of what happened," Mark said.

Dr. Lawson smiled. "I very much doubt Dr. Vannier has any incentive to be truthful about his time with Suchet. They hired him to produce a product that would have wide marketability, but he failed. Wycliffe realized the potential of Myrabin and finished developing it."

"We know he sent his work to the FDA, and someone instructed the Myrabin team to disregard it." Mark's tone was informational but not accusatory.

"I was the one who told them to ignore it. When I was

teaching at Harvard Medical School, I was involved in work on drugs for hypertension. It's a particular interest of mine because it runs in my family." He looked at Kathryn and said pointedly, "I have to take medication for my blood pressure. I studied Dr. Vannier's work. To put it politely, I knew it wasn't any good; so I instructed the Myrabin team at the FDA to ignore it. He was wrong, and I was right. There have been no deaths since Myrabin was approved."

"What about the two deaths in the clinical trials?" Rick Peyton asked.

Dr. Lawson looked startled. "Who told you about those?"

"They were mentioned in some of the discovery," Mark lied.

"That wasn't supposed to be turned over." Dr. Lawson's anger was barely in check. "That information is not relevant to Mrs. Andrews' claim because those deaths were not caused by Myrabin."

"And you investigated each one?" Rick asked.

"Of course we did! Look, you're a physician. You know your patients aren't honest with you about how much they drink and how often. Those deaths were alcohol-related liver failure. They had nothing to do with Myrabin. This is a very, very safe drug."

* * *

Per Se, evening of October 23, 2014, New York

Hugh had insisted on a table with a view of Central Park. Erin arrived at seven thirty just after they were seated. She was even more beautiful in person than in the picture her mother had shown Kathryn at Crown Manor. She, indeed, had Buffy's heart-shaped face, high cheekbones, and caramel hair that fell in luscious waves to her shoulders. But she had her father's height and expressive brown eyes. Kathryn noticed that all of the male eyes in the restaurant followed her progress to her father's table.

The menu was expensive and intimidating, but Hugh took charge and ordered the nine-course chef's tasting menu for the table. After the drinks were handed around, Erin, who was seated at Hugh's left, looked over at Kathryn on his right, and asked about her work at the public defender's office.

"It's a hard job," Kathryn said. "Much harder than I thought it was going to be."

"I've been thinking of applying," Erin said. "I'm only going to stay at Craig, Lewis for another year."

"But why the public defender's office?" her father asked. "You could come to work for me."

Erin gave him a charming smile that melted his perplexed frown. "But I won't get to try any cases if I come to work for you. I'm bored as it is. I'm not actually practicing law at Craig, Lewis. I'm pushing paper from one side of my desk to the other and writing long memos about esoteric legal questions for the partners. Admit it, Dad. It wouldn't be any different at Goldstein, Miller except for better weather to commute in." She turned to Kathryn again, excitement in her eyes. "I bet you've done a lot of trials."

"Too many to count."

"You're lucky. Nothing goes to trial in civil litigation. Everything settles."

"We settle cases, too."

"But not *all* of them."

"No, not all. But working as a public defender breaks your heart."

"How?" She looked skeptical.

"When you get that rare case where the client is actually innocent, and there aren't many, and you have to advise him to plead guilty to a lesser offense to avoid a long sentence. It's not easy to send an innocent man to prison."

Erin looked sober as if the prospect had not occurred to her.

"What can you tell us about Charles Lawson?" Hugh asked as the appetizers took center stage. For a few moments, Kathryn was lost with her companions in the prospect of Island Creek Oysters and Sterling White Sturgeon Caviar, a delicate tart of winter squash and tomatoes, and Hudson Valley Moulard Duck Foie Gras. She had never tasted anything so exquisite.

"I've never done any work for Dr. Lawson," Erin said. "His principal need is for associates who will carry his black bags when he goes to Washington to testify. That happens *all* the time."

"Where is he testifying, and who does he represent?" Hugh asked.

"In Congress, at FDA hearings. His clients are the major pharmaceutical firms. Basically he testifies in support of various drugs the companies want to market or are marketing. He doesn't seem to actually practice law. He's more of a lobbyist."

The second course arrived, as tantalizing as the first. Kathryn was lost in the delights of Fairytale Eggplant and Butter Poached Nova Scotia Lobster with petite radishes; Four Story Hill Farm's "Suprême De Poularde " with Champagne Currants and Cipollini Onion; and Carnaroli Risotto Biologico with Shaved

Australian Black Winter Truffles. The waiter kept refilling their glasses with the French champagne Hugh had insisted on. It seemed oddly like a party instead of a business meeting on the heels of a disappointing witness interview. *Tom would be smiling now,* Kathryn thought, *happy that something this exotic and expensive had taken her out of the rut that grief had plowed through her life for the last two years.*

Kathryn noticed Erin watched her father with real affection. What would it be like to have your pick of high-salaried jobs and a father who rubbed shoulders with senators and presidents? But Erin's interest in working for her office seemed genuine.

"I gather Dr. Lawson didn't tell you what you wanted to hear," she said to her father.

He shrugged. "Depends on how you look at it. He lied about investigating the two reported cases of liver failure during the Myrabin clinical trials. He also lied about Maurice Vannier's reputation as a scientist. He gave us some great material for impeachment when Wycliffe calls him as a witness. But he definitely did not admit wrongdoing in the approval of Myrabin."

"But you didn't really think he'd do that did you, Dad?"

Hugh gave Erin the impish smile that Kathryn had learned to recognize as a sign of his affection. "No, but hoping for a miracle doesn't hurt."

Kathryn looked across the street at the rich red and gold auras created by the reflection of the street lamps on the autumn leaves in Central Park and bit her tongue, so she wouldn't say what was on her mind. Hugh was wrong. Hoping for a miracle did hurt. It hurt like hell. And, in the end, hoping for a miracle hadn't kept Tom alive. And then more recently, she'd learned from Paul's betrayal and from her naïveté about Dan Ayers that hoping for a miracle only brought exquisite pain. No, Hugh was wrong when he said hoping for a miracle didn't hurt. Hoping for a miracle tore your heart out.

* * *

October 24, 2014, Friday, 8:30 a.m., LaGuardia, New York

Next morning, it was still raining as the United Airlines jet clawed its way through the ominous clouds and into the sky. Long fingers of rain trailed their way slowly across the plane's windows, ceremoniously marking each one as the big jet fought for altitude against the winds. As soon as the drink service began in the first class cabin, Hugh ordered a scotch.

"Think I have a problem?" he asked Kathryn after his drink came and he'd taken a few sips.

She was seated next to him again with Rick and Mark behind them. Even that early in the morning, he had the same air of melancholy she'd sensed when he was sitting at the bar at the Four Seasons. She sipped her coffee from the inadequate airline paper cup and considered what to say.

"That question made you uncomfortable," he said before she could answer.

She frowned. "Okay, it did. Why does what I think matter?"

Hugh smiled. "I don't know. But it matters. It mattered that first day you came to the firm, and I realized I'd lost your respect in the conference room when you saw me with Logan."

For a moment Kathryn didn't know what to say. Finally she decided on the truth.

"But I have the greatest respect for you."

"As a lawyer, but not personally."

She wished he would stop probing for her approval. "No, that isn't true. I respect you for your work as an attorney. And I know you are a man of integrity."

"Except for affairs with my associates."

"I don't think I'm qualified to judge that." She thought guiltily of the way she'd fallen for Dan Ayers and pined to see him ever since. "From what I understand, Patty was Logan's predecessor, and she has nothing but respect for you."

Hugh smiled as he sipped his too-early-in-the-morning scotch. "I'm relieved to hear that. But you still think I'm not to be trusted."

Kathryn frowned. "Not at all. I've trusted you with Tom's case, which means more to me than anything in the world now that I've lost him."

She saw his dark eyes soften behind his thick lenses. "Thanks."

She sipped coffee for a few moments and pictured Hugh as he had sat on the barstool that night at the Four Seasons. Her heart suddenly and unexpectedly twisted with sympathy for him. "Maybe you'd feel better if I told you I drank too much after Tom died. Gallons and gallons of cheap wine from Trader Joe's. I knew it was too much. I knew it was everyday. But I hurt too much to care."

"And now?"

"Some days more, some days less. I probably should stop, but I don't want to."

Hugh gave her the impish grin he'd given Erin the night before. "Me either."

He nursed his scotch in silence for a few minutes. His expression said he was deciding whether to confide in her. Finally he took the plunge. "Give me your honest opinion about Erin's interest in working for your office. Would it be a good idea?"

The question surprised her, but she was flattered because he wanted her advice. "She'd definitely learn to try cases. You know better than anyone else, you can't be a good lawyer if you're afraid to go to trial. I would say, though, she'd want to move on after a couple of years. Emotional burnout is the downside. It gets to everyone eventually."

"Did it get to your husband?"

"Sometimes. But usually when he was overwhelmed, he'd spend a few hours surfing, and he'd be okay again." She willed herself not to say "surfing with Shannon."

"What about you?"

She sighed. "To be honest, I'm beyond burnout at this point. Ever since Tom died, I've felt futile. It was different when we could talk about our cases and convince each other we were doing something good. But now I see that my professional life is nothing but a series of guilty verdicts and plea deals for guilty people."

"Then consider coming to work for us when this case is over. You'd like plaintiff's litigation the way we do it." He gave her that smile again.

"I'll think about it."

CHAPTER TWENTY-SEVEN

Monday, October 27, 2014, Office of the Public Defender, 450 B Street, San Diego

Kathryn was at her desk by seven thirty on Monday. The trip with Hugh had left her swamped at work. But she didn't care. As she shifted through the accumulated mail, she decided this must have been the way Cinderella felt the morning after the ball. She wanted to read all that mail about as much as Cinderella had wanted to pick up her broom and start sweeping her stepmother's hearth.

Someone tapped lightly at her open door, and she looked up to see her boss, Mildred Fletcher. Mid-fifties, five-eight, short curly black hair, dressed this morning in a Chanel tweed suit culled from a second-hand shop, but so impeccably tailored that it would have done Patty E. Fox proud. Millie Fletcher was a tough African-American woman who had fought her way up the ladder rung by rung until she had become one of California's leading authorities on the art and science of criminal defense.

"How was your trip?"

Kathryn smiled. "Long, interesting, and a glimpse into another world."

Did you find anything that will help your case?"

"Yes and no. At best we could see it's going to be an uphill fight to prove what we already know is true. Myrabin killed Tom."

Millie looked down at the pile of mail on Kathryn's desk and said, "I know you're trying to catch up, but I need to talk to you for a few minutes."

Kathryn felt her stomach tighten. What had she done wrong? "Sure, of course."

Millie, who had come equipped with a venti Starbuck's Café Americano, sat down in the chair across from Kathryn's desk. She took a fortifying sip of the black brew and began. "I want to talk to you about a case that came in while you were away. I want to assign it to you."

Kathryn heaved a sigh of relief because this wasn't a disciplinary interview after all. But she frowned and pointed to the stacks of files on the shelf behind her. "My dance card is pretty full at the moment."

"I know, I know. But let me tell you why I want you to have this one."

"Okay." Kathryn took a long drink of her own coffee.

"Over the weekend, three gang members from Ninth Street Crips came across a tourist who had wandered a little off the beaten path in the Gaslamp quarter downtown. Two of them assaulted the man and demanded his wallet, but the third shot and killed him. There was a surveillance camera on one of the nearby buildings that picked up the whole thing. The district attorney is charging it as a robbery-felony-murder, life-without-parole case. We're sending the shooter to the Alternate Public

Defender's Office and the first accomplice to the court-appointments panel. We're keeping the second accomplice here. His name is Tyrone Lavone Jones. I want you to take his case."

"But why, Millie? I've got more than my share of LWOP's already."

"I'm asking you to take it because this kid is only fourteen, and he's going to be tried as an adult. And he may, in fact, be innocent."

Kathryn put down her coffee cup and stared at Millie for several seconds. "Innocent? In this office? You're kidding."

"No, this is that rare case."

"But I can't, Millie. I wouldn't be able to do it justice. I only have a part-time investigator, and he's booked solid with assignments. He wouldn't be able to give me any help at all on a new case."

"I know. I know. But no one has enough investigator help, so assigning it to another senior PD won't change that."

"But why me, Millie? Why now when I'm in the midst of Tom's case?"

"Because I'd give this one to Tom if he were here." Millie's face became soft and thoughtful as she went on. "Look, Kathryn, no one knows the reality of this life better than I do. We all crash and burn at some point because we can't take the stress any more. I've got two years until retirement, and I'm counting every day. I know the bloom of 'helping the indigent' has been off the rose for you for more years than you can count, but the one person in the office who never seemed too cynical to believe in the possibility of actual innocence was Tom."

Kathryn's eyes suddenly filled with tears. She could hear

Tom saying to her over and over again, "No, this one's different. This guy didn't *do* it."

Millie ignored her display of emotion and continued. "Whenever a serious case came in, if I really thought the client might be innocent, I'd give it to Tom because, unlike the rest of us, he wasn't too jaded to believe what the client was telling him."

"But I'm not like that, Millie. Honestly, I've heard every story in the book. Nothing impresses me anymore."

"I know. I know. And I don't blame you. But since I don't have Tom now, I need you to fill his shoes. He would want you to take Tyrone's case, Kathryn. Please."

* * *

Tuesday, October 28, 2014, Juvenile Hall, Meadow Lark Drive, San Diego.

Kathryn went to see her new client at three p.m. the following day. Because he was being held in juvenile hall, she was allowed to see Tyrone in a small gray room with a table in the middle. She had already reviewed the grainy surveillance footage of the shooting. It showed three indistinct silhouettes, two beating and kicking a shorter man and a third tall, shadowy form with a gun. A second before the short man fell, Kathryn saw the fire from the muzzle. As soon as he was down, the three men ran up to him and searched his pockets. As they ran away, the shooter turned and fired one last shot. The man's body jerked once and then was still.

The tall, skinny kid in front of her in gray detention scrubs could have been one of the two shadows punching the man. He sat hunched at the table, his eyes on the floor, his face sullen.

"I understand you're fourteen, is that right?"

"Yeah." He kept his eyes on the floor.

"And where do you live?"

"Nowhere." He still didn't look at her.

"But surely—"

His dark eyes, hard and defiant, met hers. "My momma left me with my granny when I was three. Granny died last year, and the landlord threw me out of our apartment 'cause I couldn't pay the rent. Mostly I sleep on couches at friends' houses. Or on the street if I can't find nobody that will let me stay."

Kathryn's heart twisted. She felt as if Tom were in the room with her. Millie was right. Tom, the protector of the broken and homeless, would have been drawn to Tyrone's case. It was one reason he'd been protective of Shannon, because she'd run away from her abusive stepmother at sixteen, lied about her age, and learned to support herself tending bar. Living with Steve had been the first stable home she'd ever had.

"Do you go to school?"

"Not since my granny died."

"The intake form said you have one brother?"

"Marquess, yeah."

"He's a lot older than you, isn't he?"

"He's eighteen."

"I'm guessing you two didn't live together."

"Marquess lives with his baby momma. Sometimes they let me sleep on their couch. Not always though."

"Why don't you tell me what happened last Saturday night?"

"It wouldn't do no good if I did."

"Why not?"

"Because I'm gonna get convicted regardless. I'm a Ninth Street Crip. Don't matter if you guilty or innocent; if you a Crip, you gonna get convicted."

"Are you a gang member or just an associate?"

"Member." He fixed his eyes on the floor again as if he was ashamed of the admission. "I got jumped in when I was eleven."

"Isn't that kind of young?"

"Yeah, but Marquess is tight with the shot callers. He got them to take me."

"What did your granny think of that?"

"She didn't mind. The homies would bring her groceries when she didn't have no money and would drive her to the doctor's office because she didn't have no car. They helped take care of her. And me."

Kathryn nodded grimly. The story was all too familiar. Gangs were surrogate families for kids like Tyrone.

"So tell me what happened on Saturday."

He sighed. "Like I said, Miz Andrews. No offense. It won't do no good."

"Do you know Jalal Griffin?"

"Yeah. That's Big Jay. He's tight with my brother."

"Does Marquess have a gang name?"

"Pit Bull."

"What about you?"

"Lil' Pit."

"Why don't you tell me what happened on Saturday night?"

"You wear people down, Miz Andrews. You know that?"

"I know I want to help you, and I can't if you don't tell me what happened. Big Jay says you were there, and you helped rob Gunnar Thorn, who was visiting from Sweden. Big Jay says your brother Marquess was the shooter. The police found Mr. Thorn's wallet in your brother's pocket, and the murder weapon in his car."

"The cops showed me a videotape, but they didn't tell me the man's name." Tyrone looked from the floor to Kathryn's eyes and back to the floor. His face continued to be profoundly sad.

"Were you on that tape, Tyrone?"

"It don't matter what I say, Miz Andrews. The cops, they gonna believe Big Jay because that way they take some Crips off the street, guilty or not."

"But if you tell me the truth, we might be able to win at trial."

"Ain't gonna be no win."

"Try telling me your story, and I'll be the judge of whether we have a shot at winning."

"Okay, but I'm telling you now, it won't do no good."

"Try me."

"So Saturday, I spent the day at Marquess' house. He'd had a fight with Lytisha, and she'd tooken their baby to stay at her mother's."

"Where do Marquess and Lytisha live?"

"They got an apartment in Chula Vista on La Raza Street."

"So what did you guys do at your brother's?"

"Drank beer, smoked a lot of weed. Big Jay came over and a few other homies."

"Like who?"

"Freckles, Big G, Mad Dog, and Maniac."

"Are they all Ninth Street Crips?"

"All except Maniac. He's now a West Side Crip from L.A. He used to live here."

"How many of you went down to the Gaslamp?

"We didn't. At least, I didn't. We went to a night club called The Rendevous, close to Marquess's place. It's on H Street."

"Did all of you go to The Rendevous?"

"Yep. There was this girl I was hoping to meet up with there."

"And did you?"

"Yep. Her name's Tamara."

"Last name?"

"No idea. I had only met her the night before."

"So you were at this nightclub two nights in a row?"

"Yeah. I go there a lot. The older homies buy me food and drinks and shit."

"Do you have a job?"

"Yeah, I bus tables at an Applebees on H Street. I lied to get the job, and said I was sixteen."

"Okay. So when did you leave this nightclub and head down to the Gaslamp?"

"That's the thing, Miz Andrews. I didn't. Me and Tamara hit it off good, and I was there until closing."

"When was that?"

"One a.m."

Kathryn felt a tiny flicker of hope. She'd been skeptical when Millie had suggested this client might be innocent. But Gunnar

Thorn had been killed right around one a.m.

"Where'd you go after that?"

"Me and Tamara and a bunch of homies partied in the parking lot until management ran us off."

"And after that?"

"Tamara had me back to her place."

"Where is that?"

"Shoot, Miz Andrews. I don't remember the exact address. It was dark, and she was driving."

"How old is Tamara?"

"I don't know. Older than me. Old enough to have a car."

"So you went to her apartment?"

"Yeah. It wasn't too far away. Next morning, she drove me back to Marquess' place. Lytisha had come back with the baby. We was all having breakfast when the cops came and arrested me and Marquess. I didn't know about no robbery or killing or nuthin' until the cops put me in that room and showed me the tape of them shooting that guy."

"So do you know who's on the tape?"

"Not for sure. But I could guess."

"Did the police tell you Marquess' gun was the murder weapon?"

"Un huh."

"They think he was the shooter."

"Yes, ma'am. I know."

"Was he?"

"I wasn't there, Miz Andrews. And he didn't tell me nuthin' about no shooting when I got back to his place that morning. All I know is what the cops said. They think it was me and

Marquess and Jalal because Jalal told them that."

"But Jalal knows you weren't there, right?"

"Right."

"Then why did he say you were?"

"I'm guessing cause he figured out that's what the cops wanted to hear. They got Marquess and his gun, so they figured I was involved, too. I mean, I seen the tape, Ms. Andrews. The two guys with Marquess are tall and thin, like me."

"Right. But that doesn't make you guilty of murder."

"Can I ask you something?"

"Of course."

"I know I'm not real bright. But I don't get how they can say the two guys with Marquess killed that man. It was Marquess that pulled the trigger. The other two were beating on him, but they didn't do nuthn' to kill him."

"I know, Tyrone. And I wouldn't say you aren't bright. There's a really old-fashioned rule in the law that says if you are helping out with a robbery and the person with the gun pulls the trigger and kills the victim, you are just as guilty as the person who used the gun."

"That don't seem fair to me."

"Or to me. Do you have any information that will help me find Tamara?"

"Alls I know is she's a regular at The Rendevous. The owner is a guy named Ray-Ray Washington. He's a Ninth Street Crip, but he don't bang no more. Ray-Ray knows all the regulars."

"Okay, Tyrone. I'll start there trying to find her."

THE DEPOSITION

CHAPTER TWENTY-EIGHT

Tuesday, December 2, 2014, Lindbergh Field, San Diego

Jose Sanchez, his driver, was waiting to pick him up at ten a.m. when Hugh's flight from San Francisco arrived. He'd spent more than a month taking depositions in a securities fraud case involving a technology company. Being in San Francisco had given him time to hang out with Patrick and tell him why he didn't want Buffy to push him into a run for the Senate. Patrick had agreed: it was a lousy idea.

Jose made the trip from the airport to the Emerald Shapery Center in record time, deposited Hugh, and sped off to Coronado to deliver Hugh's bags to Maria, his housekeeper, who would unpack them. Hugh stood in the lobby of his building for a moment, reflecting on Kathryn's presence upstairs in the big conference room where she was being deposed. It was the second day, and Mark had called him yesterday to let him know everything was going well.

"McLaren has tried and tried to push her buttons, but she won't budge."

"That's good news. Sounds as if you and Patty did a good job prepping her."

"Thanks, but she catches on very fast."

"I bet McLaren is pissed that he can't poke holes in her happily married story."

"Pissed doesn't even begin to describe how frustrated he is."

As the glass elevator ascended to the Goldstein, Miller penthouse, Hugh decided he wanted to watch Bob McLaren's rout. He dropped his briefcase in his office, told his secretary where he could be found, and slipped into the conference room.

* * *

He sat down next to Patty. Mark, to Patty's left, looked over at him and smiled. Kathryn was seated at the end of the long table, wearing a simple green wool dress that highlighted her trim figure and her eyes. Patty had made sure she came across as a grieving widow instead of a savvy public defender.

Hugh saw Bob McLaren's steely dark eyes shift quickly from Kathryn's face to his own and back to Kathryn's. Neither he nor Annette Fry nor Emma Talbert were happy to see him. Hugh, fresh off a month-long round of striking terror into opposing counsel, chuckled silently to himself. The high of knowing he had his opponents intimidated was almost as powerful as being in love. Almost, but not quite.

Hugh was proud of Kathryn for withstanding yesterday's onslaught of questions. Mark had reported that McLaren could not make her admit that her marriage was troubled, Tom was unfaithful, or Tom drank too much. Apparently he had spent the first part of the morning circling back over yesterday's territory, trying to shake her story, because Mark was lodging asked-and-answered objections. But Hugh's appearance motivated him to move on.

"When did Dr. Myers prescribe Myrabin for your husband, Mrs. Andrews?"

"February 2012." Her voice was soft, clear, and unwavering. She looked McLaren right in the eye.

"And when did your husband become ill?"

* * *

Monday May 21, 2012, 1845 Ocean Place, Pacific Beach

Tom went surfing that morning. Kathryn lied to Bob McLaren and said that he was alone, but he'd gone with Shannon.

Whereas before Shannon, they usually drove to work together, now Kathryn was always ready to go long before Tom had disentangled himself from her nemesis. But she lied so convincingly that Bob McLaren and Hugh and everyone else present bought her excuse that she went in alone because she had to be in court earlier than Tom. And although that fact was true in a superficial sense, she still would have had time to wait and drive in with her husband had she not wanted the opportunity to show him how much she disapproved of all the time he spent with Shannon.

She was stewing about Shannon all morning as she answered the docket call for her cases. She continued some, helped clients enter guilty pleas in others, and agreed to status conference dates in the rest. When she returned to her office at eleven-thirty, she noticed Tom was now in his office. He was frowning earnestly as he talked on the phone. Likely settlement negotiations with an arrogant assistant district attorney, she thought.

She ate a quick lunch at her desk and headed for the jail to make the rounds of client interviews. When she came back at three-thirty, Beth Price, their mutual secretary, told her Tom had gone home feeling nauseous.

"Something he ate for lunch," Beth said.

Two deputy district attorneys called that afternoon, trying to negotiate settlements in cases that neither side wanted to go to trial. Exhausted by all the back and forth about who had the stronger position, Kathryn limped home by six to find Tom in deep sleep. She had smiled and pushed the hair off his forehead and kissed him lightly on the cheek before going to the kitchen and eating a slice of leftover pizza with a glass of red wine.

Tom was still sleeping soundly when she crawled into bed beside him at eleven p.m. He looked angelic and boyish in deep sleep. He stirred slightly when she kissed him on the cheek, but that was all.

She woke around two-thirty to hear the sound of dry heaves coming from the bathroom. She rushed in to find Tom slumped over the toilet. His eyes were sunken, and he was so weak he was sitting on the floor, propped against the wall.

He tried and failed to give her a smile. "Bad sushi."

"Lunch?"

He gave her a weak nod.

She managed to get him to his feet and out to the car. He could barely walk, and he had to lean on her heavily.

She drove through the empty night, praying that he was going to be okay. Red lights and stop signs flashed past in a blurred panic. Beside her in the passenger seat, Tom was just barely holding on.

By the time they arrived at Scripps Memorial, he had passed out. Kathryn parked the car in a no parking zone and ran in to the Emergency Room, her heart beating so hard, she had trouble speaking. While they wheeled Tom into the hospital on a stretcher, she hurriedly parked the car in the first space she saw, tow-away or not, and ran inside to find him.

They had taken him to one of the small examination rooms. His t-shirt and knit pajama pants were gone in favor of a regulation hospital gown. A thirty-something nurse wearing dark blue scrubs and a droopy blonde pony tail was starting an IV drip to give him fluids.

"He's badly dehydrated," she observed as she worked. "How long as this been going on?"

Her eyes wide with terror, Kathryn took Tom's free hand and recited the facts of his day. Fine in the morning. Surfing as usual. At work without symptoms mid-morning. Bad sushi for lunch followed by nausea, vomiting, and fatigue all afternoon.

A technician appeared with a cart and drew blood under the nurse's watchful gaze.

Just as the blood sample was off to the lab, the door opened and a middle-aged man in a white coat with salt-and-pepper hair and a badge that said "D. Stewart, M.D." entered. Reciting the litany of Tom's day once again reignited Kathryn's fear. Her free hand was trembling as she finished.

He gave her a reassuring smile. "Try not to worry, Mrs. Andrews. We'll know more after we see what the blood work says. But as bad as food poisoning looks at this stage, patients come back pretty fast."

Dr. Stewart vanished into the corridor, and Kathryn was left alone listening to the beep, beep of the heart monitor; the whish of the automatic blood pressure cuff as it rose and fell, and the loudly ticking clock above the door.

Three a.m. became three-thirty and then four o'clock. Kathryn's ordeal by waiting continued.

Finally, at ten minutes after four, Dr. Stewart reappeared. "We have your husband's blood work, Mrs. Andrews."

Kathryn felt her stomach tighten. "And?"

"And we're seeing elevated aminotransferases. Those are enzymes that indicate inflammation in the liver. Could your husband have been exposed to hepatitis?"

Kathryn thought sickeningly of Shannon. Had he slept with her? How many partners had Shannon had? Too many to count probably. "No, of course not."

"Hmm." Dr. Stewart was sizing her up to see if she was being truthful.

"Well, then, what medications is he taking?"

"Myrabin. For high blood pressure. Dr. Myers prescribed it."

He nodded. "I'm going to give Dr. Myers a call."

* * *

They broke for lunch. Hugh joined Patty, Mark and Kathryn in the small conference room where they picked at rubbery pasta salad and overly-mayoed sandwiches from a deli Mark's secretary favored. Kathryn drank black coffee and ate little. She reminded Hugh of a star athlete at half-time. He could see she was preparing mentally for the next round. And he knew, no matter what hearsay Mark Kelly had bought off Paul Curtis,

Kathryn was doing a superb job of hiding her secret, whatever it was.

They reconvened at one p.m.

"Tell me, Mrs. Andrews, what happened after your husband was hospitalized the first time?

* * *

Tuesday, May 22, 2012, Scripps Memorial Hospital, La Jolla

Kathryn dozed fitfully on the reclining chair in Tom's small exam room until seven-thirty the next morning. She woke with a start to find a tall, fortyish nurse in light pink scrubs wearing a name badge that said "Anna M." documenting Tom's vital signs.

"Sorry to wake you, Mrs. Andrews," Anna M. said. "Your husband is better today. His hydration is up, and his blood pressure is down."

Tom gave Kathryn a reassuring smile. "Bad sushi."

But at nine, Bruce Myers came to give them the final word. He listened to Tom's heart and lungs, prodded and poked, and finally said, "No more Myrabin."

"So it wasn't bad sushi?" Kathryn asked.

"No. Tom's had a reaction to Myrabin. But the good news is these things resolve quickly after the drug is discontinued."

"Then he's going to be okay?" Kathryn held Tom's hand tightly as she asked.

"Just fine." And Dr. Myers smiled

* * *

Memorial Day, May 28, 2012, 1845 Ocean Place Pacific Beach

They did not go to Rosarito for Memorial Day as they often did. Tom surfed that morning, but not with Shannon. He went with Paul, who was on reprieve from out-of-town-deposition hell. They met at the beach in Coronado. Kathryn and Carolyn watched from the terrace at the Hotel Del where they drank coffee and Jodie played with her Cheerios. Afterward, they all walked down Orange Avenue and had brunch at Clayton's Coffee Shop. Kathryn would forever remember the throbbing, banshee wail of the gulls that morning as they circled the hard, blue sky.

She and Tom had planned to plant vegetables and herbs in their backyard garden that afternoon, but Tom fell asleep in the car on the way home from Coronado. He didn't want to admit how tired he was, but Kathryn could see fatigue in every line of his face. In spite of his protests, she persuaded him to lie down. He was asleep again within minutes. And she was worried.

She decided to do the gardening herself to stifle her unease. But as she dug in the rich black soil of the plot she and Tom had created years ago, panic gnawed at her heart. She kept remembering how Dr. Myers had promised them Tom would be just fine when they left the hospital a week ago. She clung to that frail phrase all afternoon.

At five she stripped off her gardening gloves, caked with dirt, and crept into the house, hoping not to wake Tom. But he called out as soon as he heard her walking through the kitchen, "Why did you let me sleep so long?"

She hurried into their bedroom, where the blinds were still

closed against the strong late afternoon sun, and his long body was stretched comfortably across the bed in the half light. He opened his arms for her to come to him, and she lay down beside him, cuddling into his chest and telling herself the nap had fixed everything.

He looked down at her as he held her and smiled. "I hope you didn't do all that planting by yourself."

She smiled. "It wasn't hard. You needed to rest. Are you feeling better?"

"Much."

His arms tightened around her, and he held her close for a long time. It was, Kathryn thought later, as if he knew they were saying goodbye.

* * *

Whereas they always walked the few blocks to the Yellow Café for dinner, Kathryn suggested driving that night. Tom ate little, and went to bed again by nine-thirty. She sat up, preparing for a motion she had to argue the next day, trying as hard as she could to keep worry at bay.

But at one a.m, Kathryn woke to find Tom's side of the bed empty. She found him sitting on the sofa in the living room, clutching his belly, his face contorted with pain.

She sat down beside him and put her arms around him. "What's wrong?"

"I don't know. I woke up with the most awful pain here." He pointed to the right side of his abdomen. "I feel nauseous. And my stomach's the size of a balloon."

She put her hand on his forehead and realized he was

burning up with fever and his skin was yellow. "We'd better go to the ER."

* * *

Tuesday, December 2, 2014, Conference Room, Goldstein, Miller

"It's four o'clock," Mark said. "How much more do you have?"

"Not much," Bob McLaren said. "Just a few additional questions."

Mark looked at Kathryn, who noticed Hugh's eyes looked wet. Mark and Patty had already heard the story of Tom's last days, but he had not.

"Do you want to try to finish today," Mark asked her, "or come back in the morning?"

"Let's finish." Kathryn said quickly.

Bob McLaren didn't miss a beat. "What happened after your husband was admitted to the hospital the second time?"

* * *

May 28, 2012, Scripps Memorial Hospital, La Jolla, California

She knew it was far worse than it had been a week ago because they made her sit in the waiting room and would not let her be with Tom. At four in the morning, a tall, thin, balding man in light blue scrubs came to find her. His name badge said K. Martin, M.D.

"Mrs. Andrews, I'm Karl Martin. I'm head of the transplant team here at Scripps."

Her blood ran cold. "Transplant?"

"Your husband's liver is badly damaged. He needs a transplant."

There are moments you always remember. For Kathryn it was seeing the big clock on the wall behind Dr. Martin's head with its hands fixed at four o'clock. No matter what came after this, life as she had known it had ended in this millisecond.

"But why? Tom's an athlete. He does everything right."

Dr. Martin shook his head. "I can't tell you tonight what caused this. I only know he's critical. He needs surgery."

Her hands were suddenly clammy. "Will he be okay?"

"Transplants are very successful."

"Can I see him before he goes to surgery?"

Dr. Martin sighed. "That's the problem. He can't go to surgery right now."

"But I thought you said–"

"I said he needed surgery. I didn't say he was strong enough for it. We've got to get him to a place where he can tolerate the surgery, Mrs. Andrews. If we operate tonight, he'll die."

Die. The word rang in her head. She put her hands together and squeezed hard as if that was enough force to push death away.

"But you can't let him die."

"We're doing everything we can, Mrs. Andrews."

* * *

For three weeks, he hung on. At first Kathryn refused to leave the hospital, but eventually the nurses persuaded her to eat and rest. Millie gave her a leave of absence, so she could focus only on Tom.

He was breathing on his own, but he didn't wake up. She talked to him as she sat by his bed in the ICU, telling him news from work, reminding him always of how much she loved and needed him.

Paul was allowed in for fifteen minutes at a time. And Steve. One morning, a week after her nightmare began, she arrived at eight to find Shannon sitting in the chair by Tom's bed, holding his hand. She gave Kathryn a guilty look and slunk out. Kathryn summoned the nurse.

"Why did you let that woman in?"

"She didn't ask our permission, and when we found her, we assumed she was family."

"She's not. Don't let her in again."

* * *

Monday, June 18, 2012, ICU Scripps Memorial Hospital, La Jolla, California

She tried to tell herself he was growing stronger, but she knew the truth. His legs were useless bloated lumps; his stomach was still painfully swollen. Only the IV fluids were keeping him alive.

Dr. Martin had come to check on Tom around noon that Monday. She waited in the hallway for news. Dr. Martin looked very grave when he came out. He walked up to Kathryn.

"He's growing weaker."

"So no surgery?"

"Not now."

"Isn't there anything else you can do?"

But Dr. Martin patted her gently on the shoulder and shook his head.

She scurried past the ICU nurses, afraid they might send her home, and settled once more in the chair by Tom's bed. She lost track of time as she held his hand and listened to the thump and whir of the machines. Her prayers were now negotiations with God, telling Him that He couldn't take Tom because He had refused to give her the longed-for child.

The afternoon wore on, and she was so tired that she accidentally dozed off. When she woke, she found Tom smiling at her. Her heart turned over with joy.

"Hey, sleepyhead," he said.

She leaned over to give him a kiss. "How long have you been awake?"

"Long enough to think about how much I love you."

"You know I love you, too."

"I do." His smile trembled slightly, and he said, "I'm just so tired. I'm going to close my eyes again for a few minutes."

Kathryn squeezed his hand. Surely this had to mean he was regaining strength, and the transplant would be possible. But then, just as his eyes closed, the heart monitor's jagged line went flat, the alarm sounded, and the Code Blue team swarmed around his bed. They pushed her into the hall where a priest took her arm and led her to the nursing supervisors' office to await the news of her husband's death.

CHAPTER TWENTY-NINE

Tuesday, December 2, 2014, The Grant Grill Lounge, San Diego

Hugh had suggested they walk over to the elegant, dark-paneled bar at the Grant Hotel after Bob McLaren and his minions decamped from the Goldstein, Miller conference room. Mark, Patty, Kathryn, and Hugh walked up Broadway in the deep winter-dark that shrouded the city at seven p.m.

They sat at one of the sleek-chrome tables and ate soft pretzels with whole grain mustard and sea salt, Parmesan fries, and braised beef sliders. Hugh, Mark, and Patty laughed about various points in the deposition where Bob McLaren had been flustered by Kathryn's calm.

"You didn't give him an inch," Mark smiled at her. His admiration made her tummy flutter, but she kept her face impassive. She'd perfected that art over the last two days.

"Thanks."

The three of then continued to post-mortem Kathryn's performance, until Patty slid off her tall, chrome stool and announced she had to go.

"My nanny has fits if she has to work past eight-thirty. See you all in the morning."

The old stab of jealousy for any woman who had a child hit Kathryn hard. But she smiled at Patty as if nothing mattered as she turned to leave.

Mark stirred on his stool. "I don't have the same excuse, but I'd better get going, too. I have a hearing tomorrow in Los Angeles. I'll be on the early train."

Kathryn felt let down as he walked away. Hugh seemed to read her expression.

"You don't have to stay, if you don't want to."

She smiled. "There's no one waiting for me at home."

"Me, either. Buffy went to New York to visit Erin." He gave her a rueful smile. "Want to come back to my house and see if the housekeeper left any real food in the fridge?"

She started to say no, but she thought of how quiet her cottage would be when she got home, and how the memories of Tom and his last days would smother her in the stale atmosphere of a house that had been closed all day. She knew only too well that the price of keeping emotions in check was to be overwhelmed by them later.

"Sure, I'd like that."

* * *

Tuesday, December 2, 2014, Crown Manor, Coronado, California

The big house seemed dead inside, Kathryn thought, as Hugh opened the massive subzero refrigerator in the dimly lit kitchen. It felt as if the spirit of the place had gone to New York with Buffy.

"Not much here, I'm afraid."

"That's okay. I actually had enough to eat at the Grant."

He grinned. "Me, too. I just thought we might find something green and healthy to absorb all that grease. But no luck. How about a martini, instead?"

"Red wine if you have some."

She followed him back to the bar in the sunroom, where he found wine for her and scotch for himself.

"Would you be too cold if I lit the heaters on the patio, and we sat outside?"

"No."

A few minutes later, they had settled near the massive propane heater on the down-pillowed patio chairs. Hugh threw back his head and took a long breath of night air. "Ah," he sighed. "I never get tired of the sound of the ocean."

Kathryn sipped her wine and listened to the gentle hum of the surf. She thought of Tom, and a tear slid down her cheek.

Hugh leaned over and put his big hand over hers. "I'm sorry. I wasn't thinking."

"No, it's okay. I got through yesterday and today. I can afford to feel something now. Sometimes the ocean wakes me at night; and when it does, I always wonder if Tom is out there surfing in the dark. I wonder if dead people are able to surf at night."

Hugh took back his hand to emphasize his only intention had been a gesture of sympathy. "We're going to make Wycliffe pay, and pay big. We've got a strong case because we've got Dr. Vannier. And you'll be an excellent witness."

"Thanks. But we don't have anyone to testify that there were two deaths in the clinical trials. And we don't have anyone to say how many died besides Tom after the drug went on the market."

"We'll find someone. Don't worry." Hugh sipped his scotch and watched her face in the flickering light from the heater. Maybe she was ready to tell him what she was hiding. He said, "Sometimes it helps to talk about it."

"About what?" *I'm not going to tell you that I'm a consummate liar about my marriage*, she thought.

"Your face says you're worried about something."

She sighed. "My boss assigned me a new case at the end of October that I didn't want to take."

"Do they give you any choice?"

"It depends. But my docket is full and then some, and I didn't have any room for this one."

"Then why did you get it?"

"Because Millie said she would have given it to Tom if he were alive. Tom was the only person in the office who believed a client could be innocent. So if Millie thought the client was the real deal, she'd give the case to Tom. She said now she only had me, although she's aware I know they are all guilty."

"And did your husband get the innocent ones off?"

"No, of course not. At least, not very often. That's the heartbreaking part of this job, as I told Erin. But Millie was right. Tom would have loved this client and this case. So I had to say yes."

"And is he innocent?"

Kathryn told Hugh about Tyrone. "So, yes, he is innocent," she finished. "But I can't prove it."

"But all you need is the woman he spent the night with."

"Right, and she vanished the minute she heard my investigator was looking for her. She's a prostitute with a rap sheet as long as your arm. She's afraid of being arrested if she's found and subpoenaed to testify. And if we could find her, she'd probably lie anyway and say she never saw Tyrone in her life."

"So she's all you've got?"

"More like, she's all we *don't* have."

"What about that nightclub? Don't those places have surveillance cameras?"

"Most do, but I've got nothing but my own hunch to back that up."

"Can't your investigator check it out?"

"Our investigators are more overworked than we are."

Hugh sipped his scotch thoughtfully for a few minutes. Then he said, "I've got an idea."

"Such as?"

"Let me hire an investigator for you."

"That's very generous, but I couldn't do that."

"Oh, I don't mean me personally. Goldstein, Miller has a pro bono program of sorts. To be honest, it's not as well-developed as I'd like. But we have worked with some of the Innocence Projects on a few cases to help them exonerate clients. The firm would be paying an investigator to work on Tyrone's case. Not me, personally."

She could hear Tom telling her to say 'yes.'

Suddenly there was a light popping sound and something whizzed past her in the dark. She turned but saw nothing and no one. Then the popping resumed, and she realized someone was shooting at them. Bullets were hitting the stone patio all around them. Hugh pulled her to the ground and dragged them both behind one of the massive concrete planters that held the bougainvillea and morning glory vines.

The gunshots continued for what must have been seconds but felt like hours. Suddenly lights came on in the windows overlooking the garden. A woman screamed, and then someone turned on the flood lights illuminating the patio as brightly as the sun.

Jose came running out of the house, followed by Maria, the housekeeper.

"Señor Hugh! Señor Hugh!" They ran toward the planter where Hugh and Kathryn were huddled. Jose reached them first.

"Señor Hugh! Señora Andrews! Are you okay? What happened?"

Hugh slowly unfolded his big body as he stood up. He reached down and gave Kathryn his hand. Her legs were shaking, and she braced herself by holding onto the concrete.

"Someone shot at us," Hugh said to Jose. Maria, who was crying, had come forward to hug him. Hugh lightly stroked her hair and reassured her over and over that he was okay.

Kathryn looked down and saw at least fifteen nine-millimeter casings scattered around the patio. Whoever had been there had meant business.

Hugh reached for his cell phone and dialed 911. The Coronado Police responded within minutes.

* * *

"So you work as a public defender," Detective Richard Rodriguez said thirty minutes later as he interviewed Hugh and

Kathryn in Hugh's study. This time, Kathryn had accepted Hugh's offer of scotch, which she sipped sparingly.

"Yes."

"And you," the detective turned to Hugh. "You represent people who've been hurt by big corporations."

"Something like that."

"So the pair of you have more enemies than you can count."

"Something like that," Kathryn agreed.

"Look, you two are wasting my time. More than likely some gang scum was after you, lady, because you didn't get some guilty shit off. You get what you pay for. Sorry we can't help you."

As the detective strode off toward his unmarked car in disgust, Hugh looked at Kathryn, surprised. She gave him a small smile. "Welcome to the world of being a public defender. You might want to let Erin know before she signs up."

* * *

After the police left, they went into the kitchen where Maria insisted on making scrambled eggs. Hugh wanted her and Jose to eat, too; so the four of them sat down in the breakfast nook and devoured Maria's cooking. Afterward, she cleaned up the kitchen quickly and went back to bed. Jose, too, retired again.

Hugh poured more scotch for himself and Kathryn.

"You have to stay here tonight," he said.

"No, I'll call an Uber."

"I don't mean you should stay just because we've had a fair amount to drink. Even though the good detective blew this off, someone tried to kill you tonight. And it was probably someone who knows you live alone and is just waiting for you to come home."

She drank her scotch in silence for a few minutes, wondering if she should tell him everything. Finally she said, "This isn't the first time this has happened."

"You mean this isn't the first time in your career as a public defender someone has tried to kill you?"

"No. I've been in the office for seventeen years, and nothing like this has ever happened before; but since we filed the suit against Wycliffe, someone has tried twice."

"Why didn't you tell me?" His eyebrows shot up.

"Because the other two attempts looked like accidents, and I convinced myself they were. But now I realize someone wants me dead. Someone who has a lot of time and money to make that happen."

"Then you're staying here tonight for sure."

"There was something else about tonight that was different," Kathryn said. "Whoever was aiming at me was aiming at you, too."

CHAPTER THIRTY

Wednesday, December 3, 2014, Office of the Public Defender, 450 B Street, San Diego

Beth Price stuck her head in Kathryn's door at five-thirty and said, "If you don't need anything else, boss, I'm going home."

Kathryn looked up from the file on her desk and smiled. "No, go on. I'll see you in the morning."

But Beth lingered a moment longer. "Are you sure you're okay after last night? Shouldn't you have taken the day off and rested up?" Beth knew about the shooting because Kathryn had called her to explain why she was late and to tell her to find another attorney in the office to cover her early morning court appearances.

"I'd have just replayed it over and over in my mind if I'd stayed home. Better to come to work where I can't think about it. It's too quiet at my house, and it makes it too easy to brood about things."

"How come you aren't seeing anyone?"

Kathryn thought once again of her disappointing encounter with Dan Ayers. "I don't know. Tom's shoes are hard to fill."

"You can't fill his shoes," Beth said. "You're going to have to create a whole new pair and fill those."

Kathryn gave her a tight little smile. "I'm trying."

Beth disappeared, and Kathryn went back to reading the file. She didn't look up when someone knocked lightly on her open door. She said, "It's okay, Beth. I really don't need anything else from you tonight."

"I'm not Beth," Mark Kelly said.

She looked up, obviously surprised.

"I hope you don't mind. I just wanted to make sure you were all right. Hugh told me what happened. I didn't mean to disturb your work."

She smiled, wishing the sight of him didn't give her that funny feeling in her tummy. "I'm finished for the day. To be honest, I was hanging around to avoid a too-quiet house."

He grinned. "I have the same problem. Maybe we should hang out together. How about dinner at Martini in La Jolla? The food is not quite as spectacular as Per Se, but it's close. And they have live jazz."

"Sounds fantastic."

* * *

In a small, private booth, they lingered over drinks, steak and lobster tartare, and the music of the Chris Sterns Trio in Martini's mahogany and black UpStairs Lounge. Mark asked about her work, and she told him about Tyrone's story and Hugh's offer to hire a private investigator.

"You should take him up on it," Mark said.

They adjourned to a table overlooking the ocean, inky and

mysterious under the luminous disk of the full moon. Silvered by the moonlight, tiny white waves skipped peacefully toward the shore. Kathryn felt as if she had been transported to a magical world created for the two of them alone.

"I have a thing for appetizers," Mark smiled at her as they studied the dinner menu. "Even though we had one in the bar, I've got to order some more."

She laughed. "An appetizer freak. I remember you ordered them all at Bice."

"I'm tempted to do that again."

But eventually he settled on oysters and Point Judith Calamari. "I've got to leave room for the Georges Bank Scallops with truffle macaroni and cheese."

Time seemed to dissolve, along with the real world, as they laughed and talked their way through the exquisite meal. Kathryn was not sure where she could put the Dark Chocolate and Crushed Toffee S'Mores Mark had just ordered along with coffee, but she was happy for the extra time with him. The terror of the evening before no longer hung over her like a cloud.

"You're not holding up your end of the dessert bargain," he complained.

"I realize that. But I can't eat another bite. This place may not be Per Se, but it's close."

"Told you." His face grew serious, and he dropped his light, bantering tone. "I've got to ask you something important."

"What?"

"Are you sure you want to go on with this case?"

She frowned. The wine was making her think a lot more

about what it would be like to kiss him in the candlelight. "I don't understand."

"There have been three attempts on your life. And now one on Hugh's as well."

"The police thought it was some of my gang clients after me."

"The police were a bunch of jerks who didn't want to do their job because you're a public defender."

"Well, that, too." She smiled at him. "I told Hugh he should warn Erin before she signs up with our office."

"Look, Kathryn, I think you should take these attempts seriously."

"I do, but there's nothing I can do about them."

"You might want to consider dropping this suit."

"But we have Dr. Vannier's testimony to establish that the drug wasn't safe. And you and Hugh have said that we'll find someone who'll be willing to testify about the cover-up of those two deaths in the clinical trials and who can tell us exactly how many people have died since Myrabin was approved. I'm sure Tom wasn't the only one."

"I agree that we have some strong evidence, but our case isn't bulletproof. You know as well as I do that litigation is never anything but a crap shoot. Besides, what I'm saying has nothing to do with winning or losing. It has to do with staying alive."

"I haven't been too attached to that notion since Tom died."

* * *

December 3, 2014 Midnight, Crown Manor, Coronado

Hugh lay on the floor in his old-man pajamas, awkwardly trying to do leg raises to strengthen his back. It hurt from all the hours he'd been sitting in chairs in conference rooms taking depositions. His last scotch of the night sat beside him on the floor. Buffy knocked and opened the door at the same moment. He was annoyed to be found in such an undignified position. She had come straight to his room from the airport because she was still wearing her travel clothes.

He mustered what dignity he could as he got up and picked up his scotch.

"Want one?"

"I do." She was angry. Buffy never drank scotch unless she was furious.

Hugh handed her the drink and sat down in one of the small chairs across from his sofa, bracing himself for the onslaught. Buffy, who was opposed to wearing fur, slipped out of her nevertheless-expensive faux mink coat and sat down opposite him on the couch.

"She was here last night!"

"She?"

"Don't play me, Hugh. Kathryn Andrews was here. She ate breakfast in the kitchen *with you* this morning!"

He adopted the calm professional tone he used in the face of hysterical opposing counsel. He always enjoyed being the only rational one in the room. He was going to enjoy putting Buffy in her place.

"Your spies seem to be everywhere."

"I have a right to know what goes on in my house when I'm not in it."

"Well, did your spies tell you someone tried to kill both of us last night, and that's why Kathryn slept here? She slept in Erin's pajamas in Erin's room. She did not sleep with me. And she ate a single scrambled egg that Maria made for her this morning and was gone by nine. She was trying to keep another attorney from having to cover all of her court appearances this morning. She's not Logan, Buffy. She doesn't come into the office when she wants and leave when she wants because all she has to do is sift through documents all day. Kathryn is not a blue-chip paralegal with an Ivy League law degree. She's a hardworking lawyer with people's lives in her hands."

"So she doesn't have time for you." Buffy's sarcasm mocked him. She took a long drink of scotch. And then another. She was so angry her hands were shaking.

"No, she doesn't. She has neither the time nor the interest in me."

"And so that's why she was here in the middle of the night to get herself shot at, because she has no time and no interest in you." She polished off her scotch too fast and got up to pour herself another.

Now Hugh was angry because he'd been cornered. Since he believed his own inflated reputation, he often underestimated Buffy's intelligence and wound up humiliated and on the losing side of arguments with her. He was going to find whoever had ratted him out and fire the son-of-a-bitch. Jose. It had to be Jose because he and Maria were the only people in the house last night. And Hugh could trust Maria with his life. But then he realized Jose was new, and he'd fallen for Buffy's seemingly innocent questions on the way back from the airport. No, he wouldn't fire him. Instead, he'd train him to avoid Buffy's interrogations and to have Maria's unswerving loyalty.

"Mark, Kathryn, Patty, and I went to the Grant Grill after her deposition was over to celebrate. She did well. We ate snack food and junk. I asked her back to have something healthy with me. She was going home to an empty house. I was going home to an empty house. It was just a friendly gesture."

"Ha! When did Hugh Mahoney *ever* make a friendly gesture to an attractive woman that wasn't meant to be an invitation to sex?"

"She's a *client*, Buffy. She's a damn *client*. I can't sleep with her. I don't want to lose my license to practice, for God's sake!"

"Oh, come on. The bar's disciplinary committee is full of horny old men like you. They wouldn't disbar you for sleeping with a beautiful woman. They'd congratulate you."

"That's disgusting and untrue. You've had too much to drink. Go sleep it off."

She turned and scooped up her coat with the hand that wasn't holding the newly- poured drink. "Good night, then, Hugh. But just remember, if you don't stop cheating and if you don't run for Fred's seat, I'm going to embarrass you on every talk show in the country. Edith's publicist is just itching to line up the dates."

* * *

Hugh was shaking with rage by the time Buffy swept out of his room. He finished off his scotch and poured yet another. He paced back and forth, taking long, deep breaths and trying not to think about how high his blood pressure was. So much for avoiding stress.

As he felt his heart rate come down, the cold pain of disappointment and despair settled around him. He went over to the locked drawer of his bureau, found the key, and opened it. His pulse began to race again as he took out the small, square blue Tiffany box. He opened it, and the emeralds sparkled green fire in the low light. Four carats, fifty thousand dollars worth of pure passion suspended from delicate strands of diamonds. He'd snuck away from work this morning, and taken a cab to Fashion Valley. He didn't trust Jose with this secret. In fact, he didn't trust anyone.

Having her in the house last night had driven him mad. He could not forget those haunting seconds when he'd sheltered her in his arms, behind the planter, while the bullets flew around them. In his mind, love for a beautiful woman was always expressed by gifts of jewels. He'd learned that from his mother, who'd cherished the few diamond chips his father had managed to give her over the course of their marriage. She'd shown Hugh pictures in magazines of the jewels the dethroned king Edward VIII had showered on Wallis Simpson, the "woman he loved," and she'd told him the shining stones told the story of deep, abiding passion.

Buffy and his daughters were the only women Hugh had given jewels. Mistresses got cars and houses and partnerships. But mistress were about sex, not love. What he felt for Kathryn Andrews went so far beyond anything he had ever felt for anyone in his life that he had no words to describe it. He gazed at the earrings and imagined them dangling from her ears, making her eyes that shade of deep green that he loved. He knew he could never give these to her. Just buying and hiding them like this was dangerous. But he'd had to find an outlet for the emotions that were threatening to overwhelm him that morning.

He had lingered over the emerald rings before accepting the fact that he couldn't go that far. He knew from his mother that emeralds were the symbol of true love. Wallis Simpson's emerald engagement ring had been almost twenty carats. Now he knew what that kind of love felt like. But even if he, like Edward, offered to give up his kingdom for her, Kathryn, unlike Wallis, would never say yes.

He sighed and closed the box and locked it away again. He turned out all the lights except the one by his bed. He climbed under the covers and thoughtfully sipped the rest of his scotch. Then he turned off his lamp and dreamed of the way Kathryn's eyes would light up if only he could hand her the pale blue Tiffany box.

CHAPTER THIRTY-ONE

Monday, January 5, 2015, Juvenile Hall, Meadowlark Drive, San Diego

The rain didn't help Kathryn's mood as she pulled into the parking lot that morning at eight-thirty. She had returned yesterday from spending Christmas and New Year's with her mother in Florida. She'd accepted the invitation because traveling solo to one of the places she used to go with Tom, like Cancun or Rosarito, was depressingly out of the question. But listening to Helen and Graham Ellis finish each others' sentences the way she and Tom once did depressed her far more than traveling alone would have done. Big mistake. And now it was Monday; and she was still jet-lagged, with a headache and bad news for Tyrone.

He was waiting for her in the attorney-client conference room. Slumped in his gray scrubs in the gray metal chair, his skinny body looked like a gigantic piece of crumpled paper.

"Good morning, Tyrone."

"How 'ya doin', Miz Andrews?"

"A little wet," Kathryn smiled as she took off her overcoat and folded it over a spare chair.

"That investigator man find anything to help my case?"

"Yes and no."

"How can it be both?" He frowned.

"Well, yes, because he discovered Tamara's last name is Lopez, and he found the apartment where you spent the night with her. It's at Friar's Court Apartments, about ten blocks from The Rendevous."

"Was she there?"

"I'm afraid that's the 'no' part. She's been gone since the end of October."

"Just as soon as she found out you were looking for her."

"More likely she moved because the police were looking for her. But, either way, she's not available to help us."

Tyrone's fourteen-year-old eyes, once bright with hope, went blank. "Never mind, Miz Andrews. I tole you from the first, I got no chance."

"We're not giving up, Tyrone."

"I'm facing life, ain't I?"

"Maybe. That's a complicated question right now for someone under eighteen. The United States Supreme Court has said a life sentence can't be automatic for juveniles. They have to consider you and the circumstances."

Tyrone shook his head, "Won't do me no good. The circumstances is I'm a Crip. Courts think all Crips are bad."

"The court has to give you a fair trial and a fair sentencing decision based upon you as an individual. That means the court can't write you off as just a Crip."

But he shook his head once more. "Won't do no good, Miz Andrews. I'm never gonna get out of here."

* * *

Monday, January 13, 2015, The Four Seasons, Georgetown, Washington D.C.

Hugh gazed across the table at Logan Avery in the golden glow of the Four Seasons' renowned restaurant, Bourbon Steak. Predictably, she'd been quick to accept his dinner invitation, and she'd worn a body-hugging black sheath that revealed lots of cleavage. Her brown eyes gazed at him seductively as she toyed with the olive in her martini glass. She obviously expected an after-dinner invitation to join him in his suite.

"How did it go today on the Hill?" she purred.

"Senator Worth from New York was a jerk, but I expected that. Big corporations are the major funding sources for all his campaigns. He was leading the charge to make it harder to sue on behalf of small shareholders and people who've been injured by the death of a loved one like Kathryn Andrews."

"So exactly what would this proposed bill do?" Logan finished her martini and signaled the waiter for another without registering any emotion when he mentioned Kathryn to his great relief.

"It would allow defendant corporations to move to summary judgment before they produce discovery to a plaintiff. Exactly what Wycliffe tried in the Andrews' case. If this bill passes, the big guys could get a small plaintiff's case thrown out before it has even had a decent chance to get started."

Logan made a face. "Wouldn't be good for us."

"Not good at all," Hugh agreed.

The waiter appeared, and Hugh ordered a hundred-dollar rib eye while Logan went for seared tuna with foie gras, pommes dauphinoise, and truffles.

"Do you think it will pass?" Logan took a long sip of the new martini and leaned over slightly to allow Hugh to see more of what her low-cut gown revealed.

"It's a substantial risk. Brian Hampton, our lobbyist, says the pharmaceutical and tech giants are pouring money into the pockets of all the members of Congress who will take it from them."

"The bill is aimed at you personally, isn't it?" Logan began to play with the olive again with her long, red lacquered nails.

Hugh nodded. "Quite a compliment, in a way."

"They're terrified of you."

He grinned. "They are. And I love it."

"So what are you going to do?"

"I'm having breakfast with Hal in the morning."

"Hal as in the president?"

"Yes. I'm going to promise him a ten-million dollar contribution for his re-election campaign if he'll veto it."

"But that's illegal!"

"Not if I get the right people to front the money and divide it into legal donations."

Logan laughed. "I should have known you'd find a way around the law."

Hugh shrugged. "I'm a lawyer. My job is to get results for my client. In this case, I am the client. If Congress passes this legislation, it will hurt the work we do."

"To the little guy!" Logan held up her martini.

Hugh smiled and condescendingly clinked his scotch so the cheesy moment would pass quickly. For all the polish Logan had acquired at the University of Virginia, sometimes her small-town, Kentucky backwater upbringing still showed.

Their entrees arrived, and they devoted themselves to their expensive meal. But predictably Logan took several bites of her sixty-two dollar fish creation and put down her fork. For as long as Hugh had been involved with her, he had been painfully aware of her eating disorder.

She was now nursing her glass of Château Cheval Blanc, ignoring her plate. "How are things going with Kathryn Andrews' case?"

"Very well. We have a March 2 trial date."

"So it's going to trial? You can't settle it?"

"Wycliffe remains wedded to its offer of two million. They won't go any higher. Her case is worth a lot more than that."

Logan tossed her long blonde hair and threw back her head, eyeing Hugh challengingly. "What if it isn't? What if she and the sainted-public-defender-husband weren't so happily married?"

"Mark talked to the horses' mouth on that one. Paul Curtis swears they were the happiest couple on earth."

"Really?" Logan's voice dripped with sarcasm.

"Do you know something Paul Curtis doesn't? He grew up with Tom and introduced him to Kathryn, and he claims to know all their secrets."

"I don't know Paul, although I wish I did. He's to-die-for gorgeous. I've seen him hanging out at P & J's Brewery on Friday nights. But I could never manage to get an intro."

"I'm sure if you'd walked up to him, he'd have been very glad to introduce himself."

Logan smiled, awash in what she interpreted as Hugh's admiration. "My mistake then. He is rich and gorgeous. The ex-wife was a fool to throw that one back."

Hugh waved at the waiter for more scotch. He realized if he got too far into his cups, he might make the mistake of asking Logan upstairs for the night.

"So you have your sights set on Paul Curtis now?" He grinned although he felt a sharp stab of jealousy despite the fact sleeping with her would entangle him in an affair he didn't want to resume.

"No. Didn't I tell you? I've met someone!" She gave him a triumphant smile that said *I've won the last and final round.*

"Congratulations. Who is he?" Hugh's jealousy meter began to register in the discomfort zone.

Logan beamed. "Travis Eliot Davidson, III. Assistant U.S. Attorney, Brown University, Fulbright Scholar, and Harvard Law."

Hugh smiled in defeat. After all, Hugh Mahoney was only a top graduate of a good state law school, although his claim to fame was being the most hated and feared plaintiff's attorney in the United States. And now Big Business was shelling out millions to the members of Congress to shut him down.

"I'm glad you're happy."

"What about you?" Logan gave him her disingenuous smile. "How are you doing with Kathryn Andrews?"

"Kathryn is a client. I don't have dating relationships with my clients."

"Well, let's just say you haven't *yet*."

"Logan!"

But she knew she had pushed him too far, and it was time to change the subject. "So you think you've got a pretty solid case against Wycliffe?"

"There have been some interesting developments."

"Such as?"

"We've discovered a cover-up of two Myrabin deaths during the clinical trials that should have halted the approval process."

Logan's eyes grew big. "They'll want to settle, then, to avoid all the negative press."

"Maybe. But as I told you, they haven't yet made an offer I could recommend to Kathryn."

"Are you going to try the case?"

"I'm second chair. Mark's taking the lead. Juries like him much better than they like me."

Logan suddenly leaned back and shifted from seductress to lawyer. "You know you've got evidence of a criminal conspiracy to cover-up the number of deaths."

Hugh nodded. "I've thought of that. The trouble is, we don't know who the U.S. Attorney should indict because we don't know who ordered the cover-up. We're working on finding out."

"Well, when you do, let me know, and I'll pass the name along to Travis. A case like that would make his career as a prosecutor."

CHAPTER THIRTY-TWO

Wednesday, January 14, 2015, The White House, Washington, D.C.

"It's always good to see you," the President of the United States said next morning as they sat in Chippendale chairs over bacon, eggs, fruit and toast in the Oval Office Private Dining Room under the portrait of Lincoln and his generals. Hugh had visited Hal Edwards here more times than he could count. "What brings you to town?"

"Testifying against the Worth Litigation Reform Act." Hugh wondered how Hal kept his California tan in the depths of East Coast winter.

"Ah, of course." The president nodded his expensively coifed head of dark hair. "Edith sends her regards by the way. How's Buffy?"

"Determined to make me run for Fred Akers' Senate seat when you give him a cabinet appointment in your next term. She and Edith have it all figured out."

"You sound bitter."

"I'm a lawyer, not a politician."

"Are you still seeing that hot blonde associate, what's-her-name?"

"Logan Avery. She's been transferred to our D.C. office. No, that's over on both sides. Amiably."

"So who's the new woman in your life?"

"There isn't one." Hugh thought of Kathryn longingly as he spoke. "Buffy was upset about me taking Logan to your private fundraiser. As penance, I have to give up mistresses and make her a senator's wife."

"But wasn't there an incident with a public defender, late at night at your place? Some of her clients were taking potshots at the two of you. Or so the paper said."

"I didn't know that made the papers."

"Just the little, local Coronado one. My staff goes over all that stuff for news about my major campaign donors, trying to make sure I don't do anything stupid and step on their toes. There was a picture of her. She's gorgeous."

"And she's also a client. It was a business meeting." Hugh realized how unlikely that sounded. But Hal moved on to other subjects to his great relief.

"Some people would say you as the plaintiff have the unfair advantage in that kind of litigation. You can bring a suit without any hard evidence of fraud or wrongdoing and then poke around in their corporate documents until you find any little rash statement by an employee or an executive to exaggerate into a million-dollar verdict."

Hugh shrugged. "People say all kinds of things. I don't care what people say. I care about protecting the little guy against those corporate bastards who have bought out Worth and his cronies to give them an unfair advantage in future litigation."

"So you've come to buy me out. You want me to veto the Worth Act if it passes?"

"I've got ten million dollars broken into entirely legal campaign contributions from my partners to re-elect the People's President whose agenda is to keep the courts open to the average citizen. I wouldn't call that a buyout, but you can if you want to."

Hal sipped coffee from a flowery china cup and considered the offer. "I like that as a campaign slogan, 'the People's President.'"

"It's all yours. Supported by a veto of the Worth Act."

"Okay, Hugh. It's a deal. But tell me, doesn't Buffy's suggestion to take down your shingle sound even a little bit attractive? You've had lot of years being a corporate terror."

He grinned. "No, I love it too much."

"But what about Buffy?"

"You know about her scheme with Edith to blackmail me to run for Fred's seat?"

Hal nodded. "I take it you don't want to be a senator."

"I'm not a politician, Hal."

"What else do you think you might like to do?"

"I'd like to be on the Supreme Court."

"You'd be my first choice, but the current justices are young and in good health. I don't expect any vacancies in the next four years. Since Congress doesn't appeal to you, how about something pleasant, but not stressful, like the ambassadorship to England? Or France?"

Hugh sipped his own coffee and created a momentary

fantasy of himself married to Kathryn and living in the American Ambassador's residence in Paris. But that, of course, was an impossible pipe dream. Still, being Madame Ambassador would make Buffy happy and keep him out of Congress.

"I'd seriously consider the job, Hal, if you made me the offer."

CHAPTER THIRTY-THREE

Monday, February 2, 2015, Office of the Public Defender, 450 B Street, San Diego

"You know it's the best deal he's going to get," Sam McIntyre said at five o'clock that afternoon.

Kathryn had started to go home without taking his call. He was one of the more reasonable deputy district attorneys and therefore more willing to offer her clients a decent deal, but the thought of having to bargain away Tyrone's innocence made her stomach churn.

"Twenty-five-years-to-life is a long sentence."

"He'd be eligible for parole by age forty."

"He's only fourteen, Sam. By that time, he'd have spent his entire adult life in prison where he'd get a lousy academic education and maybe a smatter of vocational training in something like welding. He'd wind up on the streets, homeless."

"So you think he should go to trial, get convicted, and spend the rest of his life in prison where at least he'd get three meals a day and medical care."

"He's innocent, Sam."

THE DEATH OF DISTANT STARS

"Sure, they all are."

"No, they're not. You know me better than that. I don't make claims I believe aren't true."

"Sorry. I apologize. You've always been very straight with me. And I honestly can't remember when I've heard you say your client is flat-out innocent."

"Then maybe you'll listen this time. This kid didn't do it."

"Let me hear some evidence, then."

"That's the problem, Sam. He's got an alibi, but the witness disappeared. She's legit, but she's also a scared prostitute-on-the-run."

"Well, without that witness, there's no alibi."

"But he's not one of the robbers on the surveillance video. I know because he spent the night with the woman. All the details of his story check out. We just can't find the witness."

"There's no guarantee the jury will believe her."

"And there's no guarantee they won't. I don't like telling an innocent client to plead."

"Well, I can't drop this case on your word he's got an alibi."

"I wasn't suggesting that. But what about letting him plead to manslaughter, low term of three years?"

"You're kidding. A man is dead."

"But Tyrone didn't kill him."

"Well, I can talk to my boss, but I'm pretty sure he won't buy it. And if he did buy it, he'd want the high term, eleven years."

"But he's a kid with no priors."

"Maybe I could sell the mid-term of six years. Look, I hear you, Kathryn. But you know the offers come from Upstairs.

And right now, Upstairs will be running for re-election next fall, and Upstairs can't appear soft on crime. This case involved a tourist and generated a fair amount of media coverage."

"So Tyrone has to be a martyr to your boss's political ambitions?"

"Our entire office is martyr to his political ambitions. Our work has very little to do with justice. You know that."

"Try to get three years, if you can. I could recommend that to Tyrone."

"Okay. I'll get back to you. But don't hold your breath."

Kathryn put the phone down and considered going home. It had been a long day, and she was tired. She very much doubted the higher-ups in Sam's office would offer Tyrone a decent deal.

She sat back in her chair and stared at the bleak concrete city landscape outside her window. She missed Tom so much it hurt. They were exactly one month from the start date of the trial, and they didn't know who had ordered the cover-up of the clinical trial deaths or how many people had died after Myrabin had been approved.

On impulse, she picked up the phone and dialed Joe Sanders, the private investigator Goldstein, Miller had hired to help in Tyrone's case. He was a middle-aged ex-cop in a forever rumpled dark brown gray suit. But he was a good, unbiased investigator who had no problem working for the defense. "Hey, Kathryn. You read my mind. I was going to call you today."

Her heart sped up, hoping for good news. "Have you found something that helps Tyrone?"

"Yes and no."

"Tell me the no part first."

"I found Tamara Lopez. She's in state prison in Texas for drug possession and sales. Fifteen years. She's not going to be out anytime soon."

"I could get a court order to bring her here to testify."

"Wouldn't do any good. She's afraid of being killed in prison for snitching. No way she's going to testify."

"Did you at least talk to her?"

"I did, and I learned something you'll like."

"Okay. The good news, then."

"The Rendevous does, indeed, have a surveillance system."

Kathryn felt her heart lighten. "Did you get the tapes? Do they help us?"

"I didn't get them. The police did. They questioned Tamra at the club the day after the murder. They questioned Ray-Ray, too. And they took the video tapes."

"So where are they?"

"No one knows. The cops still have them. But Tamara said she and Tyrone were selling cocaine all night until the Rendevous closed. Then they did a few sales in the parking lot before spending the night at her house. And the surveillance cameras covered both the inside and the outside of the club."

"So Tyrone has some exposure for possession for sale?"

"According to Tamara. But that beats life-without-parole murder any day."

"Agreed." Kathryn drummed her fingers on her desk as she thought about this new development. "But she won't testify?"

"No way. She'd incriminate herself on the drug charge if she did."

"Then what exactly do we have to work with?"

"Not much yet. But be patient. I'm going to find out if Ray-Ray had a backup camera doing surveillance that night.

"If he did, and Tyrone is on that video, the cops have failed to turn over evidence that demonstrates our client is innocent. Maybe Sam McIntyre isn't such a good guy after all."

"Hold on," Joe cautioned. "We don't know if they've withheld *Brady* evidence yet. And it's too soon to blame the prosecutor. Look, as you know, I used to be a cop. Some of my partners didn't tell the D.A. everything."

"Okay, I'll let Sam off the hook for now. But I'm hoping there's another tape, and Tyrone is on it."

"Me, too," Joe said. "Me, too."

TRIAL

CHAPTER THIRTY-FOUR

Monday, March 16, 2015, Edward J. Schwartz Federal Courthouse, U.S. District Court, Southern District of California, San Diego, 9:00 a.m.

Mark and Hugh had chosen Millie Fletcher as their first witness. It had taken two weeks to select a jury, both sides heavily dependent upon the advice of their juror selection consultants. Kathryn had watched and listened as their psychological guru, Roger M. Thompson, Ph.D., rendered various opinions about which potential jurors looked sympathetic to their side. Above all, Bob McLaren was trying to keep women and men in their mid-thirties and early forties off the jury.

The final panel was evenly split between male and female. McLaren had managed to get four corporate executives on the jury, presumably because they would favor Wycliffe. Hugh and Mark had stood firm for the inclusion of a forty-something accountant and a fifty-something retired school teacher. They also had a thirty-something mom who was going back to school. But McLaren had relentlessly bumped off the three nurses they had wanted very much to keep.

During opening arguments, when Mark had played a montage of slides from Tom's life, Kathryn had felt all the jurors' eyes on her, sympathetic and curious. As the images rolled by, tears welled up in her own eyes and overflowed. Tom, tall and blonde, his athletic body perfectly outlined by his wetsuit, poised on his board to ride the waves. The two of them gazing at each other on their wedding day. Tom in his best going-to-court suit, threading his way through the throngs of reporters at the Pepe Jackson murder trial. The two of them in Paris on their fifth anniversary. Pictures from trips to Rosarito and Cancun. The life she'd had and loved flashed before her eyes on the courtroom's big screen, and she realized she still loved Tom too much to let go and move on.

Millie now sat poised and ready to testify. Kathryn knew that suit, the black and white no-nonsense tweed she wore on really important occasions. Hugh, sitting next to Kathryn at the plaintiff's table, fingered the blue box in his pocket and envied the way she kept her eyes fixed on Mark. He wished he were first chair so that she'd be looking at him right now.

"Please state your name for the record." Mark looked relaxed and confident as he began.

"Mildred Allen Fletcher."

"And what do you do for a living?"

"I am the Head of the Public Defender's Office in San Diego County."

"And how long have you been with the public defender's office?"

"Twenty-eight years. I've been head of the office for the past fifteen."

"And did you know Thomas Allen Andrews?"

"Yes. He was a Senior Public Defender. He joined my office in 1997 with his wife, Kathryn."

Millie's eyes met Kathryn's but showed no emotion.

"And was there something unusual about the Andrews?"

"We've had couples in the office before, but it's been a long time. We've never had a couple who went to Harvard."

"So it's unusual to have Harvard graduates in your office?"

"Yes. They can make so much more money in other jobs. Normally, we can't attract them."

"So why did Tom and Kathryn decide to join you?"

"Tom was the chief instigator, and Kathryn followed him. He felt they could do more good by serving the people who couldn't afford a lawyer."

"And did Tom Andrews fulfill that ambition? Did he serve the poor?"

"Without any doubt." Millie nodded her head for emphasis. "He was tireless in his efforts to help his clients. He was one of *the* best, if not the best, defender in our office."

"Aside from you, of course?" Mark smiled, and she smiled back.

"I believe in what I do, of course."

"Now tell me what sort of employee Tom was."

"Exemplary."

"Not even one single bad habit?"

"Well, maybe one. He liked to surf. He'd been an international champion in high school. On mornings when he didn't have to appear in court, he would surf before work. Sometimes that made him late."

"Not much of a vice?"

Millie smiled. "Not at all."

"Do you remember when Tom became ill?"

She took a sip of water from the plastic cup sitting on the edge of the witness stand. "Yes. It was in the spring, three years ago. We thought he had food poisoning. He went home early because he was nauseous."

"Was Tom under any additional stress that you were aware of in the months before he died?"

"Well, the job of a public defender is always stressful," Millie observed. "But Tom had a very high-profile murder case that began in February of 2012 and ended in March. I know he was under a great deal of stress during that trial."

Mark gave her a friendly smile. "You mean more than the stress a trial lawyer feels during a trial?"

"Yes."

"What made this trial different?"

"Pepe Jackson was accused of killing a San Diego police officer who had pulled a gun on Pepe during a routine traffic stop and threatened to kill him. Tom believed Pepe was innocent. The law enforcement community let everyone including the prosecutor know how unhappy they would be if Pepe was acquitted. Tom was under great stress to try to get Pepe a fair trial. He was facing a life without parole sentence, if convicted."

"And was Pepe convicted, Mrs. Fletcher?"

"No. It was Tom's greatest victory, in my opinion."

Kathryn could feel the sigh of relief from the jurors at this news. Good, they were hooked by Tom's story.

"Now Mrs. Fletcher, if Tom had lived, how do you think his career would have progressed in your office?"

Millie smiled and said in her soft, but powerful voice, the voice that could mesmerize a jury, "He would have had my job. Without doubt. Tom was the finest attorney in our office at the time of his death. And I would not hesitate to add, probably the best who ever worked for us."

"Thank you, Mrs. Fletcher." Mark smiled at her as she left the podium. Kathryn sensed that the jurors were enthralled. So far so good. She wondered if Tom's spirit were hovering above them in his cheap Men's Wearhouse suit, listening.

Bob McLaren took his time settling at the podium that Mark had just vacated. The jurors grew restless and looked around the courtroom instead of at Millie still on the stand. *Bad idea to lose the jury's attention,* Kathryn thought.

Finally McLaren looked up at Millie and gave her what could only be called a cheesy smile. "Tell me, Mrs. Fletcher, what did you observe about the Andrews' marriage?"

"They were exceptionally close."

"They got along then? At least at work?"

"They got along period." Millie knew better than to let him push her buttons, but her voice was firm and invited no doubts. "At work and at home."

"So you were a guest in their home?"

"Of course."

Those Christmas parties, Kathryn thought. No one had seen Shannon's excessive attachment to Tom. No one but her.

"And what about extramarital affairs? By either party?"

"None!" Millie shot the word across the courtroom, leaving

311

no doubt she was accurate and correct.

"No further questions," Bob McLaren said, and sat down.

Our first witness went well, Kathryn thought with a sigh of relief.

* * *

Mark called Paul Curtis after lunch. Hugh fingered the box of emeralds in his pocket and was consumed with jealousy as Paul described meeting Kathryn at Harvard in 1994 and his feelings for her, but how her meeting with Tom had left him out of the romantic picture. As Paul talked, Hugh thought about the night he'd met Kathryn. If only he hadn't been slightly drunk and hadn't had an equally sloshed Logan hanging on his arm. His fingers worked rapidly back and forth over the smooth little box in his pocket, which had become part talisman, part symbol of his greatest wish. He was happy the jury was hanging on Paul's every word. He was a handsome guy, Hugh reflected. Just the sort he could picture with Kathryn. Tall, blonde, confident. A lot like her husband. Did her heart lie in that direction? He couldn't tell from her expression as she listened to Paul's testimony. Deposition training had given her a real knack for a poker face.

Kathryn herself grew jealous as Mark took Paul through Tom's early life and had him tell the stories of all the years she had not been able to share with him. He explained their elementary school days of just hanging at the beach; their decision, when they reached middle school, to work on become surfing champions; and finally Tom's decision to give up competitive surfing altogether when he met Kathryn.

"He loved her. He really, really loved her." Paul looked straight at Kathryn as he spoke. She knew he wanted her to forgive him, but so far she hadn't been able to.

"So you were not aware of any problems in their marriage?" Mark asked.

"None at all."

* * *

As with Millie, it took Bob McLaren an exceptionally long time to settle himself at the podium for cross-examination.

Not surprisingly, he began with another cheesy smile. "So I gather you knew the deceased?"

"I did."

"And you say there were no problems in his marriage?"

"That's right."

"Who is Steve Cooper?" McLaren asked. Kathryn felt her stomach tighten.

"Steve grew up with me and Tom. The three of us were like brothers."

"But Mr. Cooper is no longer with us, is he?"

"Steve died in August, after Tom died in June."

"And how did he die, Mr. Curtis?"

"He drowned."

"But wasn't he an expert surfer?"

"Even experts have accidents."

"And did Mr. Cooper have a girlfriend?" Bob McLaren asked. Kathryn's blood ran cold.

Mark stood up. "Objection, Your Honor. Mr. Cooper's personal life is irrelevant."

Judge Weiner nodded. "Exactly, counselor. Move on."

"Your Honor, if you'll permit me two more questions, I can connect this up and show how it is relevant."

"Very well. But no more than two. Would the reporter please read back the last question?"

Through her rising tide of panic, Kathryn watched the reporter find the correct place in her notes and read the last question, "Did Mr. Cooper have a girlfriend?"

"Steve had a lot of girlfriends. He was a very attractive guy."

"But was there one in particular at the time of his death?"

Paul looked McLaren straight in the eye and said, "No."

"Okay, Mr. McLaren," Judge Weiner intoned from the bench, "that's enough fishing. Move on!"

CHAPTER THIRTY-FIVE

Monday, March 16, 2015, The Offices of Goldstein, Miller, Emerald Shapery Center, San Diego, 6 p.m.

Kathryn sat at the table in the small conference room, sipping a glass of red wine and listening to Hugh and Mark post-mortem the first day of trial. Hugh was drinking his usual scotch. Mark was sipping coffee. He smiled at her as he poured cream into the cup.

"Going to have a long night getting ready for tomorrow."

"Who do we have tomorrow?" Hugh asked.

"Bruce Myers and Karl Martin, although I don't think we'll get to Karl until Wednesday. I expect McLaren is going to go after Bruce pretty hard on his conclusion that Myrabin caused Tom's death. It's technical stuff, so I have to do a lot of preparation tonight."

Hugh nodded. "Makes sense."

Kathryn watched him pour himself another scotch from the carafe on the drinks tray in the center of the table. Mark frowned. "Hey, go easy on that."

Hugh laughed. "Jose is driving, thanks to you. We've had a long day; I'm entitled." He looked over at Kathryn as he spoke, and she realized not only did he want her approval, but he was desperately sad and lonely. *Poor man. He's gained the world and lost his own soul,* she thought. She smiled back and tried to damp down her nerves about McLaren's cross-examination of Paul.

It was as if Hugh had read her mind. "Hey, McLaren's desperate already! Fishing around about Steve Cooper and some unknown girlfriend. Judge Weiner really put him in his place on that one. Just stabbing in the dark to confuse the jury. Hah!"

Kathryn's stomach knotted at the same time she realized Hugh's scotch was talking. Her phone vibrated, and she looked down to see a text from Paul.

"Don't worry. It's under control. Want to talk?

She hit reply and wrote, "Yes. Can you come by the house tonight at 7:30?"

He responded, "Bad idea. They're watching your place. My house, as soon as you finish up there."

She hit reply once more, "Okay."

She looked up to find Mark's eyes on her. "Bad news?"

"No. Its just my investigator with a report on something he's found for one of my clients."

"Then we should wrap up," Mark said. "I've got to start preparing for tomorrow. We can be happy about how it went today."

* * *

Monday, March 16, 2015, 817 First Street, Coronado, California, 7:30 p.m.

Paul opened the door, and she fell into his arms. Her heart was racing. All the panic she had fought back since the moment in the courtroom when Bob McLaren began to ask questions about

Steve overwhelmed her. Tears poured down her cheeks, and she gasped for breath between sobs.

Paul patted her back and said softly over and over, "It's okay. It's okay. Don't worry, it's okay."

She cried for a long time. All the tension of the months leading up to trial overwhelmed her, and she lost control. Finally she pulled away slightly and looked into Paul's soft, blue eyes.

"I'm sorry."

"Don't be." He pulled her to him again and stroked her hair. "I understand why you're upset, but don't worry. They don't know about Shannon."

"How can you be sure?"

"Wait! First things first. Have you eaten?"

"No. I can't."

"At least try. You know what a rotten cook I am. But I can scramble eggs. Come on."

Paul made passable eggs and toast and poured a Cabernet that made up for what the food lacked. They sat at the island in the kitchen and ate. Slowly Kathryn's blood pressure and heart rate came back to normal.

"Better?" Paul smiled across his empty plate.

She nodded. "Thanks."

"Hey, that's what I'm here for."

"You did a great job for us today."

"It was all true. You were Tom's only love."

"But why was McLaren asking about Shannon?"

"He didn't mention Shannon by name, and she wasn't Steve's girlfriend when he died. She'd been moved out of his place since January."

"True. But I'm nervous because he was fishing."

"I know. But I'm telling you, no one but you and I know about Shannon. And neither of us is telling Wycliffe."

She smiled. The wine was making her relaxed and sleepy. "Okay. I feel better now."

"Good. Let's go into the living room and watch something on Netflix. It will take your mind off things."

"No, I should go home. I'm exhausted. Thanks, though."

Paul's face became serious. "Listen, call me paranoid or whatever, but I don't want you at home tonight by yourself."

She frowned. "What?"

"I've got a hunch. A feeling. Like the one I had the day Steve died. Stay here tonight. Please."

"You think someone might try to kill me?"

"Haven't they already? More than once? Wycliffe got a pretty good look at your case today. And it's very solid. Please, Kathryn."

"But I didn't bring any clothes with me!"

"Court doesn't start until 9 in the morning. You'll have time to go home and change. Besides, you don't need to be alone tonight. You need someone to take your mind off of things."

She smiled, and remembered this was Paul, who loved her and who was her last living link to Tom. "Okay. Thanks."

* * *

Tuesday, March 17, 2015, 1845 Ocean Place, Pacific Beach

Kathryn opened her red front door, framed by the white roses, at seven the next morning. She had slept soundly in Paul's guest room, and she'd decided to forgive him for everything. It took her all of ten seconds to realize her house had been turned upside down. In terror, she ran to the guest room where she found the box of Shannon's letters was missing.

CHAPTER THIRTY-SIX

Tuesday, March 17, 2015, 1845 Ocean Place, Pacific Beach

She had to be calm, she told herself as she stared at the empty drawer in Tom's desk. She had to be at court in two hours. She couldn't let anyone see she was rattled.

She fished her cell phone out of her purse and called Paul.

"Hey, Kath. What's up?"

"Someone broke into the house last night." Despite her best efforts, her voice quivered.

"Are you okay? Are you sure there's not someone still inside?"

The thought hadn't occurred to her. She'd been completely focused on the loss of Shannon's letters. "I'm shaken up. But I'm okay. I don't see any sign that anyone is still here."

"You should call the police."

"No!"

"Kath, this is serious. You should make a police report."

"No! I'd have to tell them what is missing."

"Don't be silly. The police have no idea the importance or unimportance of those letters. You just say some of your husband's personal mementoes were taken."

"But the really valuable things, the medals and trophies, weren't touched. Whoever this was knew about Shannon and her letters. I don't want anyone to know I'm upset by it."

Paul sighed. "Okay, have it your way. So I take it you aren't going to tell Mark and Hugh?"

"Of course not. You were the one who said I could say under oath my marriage was fine."

"And you can. Those letters were just Shannon in desperate mode. Tom wasn't going to leave you. But you have to realize that someone now has them who is not on your side, and they don't look good."

"But, as you said to me a long time ago, Wycliffe has no way of knowing who Shannon is. You refused to connect her to Steve yesterday."

"True. But since someone came for her letters, I wouldn't be surprised if they had figured out the connection."

"But how?"

"How doesn't matter at this point. What matters is that you're safe. You've got to let Mark and Hugh know about this, so they can be prepared if something unexpected happens."

"No! I can't talk about Shannon to them."

"Do you want me to tell them?"

"No!" *I just want to pretend there never was a Shannon. If I don't talk about her, she can't exist.*

"Should I come over?"

"No. I have to take a shower and get dressed for court."

"You shouldn't stay there tonight. You aren't safe alone."

"I'll be fine.

* * *

Tuesday, March 17, 2015, Edward J. Schwartz Federal Courthouse, U.S. District Court, Southern District of California, San Diego, 9:00 a.m.

Kathryn struggled to focus on Bruce Myers' testimony. He was a handsome, middle-aged man with thick, dark hair, kind brown eyes, and a gentle smile. His tweed jacket made him look friendly and approachable and like the healer he was. He spoke softly, but without hesitation, into the microphone as he explained Tom's medical history. It was a story she'd heard far too often. It was a story she still vainly hoped against hope would have a different ending.

Mark spent most of the morning presenting Dr. Myers and his opinion that Myrabin had caused Tom's death. Just before lunch, Bob McLaren began badgering him about his conclusions, but Bruce held firm.

After they returned from lunch, McLaren took up the cudgels again, but Bruce Myers once more refused to depart from his opinion about the role of Myrabin in Tom Andrews' death. All afternoon, as McLaren attacked Bruce repeatedly and as Mark quietly rehabilitated his opinion over and over on redirect examination, Kathryn kept seeing the empty drawer in Tom's desk and inwardly shivered at the thought of who might have Shannon's letters.

At four thirty, when the day's session ended, she walked back to the Emerald Shapery Center with Hugh and Mark, thinking about Paul's warning that she should tell them about the missing letters. But she couldn't. She just couldn't face having to say out loud that the love of her life had been involved with Shannon Freeman.

"You look tired," Hugh said as they settled around the table in the big conference room to talk over the day's testimony. *Were his eyes a shade too concerned,* she wondered. *Was his tone more personal than professional? Surely not.*

Kathryn smiled as she poured water from the carafe in the center of the table into a glass. "I am. I didn't sleep well last night. Bruce did an outstanding job for us today."

Mark nodded. "Bruce stuck to his guns on Myrabin as the cause of your husband's death."

"I think McLaren hurt himself by going after him too aggressively on cross-examination," Hugh said. "I could tell from their faces many of the jurors didn't like the way he kept attacking him. I think Wycliffe lost some points with them today."

Kathryn looked down at her phone and saw a message from Joe Sanders. "At your office. Need to talk ASAP." She stood up. "I've got to go to my office. Joe Sanders is waiting with some information on Tyrone's case."

"How is that going?" Hugh asked.

"Joe's been a great help. Goldstein, Miller's offer to pay his fees has allowed me to get information I would not otherwise have had. But so far, I haven't found what I need to prove Tyrone's alibi. Maybe this will be it."

"Let's hope so," Mark smiled.

"I'll walk you to the elevator," Hugh said as he fingered the little blue box in his pocket.

* * *

Tuesday, March 17, 2015, Office of the Public Defender, 450 B Street, San Diego

Joe was waiting for her in their bare-bones reception area when she arrived. He was wearing a light tan suit that was a radical departure from his regulation brown, but it was just as rumpled as his usual business attire. As Kathryn punched in the security code to the private area of the office and motioned for Joe to follow her, she wondered if he owned any coat hangers.

Kathryn sat down behind her desk and motioned for the investigator to take the chair opposite. She resolved to ignore the mail piled in front of her. Millie had arranged for other attorneys to cover her cases while she was in trial on Tom's case, but the mail clamored for her attention nonetheless.

"I'm hoping this is good news for Tyrone," she said.

"Mixed."

"Okay. Let's have it then."

"I've discovered the police, indeed, have the tapes from the Rendevous on the night of the shooting."

"And do they support Tyrone's alibi?"

"Yes. He's clearly visible throughout the night with Tamara."

Kathryn's heart leapt with joy. "Joe, that's not mixed news! That's the cavalry to the rescue. We can get Tyrone off with that!"

"Except we don't have it."

"What? How do you know what's on the tapes if you don't have them?"

"Because I have a confidential source in the San Diego Police Department who told me the cops are sitting on those tapes in order to get Tyrone convicted. He's a Crip, and they think that justifies a wrongful conviction to get him off the streets."

"So a clear violation of their duty to turn over any evidence which shows the defendant is not guilty under *Brady v. Maryland*?"

"Yep. They've made themselves a huge *Brady* problem."

"Then I'll call Sam McIntyre and confront him!"

"That won't get you anywhere. Sam doesn't know the cops are sitting on *Brady* evidence."

"But when I tell him—"

"They'll destroy the tapes. The only reason the cops haven't destroyed them yet is because they're afraid Ray-Ray has copies. If it comes out there are copies, they want to be able to produce the ones they took and say, "Oops, sorry. We forgot. Good faith mistake.""

"What bullshit!"

"I couldn't agree more. But a court will buy their excuse and refuse to sanction them."

"So we still have to get Ray-Ray's copies. If he still has them."

"I'm going to talk to him tomorrow and level with him. If he has the tapes and if he turns them over, he can save Tyrone. Everyone likes Tyrone. He's a Crip, but a harmless one. Besides the Crips were the only family he ever had, and he sold those drugs so he could eat. That busboy gig at Applebee's didn't pay him shit. Hey, I didn't get to ask, how are things going with Tom's case?"

"So far so good. It's just the beginning."

"I hope you don't mind that I wanted to meet in person. Since the cops are involved, I don't trust the security of my phone or yours."

"No, of course. This was best. We'll meet again when you've talked to Ray-Ray." She thought of the empty drawer in Tom's desk and the footsteps always behind her. Joe was right to be concerned about security.

"I'm thinking of going out to the club tonight. If he's had enough to drink and business is good, he'll be feeling mellow and will be more likely to cooperate."

Kathryn walked Joe back to the lobby and told him goodbye Then she went back to her desk and found a text from Paul. "Don't stay at your house alone tonight. Come sleep in the guestroom."

But she wanted to go home where she could see Tom's medals and feel Tom's presence. She unlocked the bottom drawer of her desk and took out her Glock .9 millimeter. Learning to use a handgun had been Tom's idea. They'd both taken lessons and become expert shots, although her scores were always higher than his, and he liked to tease her about it. She clicked the magazine firmly into place, put the gun in her purse, and went home.

CHAPTER THIRTY-SEVEN

Wednesday, March 18, 2015, Edward J. Schwartz Federal Courthouse, U.S. District Court, Southern District of California, San Diego, 9:00 a.m.

Karl Martin, the head of the Scripps transplant team, took the stand first thing that morning. He was tall and thin and slightly balding. His wire-rimmed glasses made him look like the medical expert that he, indeed, was. He was wearing a tweed sports coat, too, and Kathryn wondered if he and Bruce had planned to mirror each other.

She listened as, step by step, Mark led Dr. Martin through the details of death by liver failure. He described Tom's bloated belly; his swollen, useless legs; the nausea; the vomiting; his dementia; and, at last, the mercy of falling into a coma. He explained why Tom was too weak for a transplant when he was admitted to the hospital and why he never regained enough strength for the operation.

Kathryn found it nearly unbearable to listen to. Mark was focusing his questions on the details of Tom's agony to persuade the jury to bring back a multi-million dollar damage award to punish Wycliffe. A thousand times that morning, Kathryn wanted to get up and run screaming from the courtroom as she heard Dr. Martin explain how, day by day, hour by hour, and minute by minute, Tom had drifted toward death. The ordeal put her in such pain that she forgot about Shannon's missing letters for a while.

After lunch, Bob McLaren lit into Dr. Martin's conclusion that Tom had never recovered enough strength for the transplant. Kathryn knew Wycliffe intended to present their own medical expert who would testify that Tom died because Dr. Martin had been too conservative in his judgment about Tom's ability to endure the surgery. McLaren was paving the way for his hired hack by beating down Dr. Martin.

But, like Bruce Myers, Karl Martin refused to be intimidated by McLaren's bullying. He listened politely to each question and gave a calm, measured response that told the jury just how sure he was that he was right: Tom would never have survived transplant surgery.

After Dr. Martin was finally excused at two o'clock, Mark called Rick to the stand. At first his testimony about how Myrabin proceeded through the FDA approval process was a welcome relief from the pain and suffering medical testimony. But as they were nearing four o'clock and adjournment for the day, Mark began to question Rick about a theory he had developed after he and Stewart had examined the Wycliffe documents.

"Now, Dr. Peyton, who conducted the studies of Myrabin during the FDA clinical trials?"

"Wycliffe."

"So no independent researchers conducted studies for the FDA?"

"No, they were all done by Wycliffe."

"Were independent studies of the drug ever done?"

"Yes, after FDA approval."

"And how do you know these post-approval studies were conducted?"

"Because I found references to them in Wycliffe's documents."

"What kind of references?"

"Objection!" McLaren boomed.

"And what's the basis for your objection?" Judge Weiner asked.

McLaren looked flustered. "Hearsay, Your Honor."

"They aren't hearsay if they are in Wycliffe's own documents," the judge said. They are declarations against interest. You may proceed with direct examination, Mr. Kelly."

"Thank you, Your Honor. Now, Dr. Peyton, what did these references that you found say?"

"They were internal Wycliffe memoranda summarizing post-approval studies that independent researchers were doing on the safety of the drug."

"And what were the results of these studies?"

"They found deaths associated with Myrabin."

"And how many deaths?"

"It's hard to say exactly how many. The summaries said 'significant numbers of adverse effects including deaths.'"

"But you are certain these research studies reported deaths associated with taking the drug?"

"Very certain."

"And what was the cause of those deaths?"

"Liver failure."

"And that was the cause of Tom Andrews' death?"

"Objection!" McLaren was on his feet.

Judge Weiner looked at him expectantly for the basis of his objection.

"Dr. Peyton never examined Tom Andrews. He cannot say what caused his death."

"I believe he testified that he examined the autopsy reports, Mr. McLaren. Based on those, he can give his expert opinion. Next question."

"Dr. Peyton, were you able to ascertain Wycliffe's attitude toward the independent researchers who found adverse effects from Myrabin?"

"Yes."

"Could you explain that to the jury?"

"Wycliffe's internal memoranda documented payouts to them. In return for the money, they halted their studies and did not publish the results."

"Would it be fair to say Wycliffe was buying off its critics?"

"Very fair."

"Objection!" McLaren thundered.

"Overruled." Judge Weiner barely batted an eyelash.

"I have no further questions, You Honor," Mark said and returned to his seat next to Kathryn at the plaintiff's table.

Judge Weiner turned to Bob McLaren. "You may cross-examine Dr. Peyton."

"Thank you, Your Honor."

Kathryn watched McLaren settle himself at the podium.

"Now, Dr. Peyton, have you not testified that Wycliffe suppressed research studies that attributed deaths to Myrabin?"

"Yes."

"How many studies were suppressed?"

"I don't have the report in front of me. A fair number."

"More than two?"

"Definitely."

"More than ten?"

"I'm not sure."

"So between two and ten?"

"I don't have the exact number."

"And how many deaths were reported in these studies?"

"Again, I'm not sure."

"A hundred?"

"Probably not that many."

"Fifty?"

"Again, I'm not sure."

Kathryn felt her stomach tighten. Rick was not coming across well. The jurors looked skeptical and hostile.

"Now you've given an opinion that Myrabin caused Tom Andrews' death, is that correct?"

"Yes."

"And you are a medical doctor, are you not?"

"I am."

"Can a medical doctor determine the cause of death of a person whom he never examined?"

"Well, I—"

"You never examined Tom Andrews, did you?"

"No, but—"

"Just answer the question," Judge Weiner cautioned.

"So you really have no idea what caused Tom Andrews' death?"

"It is my opinion that Myrabin destroyed his liver."

"Tell me, Dr. Peyton, does the FDA agree with that conclusion?"

"The FDA has never given an opinion on the cause of Tom Andrews' death."

"But the FDA has data, does it not, on the deaths from Myrabin?"

"Yes." Kathryn could see Rick nearly choke on that answer. The jurors' faces said they saw it, too.

"And how many deaths have there been, according to the FDA, since Myrabin was approved?"

"None."

"I'm sorry, I didn't quite understand your answer. How many post-approval deaths has the FDA documented, Dr. Peyton?"

"None."

"Thank you. No further questions."

"Any redirect, Mr. Kelly?"

"No, Your Honor."

"Then you may step down, Dr. Peyton."

* * *

Wednesday, March 18, 2015, Offices of Goldstein, Miller, Emerald Shapery Center, 5 p.m.

Hugh was the first to bring up the problem when they settled around the Goldstein, Miller conference table that night. He was going heavy on the scotch; and even Mark, who never drank at their post-mortem meetings because he always had to go home and prepare for the next day of trial, accepted a red wine from Patty, who hadn't heard Rick's testimony.

"How bad was it?" she asked, looking directly at Kathryn, probably because she guessed she would give the most honest answer.

"Bad. The jury listened closely to Bruce and Dr. Martin, and I saw them making notes. But Rick's opinion sounded like desperate speculation with not much to back it up. McLaren smeared him, and the jury bought it."

"We lost our bet on presenting Rick's theory about the suppressed studies. We shouldn't have tried it," Hugh observed.

"Well, I'll do what I can with damage control tomorrow. Dr. Vannier will be here from Paris on Monday to testify. That will clean up any problems we've created with Rick."

Kathryn stood up. "I've got to go over to my office and check for messages. Joe Sanders was going to the Rendevous last night to see if he could get those surveillance tapes out of Ray-Ray."

"I take it those tapes will prove Tyrone's alibi?" Hugh asked.

"We think so. And if that's true, the state is going to be in big trouble."

"Why?" Mark asked.

"Because the cops took the first set of tapes, and they've been sitting on them. If Joe is right–"

"They're withholding *Brady* material, which is evidence that tends to prove the client is innocent. You're on to something big," Hugh said.

Kathryn smiled at him and noticed that his eyes seemed to

light up. "We think we are. And, of course, I'm very grateful for Goldstein, Miller's help."

Hugh waved his hands expansively. "It wasn't much. You and Joe are doing all the hard work. We need to set up a bigger pro bono program to help kids like Tyrone. When Tom's case is over, I'll propose it to the partners."

Except I won't be here when Tom's case is over, he thought. *Or I won't be here for long. Buffy will see to that.* He watched Patty get up to walk Kathryn to the elevator. They looked like two girlfriends. Kathryn would fit in well here. Maybe Mark could persuade her. Damn! He didn't want to be stuck in an embassy under Buffy's constant supervision while Kathryn walked the halls of Goldstein, Miller. He had to find some way to buy Buffy off. And then an even more important realization hit him. Buffy was in San Francisco and wouldn't be back until Monday. He was free to ask Kathryn to dinner that night.

* * *

Wednesday, March 18, 2015, Office of the Public Defender, 450 B Street

Joe's phone message was waiting in the middle of her desk. "Didn't want to text. Worried about security on your cell and mine. Talked to Ray-Ray. He admitted he has a set of tapes from that night. But he's reluctant to turn them over because they incriminate Tamara on the drug sales. He was her pimp, and he's in love with her. Told him she's already in jail for dealing, and those tapes are Tyrone's only shot at walking. Going back tonight to talk to him. Update tomorrow. Hope your husband's case went well today."

Kathryn smiled. Having a guy like Joe working with her made all the difference. If she took a job with Goldstein, Miller when all this was over, she'd have access to Joe and people like him all the time. It was more than worth considering.

Suddenly her cell began to ring, and she recognized Hugh's number. Her stomach tightened. What else had gone wrong besides Rick's clumsy testimony about post-approval Myrabin deaths?

"Hello, Kathryn?"

"Yes, Hugh."

"Did Joe have anything that helps Tyrone?"

"He's still working on it."

"So not yet?"

"That's right. But it looks promising. Again, I'm very grateful for the help."

"I wondered if you'd come over for dinner tonight. Buffy's in San Francisco, and I thought it would give us a chance to talk about where we go with the case after today."

"What time would you like me to come?"

"I'm leaving the office now."

"Then, say, twenty minutes?"

* * *

Wednesday, March 18, 2015, Crown Manor, Coronado, six p.m.

Jose made it across the bridge in record time. Hugh changed into tan slacks and a cozy navy sweater and slipped the box of emeralds into his pocket, stifling the fantasy that he could give them to her that night. He went down to the kitchen to see what

Maria had left for dinner. The refrigerator held a serviceable enchilada casserole and a green salad. He smiled. She fed him the way she fed her grandchildren.

He opened a bottle of merlot to go with the casserole and set the table with two place settings. The front door that Larry Lawrence's fourth wife had installed began to chime its intricate melody. He raced to open it.

She was wearing the same light gray suit she'd worn at trial with the simple white blouse. Her hair hung loose around her shoulders. Her eyes had turned that enchanting shade of emerald sea glass that he had learned meant she was very tired.

"Come in, come in." He allowed himself the air kisses that everyone in this insincere state indulged in. He wished they could be real. She was unfazed by the slight contact, and he reminded himself he was an unattractive, middle-aged male with an aggressive ego that he must learn to keep in check.

She followed him to the kitchen where he poured a glass of wine and handed it to her.

"So glad you could come."

"Thanks for asking me. The house is too quiet when I go home. Where is Buffy?"

"San Francisco. An auction for a charity whose name I forget. And a ball." She'd been really unhappy that Hugh wouldn't leave the trial to escort her to the gala.

"Sounds boring."

He grinned. "I thought so, too."

He opened the refrigerator and brought out the salads. "Let's start with these." He'd already put the casserole in the oven.

They settled opposite each other at the small kitchen table.

336

Hugh wished he could turn the lights down and light some candles, but that would be too obvious.

"You said Joe is still working on getting alibi evidence for Tyrone?"

"Yes. Ray-Ray has the tapes we need, but he's reluctant to turn them over because his former girlfriend is on them, selling dope. Along with Tyrone, I might add."

"And Joe's explained to him those tapes can save Tyrone from life without parole?"

"Of course. And he's thinking it over. The girlfriend is already in prison in Texas on drug charges. Joe's talking to Ray-Ray tonight about how helping us out won't do much to Tamara, and it will literally save Tyrone's life."

Hugh munched lettuce thoughtfully. "You do a tremendous amount of good over there in the PD's office."

"Maybe. I don't know. It doesn't feel like it most days. I'm doing Tyrone's case for Tom."

Hugh looked down at his plate and then back at Kathryn. "I admire your husband, more and more. He was an extraordinary man."

He saw tears in those exquisite green eyes. "He was." But she recovered quickly. "Mark says you are thinking of leaving the firm."

"Not exactly. Buffy wants a change. Hal Edwards' wife is very close to Buffy. She suggested Hal give me some sort of ambassadorship during his second term."

"Where?"

"England or France. Something easy."

"Would you like that?"

Only if you are there with me. "I don't know. I'd rather be on the Supreme Court, but Hal isn't anticipating any vacancies."

"Sounds as if the election is a done deal."

Hugh chuckled. "Not quite. But my ten million is solidly behind Hal." He got up to remove the empty salad plates and serve the casserole.

When he sat down again, she said, "It must be nice to have that kind of money to influence politics."

"It is," he agreed. "But I do everything in the name of my father. He was the little guy big business ran over. I exist to make them miserable for that."

Kathryn nodded. "That's the way I feel about Tom. I want them to be miserable for what they did."

Hugh sighed. "Unfortunately, they weren't miserable today. But that will change because we have Dr. Vannier on Monday."

They ate in companionable silence for a bit until Hugh's cell phone went off.

He looked down at the number and frowned. "Sorry, I have to take this. It's from Dr. Vannier's assistant. He is supposed to be flying out of Paris tonight.

"Hello? I see. Are you sure? Absolutely?" Hugh looked over at Kathryn with grave eyes. "I see. I see. We'll contact her tonight."

After he hung up, he was silent for a few moments.

"What's wrong?"

"Dr. Vannier is dead."

"Dead?" She stared at him with blank eyes. "How? When?"

"This afternoon. He was packing for the flight to America.

Someone broke into his apartment. The police are calling it robbery."

"What are we going to do?"

"Fly to Stanford and beg Aimée Girard to take his place."

CHAPTER THIRTY-EIGHT

Saturday, March 21, 2015, Gilbert Hall, Department of Biology, Stanford University

As the chartered jet took off for San Jose, Hugh sat back in his seat with his early morning scotch and blamed himself for the disaster Rick had created. He had insisted on testifying to justify the hefty fee he needed to stave off financial ruin. But now Hugh realized he should have just paid Rick under the table and gone with Dr. Vannier. If Vannier had been on the witness stand on Wednesday afternoon, he'd have been safely out of his house when the thieves had come looking for his Picasso. Or would he? Deep inside, Hugh thought "The Girl with the Red Book" had not been the real target.

Hugh fingered the emeralds in his pocket and studied Kathryn. She and Mark had the two seats facing his with the small table in the middle. They were both dressed casually in jeans. She was absorbed in reading her emails. Mark was drinking coffee and looking out the window. He'd questioned Hugh's decision to bring Kathryn on the trip, but Hugh had felt the presence of Tom's widow might overcome any hesitation

Aimée Girard might have about helping them. And, besides, he knew his own time to be with her was limited. Although Buffy had agreed to give up on making him run for Fred Akers' seat, she was already redecorating the American Ambassador's residence in Paris.

* * *

The Mercedes limo purred through the light drizzle as it headed out of the San Jose International Airport toward Stanford. Kathryn leaned back and watched the landscape grayed with rain slide past the big car. Dr. Girard had agreed to meet with them, but no more. She had refused to promise to testify.

She met them at her office on the third floor of Gilbert Hall, the home of the Department of Biology. She was barely five feet tall, thin, and stylish as Frenchwomen usually are. She wore dark slacks and a light gray sweater with a red silk scarf tied gracefully at the neck. Kathryn guessed she was about the same age as Dr. Vannier, but her complexion was still smooth; and even without make up, she looked elegant. Her chin-length light brown hair was expertly cut to lie perfectly against her jawline. She had large, deep-set, dark eyes. Even at middle age she was still a beautiful woman.

Dr. Girard led them down the hall to a small conference room. After they went in and seated themselves around the small table, Dr. Girard locked the door.

"What we say here must remain here," she cautioned as she sat down at the head of the table. She looked over at Kathryn. "I am sorry about the loss of your husband, Mrs. Andrews."

"Thank you."

"And we regret the loss of Dr. Vannier," Mark began, but Dr. Girard cut him off.

"Maurice was murdered."

"That seems very possible," Hugh agreed.

"No!" Even though her accent softened her voice, she spoke with commanding authority. "Not possible. Not probable. Absolutely for certain, he was murdered."

"Why are you so sure?" Mark asked.

"Because as soon as Wycliffe bought the rights to the drug, they began to circulate that story about Maurice being fired for sexual harassment. They thought that claiming the two of us had been lovers would make us stay quiet about our work at Suchet."

"But it didn't?"

"Of course not! Our spouses and colleagues knew it wasn't true. Wycliffe picked the wrong people to lie about."

"Dr. Vannier was going to testify about your research on Myrabin," Mark said. "He was going to testify that it was not safe and could not be made safe. Could you take his place for us?"

"I could. I'm not sure if I will."

"Because you are afraid something will happen to you?"

"Of course. Maurice told me about his meeting with you last fall, and he told me he planned to expose Wycliffe's hypocrisy. I warned him not to."

"So each of you have been subject to specific threats from Wycliffe?"

"Not in so many words. Instead of killing us, they've tried to discredit us through Charles Lawson, who, as you know, says our work is not on par with that of American scientists. Of course, he knows that's a lie. I often see him at conferences, and he takes great pains to avoid me. But when I heard about Maurice's murder, I realized they were going farther than just defaming us as scientists. I have no doubt about who arranged for those two thugs to go after the painting."

"So you are afraid to help us?" Mark asked.

"Of course I am."

"If you did decide to come back with us," Hugh explained, "I'd have you stay with my wife and me. You'd testify first thing on Monday, and my driver would be waiting to take you to the airport as soon as you've finished. A private jet would be waiting to bring you home. You'd have armed protection the entire time from the firm's private investigator."

She smiled. "Clever. So your theory is they won't have a reason to come after me, once I've done whatever damage I can do?"

Hugh nodded. "They'd be crazy to try anything after you've been a witness in a trial that's being watched nationally and internationally."

"So it sounds as if the best way to protect myself is to tell my story. And Maurice's." She was silent for a few minutes before she said, "We were not lovers, but we were close friends. He would want me to testify. I'll do it."

"And we'll do everything we can to keep you safe."

* * *

Saturday, March 21, 2015, Crown Manor, Coronado, California

At midnight, Hugh stood on the balcony outside his bedroom and surveyed his world with satisfaction as he listened to the low, soft roar of the Pacific and sipped his last scotch of the day. Aimée Girard slept safely in one of the guest rooms on the third floor of the mansion. Joe Sanders occupied the room next door with his Glock. Buffy had given him no problems about having Aimée in the house, and actually seemed to like her.

They'd have to get over the hump of witness substitution on Monday, but he knew Mark was up to the task. In fact, Hugh thought Mark's good looks and soft-spoken manor subtly influenced Judge Weiner in his favor. Bob McLaren was too abrasive for the highly intelligent judge.

His cell began to ring, and he saw the call was from Logan. He started not to answer it. Most likely she was having boyfriend problems and wanted to resume their affair.

But his intuition told him to press the "accept" button. "Hello, Logan."

"Miss me?" she cooed.

"It's over, Logan. I told you."

"I know, I know. Just testing you. Things couldn't be better with Travis. I'm calling about the Andrews case. I've got some interesting information for you."

"Such as?"

"Such as Harrison O'Connor wants to testify."

"What? Are you sure?"

"Couldn't be more positive. I talked to him myself, today. Apparently he's been watching the Andrews trial, and he saw Rick's debacle on CNN. He wants to help. He says he knows the number of post-approval deaths. It's over six hundred. They've put the reports into a private database, so they'll stay hidden from public scrutiny. He called the DC office to say he wanted to talk, and they routed him to me because I had worked on the case when I was in San Diego."

"So you are sure this is all authentic?'

"Absolutely. And I met him for a drink after work tonight at the Four Seasons to seal the deal."

"So when is he coming to San Diego?"

"In the morning. He leaves at 7:30 from Dulles. I bought him a ticket and handed it to him myself. I booked him a room at the Westgate. You're supposed to call him tonight. Here's his number."

A few minutes after Logan hung up, Hugh dialed Harrison O'Connor. The phone rang and rang, but no one answered. He tried three times and then called Logan back.

"I've got no idea," she said. "You're dialing the number he gave me. We'll just have to hope he's on that plane tomorrow."

"What times does his flight get in?

"One-thirty."

"E-mail me his flight number. I'll have Jose pick him up."

* * *

Hugh poured one more scotch and gloated over how glorious it was going to be to present both Dr. Girard and Harrison O'Connor to the jury. In fact, he couldn't think of anything more exciting except handing Kathryn the emerald earrings.

CHAPTER THIRTY-NINE

Monday, March 23, 2015, Edward J. Schwartz Federal Courthouse, U.S. District Court, Southern District of California, San Diego, 9:00 a.m.

Mark won the fight over allowing Aimée to testify. Bob McLaren argued that the plaintiff should not be allowed to present a "surprise" witness.

Judge Weiner frowned at McLaren who was at the podium. "How is Dr. Girard a 'surprise'? She is here to testify to everything her dead colleague was going to testify to. You know what the substance of Dr. Vannier's testimony was going to be."

"But we've never deposed Dr. Girard."

"But Mr. Kelly has given you a summary of her testimony. Why should I grant a mistrial just so you can depose a witness the substance of whose testimony you already know?"

"Your Honor, the Federal Rules of Civil Procedure—"

"Provide for discovery, Mr. McLaren, of the plaintiff's evidence. And I think you've had plenty of discovery. Motion denied."

Hugh breathed a sigh of relief. He looked over at Kathryn,

who was sitting next to Joe in the seat that Hugh usually occupied, and smiled. She smiled back, and his old-man's heart lit up with joy at the victory they'd shared. He noticed the slight bulge of the shoulder holster under Joe's rumpled navy suit coat. The bailiffs had let him bring the gun into the courtroom to protect Aimée only because he was an ex cop. Anyone else would have been told to leave the weapon at the door. Hugh reminded himself to see that Joe got a raise.

All morning, in her beautiful accent, Dr. Girard answered Mark's questions, explaining the development of Myrabin. She discussed the formulas the Vannier research team had tried, the effects they'd observed in animal studies, and their recommendation to give up on the Myrabin prototype.

"So in your opinion it was not safe and could not be made safe?" Mark asked her just before they broke for lunch.

"That is correct. In a high percentage of the population, the liver processes the drug so that it becomes toxic and destroys that organ."

After lunch, Bob McLaren began his cross-examination. His efforts to discredit the French team's work became personal after a while. Mark objected repeatedly to questions about Dr. Girard's marriage and about the alleged affair with Maurice Vannier.

To her credit, Aimée never lost her French cool, shrugging often at some of the more ridiculous questions.

Hugh's phone vibrated at two thirty. It as an email from Jose. "Mr. Hugh. Dr. O'Connor not on airplane. I ask airline to be sure. He never got on at Dulles. What should I do?"

Hugh emailed back, "Come to the courthouse and wait to

drive Dr. Girard to the airport to catch the private jet back to Stanford."

As soon as Judge Weiner declared the afternoon break, he found a secure spot where he could call Logan.

"Knew you were missing me," she said. "Sorry, I'm taken. Travis asked me last night. Five caret diamond that will blind you."

"Congratulations. But that's not why I called. Harrison O'Connor never got on that plane. Jose was there to meet the flight."

"I'll get Leon to run a check on the police reports. I'll call you back as soon as he lets me know what he finds."

"Okay." Hugh paced the hall, hoping the firm's D.C. investigator, Leon Abramowitz, could answer the mystery of what happened to Harrison.

Ten minutes later, Hugh's phone rang, and he saw it was Logan. "So what did you find out?"

"Harrison is dead."

"What?"

"Last night around one a.m. He hanged himself. His colleague, Mary Lancaster, called the police and asked them to do a welfare check."

"But why, then, did he contact us and want to testify if he was just planning to kill himself?"

"No idea."

"I don't think this was a suicide."

"Maybe not, but you have no proof it was murder."

"He was about to reveal the existence of the FDA's secret database where six hundred post-approval Myrabin deaths are hidden. He would have taken down one of Wycliffe's most profitable drugs if he had testified. He didn't hang himself. He was murdered."

"And now you don't have anyone to undo Rick's mess."

* * *

At three, Judge Weiner excused Dr. Girard as a witness. Jose drove her to the airport, accompanied by Joe Saunders and his Glock, where the private jet Hugh had chartered was waiting. Since Mark did not have another witness to call that afternoon, Judge Weiner recessed the proceedings early; and the Goldstein, Miller contingent, including Kathryn, headed back to the conference room at the firm to talk over the day's events.

* * *

The wine and scotch flowed freely. Everyone except Hugh thought they were celebrating Dr. Girard's triumph on the witness stand. Only Kathryn, who eyed him warily from time to time, seemed to sense something was wrong.

At five-thirty Logan texted him a picture of her hefty engagement ring and a message, "Call Mary Lancaster, ASAP."

Hugh went out into the hall and dialed the number. A frightened female voice answered. "Hello? Is this Hugh Mahoney?"

"Yes, it is. Mary Lancaster?" The name was familiar, but he was struggling to remember the contact.

"Dr. Mary Lancaster. I was a member of the Myrabin team with Harrison."

"Oh, my God. Of course. Sorry. I remember."

"Listen, Mr. Mahoney, I want to testify in Harrison's place. They murdered him. I told Harrison I didn't want to get involved. It was bad enough being followed everywhere. But now I have to do this for him. I also had access to the database where those post-approval death numbers were hidden. Harrison and I inputted the reports when they came in. Then they disappeared. He and I decided to find out what happened to them after you came around asking questions. Harrison and I both have personal knowledge of the cover-up. I can testify in his place."

"How do you know he was murdered?"

"Because he called me last night. Two men had broken into his house. He was hiding in a closet. He guessed they had followed him to the bar where he met that lawyer from your firm, the one who gave him the plane ticket. He heard them say they had to make it look like suicide. He told me to get out of my house and hide because they said they were coming after me next. He saved my life, Mr. Mahoney. I have to testify for him."

"Where are you now?"

"I'm hiding in a Motel 6 in Bethesda. I'm not safe."

"No, you're not. Listen Mary, I'm going to have our D.C. investigator, Leon Abramowitz, come out there and drive you to our D.C. office where you'll be safe. I've got a private jet in the air right now taking today's witness home to Stanford. Our San Diego investigator, Joe Saunders, is on board. I'm going to have the jet refuel in San Jose and then come for you in DC. Joe, who has a permit to carry a weapon, will accompany you to San Diego, and you'll stay at my house. Are you okay with that?"

"I am, Mr. Mahoney."

"Hugh. Call me Hugh."

As soon as he hung up, he called Leon.

"What's up boss?"

"We've got a critical witness hiding at a Motel 6 in Bethesda. Her name is Mary Lancaster. Go get her and take her to the D.C. office and stay with her until Joe and the jet arrive to bring her here. It'll be a long night because they just landed in San Jose, and Joe has got to see Aimée Girard home safely before he can leave for D.C."

"No problem, boss. I'll text you when she is safely in our office."

* * *

Hugh went back to the conference room and stood in the doorway watching Kathryn laugh with Mark and Patty and Stewart. Aimée's testimony had left them all feeling triumphant; but, as any seasoned litigator knows, things can go south in a heartbeat during trial. Killing off witnesses was an act of desperation. If Wycliffe was that desperate, Kathryn wasn't safe. At that moment, her eyes met his, and he motioned for her to meet him in the hallway.

"What's happened?" she asked.

He told her about Harrison O'Connor and Mary Lancaster. "And you're not safe, either."

"They've already tried to kill me."

"Third time's the charm."

"They've already tried three times. I've got my Glock, and I'm a superior shot. Don't look surprised. It was Tom's idea because not all of our clients admire our work. Another thing

Erin might want to consider before she joins us."

"So you've got it with you?"

"Right now it's in the car because I'm not Joe, and the bailiffs would have a fit if I tried to bring it into Judge Weiner's courtroom. But as soon as I get in the car, it goes back in my purse. And it stays by my bed all night. Don't worry, Hugh."

He fingered the box in his pocket. "Come stay at Crown Manor tonight."

"Thanks, but no. I can feel Tom in the cottage. I want to be with him."

CHAPTER FORTY

Tuesday, March 24, 2015, Crown Manor, Coronado, California

Hugh's phone rang at midnight. He had just polished off his last scotch and turned out the light. He picked up the phone in the dark and said, "Hello."

"It's Joe, Hugh. I'm at Dulles."

"Is Dr. Lancaster with you?"

"No, that's why I called. They weren't at the D.C. office when I got there, so I went out to the Motel 6 in Bethesda. But someone else had gotten there first. Dr. Lancaster and Leon are dead."

"What?"

"Dr. Lancaster and Leon. Dead. I had to pick the lock to get into the room. When I saw what happened, I got out of there as fast as I could. I didn't want to get arrested for double murder. I phoned in an anonymous tip to the cops. The place should be crawling with them right now."

"Okay, Joe. How soon will you be back?"

"By morning. They're almost done refuling the plane."

* * *

As soon as Joe hung up, Hugh called Kathryn. "Sorry to wake you."

"I wasn't asleep. Is something wrong?"

"Quite a bit, actually." He told her about Harrison and Mary. "I don't know who's killing our witnesses, but you're definitely not safe there by yourself. If they kill you, the lawsuit is over; and then they don't have to worry about our witnesses anymore."

"I'm fine at home."

"You're in danger."

"I can take care of myself. Don't worry. Good night."

A few seconds after she hung up, Hugh looked down at the text she'd sent him: a picture of her Glock.

* * *

He sighed and dialed Mark, who made a groggy noise that might have been hello.

"Sorry to wake you. We've got a crisis on our hands. Come up to the house. We need to talk."

In ten minutes, a sleepy-eyed Mark appeared at the front door in jeans and a ratty black tee shirt. Hugh led him to his study and poured scotch for them both.

"At four in the morning?" Mark frowned when Hugh handed him the glass.

"At four in the morning. You're going to need it." He proceeded to fill Mark in on the death of Harrison O'Connor and how his desperate cross-country bid to save Mary Lancaster had failed.

"Kathryn's not safe!" Mark said as soon as Hugh finished.

"I know. I told her to sleep here tonight." He showed him the picture of her Glock that she'd sent him.

"And you accepted that as an answer?"

"What was I supposed to do? She's an experienced public defender with a license for legal carry."

Mark was still angry, but he knew there was nothing else he could say. Instead, he turned to the immediate problem, "So who do I put on the stand tomorrow? Without Harrison or Mary, there's no one to testify that there were any post-approval deaths."

"I know. We let Rick get us into a mess when we allowed him to give an opinion that there were post-approval deaths without any way to say how many. I'm afraid we're just going to have to take our lumps and move on. Kathryn is the only witness left, and she'll be good. The jury will forget all about Rick's bungling after they've heard her story."

"But it's four in the morning, and she and I haven't had time to go over her testimony. I don't want to put her on the stand tomorrow without warning."

"I know. I know. Tell Judge Weiner we had planned to have Mary here tomorrow, but tragedy intervened."

"You want me to say in open court that Harrison O'Connor's death was not a suicide, and Mary and our investigator were murdered? While we know that's true at a gut level, we have not a shred of admissible evidence to present in the morning to support our request for a continuance."

"That's not true. Logan is going to email the police report as soon as she can get her hands on it through her U.S. Attorney boyfriend. Request an ex parte hearing, so you don't have to tell the story in open court in front of McLaren."

"And you think Bob is going to sit still for that?"

"He will, if the judge finds good cause to grant your request. And she will. She likes you better than McLaren. She'll let you talk to her alone in chambers about the loss of Mary and Harrison and why we need a day to pull things together."

* * *

March 24, 2015, Edward J. Schwartz Federal Courthouse, U.S. District Court, Southern District of California, San Diego

At nine a.m., Judge Weiner took the bench, and Mark stood up. "Your Honor, I would like to request a one day continuance based upon some unforeseen circumstances that have deprived us of the witness we anticipated having here today."

The judge frowned. "What is this witness' name?"

"Dr. Mary Lancaster. She was scheduled to fly in from Washington, D.C. last night but she did not arrive. I would like a few minutes in chambers, ex parte, to explain the rest."

"Your Honor!" McLaren leapt to his feet, his face bright red. "There's been no good cause shown for an ex parte hearing on the unavailability of this witness."

"I'll make that determination," Judge Weiner said "*after* I've spoken to Mr. Kelly in chambers."

Kathryn watched uneasily as Mark disappeared into Judge Weiner's chambers. At the defendant's table, Bob McLaren openly fumed in front of the puzzled jury. *Bad idea*, Kathryn thought, *to show the jury you're upset.*

In fifteen minutes, Mark came back and took his seat as first chair at the plaintiff's table. A minute later, the bailiff demanded they all rise for Judge Weiner, who swept in looking unusually serious in her black robes. She turned immediately to the jury. "Ladies and gentlemen, no one appreciates your willingness to serve as jurors more than I do, and I am committed to doing everything in my power to make sure your service is not unduly prolonged. But I have found good cause to grant the plaintiff's motion for a one-day continuance. I am letting you all go now, and we will resume tomorrow at nine."

As soon as the last juror had left, Bob McLaren stood up. "I'd like to object to this continuance, Your Honor."

"You've made your record, Mr. McLaren." The judge's face remained impassive, but Hugh smiled to himself. He'd been right. She didn't like opposing counsel.

* * *

Mark breathed a sigh of relief as he gathered his papers and turned to leave the courtroom. Behind him, he could hear Bob McLaren venting his fury to Emma Talbert, who nodded in agreement with every bit of venom that fell from Bob's lips.

Hugh came up beside him as Mark started down the hall to the front door. He chuckled, "We've got them fuming."

"Yes, but you know we've taken a risk. On appeal, the Ninth Circuit may think Judge Weiner was wrong to allow a witness to testify whom McLaren never got to depose and that granting this continuance was unfair to Wycliffe."

"I don't think that's a bridge we should worry about crossing now," Hugh insisted.

Mark glanced back to make sure he could see Kathryn and Patty behind them.

Hugh followed his worried gaze. "She's okay."

"But you know she's in as much danger as Mary Lancaster was."

"She's got a Glock that she knows how to use. Mary didn't."

"I'm not comfortable with that," Mark said.

Hugh trudged on beside him in silence and stroked the little box in his pocket. He wasn't comfortable with it, either.

When they reached West Broadway, Kathryn broke off from the group and announced she was turning right toward her office instead of left toward Goldstein, Miller and the Emerald Shapery Center.

"Since we have a day off, I've got to go to work."

Hugh was immediately nervous because her gun wasn't in her purse because she'd just come from court. But Mark preempted Hugh's plan to walk with her.

"I'll make sure you get there safely."

She smiled. "This is downtown San Diego, Mark."

"Yes, and a motorbike nearly ran you over in the heart of Paris."

Standing next to Patty waiting for the light, Hugh watched them walk away as he held on to the box in his pocket. Suddenly he felt Patty's hand on his arm in a gesture of sympathy. He looked into her soft brown eyes and realized with a jolt that she knew his secret.

"Don't worry about her," Patty said and squeezed his arm. "She'll be okay."

"Don't tell anyone."

"I won't," she smiled.

"I know it's impossible."

"You've asked her to join the firm. Maybe–"

"Buffy's on to me. She's making me leave Goldstein, Miller after Hal is re-elected. She wants to be Madame Ambassadress to France."

"What about you?" Patty asked as they walked along companionably. "Do you want to be Mr. Ambassador?"

"Are you kidding? Of course not."

"Then maybe it's time to break free."

"Of Buffy? But she's threatened to air all my affairs on national TV. You'll be horribly embarrassed."

"No, I won't. Bill knows all about you and me. He understands, and he doesn't care. I doubt anyone else's spouse would, either. The firm needs you. Don't go."

* * *

Tuesday, March 24, 2015, Office of the Public Defender, 450 "B" Street, San Diego

Mark followed her into her building.

"Hey, that's far enough," she said, turning to smile at him. "I'm here, now. I'm fine."

"I need to come upstairs and talk to you for a few minutes." His gray eyes were focused intently on hers. He was in super serious mode. So she allowed him to accompany her up the elevator, through the outer area of the office to her own inner sanctum. He watched as she removed her Glock from her desk and put it in her purse. "There. You can stop worrying now. I'm safe."

"But I don't believe that guns always keep people safe."

"I don't, either. But as things stand, this Glock is all I have."

"I'm worried about you," Mark said. "Remember when I warned you in Martini that this case could turn very nasty?"

"Of course. But that wasn't a reason to give up then, and it's not a reason to give up now."

"Even if someone is killing off our witnesses? Even if someone is trying to kill you?"

"They won't succeed."

"Aren't you a little over-confident?"

"No."

* * *

Tuesday, March 24, 2015, Office of the Public Defender, 450 "B" Street, San Diego

After Mark left, Kathryn turned to the mail that had piled up on her desk, but she couldn't concentrate. Apparently they were getting too close to the secret of how Myrabin, with all its deadly consequences, had come to be marketed. Killing Dr. Vannier and Harrison O'Connor could not make the lawsuit go away. Only killing her would end the case against Wycliffe. She looked down at the Glock in her purse.

A moment later, Beth Price appeared at her door. "Hey, boss. There's someone here to see you. A Ray-Ray Washington."

"Show him in, Beth."

A few minutes later, Ray-Ray ambled into her office. He looked like a rapper in baggy tan pants that rode way below his waistline, exposing the tops of his black boxers. He paired his extra-extra large pants with an equally over-sized Seattle Mariners jersey and matching hat, worn with the brim backwards.

"Hey, Miz Andrews. Hope you don' min' me stoppin' by."

"Of course not, Ray-Ray. I'm glad to see you." She eyed the brown, eight-by-ten envelope in his hand with caution. "Have a seat. Have you brought me something?"

Ray-Ray heaved his six-feet, two-hundred-and-fifty pound bulk into one of the chairs in front of her desk. He held out the brown envelope. "Yeah, Miz Andrews. I brung you those camera tapes Mr. Joe be want'n so bad for Tyrone. How come Mr. Joe hasn't come back to see me?"

"He's been busy on another case," Kathryn said, wondering if diverting Joe to Tom's case and leaving Tyrone's to languish was ethical.

"Well, here," Ray-Ray thrust the envelope at Kathryn, and she took it. "Mr. Joe say these can get Tyrone out of jail. I don't want no innocent blood on my conscience."

"So Tyrone did not rob Mr. Thorn?"

"Well, I can't say personally because I was drunk that night, but he's on these tapes as big as life all night long. What time did the brothers rob and shoot Thorn?"

"One a.m."

Ray-Ray grinned. "Then these will help. He's selling dope in the parking lot with Tamara at one a.m."

"Are you sure? Are the time stamps on these tapes accurate?"

"I am sure, and yes they are. I'm a good businessman, Miz Andrews. I know how to protect my shit. Protecting your shit means a top-notch surveillance system. I should know. I pay the bill for it every month."

"Listen, Ray-Ray, I'm probably going to need more from you."

"As in you'll need me to testify in court about these tapes."

"I will. I won't be able to use them without you to say they are authentic."

"I figured that when I brung them down here. I'll testify for Lil'Pit. He's a good kid. He's had more than his fair share of hard knocks."

"So you promise not to disappear on me?"

"Hell, no, Miz Andrews. The club, it does me proud. I'm mak'n good money down there. I'm not about to up and leave my major asset. I'll be around whenever you need me. And, hey, come down some night. Bring a friend. Bring a lot of friends. Have a few drinks on the house."

Kathryn walked Ray-Ray to the lobby and waved as the elevator doors closed. He waved back as he disappeared from sight. She turned back to her office, smiling at the thought of inviting the Goldstein, Miller litigation team to the Rendevous for an evening. But the simple sincerity of his invitation and his pride in the business he'd built touched her. If Tom had been alive, he'd have insisted they take Ray-Ray upon on his offer. And no doubt, he'd have begged Paul and Steve to go, too. And Shannon. *No, stop,* she told herself, *you don't have time now to think about Shannon. You have to stay focused on what matters.* And what mattered most at that moment, was viewing the surveillance tapes from the Rendevous.

CHAPTER FORTY-ONE

Tuesday, March 24, 2015, Offices of Goldstein, Miller, Emerald Shapery Center

At five p.m., as Hugh was about to leave for the day, his secretary buzzed him.

"A call for you from Senator Akers."

He sat down at his desk and considered whether or not to take it. An hour ago, Buffy had called to say she wanted to go to dinner at Juniper & Ivy and had made a reservation for six. Hugh had promised to be home by five-thirty.

But he decided to risk being late. He picked up the phone and said, "Hello, Fred."

"Hi, Hugh. I'm calling to give you an update on the Worth Act."

"Did it pass?"

"I'm afraid so. I voted against it, of course."

"Thanks, Fred."

"Glad to help you out. Don't worry, Hal's on the veto."

"That's good news. I've been distracted by this trial."

"Yeah, I can understand. I hear Rick didn't do so well for you."

"He tried, but we lost our star witness to a bunch of Paris thugs."

"You're actually thinking he was murdered?"

"Didn't want to say it, but yes."

"I'd like to hope you've got Wycliffe on the ropes, but the reports say Rick killed your case."

"We've got Kathryn left. There won't be a dry eye in the house when she's done."

"Good luck, then. Listen, I want you to come to D.C. when this is over so I can hook you up with the people you'll need for your campaign. Surely you realize how much you're needed in the Senate to vote down any more Worth Acts."

Hugh sighed. "I see your point, Fred. But Buffy has lost interest in being a senator's wife. Now she's demanding I become Ambassador to France."

"Hey, there are worse gigs," Fred said and hung up.

* * *

Dinner with Buffy was tense. He drank far too much scotch to dull the pain of listening to her plans to redecorate the residence of the American Ambassador in Paris. As she rambled on, he sucked down Glenlivet and wished that Kathryn were sitting across from him, planning their future in Paris. He fingered the emeralds in his pocket and allowed his mind to wander through his fantasy of being in Paris with Kathryn. Buffy was too self-absorbed to notice.

After they got home and went to their separate rooms like prize fighters going to their separate corners of the ring, Hugh sat outside on his private balcony and watched the night waves roll on shore. He thought of Tom Andrews and wondered if his spirit were out there against the horizon, surfing in the dark.

"I love your wife," he said to the spirit in the darkness. "You loved her, and God help me, I do, too. But I'm not even a tenth of the man you were, and she deserves so much more than the burned out old lech that I've become."

As he sipped the last of the smooth whisky that warmed his soul, he thought he heard a man's voice speaking. It said, "No one is perfect. No matter what Kathryn has told you, I wasn't either. Trust your instincts. She hasn't told you everything."

* * *

Hugh went to bed at one a.m. He tossed and turned until three before he drifted off. But not for long. His cell phone rang at five. Groggily, he reached out and punched "accept."

"Hugh, it's Rick!"

The edge of desperation in his voice pushed away the sleep cobwebs. "What's wrong?"

"Everything. I've been arrested. The feds are on to us."

"Shhh. Be quiet. Where are you?"

"I'm back home. I bailed out."

"Bailed out?"

"The feds came and arrested me at ten last night. They know about our fee sharing arrangement."

"But the statute of limitations has run—"

"Not on the Andrews case."

"But how did they know about that?"

"Logan."

"*What?*"

"Logan told her boyfriend, Travis."

"So? Logan's statement can be impeached. She's the scorned woman."

"But I'm not."

Hugh's gut tightened. "Oh, God, Rick. Not you."

"I had no choice. They offered me a two-year deal if I told them everything. Otherwise, I'd go to prison for the rest of my life. I'm sorry, Hugh."

"I took the Andrews case for you, Rick, because you were in dire financial straights. 'Sorry' doesn't exactly cut it."

"Don't give me that bullshit!" Rick shot back. "You took this case because you were tired of Logan and had the hots for Kathryn Andrews. Don't blame me because you can't keep your pants zipped. They're coming for you tomorrow." And he hung up.

Hugh sat very still in the early morning dark pierced only by the weak beam from his bedside light and remembered Patrick's prophetic words, *"Be careful, little brother. Your eye for attractive women will be your downfall one of these days."*

CHAPTER FORTY-TWO

Wednesday, March 25, 2015, Crown Manor, Coronado

Hugh slept little after Rick's call. He had been wide awake for an hour when his cell phone rang at six.

"Miss me?" Logan purred.

"Why'd you do it?" He hated himself for asking that question. Why never mattered. Only powerless people asked why.

"I told you I'd show you I'm a good lawyer."

"You haven't shown anyone you're a good lawyer. You've just demonstrated to the world you're a disloyal snitch."

She laughed the deep throaty laugh that he had once found so irresistible but which now turned his stomach. "No, I've just demonstrated to the world that I've turned the most feared plaintiff's lawyer in history into a scared cry-baby. Whining doesn't become you."

"You're terminated from Goldstein, Miller as of this instant." Powerless, he thought. Every word out of his mouth made him sound completely powerless. And he was.

"Ha!" She snorted. "Did you really think I'd be stupid

enough to give you the chance to fire me? I resigned yesterday when Travis told me he was ready to arrest Rick. And you."

"You'd better dust off your shingle then and get ready to hang it up in some seedy, executive office suite with all the other losers who couldn't make it in the Big Leagues. You'll never pull down more than fifty thousand a year until the day you die."

Her laughter was like fingernails on a blackboard. If they'd been in the same room, he'd have strangled her. "Listen to you, threatening me with money. I don't have to worry about that because Travis is a trust fund baby with more money than he'll spend in his lifetime. Besides, everyone will want to hire the attorney who brought down Hugh Mahoney. You, on the other hand, are going to have your ticket punched, removed, torn up, and burned by the State Bar."

Loss of his license, his ultimate nightmare. His stomach tightened. "You may have won this round, Logan; but you're going down in the end. You'll be begging me to take you back at Goldstein, Miller when all this is over." Only years of facing down major corporations across the battlefields of deposition conference tables gave him the chutzpah to bluff her. He punched the "end call" button to drown out her peals of derisive laughter.

To his horror, he realized he was shaking. He decided to go for a walk on the beach to steady his nerves. He watched the surfers in their wet suits waiting for waves and thought of Tom Andrews. As he began to calm down and think more clearly, he realized he wasn't as powerless as he thought. Hal Edwards wouldn't let Logan's wet-behind-the-ears boyfriend arrest one of his major campaign donors. After all, Hal had jumped at

Hugh's ten-million dollar offer in return for vetoing the Worth Act.

When he got back to Crown Manor, he dialed Hal's private cell. Edith answered. "Hugh, so good to hear from you. Did you know Justice Bloomberg is going to be stepping down from the Court, after all? You're number one on Hal's list."

"That's a relief. I didn't want to be an Ambassador."

"I know. Buffy will be disappointed. She wanted to live in Paris, but I can talk her around. After all, with the two of you in D.C., you'll be invited to all of our parties during Hal's second term."

The thought of parties at the White House was infinitely preferable to life at a federal country club prison. "That's great news, Edith. Listen, I need to talk to Hal."

"I'll certainly tell him. Unfortunately he's lunching with Justice Bloomberg right now at the Court, and he didn't take his phone with him because they don't want any interruptions. They are talking about the short-list of nominees. And, as I said, you are number one. All this is confidential, of course. There won't be an announcement until Hal feels certain that he's sure he's lined up enough Senators to confirm your appointment. It will take about six weeks."

"Sure, Edith. I understand. But, look, I need to talk to Hal urgently. The Department of Justice is out of its mind. They arrested Rick last night."

"Rick Peyton? But what could Rick possibly have done? He's a respected M.D. Buffy adores him."

"My point exactly, Edith. Look, a former employee of the firm has gone rogue and seduced a newbie Assistant U.S.

Attorney. She persuaded him to arrest Rick."

"A former female employee, I take it."

"Okay, Edith. I know how Buffy feels about the affairs. This was the last one, I swear. The two of you put the fear of God into me."

"Glad to hear it. Sorry, I've go to go. I'm already late to meet a troop of Girl Scouts from St. Louis who are here to tour the White House. I can't send Hal a text because obviously he doesn't have his phone. But I'll call the head of his Secret Service detail and tell him Hal needs to call you ASAP."

"Thanks, Edith."

"Don't worry about Rick."

After she hung up, Hugh showered and went through the motions of getting dressed while his mind whirled through Edith's news. An appointment to the Supreme Court was the best offer he'd heard in a long time. But now the threat of arrest looming over his head took on greater significance because it could deprive him of the chance to become Justice Mahoney.

He selected his navy power suit and maroon tie. He was not going to let a little twerp like Logan interfere with his career. No one could threaten him. He was always in control. He called the shots and named the tune everyone else had to dance to. He had created Logan Avery. Now, from his seat on the United States Supreme Court, he would enjoy destroying her. His vengeance would be swift and sure, and she would rue the day she was born.

He stepped back from the mirror and smiled. He looked ready to take on the world. And he was. Hal would put a stop to Logan and her schemes. There was nothing to worry about.

The last thing he did every morning was slip the emeralds into his pocket. But he paused as he reached for the box. He was confident that Hal would tell the DOJ to lay off. But Hal could be slow to take care of things, even in urgent matters. If Hal's rescue was delayed for any reason and if he was arrested today, Hugh did not want to be found with four carets of emerald earrings in his pocket. He locked them in the top drawer of his bureau and went down stairs to meet Jose, who would drive him to the courthouse.

CHAPTER FORTY-THREE

Wednesday, March 25, 2015, Edward J. Schwartz Federal Courthouse, U.S. District Court, Southern District of California, San Diego

At nine, in the green wool dress that made her eyes that fascinating shade of emerald, Kathryn swore to tell the truth and took her place on the witness stand. Mark, at the podium in front of her, gave her a reassuring smile as he asked the first question. He thought she looked beautiful. Hugh, sitting at the plaintiff's table with Joe Saunders, thought she did, too. He thought of the emerald earrings and wished for the right time and the right moment to give them to her.

"Would you state your name for the record, please?"

"Kathryn Britton Andrews."

"And your husband's name?"

"Thomas Allen Andrews."

"And when were you married, Mrs. Andrews?"

"June 10, 1997."

And they went on as they'd rehearsed the night before in the Goldstein, Miller conference room. It was the story of her marriage that she'd told during her deposition and the story of that fateful day in May when she'd made her first desperate midnight drive to the hospital, praying all the while that the person she loved most in the world would not be taken from her.

Mark had been waiting for her in the big conference room when she walked over from her office at six o'clock on Tuesday with her Glock tucked safely in her purse. They had planned for her to be there at five-thirty.

"Sorry to be so late. Something important came up today." She took off the jacket to her dark gray suit and hung it on a chair.

"Anything to do with that case Joe Saunders is working on for you?" Mark was in shirtsleeves, his tie loosened. He looked relaxed and happy. "I ordered turkey and roast beef. Help yourself."

"Yes, it does have something to do with Tyrone's case." She told him about Ray-Ray and the surveillance tapes between bites of turkey sandwich washed down with bottled water.

"Wow! So your client was on the tapes?"

"Yes, at one a.m., the exact time of the Thorn murder, Tyrone was in the parking lot at the Rendevous, dealing dope."

"Dealing dope beats life-without-parole for murder."

"Any day. And there's more."

"What else?"

"The police took the original tape from Ray-Ray's place the day after the Thorn murder, and they've never turned it over to me."

"You mean you've caught them withholding evidence that

could get your client acquitted? They've violated *Brady v. Maryland*?"

"Yes. Sam McIntyre, the Assistant D.A on the case, is pretty upset."

"So what does this mean for Tyrone?"

"Sam's going to get the felony-murder charges dismissed, and he's going to offer Tyrone a chance to plead guilty to one count of possession for sale with a recommendation for two years probation. I went to see Tyrone tonight to tell him the news. He's pretty excited, of course." Kathryn remembered Tyrone's tears of joy when she told him he was going to get his life back. He'd hugged her while he cried; and as she'd felt his thin body against hers, she had remembered that he was just a lost kid without a family who'd tried to get by the best way he could. She'd felt Tom in the room, shedding his own joyous tears, as she held Tyrone.

"But what will happen to him when he gets out? Didn't you say he's homeless?" Mark asked.

"Yes. That's the problem. He lied about his age to get a job making a little money bussing tables at Applebees' in Chula Vista. He was selling drugs that night at the Rendevous because he didn't have enough to live on."

Mark considered the problem thoughtfully. Then he said, "What if he could work here?"

"He's a fourteen-year-old kid with barely any education. What could he do at Goldstein, Miller?"

"Be a messenger. The ones we have don't stay long. And Martha McDonald, the head of the mail room, came up the hard way. I'll talk to her about Tyrone and see if we can't find somebody to take him under his or her wing."

"He'll be a ward of the juvenile court. The judge will have to approve whoever he lives with."

"I think we can find someone better than Ray-Ray Washington, with all due respect to him as a businessman."

Kathryn smiled and told him about Ray-Ray's pride in his establishment. "He invited me down with all my friends for drinks on the house. Tom would have taken him up on that." Suddenly, her eyes misted over. "Tom would be over the moon right now. I didn't want Tyrone's case, but I did it for Tom. I feel as if he's smiling at me." Her voice broke.

Mark reached across the table and put his hand on hers. "It's okay. And it's okay to tear up tomorrow on the stand. Don't worry if you do."

"I don't want the jury to think I'm faking anything."

"They won't. Believe me, they won't. When you talk about your husband, it's so obvious that you loved him very much."

Her lovely almond-shaped hazel eyes met his, and she gave him a teary smile. "I don't even have the words to say how much."

"Yes, you do. You don't realize how your voice changes when you talk about him. And then, there are the pictures of the two of you together. I probably shouldn't say this. It's not strictly professional. But we've all become friends and colleagues in the months we've worked on this. And I think every one of us in the firm who has had any contact with Tom's case wishes we had someone in our lives who loved us as much as you and Tom loved each other. The jury's going to see that, too. There's no way they could miss it."

She smiled at him. "Thanks. And thanks for finding a way to help Tyrone."

Tom would like Mark Kelly, she thought.

* * *

Wednesday, March 25, 2015, Edward J. Schwartz Federal Courthouse, U.S. District Court, Southern District of California, San Diego

It was almost lunchtime when Mark asked the question she'd anticipated since early that morning. "Now, Mrs. Andrews, do you recall the day your husband first became ill after he started talking Myrabin?"

"Yes."

Suddenly the back doors of the courtroom swung open and ten men in suits burst in. From the witness stand, Kathryn's practiced eye saw the bulge of shoulder holsters under their coats. Her stomach knotted.

"Don't come any farther!" Judge Weiner barked, partially rising from the bench. "Bailiff!" She gestured for her armed bailiff to block the aisle. He put his hand over his gun, still in its holster, as if he could single-handedly protect Her Honor and the courtroom from ten armed men.

"Who are you?" the judge demanded. "And how dare you come barging into my courtroom?"

"We are U.S. Marshals, and we are here with an arrest warrant for Hugh Sean Mahoney on charges of conspiracy and obstruction of justice. I'm Chief Deputy Anderson Baker," the leader of the group said.

"And you had to burst into my courtroom in the middle of a trial to serve this warrant, Chief Deputy Baker?" the normally unflappable judge's voice rose. She was angry and upset.

"We apologize, Your Honor. Exigent circumstances." Two of the deputy marshals had proceeded past Judge Weiner's bailiff and had handcuffs out for Hugh. Hugh thanked his lucky stars for the impulse he'd obeyed to leave the emerald earrings at home.

"Your Honor," Mark intoned, "they can't take a member of the defense team in the middle of the plaintiff's testimony."

"I agree," Judge Weiner said. "Stand away from Mr. Mahoney," she told the marshals who had surrounded Hugh.

The doors of the courtroom stirred again, and a thirty-something, brown-eyed, dark-haired, six-foot god in a navy Brooks Brother's suit walked in as if he owned the place. "I'm sorry, Judge Weiner, but the Department of Justice can take Mr. Mahoney. I'm Travis Eliot Davidson, III. Assistant U.S. Attorney. I'm here on special assignment from the Washington, D.C. office." He waived a thick sheaf of paper at the judge. "The grand jury has indicted Mr. Mahoney on twenty-two counts of conspiracy and obstruction of justice, and the Chief Justice of the United States Supreme Court, the Honorable Marion Bassett, has ordered us to take Mr. Mahoney into custody immediately."

Damn Hal for not getting on this right away. Maybe ten million was too much for his campaign. Maybe he should try to find something to like in whoever ran against him and teach Hal a lesson. Hugh tried not to flinch as the marshals applied the handcuffs. As the cold steel clicked around his wrist, he remembered Logan's litany of her boyfriend's credentials, Brown University, Fulbright Scholar, Harvard Law. *And a Ph.D. in cocky,* he added bitterly to himself. *Damn Hal!*

"Your Honor!" Now Mark, who always retained his Southern, gentlemanly calm, was angry. "This is a blatant violation of my client's due process rights and right to counsel of her choice."

"I couldn't agree with you more," Justice Weiner said. "But for now, my hands are tied by an order from the Chief Justice of the United States. We'll recess for the day and begin again tomorrow."

Kathryn came down from the witness stand and stood next to Mark as Hugh was led out of the courtroom. Mark's jaw twitched angrily. As soon as the courtroom doors closed behind them, he turned to her and said, "Let's go back to the firm and think about our options."

As they left together, Kathryn noticed Bob McLaren and Emma Talbert at the defense table, smiling at each other.

CHAPTER FORTY-FOUR

Tuesday, March 25, 2015, Offices of Goldstein, Miller, Emerald Shapery Center

They holed up like refugees in the large conference room, Patty, Stewart, Mark, and Kathryn. Stewart, as the junior member of the team, ordered sandwiches for lunch that only he ate. Mark, as senior member of the team, summoned William Hackney, the head of the firm's white collar crime section, to deal with Hugh's arrest and to arrange for bail.

After William left, Patty said, "This has got to be related to Rick. The feds arrested him on Tuesday night. Did you know?"

Mark shook his head. "No one told me."

"They promised him a two-year sentence if he'd agree to testify against Hugh about their fee-splitting arrangement. Logan ratted them out to the feds."

"What fee-splitting arrangement?" Kathryn asked.

"Hugh doesn't want anyone to know about this outside the firm," Patty said. "But for years he has shared a percentage of the attorneys' fees with Rick in the cases Rick worked on."

"But that's a violation of the ethics rules. An attorney can't share attorneys' fees with a non-lawyer."

"Right," Mark sighed. "But Hugh had this arrangement with Rick for years because Rick spotted cases like yours for him. He had a similar arrangement with a stockbroker named Eric Steiner for securities cases."

"So attorneys' fees as finders' fees?" Kathryn asked.

Patty nodded. "It's a common practice in civil litigation. Or was, until a few years ago when the feds came sniffing around all the big plaintiffs' firms. Hugh would have been safe because the statute had run on all the cases he and Rick and Eric had worked on, but then Rick begged him to take your case as the last one. Rick was in financial trouble. Again."

"So Hugh agreed to one last unethical split, and now Rick has bailed on him," Kathryn observed.

Mark nodded. "I'm afraid that's the size of it."

"But fee-splitting isn't obstruction of justice," Kathryn insisted.

"No, it's not. But Hugh and Rick swore under oath during the investigation into the plaintiffs' firms that had engaged in the practice that they, in fact, hadn't. Those declarations under penalty of perjury have come back to haunt them," Mark explained.

Kathryn looked disappointed by the news.

"I'm afraid Logan wasn't satisfied with the townhouse in Georgetown and the guarantee of partnership in the D.C. office," Patty observed. "She wanted to make it personal. And she has."

"I'll ask for a mistrial in the morning," Mark said. "The jury not only saw the arrest, they heard the charges, conspiracy and obstruction of justice. Our entire case has been prejudiced because of that."

Kathryn frowned. "No, I don't want you to ask for a mistrial."

"But Kathryn," Patty said, "the jury has been tainted. There is no jury instruction the judge could give that would undo what they saw and heard today."

"I can't face going through a trial a second time." Mark saw the strain around her eyes. "It was all I could do to answer those deposition questions; and then today I told half of the same story again. As I sit here right now, I'm wondering how I can get up there tomorrow and talk about Tom's days in the hospital, and how he looked at me the minute before he died. I believe I've got the strength to finish tomorrow. But that's all. I can't go through this again. I can't."

Mark looked at Patty, who said, "Okay. So getting Judge Weiner to grant a mistrial will mean Wycliffe wins?"

Kathryn nodded.

"Then we won't ask," Mark said. "Let's go home and get a good night's rest. And start over in the morning."

CHAPTER FORTY-FIVE

Wednesday, March 25, 2015, 1845 Ocean Place, Pacific Beach

At seven-thirty, Kathryn sat on the sofa in her living room with a tray of microwave mac and cheese in her hands and a glass of red wine. Her Glock and her iPhone were next to each other on the coffee table. She looked over at Tom's medals in their case and smiled.

"I miss you. If you were here, I'd be eating real food."

Could dead people laugh? Tom would laugh at that. Maybe it was time to learn to be a decent cook, she thought. Maybe it was time to let go of Tom and think about someone else. Someone like Mark Kelly.

Her phone rang. Although it was Paul and she'd been avoiding him, she answered.

"Hey, are you okay? Hugh's arrest is all over the news."

"I'm okay. It was, to say the least, dramatic."

"So the judge will declare a mistrial for sure."

"I told Mark not to ask for one. I can't go through this again, Paul."

"But Kathryn–"

"Don't! I've heard all the pros and cons of mistrial from Patty and Mark this afternoon. I'm going to get on the stand tomorrow and tell the rest of Tom's story, and then I'm done. I could not possibly go through this again. Too many people are dead. Tom. Dr. Vannier. Harrison O'Connor. Mary Lancaster."

"You're not safe!" Paul said.

"I've heard that before, too. I'm not leaving home. I feel Tom here. I want to be with Tom."

"But you've got to survive to testify tomorrow."

"I've got my gun."

"Kathryn–"

"I'm fine, Paul. Good night!"

* * *

Wednesday, March 25, 2015, Crown Manor, Coronado, California

"You fool!" Buffy greeted Hugh when he walked in the door at eight-thirty that evening. William Hackney had arranged for bail and had sent Jose in the Mercedes to bring him home. All Hugh could think about was a massive dose of scotch.

"Not now." He shook his head wearily as he headed for the stairs and his bedroom on the second floor.

But Buffy planted herself in his path. "You utter idiot! You've finally ruined everything because of a woman! You'll never be ambassador to anywhere now!"

I'm more worried about losing my shot at the Supreme Court, he thought as he stepped around Buffy and headed upstairs.

Damn it, Hal needed to get on this right now!

He poured a scotch and dialed Hal's cell. Eleven-thirty was not too late to call, but Hugh would have called even if it had been the wee hours of the morning. His stomach churned as he waited for the president to answer.

Finally, to his relief, Hal's smooth baritone said, "Hey, old man. Sorry I couldn't get the cavalry there in time."

"Why the hell not?" Hugh gulped his scotch. "Don't tell me the Attorney General isn't taking your calls."

"No, Liz Preston got back to me right away. The problem is your ex's boyfriend and his posse of marshals were already on their way, and the arrest warrant had been issued. Look, Hugh, if I'd known they were going after Rick even twenty-four hours before they took him, I could have stopped it cold. But it's more complicated now. He's been interrogated, and he's implicated you."

"What are you saying? Can't you stop this? Edith told me this morning I was your number one pick for Justice Bloomberg's seat on the Court."

"And you are. I've got my personal lawyer on this. He's trying to figure out what my options are. Don't worry. I'll get it fixed. I'll get you on the Court. I just can't do it as fast as either of us would like."

"So in the meantime, I'm out on bail, facing twenty-two counts of obstruction."

"I know it sounds bad. But I promise I'll find a way to stop it."

"You'd better. You know as well as I do I'm guilty as hell. I couldn't go to trial. I'd have to plea bargain and admit to at least one felony. I'd lose my license to practice law."

"Corporate America would run amuck without you. We can't let that happen. Look, I know it's hard. But stay calm, and give me some time."

"How long do you think it will take to make it go away? Do you think I'll actually be arraigned? Should I get an attorney?"

"That's probably a good idea. Just to be safe. Don't worry, Hugh. I can't lose one of my major donors right before the election. I want you on the Court a lot more than in federal prison. Have a drink and try to get some sleep. I'm on it."

* * *

After he hung up with Hal, Hugh poured himself another scotch and paced around his room. When the alcohol began to calm his nerves, he unlocked the drawer that held the emeralds and opened the box to gaze at the four carats of green magic suspended from another carat of diamond fire. Kathryn. Hal was right. He needed a criminal defense attorney. At least in the short run. He had to see Kathryn. He picked up his cell and dialed her number.

"Hugh! Are you okay?" The concern in her voice warmed his heart.

"I'm fine. I need to talk to you."

"I can be there in thirty minutes."

"No!" He realized he'd put too much force behind that word. He didn't want Buffy to know he was seeing her. "I'll come to you. Jose will drive me." He slipped the box of emeralds into his pocket.

* * *

At ten p.m., Jose parked the Mercedes in front of 1845 Ocean Place. Hugh sat in the back seat for a moment and took in the ambience of the little blue cottage with the red door surrounded by white roses. Obviously the residents had planted those flowers with plenty of love for the little house and for each other.

Kathryn had left the front porch light on. She answered as soon as he knocked. She was wearing gray sweat pants and a dark green hoodie and no makeup. Hugh's heart skipped a beat. She was breathtaking.

"Come in. I'm sorry I don't have any scotch. Would you like a glass of wine?"

Hugh produced his flask. "I came prepared."

Kathryn poured wine for herself and scotch for Hugh and invited him to sit on the sofa in the living room. She took the chair opposite. He looked over at Tom's medals in their case.

"Impressive," he said.

"Yes. He was an amazing man."

"I'm afraid I'm not." He drank a long sip of scotch.

"Patty explained a little bit of the story today when we met at the firm. Why don't you tell me yourself what happened?"

Hugh sighed. "Many years ago, I won a wrongful death case for Rick, as I told you. Antidepressant drugs killed his wife, and he recovered millions from the suit.

"But Rick likes the high life. He went through those millions and came up with a scheme to make more. Because of his work, he heard many meritorious stories from patients who'd been harmed by drugs, and he persuaded me to take their cases and to cut him a much bigger portion of the fees than he was entitled to under the Rules of Professional Responsibility.

"But every plaintiffs' firm at that time was paying finders' fees, in violation of the rules. I saw a chance to help Rick and to vindicate the people who'd been hurt by Big Medicine."

"Like your father," Kathryn said.

"Like my father."

"So why are you in trouble now?"

"A few years back, the feds started asking questions about fees and plaintiffs' firms. Rick and I, like many others, swore under oath in affidavits that we had not engaged in unethical fee sharing."

"But you had?"

"Yes, we had. But fee splitting is now the least of our problems. They've got us for lying under oath."

"Moral turpitude."

Hugh sighed. "Right. The fancy words for dishonesty which are the nail in any lawyer's coffin."

"So you don't have a defense?"

"No, I don't. Rick called me on Tuesday night and told me he'd been arrested. He's turned informer in exchange for a two-year sentence. They know everything."

"According to Patty, Logan was the one who broke the case."

Hugh gave her a sheepish smile. "The most powerful lawyer in America brought down by the woman he dumped. My brother warned me that a woman would be my undoing. Buffy called me an idiot tonight. Maybe I am."

To his surprise, Kathryn looked sympathetic. "No, you're not. You're human. To one degree or another, my clients are all in trouble because they're human."

"Your opinion matters to me." He felt as if he'd just bared his soul.

"It's not my job to judge. The jury judges guilt or innocence. The judge judges culpability when he or she hands down the sentence. I don't judge. I tell my client's story, that's all."

"This whole thing killed us in front of the jury. Mark's moving for a mistrial tomorrow, isn't he?"

"I asked him not to. I'm going to get on the stand in the morning and tell the rest of my story and Tom's, and the chips are going to have to fall where they may. I can't go through another trial."

"I wish you'd reconsider. We had a good shot at winning until this happened." He poured more scotch into his glass from his flask. "Prejudicing your case in front of the jury is Logan's form of payback. Travis Elliott Davidson III is her new boyfriend. I've talked to Hal Edwards. I'm a major campaign donor. He's working on making all this go away. When he does, we can start over with a fresh jury."

"But even the president can't force the attorney general to withdraw the indictment."

"I'm not talking about force. Suggestion. Getting Liz Preston to see that he'd like her to stay on as the Attorney General in his second term if she does him a favor."

"But you're on dangerous ground until that happens. If it happens."

Hugh sighed and tossed back the last of his scotch. "I know. What do you think I should do?"

"Hire a really good attorney."

"How about you? Will you represent me?"

"I can't. I'm a client, and you make too much money to be represented by the Public Defender."

"Then who?"

"Sarah Knight. She's in the D.C. office of Warrick, Thompson."

"The one who got Alexa Reed off on the double murder of her husband and that sleazy psychologist?"

"Yes. She's one of the best. I met her through Paul. Do you want me to ask him to contact her for you?"

Hugh sighed as he poured himself more scotch. "I'd be very grateful if you would."

"You're going through that way too fast," Kathryn observed.

He gave her a half smile. "I know. My doctor never lets me forget. But if Hal can't get Liz and the DOJ to withdraw that indictment, I'll have to plead. I can't go to trial."

"Because you're guilty."

He nodded. "And I'll lose my license. I started out seeking revenge for my dad, but after a while I got greedy. Or I should say, Rick and I got greedy. I've run after money at all costs. And I can't even show that I'm much of a philanthropist."

"You've helped Tyrone. You've saved his life. Joe came up with surveillance video that the cops wrongfully withheld. The video shows Tyrone is innocent. If you hadn't paid Joe, I would have never found the truth for Tyrone."

Hugh brightened a little. "Really?"

"Really. He's on the surveillance tape dealing drugs at the time of the murder. He'll plead to one count of possession for sale in return for two years probation. Mark's going to find him a job at the firm as a messenger. You've done a lot of good, Hugh. I wouldn't be in court right now, telling Tom's story, if it weren't for you."

Hugh gulped the last of the scotch and let it fortify his courage before he reached into his pocket and brought out the box and put it on the coffee table between her Glock and her iPhone. "This is for you."

Kathryn looked down at the little blue box and frowned. "For me? Why?"

"Just open it. Please." *I wish I were young at this moment,* Hugh thought. *I wish I were Mark Kelly, and I could say, "marry me."*

She picked it up carefully and opened the box. Her eyes grew wide when she saw the emeralds. She picked one up and held it up to the light before she put it back in the box and pushed it gently back toward Hugh. "They are quite lovely, but I couldn't possibly accept anything this valuable."

"Please." He knew he was pleading with her. He wasn't the most powerful plaintiff's attorney in America anymore. He was an old man, begging to be loved, even at a distance.

"No, Hugh. Really. Thank you. But no." *At least she smiled when she said it,* he thought.

Hugh picked up the box and held it in his big hands. "I didn't do this because I thought you were like Logan. Or even Patty."

"I'm glad to hear that. But I have the utmost respect for Patty."

Hugh nodded. "We are friends. I thought Logan and I would be friends, but I was wrong."

"Patty loved you. Logan was only ambitious."

Hugh smiled at her. "Were I as wise as you, I would not be on bail right now."

"Real love forgives a lot."

As she spoke, Hugh wondered if that was her secret. Had she forgiven Tom for something nearly unforgivable? He wondered what it was. But he dared not ask. Instead he said, "If we are talking about real love, I want to be honest with you."

"All right. Be honest."

He would never forget the moment of looking into her beautiful face, free of makeup, open and compassionate. He said, "The truth is, I love you. I'd give all my millions to have you love me. I know that's impossible. I know what I am. I'm arrogant, overreaching, and vindictive. I've done good for Tyrone, but I've also done bad things in the name of vengeance. I drove a small law firm out of business last year because I imagined that their senior partner, my colleague, threatened my control of a case. He didn't do that. And Mark told me he didn't. But I punished him anyway.

"I have never been in the same league as your husband. I've never been unfailingly honest and just and compassionate like Tom. I've never deserved anyone like you. Look, I'm not asking for much. I just want you to take these emeralds and let me be happy that I could give you something that says how much I love you. Please."

His heart beat faster when she picked up the little blue box and opened it once more. There were tears in her eyes. "Okay," she said. "Okay, I'll take them because it will make you happy."

"And promise me you'll wear them. Don't just put them in

a drawer somewhere. Wear them. Because you are a beautiful woman, and you deserve beautiful things to wear."

She gazed at the box in silence, while tears rolled down her cheeks.

Hugh stood up. "I should go. You've had a long day. And tomorrow will be another."

Still holding the little box, she walked him to the front door. She stopped and looked up at him. "I'll call Paul tonight before I go to bed and tell him you need Sarah."

"Thanks."

They stood looking at each other in silence for a few seconds. Then Hugh asked,

"Would you mind if I hugged you?"

She smiled and opened her arms.

He went out into the night and got into the car where Jose waited. He looked back at the little blue house with the light shining on the red door and the white roses, and his heart broke as he realized how much she had lost when her husband died. She could never be his, but she could wear his emeralds And the thought of that would forever bring joy to his old-man's heart, eternally longing for her love.

CHAPTER FORTY-SIX

Thursday, March 26, 2015, Edward J. Schwartz Federal Courthouse, U.S. District Court, Southern District of California, San Diego

Judge Weiner took the bench promptly at nine and looked over at Mark expectantly. "Does the plaintiff have any motions for the court to hear before the bailiff brings in the jury?"

She thinks we're going to ask for a mistrial, Hugh thought; *and since she's anticipating it, she's prepared to grant it. He wished Kathryn hadn't been so dead set against a new trial.*

"No motions, Your Honor, but we do have a request for an instruction to be read to the jury when it comes in this morning."

Surprise registered on the judge's face. Mistrial had been the only thing on her mind. "I assume you've drafted the instruction you want me to read?"

"Yes, Your Honor." Mark handed copies to the bailiff to give to the judge and opposing counsel.

Judge Weiner read it over, nodding in agreement as she read. When she looked up she focused on Bob McLaren. "Anything you want to say, Mr. McLaren?"

"No, Your Honor."

"No objections?" The judge raised her eyebrows.

"None, Your Honor."

"Then if the bailiff would please bring in the jury."

All sixteen pairs of eyes focused on Hugh, the minute the jurors entered the courtroom. They hadn't been expecting him.

When the jurors were seated, Judge Weiner began. "All of you witnessed an unfortunate event yesterday that, quite frankly, should never have taken place in anyone's courtroom. I'm going to read you a jury instruction now about how you are to treat what went on yesterday.

"Ladies and gentlemen of the jury, the plaintiff in any civil case is entitled to a fair trial. Mrs. Andrews, the plaintiff in this case, is entitled to a trial untainted by bias or prejudice from matters outside the evidence. The scene that the U.S. Marshals and the United States Attorney created in this courtroom yesterday is not a part of the evidence in Mrs. Andrews' case, and you are to ignore the events of yesterday in deciding this case. Mrs. Andrews' attorney, Mr. Hugh Sean Mahoney, is a member in good standing of the California State Bar, and Mrs. Andrews is entitled to have his assistance at trial as one of her federal constitutional due process rights." The judge finished reading and leaned slightly toward the jurors in the box. "Is there anyone who will be influenced by what happened here yesterday? I see no hands," Judge Weiner intoned for the record. "Mr. Kelly, please call your next witness."

"Kathryn Britton Andrews."

And so, throughout the morning and into mid-afternoon

after the lunch break, Kathryn told the rest of Tom's story. His swollen, bloated limbs; the dementia relieved only by slipping into a coma; his last breath spent telling her that he loved her. There was not, as Hugh had predicted, a dry eye in the house.

Bob McLaren moved quickly on cross-examination to dispel the jury's sympathy.

"Good afternoon, Mrs. Andrews."

"Good afternoon." His oily, insinuating tone made her stomach knot.

"Now, if I understand correctly, you and your husband chose not to have children."

"We tried to have a child, but we were never successful."

"Your husband's medical records indicate you tried in vitro fertilization."

"Yes, we did. It was unsuccessful."

"And was your inability to conceive a source of conflict between you and your husband?"

Mark saw the startled look in Kathryn's eyes before she quickly suppressed it. McLaren smiled. He knew he'd hit a nerve. *But what nerve,* Mark wondered. *She had never told anyone at Goldstein, Miller that being childless had been a strain on her marriage.*

"No, of course not. Tom and I were that much closer because we had no children."

"I see." Sarcastic skepticism dripped from every vowel. "So tell me, Mrs. Andrews, how did you and Tom celebrate your holidays, as a childless couple?"

"We traveled, usually to places where Tom could surf."

"And did you also give holiday parties?"

The wary look in Kathryn's eye warned Mark that McLaren was close to something else she did not want known. *Damn! Why hadn't she trusted him and Patty enough to tell them everything?* He sensed disaster on the way.

"Yes, we did."

"And wasn't your Christmas party always a large affair?"

"Well, the guests filled up the house, if that's what you mean. But our house was very small."

"I see." More dripping sarcastic skepticism. "And I assume that Paul Curtis and Steve Cooper, your husband's childhood friends, were at these parties?"

"Yes, although sometimes Paul was not in town."

"I see," McLaren intoned once more.

Mark smiled as he noticed the jury was growing restless and looking uncomfortable in the face of McLaren's rambling questions and open rudeness. Opposing counsel's bad manners were winning points for Kathryn. Maybe disaster was not imminent after all.

"And I assume Paul Curtis and Steve Cooper brought their significant others to these holiday parties?"

"Yes, although Steve was often single and came to the parties alone."

"But didn't Steve have a very serious relationship with someone in December 2011?"

Mark saw her deer-in-the-headlights expression once more before she managed to wipe her face clean of emotion. "Not a 'very serious relationship,' no."

"You mean he wasn't seeing someone at Christmas 2011? Someone that he wanted to marry?"

Suddenly Mark knew from her expression that Kathryn was in trouble. He stood up and intoned, "Objection, Your Honor. Steve Cooper's social life is irrelevant."

"I couldn't agree more," Judge Weiner said. "I thought I made that clear, Mr. McLaren, when you were cross-examining Mr. Curtis."

Bob McLaren gave the judge an insincere smile. "I apologize for being a bit slow, Your Honor.

"Now, Mrs. Andrews, did your husband drink at these parties?"

"Well, everyone did."

"So you would agreed that your husband consumed alcohol with his friends at holiday parties?"

"Yes."

"Wine, beer, cocktails?"

"Tom preferred beer. But he drank wine with me when we went out to dinner. He didn't like mixed drinks."

"And what about surfing? Did your husband often drink beer with his fellow surfers?"

"I don't know what you mean by 'often.'"

"Well, how many days a week did your husband surf?"

"As many as he could."

"And on those days, did he come back with his companions and have a beer or two?"

"Not on weekdays. He had to go straight to the office in the mornings."

"So on weekends?"

"Sometimes." *Where were these questions coming from?* Kathryn struggled to keep panic at bay and to stay focused on clean, sharp answers that would give nothing away. But she looked over at Mark at the plaintiff's table and realized he knew she was in trouble.

"Did your husband surf every weekend?"

"Most of the time."

"Did he surf alone?"

"Steve or Paul usually went, too." *And, God forbid, Shannon.*

"And did your husband drink beer with them on the weekends after surfing?"

"Sometimes." *He knows you're lying. Tom and Steve and Paul always had a beer, sometimes two, after surfing. But Paul would never have given away this secret. Only Shannon knew because she was usually with them.*

"So just to sum up, Mrs. Andrews. You and your husband were very happily married. Being childless brought you closer together, and failure to conceive was not a strain on your marriage. And you liked to entertain your friends at holiday parties where your husband drank beer and wine, and he also drank beer on a weekly basis with friends after surfing. Did I fairly summarize the facts, Mrs. Andrews?"

"Yes, Mr. McLaren." She worked to keep her composure while panic chipped at her soul.

"Thank you. No further questions." And Bob McLaren sat down.

Judge Weiner turned to Mark. "Any follow up, Mr. Kelly?"

"Briefly, Your Honor."

Mark resumed the podium and gave her a friendly, reassuring smile that the jury could not see. "Now, Mrs. Andrews, just to be clear. Your husband enjoyed an alcoholic beverage with friends from time to time?"

"Yes."

"And when he consumed beer or wine with friends, did he exhibit symptoms of intoxication?"

"Objection, Your Honor." Bob McLaren leapt to his feet. "Calls for an opinion the witness is not qualified to give."

Judge Weiner looked at McLaren with an amused glimmer in her eyes. "Oh, I believe any wife is qualified to give an opinion on when her husband is drunk, Mr. McLaren. Overruled."

"No. Tom was a very moderate drinker."

Mark smiled. "Thank you, Mrs. Andrews."

Bob McLaren was on his feet immediately. "I have some additional questions."

"Very well," Judge Weiner said.

"Did your husband consume alcohol on a daily basis, Mrs. Andrews?"

"No." *But in those days after the 2011 Christmas party, he did. As the Pepe Jackson case approached, he drank daily. But I'm the only person who knows. Except Shannon.*

"What about when he was upset? Did he tend to drink more then?"

"No." *It's lie I can get away with, she told herself.*

"Thank you. No more questions." Bob McLaren gave her his oily smile and sat down.

Kathryn realized her knees were shaking as she climbed down from the witness stand. It took all her strength to cross the courtroom confidently and resume her place between Mark and Hugh. Both of them smiled, so maybe she had done a better job than she thought she had.

Judge Weiner looked at Mark expectantly. "Any more witnesses, Mr. Kelly?"

He stood up. "No, Your Honor. The plaintiff rests, subject to admission of the exhibits."

CHAPTER FORTY-SEVEN

Thursday March 26, 2015, 1845 Ocean Place, Pacific Beach

"I don't think you have to worry," Paul said that night at eight-thirty. Kathryn had called him to come over after she'd gotten home from court, her nerves on edge and her pulse racing. He refilled her glass with the French Bordeaux he had brought to go with the pepperoni pizza they had ordered from New York Pizza Kitchen. She was drinking more than usual.

"But he started questioning me about things only Shannon would have known."

"What kinds of things?"

"Like how much beer Tom drank in a week. Whether he always drank after surfing. Whether Steve brought his girlfriends to our holiday parties."

Paul shrugged. "Well, Shannon isn't the only one who knows about your holiday parties and Steve's dating habits. As for the rest of it, McLaren was just stabbing in the dark. You already know Wycliffe wants to claim alcohol destroyed Tom's liver, not Myrabin. McLaren was hoping he'd get some facts out of you to support the defense theory. Actually, I'd be happy if I were you that McLaren went fishing. That means he doesn't have the evidence he needs to back up his case."

She gave him a weak smile. "I hope you're right."

"I'm absolutely right. What did Mark say about your performance?"

"He thought it went well. And Hugh did, too.

"How is Hugh? Sarah called today. She agreed to talk to him about taking his case."

"I'm glad. I think he's going to need her. He's in denial. He thinks Hal Edwards is going to get the indictment withdrawn because he's such a big campaign contributor."

She thought about the emeralds in their box in the bottom of her jewelry chest and wondered if she should have agreed to accept them.

Paul shrugged. "It could happen. Word on the street says the whole thing is Logan's doing. She and her boyfriend are far enough down the totem pole to have their plan foiled by the higher-ups. You look tired."

"I am. Long day. They start their case tomorrow."

"Who are they calling first?"

"Fred Butler, the head of the Myrabin approval team at the FDA. He'll testify that the approval process was all routine and done correctly."

Paul smiled. "That ought to put the jury to sleep."

"Our main worry is that he'll harp on Rick's inability to name the number of post-approval deaths. We thought we'd have Harrison O'Connor or Mary Lancaster to give first-hand accounts of how many people have died since Myrabin was approved and to explain how the deaths were covered up.

Harrison had told us there were at least six hundred. But we lost them both."

"Wycliffe is desperate."

"Except Harrison's death has been ruled a suicide, and Mary and Leon Abromowitz were supposedly the victims of a botched robbery."

I've been worried about you, too."

"I'm fine." Kathryn pointed to her Glock on the coffee table, next to the pizza box.

"I know you're good with that thing," Paul acknowledged, "but it's no guarantee you'll be safe. I wish you'd come stay with me until the trial is over."

But she shook her head. "No. I have to be here. I feel Tom here. I can't be anywhere else."

"Please reconsider."

"No."

He sighed. "What about taking a trip together when this is all over?"

"Could you take the time away from work?"

"If Alan won't give it to me, I'll quit."

"You wouldn't do that!"

"I won't have to. I'm long overdue for a vacation. I'll have no problem getting the time off."

Kathryn considered the idea as she sipped Bordeaux. "Where do you want to go?"

He smiled. "Somewhere we've never been before with anyone else. What about Tahiti?"

"Or the South of France."

"You decide. But I'm completely serious, let's go away

together when it's over. What do you say?"

"I'll have to think about it." He knew the question that was coming next, and he dreaded it. "When was the last time you saw Shannon?"

"Not since that night when you came by and her car was in the drive. A night I continue to regret, by the way. She called a few times after that; but I put her off, and then finally I told her the truth."

"Which was?"

"Just what I told you. We were tired and lonely and drunk, and it was sex and nothing more. I told her I'm in love with you and always have been. And I told her I had problems with the way she'd treated you when Tom was alive."

"What did she say?"

"Nothing. What could she say? She was wrong to go after Tom the way she did, especially while she was still living with Steve."

"After the way McLaren questioned me today, I'm worried Wycliffe found her and talked to her about Tom and me."

"There's no way they could have. We're the only ones who knew about that."

She sipped wine thoughtfully for a minute. Then she said, "I keep racking my brain to make sure you're right."

"I'm right. I'm the only one Tom talked to about those letters."

"But Shannon's friends knew she moved out of Steve's place in January of 2012."

"True, but her friends didn't know Shannon's interest in Tom had anything to do with her move. Shannon realized Tom was very confused about what he wanted, and she knew he would break things off in a heartbeat if she told anyone they were a couple. Because they weren't a couple, Kath. He wasn't committed to her. I don't know how many times I have to tell you: Tom wasn't going to leave you."

She was silent as she studied the medals in the case. The silence lengthened until he became uncomfortable. Paul poured the last of the Bordeaux into her glass to give himself something to do.

Finally he said, "You aren't going to forgive me for not telling you about Shannon and Tom in the winter of 2012, are you?"

She shook her head impatiently and her eyes met his, dark and troubled. "I don't know. I keep trying to forgive you. Part of me wants to forgive you, and part of me says I shouldn't. The part of me that knows you are the only person left who knew Tom the way I did wants to forgive. But the part of me that says you betrayed me says I should never trust you again."

Paul looked down at his own glass as disappointment cut his heart in two. "Look, I thought I was doing the right thing. I knew Tom wasn't going to leave you because he loved you, and he didn't love Shannon. I knew the whole Shannon thing was going to blow over, so why upset you needlessly? What good would it have done for me to tell you, Kath? What would you have done differently?"

"I would have fought harder to keep Tom!"

"But you didn't have to fight to keep him. He was always yours!"

CHAPTER FORTY-EIGHT

Wednesday, April 1, 2015, Crown Manor, Coronado

Hugh's cell rang at midnight as he was standing on the balcony of his bedroom, drinking scotch and staring at the Pacific. The ocean always calmed his nerves. He was waiting for a progress report from Hal Edwards. It had been three days since Edith had telephoned to say Hal was in negotiations with Liz Preston.

"Hey, old man!" Hal could have worked as an announcer with that voice.

"You're up late." Hugh felt as relieved as a teenage girl who'd been waiting for her boyfriend's call.

"Presidents never sleep. That's one of the downsides to the job. In case you're ever tempted to run."

"No thanks. Any news?"

"Liz has said she's willing to work with me on it. She's been talking to Davidson's boss. He's not happy that Davidson went before the grand jury without his permission. Maybe we can turn the tables on your ex and her honey, get the indictment dismissed, and get him fired."

Relief washed over Hugh. "Sounds good to me."

"Have you been arraigned?" Hal asked.

"Yeah. I had to appear with Bill Hackney last Monday morning. Took all of ten minutes to plead not guilty."

"Okay. I was hoping things hadn't gotten that far."

Hugh felt his gut tighten again. "Does that mean you can't get Liz to withdraw it?"

"No. But the more they accomplish procedurally, the less willing they are going to be to let it go. Do you have an attorney or is Bill representing you?"

"God, no, not Bill. Sarah Knight has agreed to take it on."

"Ah, the best of the best."

"I'd expect to win if I had a defense."

"Alexa Reed looked as if she didn't have one, and she walked away, charges dismissed. I'd say Sarah will help you become Justice Mahoney."

"So that's still in the works?"

"Absolutely. But top secret until we get this other matter cleared up."

"Thanks, Hal."

"Hey, like I said, I need your money for my next campaign, and I need your vote on the court during my second term. Don't worry, Hugh. I'm on it. How's the Myrabin trial going? Aren't you guys about ready to wrap things up and send it to the jury?"

"I'd say we're close. Last Friday Fred Butler testified in excruciating detail about the FDA's approval of Myrabin. His testimony was full of dates and numbers and the jurors' eyes glazed over. It was the same story Butler told us when we went to FDA headquarters last October and met with him and his team. Since we lost our two best impeachment witnesses,

Harrison O'Connor and Mary Lancaster, we didn't have any way of showing the jury that Butler was lying when he swore the approval process was conducted according to FDA regulations."

"It wasn't?"

"No. Someone ordered a cover-up of two deaths in the clinical trials and of all the post-approval deaths. But without Harrison or Mary, we have no evidence to show that. And then on Monday, McLaren called Charles Lawson who proceeded to assassinate the reputations of Dr. Vannier and Dr. Girard. Mark did a great job on cross-examination of getting Lawson to admit his bias because of his work as a lobbyist for Big Drug. The jury did not look impressed when he left the witness stand, so I think we won that round.

"Then yesterday and today, they put on Winston Wilhite, the head of Wycliffe's research division. He did what we expected and gave an opinion that alcohol, not Myrabin, caused Tom Andrews' death. He also insisted that Wycliffe had completely reformulated Myrabin after purchasing it from Suchet, but Mark shot that down pretty hard on cross-examination. Wilhite more or less admitted that he'd lied about a new formula."

"Sounds like closing argument tomorrow," Hal said.

"That's what we are thinking. Mark is preparing tonight."

"Aren't you doing the closing?"

"No. Juries don't like me. And now I'm a jailbird to boot."

"Hey, you definitely are not, and that's almost behind you. Good luck tomorrow. I'll keep working on Liz and DOJ. Don't worry."

* * *

Thursday, April 2, 2015, Edward J. Schwartz Federal Courthouse, U.S. District Court, Southern District of California, San Diego

Next morning, as they took their places at the plaintiff's table, Kathryn glanced at the back of the courtroom and saw someone who looked like Dan Ayers seated in the last row of public seating. She immediately felt uneasy.

A few minutes later, Judge Weiner took the bench and asked, "Does the defense rest at this time, Mr. McLaren?"

"No, Your Honor. We have one further witness."

"Please call your next witness, then."

Bob McLaren stood up and said, "The defense calls Shannon Lynn Freeman."

Mark felt Kathryn, who was seated next to him, tense up even before the tall, beautiful blonde in the tight navy dress strode through the courtroom. As Kathryn turned to see Shannon approach the witness stand, the man who had called himself Dan Ayers held her eye and gave her a faint smile. She felt sick.

Shannon tossed her long blonde hair, and swore to tell the truth. She looked older and harder than the last time Kathryn had seen her. Too much time in the sun had etched fine lines around the corners of her eyes and around her mouth. She looked around the courtroom until she caught Kathryn's eye. She gave her a contemptuous little smile.

"Who is she?" Mark whispered in Kathryn's ear.

"Steve's ex-girlfriend," she whispered back. Mark hoped the

jury didn't notice the terror in her eyes. Clearly Shannon Freeman wasn't going to be good for their case. Mark stood up. "Objection, Your Honor."

"On what grounds, Mr. Kelly?"

"We've had no notice that Mr. McLaren intended to call this witness, and we've had no opportunity to take her deposition."

"We only just located Ms. Freeman," Bob McLaren countered. "And as for deposition, the plaintiff was allowed to present Dr. Girard, without giving us an opportunity to depose her."

Judge Weiner turned back to Mark. "Mr. McLaren has a point, Mr. Kelly. I'm going to let this witness testify."

As Mark sat down, Kathryn could see him clench his jaw. He was furious. Panic seized her. *I should have told them about Shannon. But now it is too late.* In a split second, she realized the terrible truth: she had told Dan Ayers her secret. Except, of course, that probably wasn't his real name. Kathryn's heart began to race. Her hands were trembling uncontrollably. She felt like an idiot. How could she have been so careless?

"Ms. Freeman, are you employed?" Bob McLaren began.

"I run the Coronado Youth Surfing Academy for children ages three and up. And I'm also a bartender at O'Brien's Pub in Coronado."

"And are you acquainted with Mrs. Andrews and her husband, Tom?"

"Yes, I dated Steve Cooper, Tom's friend, for about two and a half years."

"When did you first meet Mr. Cooper?"

"The summer of 2009."

"And when did your relationship with him end?"

"Around January 2012."

"Why did your relationship with Mr. Cooper end?"

"I became involved with someone else."

"And who was that person?"

"Tom Andrews."

Kathryn's stomach knotted. Out of the corner of her eye, she saw Mark's jaw tensing in angry little waves. She kept her hands clenched together in her lap to control their trembling. She felt the jurors' eyes on her, and she worked to keep her face impassive.

"Now, Ms. Freeman, Mrs. Andrews has testified that she and her husband were very happily married. If that is true, how did you come to have an affair with Tom Andrews?"

"They weren't happily married in 2009 when I got to know Tom."

"How did you become acquainted with Mr. Andrews?"

"Through Steve. I met Steve at Black's Beach one morning, and we started surfing together regularly and then dating. After a while, he invited me to surf with his friends, Tom and Paul Curtis."

"So you knew Paul Curtis, as well as Steve Cooper and Tom Andrews?"

"Yes."

"Now you've said that in 2009, the Andrews' marriage was not a happy one. Do you know why that was true?"

"Because Kathryn wanted a baby, and they couldn't have one. In the beginning, Tom had wanted children, too; but he'd grown tired of trying."

"So Tom Andrews had changed his mind about having a family, but Mrs. Andrews felt differently?"

"Yes."

"Would you tell the jury how you happened to become close to Tom Andrews?"

Shannon paused to drink water from the glass next to her chair. She gave her long blonde hair a shake. Kathryn could see the jury was waiting intently for her answer.

"In the beginning, as I said, I always surfed with Steve. Then Tom joined the two of us more and more often, sometimes with Paul. But usually it was me, Steve, and Tom. Toward the end of 2009, Steve got busy with work and couldn't surf in the mornings very often. So that left Tom and me alone most days."

"What kind of work did Steve do?"

"He was an attorney for the Natural Resources Defense Council."

"So an environmental attorney?" Bob McLaren gave her a friendly, conspiratorial smile.

"Yes."

"So what happened when you and Tom Andrews were left alone in late 2009?"

"At first we were just good friends."

"What kinds of things did you talk about as good friends?"

"Tom talked a lot about his work. He loved his job. He talked a lot about Steve, too. They'd been friends since childhood, and they were really close. I could see that he was hoping things would work out between me and Steve."

"Why did you draw that conclusion?"

"Because Tom actually said so many times. He kept saying

that he and Paul were happily married, and he wanted Steve to find someone, too. He didn't understand why Steve was having such a hard time, and he thought we'd be perfect for each other."

"And how did you feel about that?"

"In the beginning, I listened to him. I had an open mind about having a relationship with Steve. But the more time I spent with Tom, the more I realized Steve and I would never be anything more than friends. Whereas, with Tom—"

"Objection, narrative," Mark intoned.

"Sustained," Judge Weiner replied. "Ms. Freeman, wait for Mr. McLaren to ask you a question."

"When did your relationship with Tom Andrews cease to be a friendship and become, instead, a love affair?"

"In January 2012."

"Was there an event that precipitated the change in your relations with Mr. Andrews?"

"Yes, Steve asked me to marry him in December 2011, the night of the Andrews' annual Christmas party."

"And did you agree to marry him?"

"No. That was when I realized that I wasn't in love with Steve. I loved Tom."

"And did you tell Tom that?"

"I did."

"How did you tell him about your feelings?"

"I wrote him a letter on New Year's Day of 2012."

McLaren held up a piece of paper. "Your Honor, I'd like this marked as Defendant's Exhibit G."

Judge Weiner simply nodded.

McLaren handed Shannon the paper. "Do you recognize this, Ms. Freeman?"

"Yes. It's the letter I wrote to Tom on January 1, 2012."

"Would you read it for the jury?"

As Kathryn listened to those now-familiar words, "I can't go on pretending I do not love you. I've realized I can't say yes to Steve," she felt the man who had pretended to be Dan Ayers watching her. He must have come back for the letters after he talked to Shannon.

"And what was Tom Andrews' reaction to this letter?"

"At first he was upset. He insisted he was in love with Kathryn and would never leave her. He said we shouldn't see each other anymore."

"How long did not seeing each other last?"

"About two weeks."

"Did you ask to see him at the end of two weeks or did he contact you?"

"He contacted me. He said he missed me too much."

"And is this the letter you sent him after he contacted you in mid-January?"

"Yes."

"Would you read it for the jury?"

The words, "we belong together," pierced Kathryn's heart. She struggled to keep back tears.

"What did you do after Tom Andrews resumed his relationship with you?"

"I moved out of Steve's house and got my own apartment, so Tom and I could spend time together."

"And how much time did you spend together after you got your own apartment?"

"As much time as we could. Tom was defending a high-profile client who was on trial for murder throughout February. He would tell Kathryn he was going to the office to work at night when, in fact, he was coming to see me."

"So at least three nights a week?"

"More like four or five."

"And I assume the two of you had sex?"

"Yes, we did. Tom felt very guilty about that."

"Why?"

"Kathryn was still trying to get pregnant, but on the nights when she knew she was ovulating, Tom would spend that time with me."

"And did Tom Andrews agree to leave his wife and move in with you?"

"Yes, he did."

"When was that?"

"In early March when the murder trial ended. He couldn't use that as an excuse to be with me anymore, so he agreed we should tell Steve and Kathryn that he was coming to live with me."

"And did you tell them?"

"No. Paul Curtis intervened."

"How did Paul know that Tom intended to move in with you?"

"Tom was wracked with guilt over Kathryn. He needed someone to talk to, and he couldn't talk to Steve, so he told Paul what had happened."

"And did Mr. Curtis give him some advice that he followed?"

"Yes, after talking to Paul, Tom decided to give his marriage six more months."

"And how did you feel about that?"

"I was devastated."

"So you wrote to him several times, begging him not to heed Mr. Curtis' advice?"

"I did."

"And are these the letters that you wrote?"

"Yes, they are."

"And did you continue to see each other?"

"Yes, although it was harder. Kathryn thought we were surfing together in the mornings when we were actually at my place."

"Having sex?"

"Yes."

"And your last letter to Tom Andrews was dated when?"

"April 30."

"How long was that before he got sick?"

"Three weeks."

"Why did you write the letter?"

"Tom had decided we should tell Kathryn and Steve. He wasn't going to wait to move in with me. But then he talked to Paul again and got cold feet. I was trying to get him to see the sooner we told the truth, the better for everyone involved."

"When was the last time you saw Tom Andrews before his first hospitalization on May 21?"

"The day before, Sunday. He told Kathryn he was going to the office for a few hours, but he was with me."

"And did you continue to see him after that first hospitalization?"

Shannon shook her head. "He didn't feel well the entire

week of May 21, so he couldn't find an excuse to see me. Then May 28 was the day he became critically ill. I managed to sneak into his room once, but only once, when he was in intensive care."

"What happened when you did see him in the hospital?"

"He was in a coma. I sat by his bed and talked to him, but he didn't respond. Kathryn found me there, and told the nurses I wasn't family, so they wouldn't let me come back."

"Did Mrs. Andrews know that Tom intended to leave her for you?"

"She suspected. She didn't like the amount of time Tom spent with me."

"And did she tell you that?"

"Not in so many words, but Tom said–"

"Objection." Mark stood up. "Hearsay."

"Sustained," Judge Weiner said. "How much more do you have, Mr. McLaren?"

"Just one more, Your Honor."

"Very well, proceed."

"Ms. Freeman, did you observe Tom Andrews drinking heavily in the months leading up to his hospitalization in May?"

"Yes. He was very upset about ending his marriage and worried about the murder trial in February."

"Thank you, Ms. Freeman. No further questions."

"Mr. Kelly, you may begin your cross-examination after lunch."

Except I have none, Mark thought desperately, as they all rose for the judge's exit from the courtroom.

CHAPTER FORTY-NINE

Thursday, April 2, 2015, Edward J. Schwartz Federal Courthouse, U.S. District Court, Southern District of California, San Diego

Judge Weiner glanced at Mark as she left the bench, and he saw a flicker of sympathy in her eyes. She understood he'd been caught in a trial lawyer's worst nightmare, a surprise witness whose testimony he was completely unprepared for. At least he had the lunch break to try to pull some sort of cross-examination together.

He looked at Kathryn, who had managed to get to her feet, although he could see she was shaking. She was looking at the back of the courtroom where a man in a suit was standing. He seemed to be smirking at her. Mark hoped the man wasn't going to turn out to be another surprise witness for Wycliffe. He took her arm to steady her, but his grip was tight enough to let her know just how angry he was. He should have listened to Hugh: she'd been hiding a secret that was going to kill their case.

Firmly, and without a word, he kept his hand on her arm and guided her out of the courtroom, down the corridor, and out the front door. Hugh and Patty followed. In silence they walked back to the firm, went up the elevator, and took their places around the table in the big conference room. Stewart had ordered sandwiches. Kathryn shook her head when he passed the tray to her. Mark took one but was too angry to think about eating and left it on his paper plate still unwrapped. At that moment, he felt Patty looking at him. She shook her head slightly, a warning that he needed to calm down. She and Hugh took sandwiches and opened bottles of water; and to his relief, because he was still too angry to speak, Hugh took charge.

He began far more gently than Mark would have done. "Why didn't you tell us about Shannon and your husband?"

"Because I was never sure it was true. I always told myself I was just imagining Tom's interest in her. Whenever we talked about it, he told me he was trying to get her together with Steve. I found those letters in Tom's desk last September and confronted Paul with them. That was the first time I knew Shannon had moved out of Steve's house in January and that Tom was spending time alone with her in her own place. Paul insisted the letters were just Shannon in desperate mode. He was sure Tom never intended to leave me. He said Tom was upset about the Pepe Jackson trial and about our inability to have a child, but he didn't think Tom intended to end our marriage."

"Who knew about Tom and Shannon besides you and Paul?"

"We were the only ones. Steve didn't know that Shannon was interested in Tom. Paul didn't think Wycliffe would find Shannon; and if they did, they would only know she was Steve's girlfriend. He said I shouldn't tell you because he and I were the only ones who knew."

"How did they find out, then?" Mark asked.

Kathryn looked down at the highly polished table and said nothing for a long time. Then she looked at all of them and said, "I'm embarrassed to tell you, but here's what happened. I was so angry with Paul for keeping the truth from me about Tom and Shannon that I went out one night in September, determined to pick up someone in a bar."

Hugh nodded wisely. "And you were being tailed by a private investigator who played you."

Kathryn nodded, overcome with humiliation.

"Hey," Hugh said, "Don't let it get you down. You couldn't have known."

"No, I should have known. There was something about the whole thing that was too slick and cheesy."

Mark sighed. "There's no way we can get sanctions against Wycliffe for this."

"It wasn't Wycliffe," Hugh said.

"What?" Patty frowned at him.

"I said, 'It wasn't Wycliffe.'"

"But of course it was Wycliffe," Mark insisted.

"No, it wasn't," Hugh repeated. "He wasn't sitting with McLaren and Emma Talbert today at the defense table. If he'd been their investigator, he'd have been with them."

"Then who was it?" Mark demanded.

Hugh sighed. "I'm going to bet it was Buffy."

"*Buffy?*" Mark couldn't keep the disbelief out of his voice.

"She met Kathryn the night she came to dinner at Crown Manor and got the wrong impression about my interest in her."
Except she didn't get the wrong impression. I'm so in love with her

that I was tempted get up and tear Shannon Freeman's heart out on cross-examination.

"Aren't you reading too much into the situation?" Patty began reasonably.

"No, I don't think so. I know that Buffy's been paying someone to follow me. Hal Edwards' wife Edith put the idea in her head. She probably paid Ayers, or whatever his name is, to follow Kathryn, hoping to find some dirt. Look, we have to put my wife's idiotic jealousy aside for the time being. We've got to mount some sort of cross-examination of this very damaging witness in less than forty-five minutes. Let's get focused on getting the job done."

"We need Paul Curtis," Mark said. "Kathryn, do you know if he's in town?"

"No, but I have his cell."

"Let's get him on speaker phone, then, and figure out how to shake this woman's story." Mark looked over at Kathryn, his eyes now warm and sympathetic. "I, for one, don't believe a word of it."

* * *

Thursday, April 2, 2015, 1845 Ocean Place, Pacific Beach

When Paul phoned at eight that night, Kathryn decided to answer.

"How are you holding up?"

"I'm sitting here looking at his medals and wondering if I should take his surfboard and smash the case!"

"Don't!"

"But I want to!"

"How much have you had to drink?"

"Too much! Shannon Freeman told the whole world in open court today that my husband didn't love me!"

"It's a lie, Kathryn; and you know it."

"I don't know what I know anymore. Tom's gone, and Shannon won't go away!"

"Shannon will go away. How did Mark's cross-exam go after we talked to him on that conference call at lunch?"

"Middling-to-fair. He couldn't shake her claim that Tom was about to leave me when he got sick."

"Don't worry. I'll be first on rebuttal on Monday. I'll tell the jurors the truth."

"But they have three days to think about what Shannon said. We're dark tomorrow because Judge Weiner has a mandatory judge's training conference."

"Don't worry," he repeated. "Mark and I can undo Shannon on Monday. She's a big liar, Kath. She always has been."

"She wasn't lying about sleeping with Tom."

"It was just sex, Kath."

"*How do you know?*"

"Damn, it! Because I slept with her, too. *And it was just sex!*"

"So from the horse's mouth?"

"If you say so. Aren't you ever going to forgive me for that one stupid, stupid decision?"

"Honestly, I don't know. I don't know anything right now except how much this hurts. You tried to warn me."

"I did. But I had no idea they'd find Shannon."

"Because of my stupidity, they found her."

"Don't be so hard on yourself."

"I can't help it. I wanted to vindicate Tom, but all I've done is show the world our marriage was all but over when he died."

"Kathryn, stop it! What was the last thing Tom said to you?"

She was silent for a few moments, realizing he had cornered her in her maudlin wallow in self-pity. "That he loved me."

"Right. That he loved *you*, not Shannon."

"You're sure he wasn't going to leave me?"

"As sure as I've ever been of anything in my life. Don't you think I wanted him to leave, so I'd finally have a chance?"

"I never thought of it that way."

"Look, you need some sleep, and you aren't safe there alone. Come stay in my guest room tonight. Please!"

"No, thanks. I want to be alone with my Glock and these medals, wondering if Tom ever loved me."

"Stop it, Kath! You know he did."

"I'm not sure what I know anymore."

"Well, if you won't come here tonight, I'm coming over there first thing tomorrow to take you to breakfast and to make sure you're okay."

"I'm not okay. I'll never be okay again."

* * *

After Paul hung up, Kathryn turned out the lights, poured one more generous glass of wine, and crawled into bed. She sipped the wine in the dark and said to Tom, "We're losing. Wycliffe is not squirming in front of the jury the way I planned. And not only are we losing, I see now that I lost you. I wanted a child so much that I drove you to Shannon. Paul warned me not to open this can of worms. But I wouldn't listen. We're losing, Tom. We're losing big time."

CHAPTER FIFTY

Friday, April 3, 2015, Motel 6, Arlington, Virginia

Dr. Frank Reynolds had been on the run for ten days. On March 22, his colleague Harrison O'Connor had been found dead in his Maryland townhouse. Two days later, his colleague Mary Lancaster was shot to death in a Bethesda motel room. The three of them had been single and close. And Frank did not buy for one minute the story that Mary was the victim of a botched robbery or that Harrison had hanged himself. The three of them had seen the hidden database. The three of them had known that there were more than six hundred post-approval deaths from Myrabin, and the numbers were increasing rapidly. Frank knew they were coming for him next, so he found his ancient college fake ID in the name of his former roommate, Larry Gwen, in the bottom of his desk drawer, packed his bag, and left his Fairfax townhouse, probably for good.

He'd rented a car in Larry's name and tried to figure out what came next. For ten days he'd evaded the black Suburbans that tailed him. He was, after all, a Ph.D. organic chemist, Yale undergrad, Stanford Ph.D. He should be smart enough to outwit the mid-level government operatives following him, he told himself.

But now at eight p.m., he sat in a dark room that smelled of urine and stale smoke at the Motel 6 in Arlington next to the Iwo Jima Memorial and thought about what came next. He had a ticket to San Diego in his pocket for the red-eye out of Dulles at 11:30 p.m. He could see the goons in their SUV in the parking lot through the crack he had made in the blinds. He was afraid to turn on the lights. They had knocked earlier but decided he was out because the lights were off. He went to the bathroom and painfully scraped the stubble off his face in the dark. The TSA operatives would be unlikely to let him on the flight with ten days worth of ragged beard that made him look like a terrorist.

When he finished shaving, he turned his attention to the bathroom window. Fortunately for him, it both opened and was big enough for him to crawl through. He pushed his bag out first. When it plopped onto the asphalt in the rear parking lot and produced no reaction, he climbed up on the chair he had pushed against the wall and followed his bag. He crept through the rear of the lot, his heart in his mouth, praying the SUV remained parked out front. He climbed into his rented black Kia Soul and began his desperate drive to Dulles with his ticket and Kathryn Andrews' address and phone number in his pocket.

* * *

Monday, April 6, 2015 Edward J. Schwartz Federal Courthouse, U.S. District Court, Southern District of California, San Diego

"Good morning," Judge Weiner smiled as she took the bench on Monday morning.

"Mr. McLaren, does the defense have any additional witnesses?"

"No, Your Honor. The defense rests."

"Very well." She turned to Mark, in the lead chair at the plaintiff's table. "Mr. Kelly, does the plaintiff have any rebuttal evidence?"

"We do, Your Honor. We would like to call Dr. Frank Reynolds."

"Objection, Your Honor!" Bob McLaren was on his feet immediately. Hugh smiled inside when he saw that Emma Talbert suddenly looked very worried.

"Your Honor, I have prepared a witness summary for Mr. McLaren, but we believe you will see that Wycliffe is already intimately acquainted with the subject of Dr. Reynolds' testimony."

"Very well, Mr. Kelly. You may proceed."

Frank was only a little nervous as he took the stand in one of Paul Curtis' suits.

"Please state your name for the record."

"Franklin David Reynolds."

"And how are you employed?"

"Until March 20, I was employed as an organic chemist by the Federal Drug Administration."

"And what is your background and training?"

"I graduated from Yale with a degree in organic chemistry and earned my Masters and Ph.D. from Stanford."

"And were you part of the team assigned to work on the approval of Wycliffe's drug, Myrabin, in 1997, Dr. Reynolds?"

"Yes, I was."

He had literally shown up on Kathryn's doorstep at nine-thirty on Saturday morning, tired, distraught, and hungry, and clutching a gym bag and a briefcase.

"Do you remember me? Frank Reynolds of the FDA Myrabin team?"

She'd crawled out of bed when she'd heard the front door bell. She was uncomfortably aware that she was wearing the sweatpants and camisole she slept in and had bed hair.

"Please let me in. If I've been followed, our lives are in danger."

They went to the kitchen where Kathryn made coffee and scrambled eggs.

He sat at the table and described his ten days on the run.

Finally she asked, "Why have you come?"

"For Mary and Harrison. They were killed because they knew the truth about Myrabin. And I'm about to be next."

"What is the truth?"

"It's all in here." He tapped the briefcase sitting next to him at the table.

* * *

Monday afternoon, April 6, 2015, Edward J. Schwartz Federal Courthouse, U.S. District Court, Southern District of California, San Diego

"And so you are saying that there were deaths associated with Myrabin in the clinical trials before the drug was approved by the FDA?" Bob McLaren wiggled his eyebrows skeptically as he cross-examined Frank Reynolds to show the jury just how unbelievable his story was.

"Yes, there were two."

"But weren't those caused by alcohol abuse by the two patients who died?"

"No. We were instructed to say that, but it was a lie. Myrabin caused those two deaths."

"What reason, Dr. Reynolds, would anyone have to order you to lie about deaths during a clinical study?"

"Because if we had told the truth, the clinical trials would have been shut down, and Myrabin would never have been approved."

McLaren frowned. He had clearly lost on that point. But he went on. "Now, Dr. Reynolds, you are also claiming that there were deaths after Myrabin was approved?"

"That's right. More than six hundred have been reported to the FDA."

"Then why didn't your team at the FDA act on those reports?"

"Because we were instructed not to."

McLaren paused for effect and gave the jury his best deadpan. "So you want us to believe, Dr. Reynolds, that someone directed the Federal Food and Drug Administration to ignore a large number of deaths from a drug the agency had found safe?"

"I have the memo that was directed to us right here." Dr. Reynolds pulled a folded paper out of the inner pocket of his borrowed suit.

Kathryn felt Mark tense up beside her. Reynolds had never shown them that document when they interviewed him over the weekend.

"Objection. Hearsay!" McLaren boomed.

Judge Weiner looked over at Mark, who said, "We haven't seen this document before. May we approach the bench?"

Kathryn watched as Mark and McLaren huddled in front of the judge, each of them examining the paper Frank Reynolds had produced. McLaren looked angry. Mark looked grave. After a few minutes, Mark came back and sat down beside Kathryn. Hugh, seated at Kathryn's right, gave him a questioning look, but Mark didn't respond.

Judge Weiner addressed her courtroom. "I am going to allow this memo. It appears to me to be a business record, and Dr. Reynolds has testified that his job duties include the preservation of memoranda directed to his team about the drug approval process. You may continue cross-examination, Mr. McLaren."

"No further questions," McLaren said, and sat down. He looked bleak. Mark was on his feet immediately for redirect.

"Your Honor, we'd like Mr. Reynolds' document marked as Plaintiff's Exhibit No. 106."

"The exhibit will be admitted," the judge intoned.

"So, Dr. Reynolds, if I understand you correctly, someone ordered a cover-up of the number of deaths from Myrabin after it was approved by the FDA?"

"That's right."

"And did the same person give the order to cover-up both the pre- and post-approval deaths?"

"Yes."

"And is that person's name on the memo that you have in your hand?"

"Yes."

"Who ordered the cover-up, Dr. Reynolds?"

Kathryn held her breath. The jury was riveted on Frank.

He took a deep breath and then said, "Senator Hal Edwards."

* * *

April 6, 2015, Monday, 2015, 4151 Opal Court, Pacific Beach

At seven p.m., Amanda Cooper sat alone on the porch of the cottage that had belonged to her brother Steve and sipped the martini she had made for herself in the kitchen as she watched the sun slide into the ocean. His little two-bedroom house sat on a moderate hillside facing the Pacific, and every afternoon there was a spectacular end-of-day view from the porch.

If Steve had lived, he would have been coming up on his forty-third birthday. Her heart ached whenever she thought of him. She could hardly believe she had just cleared forty-five. She knew she didn't look it. She didn't surf, but she was athletic like her brother. She was five-eight, one hundred twenty pounds. She ran marathons. She had the grays removed from her shoulder-length blonde hair by an expensive stylist in La Jolla. She had, according to the men she met in bars, melting brown eyes to go with her hot body. But her left hand remained distinctly bare, and her life was devoted to teaching the fifth grade at Bird Rock Elementary. Dogs and children adored her, she often said, but never the right man.

She had moved from her La Mesa rental to Steve's place after he died. He had left her the cottage, and it was much closer to her work than her old apartment. She would never have been able to afford the mortgage on her teacher's salary. But Steve, ever the financial wizard, had paid it off. And now it was hers.

The house, of course, did not make up for losing her brother. Or Tom. Her eyes teared up as she thought of Tom and Steve and Paul in high school, traveling the world as champion surfers. She could see a few of the black dots now on the distant horizon waiting for the next wave. Steve was there in spirit. With Tom.

The news for the last few nights had left Amanda furious. Watching Shannon simper as she left the federal courthouse last Thursday had turned Amanda's stomach. She had never liked Shannon. From the first time she had met her, she had sensed the hard-nosed, bar-tending opportunist was out to take advantage of her brother. Since Thursday, she had balanced her hatred of Shannon's bold-faced opportunism against her own resolve to put the past behind her and move on from her brother's death. Now, as she watched the black specks of the surfers in the water in the soft spring twilight, she heard Steve's voice as plainly as if he'd been in the room. "I left you the truth, Amanda. I left you that note. Please go tell them my truth, sis. Please don't let Shannon get away with this."

Amanda polished off her martini and phoned Paul, who saw her number and answered on the first ring. "I need the phone number of the attorney who is trying Tom's case."

"Mark Kelly. He lives just down the street from me."

"Would you call him and tell him I'll be over to see him in thirty minutes? You can come, too. Steve would want you to know. I'll pick you up."

* * *

Monday, April 6, 2015, Crown Manor, Coronado, California

Hugh had begun phoning Hal as soon as he'd reached his office late that afternoon, but the president did not answer his cell. Edith picked up one of the calls and said Hal was in a cabinet meeting. But as the hours slid by, Hugh's phone remained frustratingly silent.

Until midnight. "Why didn't you tell me?" Hugh shouted into the phone when he answered.

"Calm down. I tried to. I used Fred to try to get you interested in a run for his seat by offering to kick him upstairs to the Attorney General's office. I hoped you'd turn the case over to your junior partner and let him lose it for you."

"Mark's better in a courtroom that I am. He never loses."

"Well, it would have been to your advantage if he'd lost this one. I gave you your chance to get out from under this suit. You didn't take it, and now you're finished as a lawyer, thanks to your former mistress. Hope you enjoy retirement."

"So you were just stringing me along? You were never going to withdraw that indictment?"

"God, no. Logan Avery didn't come to us. We went to her. Davidson was instructed to get cozy with her and persuade her to spill the beans."

"But hundreds of people are dead because of Myrabin."

"Yeah, I know. But it doesn't kill everyone. And besides, it's about the money, Hugh. You know what that means. You'd do anything for money. Hell, you have done anything for money."

"I haven't killed anyone."

"Well, then, maybe you're a slightly better crook than I am. But not much. You've shaken down too many corporations. They want you off the streets, and I'm the one whose taking you off."

"So you're not acting just for Wycliffe?"

"Let's say 'Wycliffe and friends.' Corporate America is rejoicing that their biggest enemy has finally fallen by his own sword. You and Rick were pretty stupid to keep up that arrangement after the Department of Justice started sniffing around."

"This was the last one. Rick was in financial trouble."

"Well, now he's going to be in 'convicted felon trouble.' And you are, too. You should have done your homework, Hugh, before you filed suit for the pretty widow. Then you'd have seen that I chaired the committee that approved the FDA's work on Myrabin. Wycliffe has been paying me ever since I was in the Senate to get them what they want. And I always deliver."

"So this is how you treat old friends who have helped you all the way to the presidency?"

"I'm grateful for your support, Hugh. But you only offered ten million."

"I'll double that to twenty."

"Try fifty million. That's what Wycliffe is giving me. In legally correct donations, I might add. And I'm going to be on Wycliffe's board when I leave office after my second term. I like you, Hugh. Edith does, too. I tried to warn you to stay out of the Andrews case. But the pretty widow was too tempting."

"Kathryn is a *client*. I don't sleep with my *clients*."

"Like hell you don't. Look, do everyone a favor. Call McLaren and settle it right now for a half mil. The sainted hubby was nothing more than a public defender. They make peanuts. If you dismiss the suit in the morning, I'll get DOJ to withdraw the indictment."

"You know I can't do that. I can't put my interest ahead of my client's."

"Well, listen to Hugh Mahoney hiding behind the ethics rules he's broken more times than anyone can count."

"Don't be insulting. Kathryn Andrews has a right to justice for her husband."

"So get her some cheap justice before in the morning. Look, Hugh, how did the lovely widow kill the hard-headed businessman in you? Myrabin is one of Wycliffe's most successful drugs. My so-called 'blind trust' is weighted with Wycliffe stock. If Myrabin goes down, I'm going to lose millions along with Wycliffe. And if Myrabin goes down, there'll be class actions that could bankrupt the company. Did you really think I would stand by and let that happen?"

"Lawson told us that he was the one who gave the order to ignore Vannier and Girard's work."

"That was our cover story. I told Lawson what to do because Wycliffe paid me to."

"So hundreds of people have died so you can line your pockets?"

"More like thousands, actually. Lawson developed a system to hide the majority of post-approval complaints that reached the FDA."

"You'll reap what you've sowed. I'll call you as a witness."

"Go ahead and try. You'll never get me on the stand. My attorneys can keep you tied up for years."

"You knew Suchet gave up on Myrabin because it wasn't safe."

"Sorry, Hugh. I have to go. You've played with the Big Boys for a long time, but now you're out. I hear a couple of years in a federal country club prison isn't so bad. And after that, you can learn to play golf. Or something."

The phone went dead. Hugh found himself shaking with rage.

CHAPTER FIFTY-ONE

Tuesday, April 7, 2015, Edward J. Schwartz Federal Courthouse, U.S. District Court, Southern District of California, San Diego

At nine a.m. the next morning, Judge Weiner addressed Mark from the bench. "Mr. Kelly, do you have any further rebuttal evidence to present?"

"I do, Your Honor. The plaintiff calls Amanda Cooper."

Kathryn watched Amanda cross the courtroom to the witness stand and take the oath. Her trim figure was perfect in her black suit. She had bundled her lovely blonde hair into a neat but soft, professional bun. She usually did not look like a fifth grade teacher, but today she had all the charisma and credibility of one. Mark had told her he was going to call Amanda instead of Paul to rebut Shannon, but Kathryn had no idea why.

"Please state your name for the record."

"Amanda Rose Cooper."

"And how are you employed, Miss Cooper?"

"I am a fifth grade teacher at Bird Rock Elementary in La Jolla."

"And do you have siblings, Miss Cooper?"

"I did. A brother."

"And what was his name?"

"Stephen Shepard Cooper. Shepard was our mother's maiden name."

"And did you know the deceased, Tom Andrews and his wife, Kathryn?"

"Yes. Steve and Tom and I grew up together. And I met Kathryn when she started dating Tom."

"Did your brother Steve have a girlfriend named Shannon Freeman during 2009 and 2012?"

"Yes."

"And did your brother ask Ms. Freeman to marry him in December 2011?"

"He did."

"And did Ms. Freeman agree to marry your brother?"

"No. She turned him down."

"Do you know why?"

"Not at the time that it happened."

"But did you find out later why Shannon refused your brother's proposal?"

"Yes."

"And when did you find out why Ms. Freeman turned your brother down?"

"After Steve died."

"When did your brother pass away, Ms. Cooper?"

"On August 1, 2012."

"And what was the cause of his death?"

"He committed suicide."

Kathryn's heart lurched and seemed to stop beating for a full second before it recovered its rhythm. She focused intently on Amanda's deep blue eyes, so like Steve's. And Tom's.

"Ms. Cooper, are you aware that the coroner concluded your brother died by accidental drowning?"

"I know about his conclusion, but I also know it is incorrect."

"And how do you know that?"

"Because Steve wrote a note to me the morning before he went to Black's Beach. He posted it on the way to his death."

Kathryn's heart skipped another beat.

Mark continued. "And have you brought with you today, that note your brother posted to you on August 1, 2012?"

"Yes. With the envelope that I received it in."

"And is this the handwriting of your brother?'

"It is."

"With the court's permission, I have copies to hand to the jurors."

Judge Weiner nodded. "That's fine, counsel."

"Objection," Bob McLaren boomed. "Hearsay."

"Your Honor, Mr. Cooper's statement to his sister qualifies as a dying declaration. According to the postmark, it was composed and sent just before he drove to Black's Beach to take his life."

"Objection overruled. You may continue, Mr. Kelly."

"Thank you, Your Honor."

"Ms. Cooper, would you read your brother's last letter for the jury?"

"Dear Manda. I love you so. Sorry for what I am about to do to you. I know with Mom gone, it's just the two of us. But I can't go on, Sis. I would if I could, but I can't.

"I feel so guilty for what I did to Tom and Kath. I never meant to bring anyone into their world who would try to come between them. The truth is, I've been in love with Tom my whole life. I tried not to feel that way, but you can't control who you fall in love with.

"I told Tom how I felt during our senior year at Stanford. He said he'd think about it, but then he met Kath the following year at law school. There was never any question after that. She was the love of his life.

"I thought when I met Shannon I might get over Tom. She was beautiful and a world-class surfer like Tom. I tried my best to fall in love with her, but I couldn't.

"Last Christmas, I realized she was just using me to get close to Tom. I thought I could protect him and Kathryn by marrying her, but she turned me down because she was determined to have Tom. She moved out, and she pursued him relentlessly.

"Tom was so sick, Manda. That drug ate up his insides, and he was so weak he could barely talk. I went to see him the day before he died. I got Kath to take a break and go get something to eat. He opened his eyes after she left, and I got to tell him how sorry I was for bringing a destructive force like Shannon into the lives of the people I loved the most. He smiled and said that it didn't matter because he could never leave Kath. I told him I loved him, and he just barely squeezed my hand and said he loved me, too. And then he closed his eyes and went back into the coma.

"I've tried to live without him, but I can't. Knowing he was in the world was enough for me. But now that he's gone, I don't want to be here anymore.

"Forgive me, Manda, for leaving you alone like this. But it will be easy for me to go today. I'll slip off the board and into the waves, and Tom will be waiting for me."

Always with love,
Steve"

When Amanda finished, Kathryn wiped the tears that clouded her eyes and looked across the courtroom at the jurors who were doing the same.

"And 'Manda' is a special name your brother had for you?" Mark asked gently.

"Yes. He couldn't say 'Amanda' when he first began to talk, so he called me 'Manda.' He's the only person who shortened my name like that."

"Thank you, Ms. Cooper. I know how difficult this has been

for you. I have only one final question. Ms Freeman has testified that if Tom Andrews had not gotten sick, he would have left his wife of fifteen years, the plaintiff, Kathryn Andrews. Do you agree with that statement?"

"Absolutely not. Kathryn was the love of his life. Tom would never have left her."

CHAPTER FIFTY-TWO

Wednesday, April 8, 2015, 1845 Ocean Place, Pacific Beach

At midnight, Kathryn sat on the sofa across a red wine nightcap and studied Tom's medals in their case. He'd been wearing one of them in the series of slides Mark had shown the jury during closing arguments yesterday morning.

As counsel for the plaintiff with the burden of proof, Mark had led off. He had created yet another slide show of Tom's life, and Kathryn had noted with satisfaction that the jury focused intently on the images of Tom as he had once been, powerful, athletic, and unbelievably handsome.

Bob McLaren argued after lunch, insisting Myrabin was safe, alcohol had caused Tom's death, and Kathryn's marriage had been over by the time her husband died. He portrayed Myrabin as a lifesaving drug and Kathryn as a money-hungry liar.

Then Mark had the last word in rebuttal argument as he showed the most important slides again: Kathryn and Tom on their wedding day; Tom as a high school international champion, medal around his neck, Steve and Paul on either side of him; Tom giving a news conference with Pepe Jackson beside him the day Pepe was acquitted.

The jury left the courtroom to begin deliberations at three-thirty. Kathryn went back to the Goldstein, Miller conference room to listen to Hugh and Mark and Patty post-mortem the closings. They were hopeful that the rebuttal case would undo the damage that Rick's clumsy testimony and Shannon's claims had done. She went home and slept long and deeply, grateful that the ordeal of the trial was over.

For the first time since the trial had started, she slept past six a.m. on Wednesday morning. She opened her eyes at eight in a panic because she wouldn't be at court to meet Hugh and Mark by 8:30. But then she remembered it was all over, and they now were waiting on the jury to decide. They would not go back to Judge Weiner's courtroom until the jury announced that it had reached a verdict.

She was tempted to take the day off, but she had work to catch up on. Tyrone still needed her, and she knew Tom would want her to make sure his future was secure. She went to her own office and called Sam McIntrye to make the final arrangements for Tyrone's release into the custody of Martha McDonald the following day. The court had agreed that Martha should have custody of him while he was on probation, and he would work with her in the Goldstein, Miller mail room.

Mark had been instrumental in arranging a new home for Tyrone. Kathryn realized that now the trial was over, she'd miss seeing him every day. And Patty. And, of course, Hugh. And his emerald earrings, locked in her jewelry box. For all their Big Firm lawyer foibles, they had good hearts. Even Hugh.

By noon she had Tyrone's life squared away for the next two

years and was ready to tackle the accumulated mail. She worked her way through it slowly during the long afternoon and then left at six so she could meet Amanda Cooper for dinner. She stopped by Tom's old office on the way out, remembering the slide Mark had shown the jury yesterday of Tom seated at his desk. *I just want him back,* she told the Universe. *I don't want millions of dollars. I just want Tom.*

At the Yellow Café, the waitress had given Amanda and Kathryn the same booth she had occupied with Tom the night he'd told her he no longer wanted a child. After dinner, she had let Amanda talk her into going back to Steve's cottage for another glass of wine. It was odd to step inside Steve's place and see feminine, flowery prints on the sofa and chairs next to small, antique pine tables. Kathryn remembered how the living room had always been full of surfboards, Ikea furniture, and piles of Steve's legal work. The transformation made it seem as if Steve had never lived there.

And now, at just past midnight, after her first day back on the job she had shared with Tom, she looked around her own house where nothing had changed since he died. His medals were in their case. His clothes were in their closet. His desk drawers were undisturbed except for the removal of Shannon's letters. And now she was about to go to bed alone in the bed she had shared with him throughout their marriage. She had told Paul the truth: she had kept everything the same, so she could pretend that nothing had changed and that Tom was on his way back to her.

Except, of course, he wasn't.

Tears welled up and overflowed. She fled to the kitchen to escape the emotion that threatened to overwhelm her and topped off her drink. She wandered into her bedroom and impulsively unlocked the box where she kept the emerald earrings. She carried them back to the living room and curled up on the sofa again. She opened the box and stared at all that green fire. She thought of how Hugh had begged her to take them. She thought of Tyrone on his way to a new home tomorrow because of Hugh. He wasn't a perfect man, as he'd confessed to her the night he'd been arrested. But without him, Tyrone wouldn't have this second chance. He'd have been another plea-bargained statistic on the public defender's docket. And without Hugh, she would have never been given the chance to rub Wycliffe's nose in the story of Tom's suffering. And hers.

I can't let go of you, Tom. I can't.

She drained the last of her wine, put the glass on the coffee table, and got up. She walked over to the trophy case and put the little blue Tiffany box next to the medal Tom had been wearing in the photographs that Mark had shown to the jury yesterday. She closed the door and twisted the key in the lock. Was she keeping the memories in that case safe, or was she locking them away where they could do no further harm?

She turned out all the lights, went into her bedroom, crawled into bed, and went to sleep.

* * *

Early Morning Hours of Thursday, April 9, 2015, 1845 Ocean Place, Pacific Beach

Kathryn dreamed the cottage was on fire. Black smoke billowed through every room. Tom was shaking her gently and telling her it was time to wake up and leave the house.

Her eyes suddenly opened. The smoke was all around her, but Tom was not there. This was not a dream; her house was on fire. She sat up, but began to cough so violently that she had to lie down again. But only for a moment. Carefully she climbed out of bed and, staying close to the floor, crept to the doorway to see if there was anyone else in the house. The smoke was so thick, she could not tell if anyone was nearby.

She had to get out of the house. Her bedroom windows were the closest exit. She grabbed her Glock and her cell phone and crawled along the floor until she reached the windows. They were nearly floor length, side by side. She unlocked them and attempted to pull them open. But no luck. She tried more times than she could count, all the while breathing in the acrid smell of smoke and burning wood. As she worked at trying to make the windows open, a rising tide of panic began to engulf her.

Both windows were still hopelessly stuck. Heat from the flames was beginning to scorch her back. The latches opened, but the windows would not budge.

She resisted thinking what she already knew to be true: someone had set this fire and nailed the windows shut.

Then she heard a small explosion. It seemed to come from the kitchen. The smoke was so thick now that she could barely breathe. She lay down on her tummy on the floor for a few seconds to try to catch a cleaner breath of air. Her only chance of escape was through those windows. Smoke and fire blocked her paths to the front and back doors.

She still had her Glock in her hand. She considered whether she could smash the glass cleanly enough to allow herself to get through without being cut. She began to feel dizzy. She gasped for breath.

And then Tom was standing over her. Steve was with him. They were wearing their wetsuits and had just come from surfing. *Except that can't be right because they can't surf in the dark.*

Kathryn heard another explosion. And another. And another. The fire and heat were intensifying. Beside her, Tom reached down and pulled her to her feet. He took her gun, and smashed the glass in one of the windows. As Kathryn stood in front of the now-open window, an explosion rocked the house like an earthquake. It hurled her through the opening Tom had created. When her head hit the ground, it felt like someone had hit her with a sledgehammer. Dazed and unable to move, she looked up at the stars and then shifted her eyes back to the burning house. Tom and Steve were still inside, looking down at her through the shattered window. She opened her mouth to call to them; but before she could make a sound, another explosion ripped through the house, followed by another and another. The ground shook violently, and then everything went black.

CHAPTER FIFTY-THREE

Early Morning Hours of Thursday, April 9, 2015, 610 First Street, Coronado, California

Mark's cell went off at 2:30 in the morning. He struggled awake and said, "This is Mark Kelly."

"Mr. Kelly, I'm Detective Tim McIntosh of the San Diego Police Department. I understand you are the attorney for Kathryn Andrews."

"That's right."

"Her house is on fire. We suspect arson, probably multiple explosive devices."

His stomach tightened. "Where's Kathryn? Is she all right?"

"No, I'm afraid not. She's on the way to Scripps Memorial with the EMT's. When the house blew up, the blast sent her through the bedroom windows. She was knocked unconscious. Looks like severe head trauma. Does she have any family in town?"

"No. Her mother's in Miami. We'll get her here as fast as we can. I'm on my way to the hospital now."

Hugh was waiting for him in the drive at Crown Manor,

wearing a pair of sweatpants, one of his sloppy, knit collared shirts, and a rumpled trench coat.

As soon as he got into the car, Mark tossed him his cell phone. "Call Paul Curtis. He's number six on my speed dial. He's the closest thing to a family member I could think of for her."

"There's us." Hugh said stubbornly. "She feels like family now."

Mark sighed. "I know. But call Paul. We've got to get her mother here from Florida, and we don't know how to contact her. He'll know."

* * *

Thursday, April 9, 2015, Scripps Memorial Hospital, La Jolla, California

At six a.m., Hugh, Mark, and Paul were huddled together in a waiting room on the intensive care floor. Kathryn's mother and her husband were just taking off on the jet Hugh had chartered to bring them to California. Paul insisted that he, and not Jose, should be the one to meet them at the airport when they arrived in the early afternoon.

Restless and tired of waiting, Mark got up and wandered over to the window where the first rays of new sunlight had turned all the scattered bits and pieces of clouds soft pink against the pale blue sky. He could barely see the outline of the ocean against the horizon. He thought of Tom Andrews. It was the hour when surfers paddled out to catch the first wave of the day.

"She's been in surgery now for about four hours," Hugh

broke the silence. He wished he hadn't forgotten his flask. He needed his scotch to take the edge off the cold, unrelenting fear that was eating him.

"I've gone to the nurse's station twice and asked," Paul said. "But they always say she's still in surgery, and that's all they know."

Mark sighed. "I've received a text from Bob McLaren. He has asked Judge Weiner to convene this morning so that he can make a motion for a mistrial. He is assuming the jury has heard about Kathryn and will bring in a sympathy verdict. I'm going to have to make that court appearance, but I don't want to leave without any news."

"We'll text you as soon as we hear anything," Paul said.

"If the judge grants a mistrial, that means Wycliffe wins if Kathryn was serious about refusing to go through another trial," Paul said.

"That's a bridge we don't have to cross right now," Hugh cautioned. "Kathryn may feel differently after everything that's happened." He didn't add what they all thought, *if she survives.*

At that moment, a man in green scrubs with a surgical mask dangling around his neck entered their enclave. "Are you all here for Mrs. Andrews?"

Three heads nodded.

"I'm Dr. Belinsky. I was the on-call neurosurgeon when she came in last night. Which of you is family?"

"None of us," Paul said. "We're close friends. Her mother is her only family, and she's flying here from the east coast as we speak."

"Okay, then you can pass along the updates when she arrives.

Mrs. Andrews has suffered a severe concussion. We've had to do surgery because of swelling in the brain. Her less severe injury is a broken arm. Her head hit something pretty hard."

"The fire captain told me she was blown through a glass window when her house exploded," Mark said. "She hit her head when she hit the ground."

"Well, then, she's lucky she didn't break her neck. But if she was blown through a glass window, she should have been horribly cut up. She wasn't."

"But she's going to be all right, isn't she?" Mark saw the tension in Hugh's face as he asked.

"We don't know yet." Dr. Belinsky looked very grave. "We'll have to wait and see."

* * *

Thursday, April 9, 2015, Edward J. Schwartz Federal Courthouse, U.S. District Court, Southern District of California, San Diego

Judge Weiner took the bench promptly at nine a.m. and looked down at Bob McLaren and Emma Talbert at the defense table, and Mark and Patty on the plaintiff's side.

"How is your client, Mr. Kelly? We're all very concerned about her."

"When I left the hospital, she was still in surgery. I haven't heard anything more."

"I see. Well, we all hope she's going to be fine. Mr. McLaren, I'll hear from you. You wanted to bring a motion?"

"Your Honor, on behalf of my client, I move for a mistrial. Even if the jurors have followed the court's instructions and stayed away from news reports, and I highly doubt that is true, we are still going to have to explain to them why Mrs. Andrews is no longer in court. Any verdict they bring in now will be tainted by sympathy for her. They will think that my client is responsible, and that is simply not true."

Judge Weiner looked over at Mark. "I'm afraid I'm going to have to grant his motion, Mr. Kelly. Unless, by some unlikely chance, the jury has already reached a verdict. Bailiff, bring the jurors in, and let's ask them."

Mark watched the jurors file into the box, but his mind was miles away at the hospital with Kathryn. His phone remained maddeningly empty of text updates.

"Good morning, ladies and gentlemen."

"Good morning, Your Honor." Juror No. 10 spoke up.

"I am assuming you are the foreman," the judge responded.

"I am. We reached our verdict yesterday at 4:15. We were going to give this note to your bailiff first thing this morning."

The bailiff took the paper from the foreman of the jury and handed it to Judge Weiner, who studied it in silence for a few minutes. Then she read it aloud. "It says, 'We the jury have reached a verdict.' And it is dated April 8, 2015 at 4:30 p.m."

"Your Honor," McLaren sputtered. "This is completely wrong. The jury should have given that note to the bailiff yesterday afternoon."

"We didn't know that, Your Honor," the foreman spoke up. "We thought first thing this morning would be better. It was a long day, and we wanted to go home."

"That's fine. I understand," the judge said. "Have any of you seen or heard any news reports in the last twenty-four hours?"

Twelve heads shook 'no.'

"Good, then you've followed my instructions. Bailiff, let me see if the verdicts are in order. Mr. Foreman, please hand the signed verdict forms to the bailiff."

Mark's stomach became a knot as he watched Judge Weiner study the verdicts. He looked over at Patty, who gave him a tense smile. Their chance of victory hung by the slender thread that the jury had not made any mistakes in filling out the forms. Otherwise, McLaren's motion would be granted; and if Kathryn really meant what she had said about another trial, Wycliffe had won.

Judge Weiner looked up from the papers in front of her. "The jury's verdicts are in order. They are signed and dated yesterday at 4:15 p.m. I am going to accept them."

"The defense objects!"

"I'm sure you do," Judge Weiner said without the least show of emotion. "But I am accepting these verdicts. If you have a problem with that, Mr. McLaren, you can take it up with the court of appeal. Bailiff, if you will hand these to the clerk to read, please."

Mark sucked in his breath and waited.

"We, the jury, find for the plaintiff on count one, negligence causing wrongful death, in the amount of fifty-five million dollars, twenty million for the lost wages and economic contribution of Thomas Allen Andrews, and thirty-five million for the plaintiff's loss of companionship and care."

Mark felt dizzy with joy.

But the court clerk continued, "We the jury also find punitive damages to be awarded to the estate of Thomas Allen

Andrews in the amount of thirty million dollars."

The judge turned to the jurors. "Is that your true and correct verdict?"

Twelve voices replied, "Yes, Your Honor."

* * *

"How is Kathryn?" Mark had gone back to the privacy of his office to telephone Hugh with the news.

"She's in ICU. They let me and Paul go in for five minutes each. She's in a coma, and they don't know if she'll wake up."

"Eighty-five million dollars."

"What?"

"That was the verdict. Thirty million in punitive damages. Patty and I talked to the jurors. They were pretty outraged about the cover-up, particularly about Hal Edwards' role in ordering the FDA to sanitize the data about deaths from the drug."

"I assume we're looking at an appeal?"

"McLaren huffed back to his office to prepare his notice. I've told the Appellate Department to be prepared for their filing."

Hugh didn't feel any of the joy he usually felt at a major win. "It should be good news, but we may lose her. We shouldn't have let her go home alone."

"We all tried to get her to see the danger," Mark said. "She wouldn't listen."

"It had to be Wycliffe."

"McLaren insisted they had nothing to do with it. The trouble is, even if it was Wycliffe, we have no way to prove it."

* * *

454

By four o'clock, Helen Ellis was with Kathryn, so Hugh decided to go home to shower and have a drink. He was surprised he'd lasted this long without his scotch.

The big house was quiet and empty. Buffy had been so outraged by his arrest that she had gone to stay with Elise, and Hugh was pretty sure she wasn't coming back.

He showered and put on fresh clothes and sat on the balcony outside his bedroom to eat the meal Maria had brought him on a tray. He sipped scotch and watched the ocean and tried to find the words of a prayer in the depths of his discarded Catholic faith. He wished for the comfort of saying the rosary. At least it made you feel as if you weren't powerless. Even though you were.

His cell phone rang, and he picked it up without looking at caller ID because he was anxious for news about Kathryn.

Hal Edwards said, "She's a tough one to get rid of."

Hugh's blood ran cold. "What are you saying?"

"Look, old man. I thought you'd figure it out eventually. I've been trying to take her out since you filed that ill-advised suit against Wycliffe. Who knew she could drive like a NASCAR competitor and had the instincts of an international operative? My guys failed on the bridge early on and failed again in Paris."

"Are you telling me you ordered the Secret Service to kill my client?"

"God, no! Don't be naive. I would never risk anything in my official capacity. But I have access to former operatives who are more than willing to do special ops at a price."

"You failed to mention shooting at her in the garden of my house that night."

"Oh, that wasn't me. At least directly."

"What do you mean 'directly'?"

"Your dear wife set that up. With the help of Edith."

"What?"

"She was fed up with the affairs. You dumped the blonde in favor of the pretty widow."

"That's not true. Kathryn is a client. Besides, Buffy wouldn't know how to buy a hit man."

"But Edith does. Never underestimate the power of a wife with money of her own. FLOTUS makes me walk the straight and narrow when it comes to being faithful. Besides, it would have been to my advantage if their scheme had succeeded. It would have saved me the trouble of last night."

"But you failed. The jury returned a verdict. A big verdict."

"It would have been better if they hadn't. But eighty-five million is way too much. It will never stand up on appeal. Plus all the witness shenanigans you guys pulled."

"We'll come after you."

"Hah! Like hell you will. You have no shred of proof that I was responsible for anything. I keep my special ops neat and clean. You can't prove my guys took out Vannier or O'Connor or Lancaster. Unfortunately, Reynolds gave them the slip."

"That's going to cost you politically."

"No, it won't. He's a disgruntled employee who lied under oath. And you're on your way to becoming a convicted felon."

The line went dead.

CHAPTER FIFTY-FOUR

Monday, April 13, 2015, Scripps Memorial Hospital, La Jolla, California

When Kathryn opened her eyes, light was streaming through half-closed blinds. Her head ached and seemed to be wrapped in some sort of bandage. Her left arm was heavy and immobile. It throbbed, and she remembered the agony of a broken bone from her gymnastics days.

In the darkened room, it took a moment for her eyes to focus on the male figure in the chair by the bed. Hugh, customarily sloppy in a knit collared shirt and casual tan pants. He had been writing something on a laptop. He looked up, and his face broke into a luminous smile.

"Finally, you're awake."

"How long has it been?"

"Four days. We weren't sure you were going to wake up. Your mother is here. Patty and Mark and Paul and I have been taking turns giving her some rest. She'll be back in a few minutes. She went down to the cafeteria with your stepfather for lunch."

Graham. He was her stepfather, she guessed. No one ever called him that. He was always just "Graham." She felt as if she'd awakened in an entirely different world. Could she be dead after all? "What time is it?"

"Around one-thirty."

"I'm thirsty."

"That's good news." He pressed the call button for the nurse, who appeared almost immediately.

"Awake at last!" The salt and pepper haired nurse in creased green scrubs smiled as she hurried to check Kathryn's vitals.

"I'm thirsty. I want to get up."

"I'll bring you some water, but no getting up. Not yet. You might fall."

The nurse whisked out the door with the pink plastic pitcher from the bedside table.

"I need to get up. I want to go home."

"You're not going to be able to go anywhere for a while. They had to do surgery."

"Surgery?" She tried to reach up with the hand locked into the IV.

"Yes, to relieve the pressure from the swelling in your brain. You hit your head pretty hard when you were blown out of the house. Do you remember any of it?"

She thought for a minute, trying to pull her memories out of the fog. "I was asleep. And then I woke up and smelled smoke. Someone had nailed the bedroom windows shut. And then Tom was there with Steve. They had their wetsuits on. Tom broke the glass with my gun. There was an explosion, and it blew me through the open windows onto the back lawn. Tom and Steve were still in the house, looking down at me. Then there was another explosion, and that's all I remember."

Hugh looked very grave.

"What's wrong? Why aren't you saying anything?"

"Because we couldn't figure out how you could have gone through that window when it exploded without being horribly cut up."

"It didn't explode. Tom broke the glass."

He remained silent, thinking over what she had said.

"You don't believe me, do you? You don't think Tom and Steve were there."

"No, that's just it. I do believe you. They were there to save your life. And they did."

"And now I want to go home."

"The cottage isn't there to go home to," Hugh said gently.

"Couldn't they save any of it?" Tears stung her eyes.

"I'm afraid not. It wasn't just one explosion. It was a series of devices planted throughout the house. The first one triggered the second which triggered the third and the third triggered the fourth."

"They must have set them when I was out with Amanda that night."

"That's right."

"It was Wycliffe, wasn't it?"

"Indirectly."

"What does that mean?"

"I was going to wait to tell you all this; but if you feel up to it, I'll explain."

"Go on."

"A group of ex-CIA operatives, now mercenaries for hire, set the bombs in your house. Their first attempt to kill you was on the bridge that night. When that failed, they tried again in Pairs. They were more successful with Dr. Vannier and Mary Lancaster and Harrison O'Connor. They came after Frank Reynolds, too; but he managed to escape and make his way here. Hal Edwards is the one who hired and directed them."

"The President?"

Hugh nodded. "His personal fortune is tied up in Wycliffe's stock, and he intended to be on their board of directors after he left office. He knew that if the jury returned a verdict for you, Wycliffe's stock would go down, and he'd lose millions. And a plaintiff's verdict would be followed by thousands of other lawsuits and would lead the FDA to recall Myrabin, which, as you know, is one of Wycliffe's biggest profit centers. If Hal had managed to kill you last Wednesday night, he thought Wycliffe would get away scot-free because the jury had not yet reached a verdict. With you dead, Judge Weiner would have had to send the jurors home with no verdict, and the case would have been over."

"But how do you know it was Edwards?"

"Because he called me last Thursday afternoon and bragged about what he'd done. And the trouble is, he's not going to be held accountable because I haven't any proof outside of his own admission, which he would deny, that he tried to kill you."

"Are you sure the house is all gone? Weren't any bits and pieces of our things blown clear by the explosions?"

"Afraid not. All that's left are the photo albums you brought down to the firm so that Mark could select pictures to use in his opening and closing arguments. You still have those. And these." He reached into his pocket and pulled out another small blue Tiffany's box, opened it, and placed it in her hand. The familiar green fire of the emerald earrings twinkled serenely as if the fire had never happened.

"They're beautiful. But how did they survive?"

"They didn't. I had new ones made. It meant a lot to me that you were willing to accept them the first time. I didn't want you to be without them." His eyes were full of tears.

The door swung open slowly, and her mother and Graham entered.

Hugh left the box in her hand, and got up. "I'm going to leave, so you can have some time alone with your family. Mark has news from the trial for you, but I promised I'd let him tell you. He'll want to come by later."

CHAPTER FIFTY-FIVE

Monday, April 13, 2015, Scripps Memorial Hospital, La Jolla

When Kathryn woke again, the weak light streaming into the darkened room suggested twilight. She'd drifted off after telling her mother and Graham that she was just fine. She was still overwhelmingly sleepy, but she was determined to stay awake.

Mark was sitting in the chair that Hugh had occupied earlier. He was dressed in jeans and a seen-better-days black t-shirt. He looked up from his laptop and a big smile broke over his face.

"I was afraid Hugh had been wrong when he said you were better."

"I'm fine."

"Well, as fine as someone could be who survived being blown out of a burning house."

"Tom and Steve were there."

"Hugh told me."

"I thought they were going to take me with them."

"Did you want to go?"

Her face grew thoughtful because she didn't have a quick answer. "I—I thought I did, but now I'm thinking maybe not. It felt as if I wasn't finished here."

"I would agree with that. The jury returned an eighty-five million dollar verdict. Twenty million for Tom, thirty-five million for you, and thirty-million in punitive damages."

"When?"

Mark smiled. "That's an interesting story. The morning after the explosion, Hugh was here at the hospital waiting for your mother to arrive, and Patty and I went to court. Bob McLaren immediately moved for a mistrial, claiming any verdict from the jury would be tainted by sympathy for you."

"So how did you avoid that?"

"I didn't have to. The jury foreman spoke up and said they had reached their verdict the day before at 4:15. And sure enough, when the judge looked at the verdict forms, they were signed and dated April 8, 4:15 p.m. McLaren was apoplectic."

Kathryn was silent for a few moments. Then she said, "I can't even imagine eighty-five million dollars."

"Well, it's likely to be reduced somewhat in the end. Wycliffe has already filed its notice of appeal. They'll rattle their appellate swords for a while and then try to settle for something less. Maybe fifty-five million."

"That's still more money than I can grasp."

Mark grinned, "How does thirty million sound, then? The firm gets one-third."

"Still a lot of money."

"It won't come for a while. You know that. Appeals take time. We've got our appellate team on it. By the time you get a check, you'll have had time to get used to it."

The light had grown dimmer through the slats in the blinds.

"What time is it?"

"Seven o'clock. The sun's about down. You slept through supper. Are you hungry?"

She thought for a moment. She had the feeling again that she'd been blown through the window into an entirely different place. She had forgotten what hunger felt like. "Yes, I guess I am."

"Then I'll go tell them to bring you something. Paul's outside. Are you too tired to see him?"

She tried to remember what she felt for Paul. Love? Friendship? More? Less? She wasn't the same person she'd been before the blast, but she couldn't say exactly why.

"No, I'm fine. Tell him to come in. But before you do, would you hang on to that little blue box on the bedside table? They're from Hugh."

"I know. He told me the story. You made him very happy by taking them. I'll keep them safe for you."

"Thanks."

She watched Mark cross the room and open the door, but just as he was about to leave, she called out, "Wait!"

He turned, a concerned look on his face. "What's wrong?"

"Nothing. I'm not sure. No, nothing. I just wanted to ask– will you come back soon?"

That grin again, and his eyes lit up. "Of course. Is tomorrow soon enough?"

"Tomorrow is terrific."

* * *

Paul hurried in, gave her a kiss on the cheek, took her hand, and pulled the chair closer to the bed. "It's getting dark in here, want the light on?"

Kathryn nodded.

"They're bringing you something to eat."

"Good."

He reached out and stroked the part of her forehead visible under the bandage. "Mark told you the news, right? Eighty-five million?"

She nodded.

"That's more than enough for a new life."

"It won't be that much in the end."

"Close to, I bet. You're going to be well taken care of. Tom would be pleased."

She nodded. "He was there, Paul. He and Steve were there that night." She told him about the minutes before the explosion.

Paul listened quietly. "I'm not surprised. I have times when I feel them near me. But I'm glad it wasn't time for you to go with them."

"But I've woken up to an entirely new life. I just don't know exactly what it's going to be yet."

"Still want to take that vacation when you're out of here? Did you decide, Tahiti or the South of France?"

"Neither, I'm afraid."

His face fell. "Then somewhere else?"

"No."

"What are you saying?"

"Paul, I love you. I will always love you. But you're part of the past. You're part of my life with Tom. That's over. Whenever I see you, I see Tom, and I think about how much I miss him. And as long as I keep thinking about the hole in my heart, it can't heal. You were right. I wanted to sue Wycliffe, so I could keep wallowing in my grief. But looking for that kind of vengeance destroyed everything I had left from Tom. Our house is gone. His clothes, his books, the bed we shared. All in ashes. It took losing everything that way to make me understand I can't keep hanging on. And if I try to start a relationship with you, I'm still hanging on."

His mouth twisted as if in pain. "You blame me for that night with Shannon. And for not telling you that she had moved out of Steve's place."

"No, I don't. I understand why you did what you did, and it doesn't matter. But we both need to get beyond that old life in order to make a new one. And we can't do that together."

The door swung open and the nurse appeared with a tray. Her mother was right behind her.

Paul got up at once and offered Helen the chair. He leaned over and kissed Kathryn's cheek. "I have to go."

CHAPTER FIFTY-SIX

Tuesday, April 14, 2015, Crown Manor, Coronado, California

At eight-thirty, Hugh grew restless in his house, empty except for Maria and Jose, whom he had sent to bed. Frank Reynolds had been summoned to Stanford where Aimée Girard had offered him a job in her laboratory. Hugh went out into the dark and lit one of the butane heaters on his magnificent patio. He settled into one of Buffy's chaise lounges and listened to the soft purr of the waves rolling onshore across the street. A sea gull's cry throbbed through the night.

He had been to see Kathryn that morning. She'd been sleeping, and hadn't awakened while her mother went to the cafeteria for breakfast. Helen Ellis still refused to leave her daughter overnight. She slept on a cramped cot beside her bed.

When Helen came back, Hugh left, disappointed that he'd had no opportunity to talk to Kathryn. Still, her color was improving. The bandage around her head was gone. He allowed himself to believe she was going to get well.

At three that afternoon, he'd met with Sarah Knight in his office at Goldstein, Miller. She had flown in from D.C. to discuss what came next for him.

"I've been in negotiations with Travis Davidson since you retained me, and I haven't made much headway."

Hugh looked into her large, dark eyes and saw sympathy for his plight. Her cell phone rang, and she exchanged a few words with her husband, Jim Mitchell, the FBI agent, who had helped her crack the Alexa Reed murder case and save Alexa's life. He heard love and genuine passion in her voice, and felt bereft. Why couldn't he have these things, too? *Because you've been a shallow, self-absorbed bastard since you started winning lawsuits,* a voice inside reminded him.

"Sorry. That was my husband. He's here on business, too; and we're deciding on time and place for dinner. At any rate, Davidson won't budge off requiring you to plead to two felony counts for a sentence of three years."

"God, no! I'm not going to be able to stand prison for three years. I'll offer to plead to one count of obstruction, sentence fifteen months."

"That's going to be a hard sell. But you know that. I've got an appointment with Davidson in the morning. I'll try."

Now, sitting under the bright stars in the chilly air with the soft sound of the ocean to calm him, Hugh grimly considered his future. It wasn't the money. He had plenty of that. But he had worked his way up from being a nobody to being one of the biggest somebodies in the game. The horror for him was being a convicted felon, and being demoted to a position even lower than the one he started from. He could work his way back from being a nobody. But there was no comeback from being convicted of a crime that involved lying to a court. He felt empty inside. His legal career was finished. He was deeply and thoroughly in love with a woman who regarded him only as a good friend. And, both personally and professionally, his heart was shattered into a thousand pieces and could never be mended.

At that moment, he saw a shadow behind one of the morning glory planters. As his eyes focused in the dim light, he realized a man was hiding there. He was dressed entirely in black and had a ski mask pulled over his face. *So this was how he was going to die.* Buffy had tried again, and this time she would succeed. Well, he had nothing left to live for, anyway. She was doing him a favor.

The dark figure emerged into the dim light and pulled off the mask. *Okay, so he wants me to see his face before he kills me.* Hugh saw the shoulder holster bulging under the man's black sweater. Why didn't he have the gun out?

"Hugh Mahoney?" an Irish accent made his name sound all the more authentic.

"Let's get it over with."

"I haven't come to kill you. I've come to tell you who blew up Kathryn Andrews' house."

* * *

Thirty minutes later, Hugh and Sean Boyle were sitting in Hugh's kitchen. Sean had showered in one of the guest baths and changed into one of Hugh's too-big sweat suits. Hugh was watching him devour an enormous plate of bacon and eggs that Hugh had managed to cobble together without summoning Maria.

"I've been on the run since we did the job," Sean explained. "I haven't had any real food in six days."

"How'd you get by?"

"Lived off what I could find. I'm a trained special ops commando. When I left the army in Ireland I started picking up side jobs."

"Like Kathryn's cottage? How much courage does it take to blow up a defenseless woman's house?"

"Okay, okay. Calm down. I understand. I was told she wouldn't be there."

"Then why did the explosives go off when she was obviously home sleeping?"

"Look, there were three of us on the job. An American was the leader, a guy named Ed Parker. Used to be a Navy Seal. Seals kicked him out for beating a man nearly to death in a bar fight.

"Me and the other guy, Jeff Griggs, another American, set the charges to go off at ten the next morning when we thought she'd be out of the house. But Parker overrode everything we did after we finished."

"Who hired you?"

"Hal Edwards."

"Not Wycliffe?"

"Nope. The president himself put out a call to our organization, and we three agreed for a million apiece."

"Then why are you sitting in my kitchen ratting out Edwards?"

"Because unbeknownst to me and Jeff, Ed was tasked with taking me and Jeff out after the job."

"And is he still after you two?"

"No. Jeff and I took care of him. But then we split up because we knew Edwards had double crossed us, and he'd send more guys after us to make sure we didn't talk."

"And I gather you got no money?"

"Not a penny."

"So why did you come to me?"

"Because the only way I'm going to stay alive is if I turn myself in and negotiate a deal. You have the biggest stake in bringing down the president."

"But you can't prove it was Edwards."

"Oh, yes, I can. I never take a job without meeting directly with the client while I'm wearing a wire. Listen." Sean Brady pulled out his cell phone, opened an app, and Hugh heard Hal Edward's familiar baritone detailing what he wanted.

"Can you send me a copy of that?"

"Absolutely. It's going to your inbox right now."

CHAPTER FIFTY-SEVEN

Thursday afternoon, April 23, 2015, 1845 Ocean Place, Pacific Beach

Mark drew up to the curb and parked. "Are you sure you want to do this?" he asked Kathryn.

She thought of that first night when he had driven her to Petco Park in the rain after dinner at Bice. Over the last two weeks, he'd been to see her at the hospital every day, and she'd come to realize that first evening had never been a strictly business occasion. She'd asked him to bring her here today for one last look. Tonight she would stay with Amanda, and tomorrow he would put her on a plane to Miami where her mother and Graham had gone ahead to arrange a room for her in their condo.

"I'm sure." But she wasn't completely.

He came around and opened the door for her, and helped her out. She was still a little unsteady on her feet. She leaned on him as she stared at the destruction.

Where the little blue cottage had stood with the delicate white roses around the red door was nothing but a sea of ash.

The burnt-out hulls of Tom's Jeep in the garage and her Mini in the driveway completed the loss of all her earthly possessions.

She stared in silence for a few minutes. Finally she whispered, "There's really nothing left."

Mark gave her a reassuring hug. "I know. I started the ball rolling with the insurance company for you. You'll have plenty of money to rebuild when you're ready."

But she remained silent. She left the sidewalk and moved unsteadily toward the blacked rectangle of ash. As she went, she recalled each memory: the day she and Tom had seen the cottage for the first time, the day it had become theirs, the day they'd planted the roses, the crib in the nursery, their vegetable garden, their bedroom, the mismatched chairs in the kitchen, all the parties they'd given. Most of all, she remembered leaving the little house behind as she'd driven Tom to the hospital on that last desperate trip to save his life.

"It's all gone," she repeated softly as if trying to make herself believe what she was seeing. This was a new life, she realized. Her past with Tom had burned up in the early morning hours of April 9.

Mark had followed her as she walked toward the ashes. He put his arm around her sympathetically and repeated, "You'll have plenty of money to rebuild."

But she shook her head. "No, I want you to arrange for the sale of the lot. I couldn't put another house here and live in it. This place belonged to Tom and to me, and now I finally understand that's over."

"Does that mean you aren't coming back from Miami?"

She kept staring at the black dust. "I'm sure I can find a job there."

"I want you to come back," he said.

Slowly she turned to meet his eyes. There was that familiar feeling as if she were melting inside. *Could she ever trust anyone again?* Then she heard Tom's voice in her head. *"Yes, you can. He understands, Kathryn. You heard that in his closing arguments. You're safe with him. He understands."*

She smiled up at him. "I'll think about it. That's why I need to go away for a while. To see how it feels. To think about what kind of future I want now that I'm not waiting for Tom to come back."

The thought of not seeing her again made Mark's heart hurt. But he had always known that was a possibility. He took both of her hands. "I wasn't going to get into all this today because you've just gotten out of the hospital, and I know you have a lot to think about. But some things have changed in the last few days."

"What kinds of things?"

"Hugh isn't going to lose his license. Erin's leaving Craig, Lewis and coming with Goldstein, Miller. The two of them are going to start an Innocence Project. It's going to be a very large scale pro bono project for the wrongfully convicted. Hugh wanted to tell you himself, but he thought you'd be coming back. Hugh and Erin want you to work with them, and I can give you anything else you want to do. Hugh is still putting me in charge of the firm. Things are going to change under my direction."

"But how did this happen?" The news was so good that Kathryn was afraid to believe it.

"Sarah told Logan's stuck-up boyfriend that she would take

Hugh's case to trial and would call Sean Brady as a witness to air all of the president's dirty laundry in public. The Department of Justice instructed Davidson to withdraw the indictment. That saved Hugh's career, but it didn't save Hal Edwards. Sarah's husband was pretty sure what she'd found so far was just the tip of the Edwards' iceberg, and so the Bureau is investigating him. The House is drawing up articles of impeachment in case he refuses to resign."

Kathryn turned back to look at the ruins of the cottage. Her eyes teared up. She said, softly, "It's so strange to think Tom died because of the President of the United States, a man we never met. I'd like to contribute the money from Tom's case to Hugh and Erin's Innocence Project. It's what he would have wanted."

Mark smiled. "I'll tell them. "Are you done here? You look a little tired."

Kathryn turned back for one last look at the ashes. "We were happy here," she said.

Mark hugged her gently. "I know. I'd like to think you might be happy with me. Some day. When you've had time to think about it."

She turned away from the ruins of the little house and laid her head on his shoulder. "I don't need any more time to think about it. The answer is yes."

EPILOGUE

San Diego, California, December 28, 2016, Breaking News

The Andrews-Cooper Innocence Project has announced today the exoneration of Mr. Saul Rodriguez. Mr. Rodriguez, a member of the Los Angeles gang Rollin' Sixties, was convicted of the first degree murder of a rival gang member in 1996, and was given a life without parole sentence. Mr. Rodriguez was ordered released from custody today after Erin Mahoney and her father, Hugh, persuaded the Ninth Circuit Court of Appeals that DNA evidence proving Mr. Rodriguez innocent of the murder had been wrongfully suppressed by the Los Angeles District Attorney's Office.

The Andrews-Cooper Innocence Project was founded in August 2015 to honor Thomas Allen Andrews, a long-time member of the San Diego Public Defender's office, and his close friend Stephen Cooper, an environmental lawyer for the Natural Resources Defense Counsel. Mr. Andrews' widow, Kathryn Andrews Kelly, is the director of the project, which is sponsored by the law firm of Goldstein, Miller, and Mahoney. Mark Kelly, managing partner of the firm, calls the Andrews-Cooper Innocence Project one of the firm's finest achievements. To date, ten wrongfully convicted clients have been released from prison because of the work of Mrs. Kelly and her team.

AUTHOR'S NOTE

I hope you enjoyed *The Death of Distant Stars* and that you'll let other readers know on Amazon.com. I chose this title because when we first meet Hugh Mahoney, he is at the height of his power in the legal and political realms. Little does he know that his decision to help Kathryn Andrews will bring about his professional downfall. At the beginning of the book, he is a star whose "light is shining the brightest," and he doesn't yet know that Kathryn's case is the beginning of his star's collapse.

I hope that as you read, you spotted the influences that brought about the changes in Hugh. Of course, his feelings for Kathryn influenced him to see life differently. But Hugh also changed because he respected Kathryn's dedication to Tom. And he changed because he respected Kathryn and Tom's dedication to their often thankless careers as public defenders.

I really enjoyed writing about Kathryn Andrews. When the story opens, she has reached a point in her career where she feels utterly burned out, and the loss of Tom and her uncertainty over his fidelity to their marriage has left her hollow and empty.

479

Nevertheless, her fierce devotion to her husband pushes her to approach Hugh and the intimidating world of Big Law, a world she and Tom decided not to join. And her determination to prove the truth about her husband's death inspires everyone around her to join her cause.

I'd love to hear your thoughts about the characters and the story of *The Death of Distant Stars.* Write to me at dhawkins8350@gmail.com. And sign up for my email list at deborahhawkinsficton.com so you'll be the first to know when new books in The Warrick, Thompson Files are released.

A PREVIEW OF BOOK FIVE

In *Vengeance,* newly widowed Charlotte Estes must defend the son of Lucas Owens, one of Goldstein, Miller's most important clients. Assisting her is trial attorney Sean Donovan whose partnership at Goldstein, Miller is hanging by a thread because he's been on a three-year losing streak in front of juries. Rich, spoiled Andy Owens is a thirty-two-year old party boy who has tried to cover up the murder of his best friend by making it look like a drunken boating accident. Although Andy swears he wasn't on the boat when Nate McClellan died, Charlotte can see that Andy is an accomplished liar, and all the evidence points to him. Party-boy Andy's conviction is inevitable. But Sean Donovan needs a big win to save his career. And Andy isn't willing to take Charlotte's prejudice against him lying down.

Enjoy the following preview of *Vengeance.*

PROLOGUE

Monday, January 8, 2018, Georgetown, District of Columbia

Someone was trying to kill her. But Charlotte Estes had no idea who. Or why.

It was freezing outside when Charlotte closed the door of her townhouse on O Street at four o'clock, ready to do her favorite neighborhood run for the last time. The ink had been dry on the merger agreement with Goldstein, Miller for months. The Estes Law Firm's offices on K Street had long been emptied, and the firm's sixty-five attorneys had been disbursed throughout Goldstein, Miller's web of national and international offices. She, alone, had remained behind to oversee the final arrangements for the end of the criminal defense firm that she and Matt had built together. Now The Estes Law Firm and Matt were dead, and the bits and pieces of her life with her husband were boxed and ready for the moving van in the morning. She was headed back to San Diego where she had been born.

She began to run slowly to warm up but also so that she could savor the quaint, European atmosphere of her neighborhood for the last time. When she reached M Street, she passed the red brick townhouse, sandwiched between the antiques store and the Thai takeout joint, where she and Matt had started their firm in 1985. Her eyes misted over as she pictured her husband as he'd been in those days. Dark hair, gentle gray eyes. A trim five feet, eight, with a ready smile, a generous disposition, and a keen intelligence. She had never imagined her life without him. Yet here she was, running from their shared past, looking for the comfort of oblivion a continent away.

When she reached Wisconsin, she turned left and headed for the path along the C & O canal. The late afternoon light was thinning, and she knew for security reasons she shouldn't go far because sunset was imminent. But she wanted to say goodby to one of her favorite places, a place where she and Matt had often run together in the days when she'd never imagined anyone or anything coming between them.

She increased her pace when she reached the canal path. Her father, the track coach, had taught her how to maximize her endurance. Obviously she hadn't the speed or the mileage she'd had at UCLA all those years ago when her track scholarship had paid for her undergraduate degree. But if her father were still alive, he'd have been proud of the distance she still covered every week at age fifty-eight.

Overhead, the trees were bare and brown. It was hard to believe that in twenty-four hours she'd be in the lush, eternal sunshine of Southern California. She had mixed feelings about leaving her home of more than thirty years. But Matt had been gone since mid-November, and she wasn't making any progress with moving on with her life. Every street corner, every restaurant, every nook and cranny of their house on O Street was full of memories that haunted and tormented her because she could not understand why Matt, the one person she had trusted without question for over thirty years, had died in another woman's bed.

There had been no sign that anything was amiss in their marriage, she thought as she ran. Or had she been too quick to overlook the nights he'd stayed late at the office in the months leading up to his death and the trips he taken to London, ostensibly alone?

The sunlight was dissipating rapidly. The D.C. detectives had warned her about what she was doing at that very minute. Another reason to leave town. Surely whichever disgruntled, but unidentified client, had tried to run her down on K Street in early December wouldn't bother to follow her all the way to San Diego. Today was her anonymous assassin's last chance. Death threats came with the territory of criminal defense work. But actual attempts were rare. Charlotte turned back toward home, suddenly aware that she'd pushed the envelope farther than she'd intended. She quickened her pace yet again. And then she heard the crack of the rifle shot coming from the trees behind her.